Traitor's and Heroes

Born of Hitler's savagery is a largely new idea,
offering a new hope—that basic human rights are the
proper concern of people everywhere. This idea has
been central to Martin Garbus' life as a lawyer. His
memoir revisits the sham trials of blacks in South
Africa and dissidents in Chile. He has acted in behalf
of Sakharov and Shcharansky as well as the lesser
known dissidents and refuseniks resisting Soviet
brutalities. Epic struggles are told here—inspiring
tales of those who challenge repressive and seemingly
impregnable state forces. They are the ''traitors'' and
''heroes'' of the book's title.''

—*ABA Journal*

Also by Martin Garbus from Carroll & Graf

Ready for the Defense

TRAITORS
AND
HEROES

TRAITORS AND HEROES

MARTIN GARBUS

Carroll & Graf Publishers, Inc.
New York

First Carroll & Graf edition 1989

This edition reprinted by arrangement with Atheneum Publishers, an imprint of Macmillan Publishing Company.

Carroll & Graf Publishers, Inc.
260 Fifth Avenue
New York, NY 10001

ISBN: 0-88184-540-X

Manufactured in the United States of America

For my wife,
RUTH,
and my daughters,
ELIZABETH
and
CASSANDRA ANNE

AUTHOR'S NOTE

THERE ARE DOZENS of people in South Africa, Chile, the Soviet Union, Spain, Pakistan, Israel, Egypt, and China whom I would like to thank by name. I cannot do so because I do not want to endanger their lives. Often, at great personal risk, they took care of me, permitted me to invade their homes and intrude on their lives, so that I could learn and tell their story.

I thank Susan Leon, my editor, for her friendship and skill.

I thank many friends who encouraged me in the writing of this book: Michael Frankfurt, Peter Shepherd, Sue Woodman, Gabe Motola, Peter Winn, Harry Streifer, and Sue Gronewold. My brother, Albert Garbus, and sister, Robin Baker, also deserve mention.

CONTENTS

PREFACE

WHEN I WAS IN the Army, I came close to being charged with treason. That was in 1955. The Korean War had ended a year earlier and the McCarthy era was just about over, but the mood of the country remained brittle. If the grip of paranoia had loosened a bit, its touch still could be felt. The fifties was not a decade that easily welcomed controversy.

Of course, I was not unaware of the climate at the time. I was twenty-two years old and a recent graduate of Hunter College in New York. As a private first class I was sophisticated enough to know that the Army was not the best forum for the airing of ideas, but I was also naïve enough to underestimate the violence of its response. Still and all, the very notion of treason was beyond my contemplation, especially since I had done nothing even remotely treasonous. Here is what happened:

After completing basic training, I was assigned to Fort Slocum on David's Island off New Rochelle, New York, where I taught current events to enlisted men. Most of the time I commented on news stories in the *New York Times*, but on occasion I devoted a full hour to a specific topic, always with a point of view. I gave one hour to the reasons why the United States should recognize Red China, another to explaining that those who stood on their Fifth Amendment rights before the House Un-American Activities Committee should not be removed from their jobs or be jailed. The commanding officer, acting on complaints from junior officers, told me to stay away from controversial subjects. I responded by holding sessions on the Sacco-Vanzetti case and the prosecutions of Eugene Debs during the First World War and Eugene Dennis after the Second.

Soon after, when I returned to the base a half an hour late one night—a common enough practice at Slocum—I was charged with being AWOL and with disobeying orders "relating to the performance of my duties." Court-martial proceedings were begun. I faced a jail term and a dishonorable discharge.

The court-martial attracted just one spectator, a rugged, commanding-looking, fifty-two-year-old master sergeant named James Hatch. Hatch regularly attended my current events class, but I knew him only slightly, and I was unacquainted with his political views. I knew only that, unlike most of the commissioned and noncommissioned officers at the base, he was a much-decorated combat veteran of both World War II and the Korean War, and thus he had a special standing among his peers. I did not know why he was at the trial, and when he suddenly rose, interrupting the three young officers who were my judges, and asked to be heard, I listened with trepidation.

As it turned out, Hatch was on my side. His plea to the officers was that someone who felt the need to express his beliefs as strongly as I did should not be punished. He went further. The best soldiers, he said, were those with minds of their own who were ready, on occasion, to violate orders. "Garbus is the kind of person I would pick to lead a patrol, because he would keep his men safe," Hatch said. "He would respect the rules, but he would be willing to break them when he felt he had to." Then he added that he believed the AWOL charge was a pretext and that I was being tried for my political beliefs.

The three officers declared a recess. They met with Hatch outside the courtroom. Ten minutes later he returned and called me aside. The court-martial was a cover, he told me. The officer who instigated the trial had visions of darker demons. He believed I was guilty of treason.

Through the good offices of Sergeant Hatch, a deal was struck. In exchange for the Army's dropping the charges against me, I agreed to leave Fort Slocum, stop teaching troops, give up my security clearance, and be reclassified to finish my service in a radar unit on Long Island.

Never before those days in the Army could I have imagined that I would place myself in such a dangerous situation.

As a poor Jewish boy, growing up in a gentile neighborhood in the Bronx during World War II, I was terrified both by the people who ran this country and by the specters of Nazism and anti-Semitism. My father's back had been broken at age fourteen during a pogrom in Poland when a soldier had thrown him from a hay wagon. His hunchback was a painful, daily reminder to me of the penalty of being a helpless outsider. All I wanted to do was hide.

Because he expected a great pogrom in America, so did I. Only Franklin Delano Roosevelt, I thought, prevented slaughters in the United States in the 1940s.

A quiet, withdrawn man, who spoke English badly, my father despised Jews who were too loud, and who were either misers or spent money lavishly. Trying to disappear into his eighteen-hour-a-day, six-and-a-half-day week at his Bronx candy store, he was angry at Jews who allowed themselves to be noticed. Even in those moments when he was out of that store, he seemed to be hiding— shielding himself from the Storm Trooper about to beat him.

Growing up, I feared that my safety was a fragile thing. When I helped my father in the store, I thanked the gentiles who put food on our table with their nickels and dimes for their cigarettes and newspapers.

As a young boy I could never understand why such Jews as Marx, Freud, and Einstein foolishly allowed attention to focus on them. Didn't they understand that they could be killed because they talked so loud?

I felt, as my father did, that Jews should keep low profiles and not speak out at all. In college during the McCarthy years, I admired those who spoke out, but I never did. When Jews became embroiled in political controversy in the 1950s, they were, I thought, quite insane and also heroic.

At the same time, I had romantic images of those who joined the fight against Franco and those who fought in the French Resistance. George Orwell, who had fought in Spain, became my hero.

After I left the Army, I enrolled at Columbia University to do graduate work in economics. But my Army days, and my experience there of being called a traitor, influenced me. I began reading about people who had been similarly called—Galileo, Joan of Arc, Eugene Debs—but who had long since been redeemed by history.

When I was in the army, age twenty-two, I, for the first time, stood up for something I believed in. And I began to believe that only a system of law could stand between both physical beatings by police and false accusations of treason from Army officers. I decided finally to make a career of law. My intention was to represent political dissidents and insist, as Sergeant Hatch had done, that conscience reasonably exercised and deeply felt should transcend the demands of democratic government.

Not surprisingly, after law school and then after brief teaching appointments at Columbia and Yale, I became associate director of the American Civil Liberties Union. There I wrestled daily with the question of how far authority can and should go in permitting people to speak against a government and even call for its overthrow.

This issue was dramatically presented to me some years ago when the Civil Liberties Union was supporting the right of Nazis to march through a Jewish suburb near Chicago, calling for the return of fascism and the killing of Jews. I found myself in the unlikely position of defending Nazis' right to speak and demonstrate.

It is true, as others pointed out, that if the Nazis are permitted to hold rallies and marches, as they did in Skokie, Illinois, they may win converts and obtain the power to abolish freedom and to finish what Hitler had left undone. This possibility terrifies me. The town my father grew up in was wiped out by the Germans. His father and mother and eleven brothers and sisters were killed in the camps. I was twelve years old in 1946 when I learned that my father's entire family had been murdered. My friends' parents' families had shared similar fates. We were all affected by Hitler's final solution—few of us had uncles or aunts, and many people we later met had gray numbers tattooed on their skin.

And yet I believe those who harbor those repulsive thoughts ought to be permitted to speak out clearly.

Why? Not because I support them. Because it is in my self-interest to protect them. Because if they start to acquire power, the only chance those who oppose them have is to demonstrate, to speak out against them—to get the attention and support of the world in the way that the victims of genocide and oppression seldom do.

The only alternative to freedom for any group is power. But minority groups will rarely have the means sufficient to avoid injustice. If shutting down printing presses or banning demonstrations would better lead to freedom, or ensure it, I might want the state to have that power. Unfortunately, history has shown us that we are correct to be skeptical of those who have that power. This is why it is so important for any group that is being oppressed to have the right to let the rest of the world know its agony.

Does an absolute commitment to the protection of free speech ensure there will not be another era of mass killings? Of course not. But on balance there is a better chance of its not happening again if the government is not given the power to decide what we can say. It is a dangerous business, Supreme Court Justice Robert Jackson warned years ago, when he cautioned against turning our Constitution into a "suicide pact."

My experience in the Army was the first time, though not the last, I heard the term "traitor" attached to my name, and it had a profound and long-lasting effect. The very notion of what it meant to be a traitor fascinated me. Treason, after all, was unlike any other crime, for it represented a transgression not against person or property but against those who represented the regime in power. In most common criminal cases—homicide, assault, robbery, burglary—the fact that a crime has been committed is not at issue. Tangible evidence speaks to the point: someone is dead or injured, property is missing or damaged. The question to be determined at trial is whether the defendant was the perpetrator. When it comes to treason, however, the issue most often is whether the acts of the defendant constitute a crime at all.

You can also be a traitor to a people—or to a set of ideas.

Historically, there are two types of treasonous acts: those of commission and those of advocacy or expression. The first type is more easily defined—individuals make war against the governors of their country by performing acts of violence: bombs are planted, buildings are torched, officials assassinated. As opposed

to the murder and mayhem of terrorists, the second type of treason concerns those who defy their regimes simply by speaking out
against specific acts or policies. Here dissenters express ideas
contrary to those of the people who run the government; they
advocate resistance to the course on which their country is em-
barked. Such dissidents, branded traitors by some, are often seen
as heroes, even patriots, by those who share their views.

These emotion-laden words were very recently hurled about
when Lieutenant Colonel Oliver L. North, called a hero and a pa-
triot by his president, accused the press of being "traitors" when
they first started to explode the wall of secrecy around the Iran
arms deal. "What the press is doing," North said, "would, in another time, be considered treason."

In the twenty-five years that I have been practicing law, I
have observed by traveling in many countries all over the world
the degree to which politics can preempt the legal process. In most
countries "treason" means whatever those in power say it means.
Throughout the globe the great conflicts between the state and the
individual, between the rule of law and the forces of political
opposition, are played out in political trials. Treason trials are
often "show trials"—dramatic renderings, sometimes open, sometimes closed—stages on which politics and the law nakedly confront one another.

The person on trial frequently is no more than a symbol. At
issue is what he represents, rather than the nature of the act he has
committed, and in this way a treason trial is different from any
other criminal case. The accused's "disloyal intent" is classified as
a political offense that justifies punishment that would be improper under "normal" legal standards. The trial's main purpose
is to intimidate. It is too often held solely to intimidate political
foes and deter further antigovernment behavior, as in the trial of
South African poet Breyten Breytenbach, or, on occasion, to im-
press the outside world with the appearance that justice is being
done, as in Chile's "Nuremberg trial" of supporters of Chile's late
president, Salvador Allende. There is almost never a commitment
to either serve justice or guard the rights of the accused.

My deepening commitments to the legal concepts of free
speech and treason led to a personal involvement in human rights
battles throughout the world. It is a direct path. Those who are

called traitors are attacked most savagely by the guardians of the regimes under siege: its prosecutors, courts, soldiers, police and prison guards. In order to expand the power of people to speak out against their governments, I found myself fighting not only to enlarge free speech laws but also to make sure dissidents were not killed, tortured, or imprisoned at will.

Some regimes do not even bother to try to prove to the world that they act in the name of justice. In the sixties and seventies, when I traveled to Chile, Brazil, El Salvador, Argentina, and Iran—all nearly totally lawless nations when they deal with the opposition—I took part in trials of dissidents that were no more than token rituals.

At times, as in Iran, I was retained directly by the father of a young man facing a death sentence because he published articles too critical of the shah. But most times I represented international organizations: Amnesty International, the Committee to Free Prisoners of Apartheid, the Committee to Free Soviet Jewry and PEN, a writers' organization.

Often all I could do was to plead that written legal procedures, traditionally ignored, must be followed. Sometimes the outcome was changed, sometimes not. On many occasions the foreign authorities lied about its legal system and at other times a government tried to prevent my meeting with or representing a defendant. In Beijing, China, toward the end of the Cultural Revolution in 1977, for instance, a few months after Mao's death, the new regime falsely described with meticulous detail legal proceedings and trials that never were held. When, after meeting with Anatoly Shcharansky in the Soviet Union, I tried to return to attend his trial and help represent him, the Soviet government refused to allow me to enter the country.

These are not, unfortunately, aberrations in the legal machinery of just a few countries, but rather the norm. I have seen justice bent in courtrooms in Bangladesh, India, Spain, the West Bank of Israel, Cuba, and Nicaragua as well. In writing this book I have chosen to focus on trials in South Africa, Chile, and the Soviet Union because I was most moved by my experiences there and because, taken together, they help to illuminate a good deal of what is going on in the world at this time.

The men on trial in each of these countries were once national heroes of a sort. Breyten Breytenbach was acclaimed one of the foremost poets in his native tongue; many of the men on trial in Chile helped to run the government before Pinochet came to power; Andrei Sakharov was twice awarded Russia's highest honors.

The fates of Breytenbach, the Allende supporters, and Sakharov and Shcharansky were all predetermined by political considerations rather than any fair assessment of their guilt or innocence of properly defined crimes. Despite the elaborate façade of legal procedures and trials, the defendants were selected by the state to serve as examples; they were prosecuted for what they stood for. Their alleged treasons were, at most, expressions of political dissent.

These cases stirred deep interest in the United States and Western Europe, signaling the growing feeling in the world that human rights was not merely a political issue to be addressed by governments but a *human* issue concerning us all; that individual governments should not be allowed unlimited discretion in their treatment of political prisoners. Where international figures such as Breytenbach and Sakharov are concerned, citizens of other countries have felt a clear obligation to try to ensure their humane treatment.

As in the Army, my efforts on behalf of free speech often put me in frightening situations. For example, agents of the South African government responded to my efforts on behalf of Breytenbach and for members of the African National Congress by following me back to the United States and attempting to have me disbarred.

But the movement of the law across national boundaries has afforded benefits that far outweigh any brutal consequences to me and others involved in the fight. A law of nations is developing. Treason laws once created to protect the king and the king's men are now being supplanted by new legal theories holding responsible the king's successors—those who run today's governments. Court argument opposing American involvement in Vietnam, Chile, and Central America has drawn on the reasoning in legal briefs protesting Czechoslovakia's and Poland's mistreatment of dissidents. Argentina, in putting the generals on trial, drew on Nuremberg principles.

One of the more pivotal of these was a 1982 United States court decision allowing the widow of Orlando Letelier, then living in the United States, to sue the government of Chile for the assassination of her husband, Chilean ambassador to the United States under Allende, who was killed by a car bomb in Washington, D.C., six years earlier.

The Letelier case and other recent decisions by American courts constitute important precedents in efforts to extend the demands of justice and personal rights to areas once considered legally out of bounds. There is even hope today for the formulation of standards for a global bill of rights, establishing basic, inviolable standards of treatment applicable to political prisoners.

Throughout the world there is an increased awareness that the lives of all the world's people are interrelated. American, German, and British students rally against South African apartheid; antinuclear demonstrators in Europe swelled in the aftermath of the nuclear disaster at Chernobyl; and human rights issues are on the bargaining table at superpower summit conferences. We see posters in South Korea not only applauding the overthrow of the Marcos government in the Philippines, but also seeking fair trials, due process, and better prison conditions.

The need for a world-wide commitment to human rights is apparent and urgent. The best guarantee against tyranny everywhere, but especially in countries where tyranny has often seemed acceptable to the majority, is a heightened public sense of why it is repulsive.

The human rights movement is now international in scope, and even nations that routinely violate those rights now face threats from abroad. The most prominent new leaders in Latin America, President Raúl Alfonsín of Argentina and President Alan García of Peru, owe a significant part of their election to reputations flowing from their efforts to promote human rights.

Even President Ronald Reagan was forced to reverse himself in Chile, Haiti, and the Philippines, picking up the pieces of a human rights policy he and Jeane Kirkpatrick tried to destroy in his first days as president.

But if the peoples of the world could agree on which rights were inviolate, their enforcement would transcend the tempestuous currents of domestic and foreign politics. Then the day might yet dawn when those who dare to dream new dreams will have cause neither to distrust the truth of their vision nor fear the consequences of uttering its name.

The subject of this book is freedom. It fulfills part of my obligation to bear witness. The book is dedicated to the brave men I met and defended. Some of them are dead, but I can still see their faces and hear their voices.

THE
STATE
OF
SOUTH AFRICA
AGAINST
BREYTEN BREYTENBACH
AND THE
AFRICAN NATIONAL
CONGRESS

1

Too much harm has been done, we have been driven too far apart.

—Winnie Mandela, 1986

I N   T H E   S U M M E R of 1977 South Africa was in turmoil, the threat of violence bubbling just below the surface. The uprising in the black township of Soweto one year before, which left seven hundred people dead in months of rioting and unrest, caused an unprecedented exodus of young black refugees angry and impatient to fight back. The white mood, both within and outside the country, was restless. Little has changed in the past years. Nationally, the government's handling of the Soweto disturbances brought it severe criticism from both white liberals and conservatives as well as spearheading the increasingly virulent dissent among the blacks.

Internationally, the changing politics of the region also threatened the Afrikaner rulers. A proclaimed fresh invasion by South Africa of Angola, foreshadowed by a massive build-up of troops in the Namibia area, was called off because of unexpected international pressure. South Africa was being forced to the conference table on the vexed subject of its possession of Namibia. It had also learned that its ability to control the price of gold had been wrested away by foreign powers.

It was in this climate that in June the International Commission of Jurists, the International League for Human Rights, and PEN, asked me to go to South Africa to attend and report on two potentially politically explosive South African trials set for that summer.

The International League had gotten my name from some of my friends in the American civil rights movement. They believed I could function well and responsibly as a lawyer and furnish them with an unbiased, objective report of what I had seen. When they asked me to go, I jumped at the chance. South Africa had been in my consciousness for years, first when I was a student and then as a civil rights lawyer in the South.

Alan Paton and his *Cry, The Beloved Country* had left a deep impression on me when I was a high school student. I knew, in the 1940s and 1950s, that Paton spoke out nearly alone against the white South African government—often at great risk to himself. His stirring books about oppressed but not defeated blacks looked to the legal system as a place to soften injustice. I could not know when I agreed to go to South Africa that, surprisingly, it would be none other than Alan Paton who would attack me for what I did there.

The South African example of brutality to blacks had come up again and again when I was in Mississippi and Alabama working as a lawyer in the 1960s. There were both similarities and differences between the United States and South Africa in the way racism developed and existed and the way in which the legal system of each country was then dealing with racial injustice. The legal system in both countries was originally used to degrade blacks. But in those years American legal force was being used to break down racial barriers, whereas South Africa continued to use the law to foster apartheid.

Interesting enough, early South Africa took a much more relaxed attitude toward racial mixing than the American South did. Some people of mixed origin infiltrated the "white" settler community and a separate category of population called the Cape Colored eventually emerged.

Racial slavery came to both societies, but in different forms. The rich soil and extensive inland waterways of North America made possible a wealthy and expansive plantation economy, with many slaves, while the Cape Colony's generally arid climate and poor agricultural resources resulted in modest and poor farms that could not support a slave society.

4

Both countries had civil wars. The Anglo-Boer struggle for control of the interior of South Africa, like our civil war, involved differences over racial issues. But with the coming of industrialization, the paths of the two countries diverged dramatically. Free white immigrants comprised the bulk of the factory work force in the United States, while in South Africa's gold and diamond mines, whites supervised a low-paid and ill-treated black labor force.

Martin Luther King in 1963 told me he thought South Africa's system of apartheid was only an exaggerated form of America's system of racism. Professor George Frederickson reached the same conclusion in his excellent book *White Supremacy* when he suggested "the phrase 'white supremacy' applies with particular force to the historical experience of two nations—South Africa and the United States." White supremacy, he wrote, "suggests systematic and self-conscious efforts to make race or color a qualification for membership in the civil community"—it is a justification for brutalization.

By looking at what South Africa does to its blacks, I knew I could better understand how blacks felt racism operated in this country.

The two treason trials I was to attend were being used by the South African government to show South Africa's friends and enemies that neither black unrest at home nor the hard line adopted by the new United States government under President Carter would stop South Africa's crackdown against the more active African National Congress in the aftermath of Soweto. First the government put Breyten Breytenbach, a white Afrikaner poet, on trial for treason and attempting to escape from prison. Breytenbach had been jailed the previous year for attempting to overthrow the government. Because the charge this time was high treason, a guilty verdict could mean the death penalty. Then the government charged twelve black members of the banned African National Congress with treason, sabotage, and attempted murder after an attack on a police station. They demanded the punishment of death.

The Afrikaner government sought to prevent either trial from benefiting its enemies. Both trials were held in the capital, Pretoria, rather than Johannesburg, because the capital was farther away from the smoldering black ghettos, and there was less likelihood of

5

demonstrations taking place. The government also hoped that by placing the trial in Pretoria—miles away from the offices of the press—the trials would get less foreign publicity.

The government was still smarting from the effects of a bad press the year before, during the controversial 1976 prosecution of the SASO Nine (the South African Students Organization), which revealed to the world, perhaps for the first time, the vitality of the burgeoning Black Consciousness movement. Even though the SASO Nine were convicted and sentenced to long terms on Robben Island, the case proved a psychological defeat for the government. For instead of helping to suppress the Black Consciousness ideology, the trial afforded the accused a public platform to proclaim their defiance of the state.

Throughout the proceedings, they had seized headlines by singing freedom songs and raising clenched fists in the courtroom. The trial helped inspire the uprising that broke out in Soweto. There black children's courage in facing down policemen's bullets shook the apartheid state to its roots. In township after township the old people kept saying "the youth have taken over." An old wizened man in Johannesburg said, "They are ready to die, the youth. They say 'Why not go to be part of the struggle? We will die anyway, even if we stay at home.' "

And yet for a growing number of people in white South Africa, Steve Biko's Black Consciousness movement was the dominant political force, far more relevant to the country's majority than black revolutionaries or white resistance. Biko, who had eloquently defended the SASO Nine, was already a national figure, fast gaining international status and a reputation as a spokesman for black Africa. Though hardly thirty, he was touted as a future prime minister. But those whites who believed that the new black movement was nonviolent, or that Biko was another Gandhi, deceived themselves. Steve Biko at the trial spelled out exactly what Black Consciousness meant for blacks:

> The claim by whites of monopoly on comfort and security has always been so exclusive that blacks see whites as the major obstacle in their progress towards peace, prosperity and a sane society. Through its association with all these negative aspects, whiteness has thus been soiled beyond recognition. At best there-

fore, blacks see whiteness as a concept that warrants being despised, hated, destroyed and replaced by an aspiration with more human content in it. At worst, blacks envy white society for the comfort it has usurped and that the center of this envy is . . . the secret determination . . . to kick whites off those comfortable garden chairs that one sees as he rides in a bus out of town, and to claim them for themselves.

It was under this threat that the Breytenbach and ANC trials began. As it happened, I almost missed the proceedings. I had considerable trouble obtaining a visa. It was only after Congressmen Stephen Solarz and Benjamin Rosenthal, and Allard Lowenstein, then a United Nations official, appealed to the South African passport office that I finally got my visa. I left for Johannesburg immediately. It was June 18, 1977.

Apartheid slams you in the face the moment you arrive at the very modern glass airport terminal in Johannesburg. There are no conveyor belts or carts for the passengers' suitcases. Instead, large numbers of black men with wool caps descend like ants on the mounds of luggage. Calling me "boss," one black found my heavy suitcase, and with shuffling feet and eyes rooted to the floor ran with it an extremely long distance to the taxi.

I drove through Johannesburg to a hotel in the center of town. Hard, gritty, ugly, fast, the city is set on the topmost ridge of a reef six thousand feet above sea level, the richest of a string of South Africa's industrial cities, with more days of sunshine than Southern California.

Because it started as a mining camp in the 1880s, Johannesburg was laid out quickly, efficiently, and without imagination. The buildings are starkly contemporary—they are pulled down and replaced by bigger ones every thirty years. The great mines south of the city center are grand in their way, even beautiful. They give off great quantities of fine dust which blows, when the wind is up, and penetrates everything. The mines are the only real reason for Johannesburg; that's where the money is and that's where the gold is, or what's left of it.

A century ago, in 1886, when the first mines were opened and the first streets laid out, there were few whites there. In the years since, the rand had yielded more than ten billion dollars in gold;

and some of those same mines are still producing. The whites, while still few in number, have prospered royally. The blacks, who worked in the mines, share not at all in the riches they made possible.

What gives Johannesburg its unique flavor is its social engineering—its segregated entrances and exists, its segregated public conveniences, its carefully regulated neighborhoods, and its "pass laws" which, in order to restrict the migration of rural blacks to urban areas, require that blacks carry documents proving they have legitimate business in the white areas. The subject of race— laws about it, signs about it, talk about it, thought about it—was all-pervasive. The blacks who gave me a wide berth as I made my way along the sidewalks were surely thinking of race, and the whites who made unconscious detours around outdoor trash baskets (sites of numerous bomb blasts) were also thinking about it. The police patrolling the streets, the guards in front of the banks, the nervous salespeople in the diamond shops, the drivers of the segregated buses, the proprietors of the corner kiosks were all thinking about race. A white university professor caught this mood. "It's so tiresome having to think about race all the time. But then, how can you not in a place like this? Still, it would be nice to move on to something else and think about something a little more interesting and complex."

The day after I arrived, I drove to Pretoria. It is very different from Johannesburg—gracious, staid, good-looking, and peaceful. It is also a thousand feet closer to sea level, which makes it considerably hotter. Some white people live in ordinary suburban houses with front gardens and backyards right in the middle of the city, although such dwellings are outnumbered and overshadowed by tall new office buildings, hotels, and blocks of flats.

But it is a city which has been quite obviously planned. Like Washington, D.C., it has a certain dignity befitting the nation's administrative capital. There are handsome squares surrounded by fine buildings, sweeping avenues of jacaranda trees that look down on many acres of formal gardens with cool expanses of lawn. The tenor of the city and its way of life are dominated by the presence of the government and the Afrikaner majority. The streets are full of muscular policemen and sunburned schoolchildren in khaki. There is relatively little crime. Indeed, one feels that, unlike Johannesburg, Pretoria has nearly bleached the blackness off the streets. As I walked, I heard the Dutch-based Afrikaans language, with its rolled r's sounding somewhat like a Scottish burr, intermingle with the sounds of English.

When I arrived at the Pretoria courthouse to try to find out where the Breytenbach and ANC trials were to be held, my queries were met with reticence and hostility from the Afrikaner civil servants. Their reticence seems to stem from a strictly hierarchical system in which opinions or information come only from the top. Laws seem to govern every aspect of life, and people seem afraid of saying the wrong things. Part of their reluctance to talk to me also came from their antipathy toward the English language, the language of their former oppressors.

But when we did talk, nearly every court clerk and judge that I spoke to, then and over the next few weeks, brought up the British-Boer war early in our conversation. One clerk choked with rage as he told me about the treatment in the British concentration camps of Boer women and children. Another clerk remembers stories of his father and uncles being punished in school for daring to speak Afrikaans.

I finally learned that the Breytenbach trial was scheduled to begin in the spacious Hall of Justice the following Monday. The formal charges against him were two: one, under the Terrorism Act, for helping to set up Okhela, an illegal organization to promote armed struggle, and the other, for trying to escape after serving two years of his earlier sentence.

The Terrorism Act punishes by death or life imprisonment anyone who intends "to endanger the maintenance of law or order in the republic" or who commits acts "to endanger the republic." The Suppression of Communism Act also punishes by life imprisonment or death anyone who advocates socialism or communism or who advocates or tries or has tried to set up "the establishment of a despotic system of government based on the dictatorship of the proletariat."

South Africa does not have the separation of powers and the system of checks and balances we have. Its Parliament creates all law. As a result, there can be no attack on the constitutionality of

South African laws, for its constitution forbids the courts from entering into "a pronounciation upon the validity of any Act passed by Parliament."

The government prosecutor, after a long debate within his office, chose not to seek the death penalty as the law entitled, but rather only life imprisonment. Had Breytenbach been an English writer critical of the regime, he probably would never have been arrested. Although the Afrikaners despise their former "colonials," they reserve a deeper hatred for their own traitors to the new ruling class, and they persecute them with a peculiar ferocity. Still, no one of Breytenbach's prominence had ever been sentenced to death, and the government was not about to risk international censure by doing that now.

Unlike the British, who always retained the option of returning to the mother country when a colonial outpost went up in flames, Afrikaners had neither a Dutch nor English homeland to return to. The Europe their forebears left was preindustrial, and now if southern Africa were to become inhospitable to Afrikaners' social and economic agendas, no nation on earth would be home to them. The Afrikaner establishment had grown used to crushing nonwhites who opposed ministry rule, and it had even come to expect some of South Africa's British descendants to drift occasionally from the tenets of white rule. But to have the country's leading white Afrikaans poet, whose welfare the entire society has been organized to protect, become interested not only in reform but in armed revolution put a crack in the wall that a vigorous prosecution must try to seal.

Breytenbach, thirty-eight years old, sallow-faced, with a neat prison haircut, a slim and thoughtful-looking man, sat in Pretoria's stately courthouse the first day, taking notes in a schoolboy's notebook and looking more like an observer than a man on trial for his freedom. He sat quietly in the dock, but his extraordinary, piercing, intense eyes moved incessantly, making contact with members of the crowd of more than two hundred spectators, many of whom were friends or admirers, anxious to know how this sensitive white man had survived his ordeal in jail.

Breytenbach was born in 1939 into an archetypal Afrikaner family, part of "the Tribe," as the Afrikaners call themselves—the tribe of 2.1 million that rules a nation of 26 million. But in

1957, when Breytenbach graduated as the leading student at Huguenot High School in Wellington, he chose not to attend Stellenbosch, the traditional Afrikaner college, and instead enrolled in the liberal English-speaking University of Capetown, where he pursued his interests in art and literature, and, as he later noted, "met on a base of equality fellow countrymen of a different skin color." Some of his poems had already appeared in magazines, and when in 1960, at the age of twenty-one, he left South Africa for Paris, he was already a painter and poet of considerable promise.

In 1962, in Paris, he met and married a beautiful Vietnamese woman of aristocratic background, Hoang Lien, or Yolande, who had spent most of her life in France and was distinctly apolitical. By that time, his paintings were selling well in Paris galleries and he was writing poetry of such exceptional beauty that in 1963, when the Afrikaans writer Christian Barnard visited, he arranged for a selection of Breytenbach's works to be sent to Afrikaanse Pers, a South African publisher. Two books published the following year, one a collection of verse, the other of prose, won him the Afrikaanse Pers Boekhandel (APB) Prize for 1965, the first of five major Afrikaans literary awards he was to receive in the years to come.

Much of Breytenbach's force comes from the author's understanding and passion for Afrikaans culture. He understands intimately what he is rejecting, and it is this understanding that is most traitorous. That Breytenbach was able to publish his virulently antigovernment verse in South Africa is not wholly surprising. As Harry Minetree, who has written on South Africa and who knows Breytenbach intimately, explained, the government had been eager, for propaganda purposes, to nurture an Afrikaans voice to challenge the country's English-speaking writers.

The Afrikaners have an intense love of their language which dates from before the Boer War, when the old colonial rulers tried to force English down the throats of the Afrikaans poets. Those poets and writers who refused to adapt—many of whom were persecuted because of it—are part of the proud history of the Afrikaners. Breytenbach was in the honored tradition of brave poets who emerged to use their native language to write about their people's glories, past and present.

11

In 1965 Breytenbach's publishers invited him to come back to South Africa. But his wife, considered a nonwhite under the country's apartheid laws, was denied a visa. Breytenbach was shocked. "Perhaps one should ascribe this to naïvete or innocence," he said afterward. In any case, it was what he called "the beginning of my ambivalent relationship with my country." In a letter to the Cape Town newspaper *Die Burger*, he lashed out at the government for its decision:

> If I could give up my Afrikaanerhood today, I would. I am ashamed of my people. I am shamed by the humiliation of my wife, my family and friends and her family. I hate and abhor apartheid with all its implications, and if it is representative of Afrikaanerdom, if the two cannot be separated, then I see no future for the Afrikaaner in our beautiful country. I hope my case makes more Afrikaaners conscious of what current ideology, and specifically the Immorality Act, means in term of the most elementary human rights: everyday life. And I don't even want to think of how the existing laws of the land rule the daily life of the non-whites in general.

Thereafter, Breytenbach became more outspoken. At political meetings in Europe, his remarks attracted several antiapartheid groups, as well as the militant African National Congress and an underground terrorist organization called Solidarité. Though he was not yet an activist, his demands were so explosive that the Afrikans Academy accused him of having links with the Communist Party and in 1968 denied him the Herzog Prize, the most important South African literary award. It was conferred posthumously on another poet.

Breytenbach pressed on. He issued a statement to a Dutch newspaper, designed to be inflammatory: "Our freedom fighters in Zambia and Tanzania are beginning to infiltrate South-West Africa," he wrote. "They will never be stopped."

This statement incensed not only Breytenbach's literary colleagues in South Africa, but his family as well. His brother Cloete was a prominent photojournalist who had defended Breytenbach against the government on many occasions. Now Cloete was torn between loyalty to Breyten and to their elder brother, Colonel Jan Breytenbach, commander of the country's crack antiguerrilla unit, who was then fighting the very guerrillas the poet said could not be overcome. Jan appealed to his younger brother to come home, and to join the "fight against the freedom fighters." Breytenbach refused, claiming Jan had "decidedly fascist sympathies."

Evidence of the support Breytenbach enjoyed at home from liberals appeared in November 1971, when the National Union of South African Students (NUSAS) made him its honorary vice-president and praised his antiapartheid stance. He, in turn, encouraged them to align themselves with other student organizations, particularly Steve Biko's Black Consciousness group.

Considering the nature of Breytenbach's poetry, and the form his public statements were taking, it was inevitable that the government would move against him. In 1972 it banned his volume of poetry, *Skryt*, which featured a poem entitled "Letter from Abroad to Butcher." The seering cry of a tortured man, it was dedicated to "Balthazar," referring to Prime Minister Balthazar Johannes (John) Vorster.

I stand on bricks before my fellow man
I am the statue of emancipation
with electrodes on my balls
trying to scream light in the gloom
I write slogans in crimson urine
on my skin and on the floor
I keep watch
strangle on the ropes of my intestines
slip on soap and break my bones
murder myself with the evening paper
tumble from the tenth floor of heaven
to deliverance on a street among people

and you, butcher
you who are entrusted with the security of the state
what do you think of when the night reveals her
framework
and the first babbling shriek is squeezed out
of the prisoner
as in a birth
with the fluids of parturition?
are you humble before this bloodied thing

13

with all its manlike tremors
with the shattered breath of dying
in your hands?
does your heart also stiffen in your throat
when you touch the extinguished limbs
with the same hands that will fondle your wife's
mysteries?

Skryt shocked even his admirers, 30 percent of whom told a public opinion poll they thought Breytenbach should not write again. With this poem the poet had made a definitive break with his people. In Paris he tried to come to terms with the life of an exile.

2

DESPITE HAVING BANNED *Skryt*, the government soon realized that it had more to lose than to gain by alienating its most popular Afrikaans poet. Breytenbach was having a great impact on the younger generation. Using Breytenbach's brother Cloete as an intermediary, the government extended an invitation to the poet and his wife to visit South Africa for three months—on the condition that neither would make any political statements during the visit.

For the most part, Breytenbach complied; he limited his comments to the press (which followed him everywhere) to platitudes, and used the visit to revel in the beauty of the country and the quiet enjoyment of being once again among family and friends. Nevertheless, before returning to Europe in April, he agreed to address a reunion of the Sestigers (Writers of the Sixties) group, sponsored by the Summer School of the University of Cape Town. The Sestigers, as the leading Afrikaner novelist André Brink wrote in his invitation to the reunion, "had been responsible for the total renewal of Afrikaans literature in the course of the previous decade . . . an event of much more than literary importance since it implied a challenge to all the icons of Afrikanerdom—in politics, in religion, in morals, in esthetics." It had become customary in South Africa to identify pro- and anti-Sestigers with political progressives and conservatives.

The anti-Sestiger conservatives feared their potential power as a revolutionary force. Ruling whites were confident that neither the blacks nor foreign intervention could bring about the overthrow of apartheid. But they feared that their own white intellectuals could mobilize such change by appealing to the country's youth. The Sestigers were often criticized for not using their intellectual clout politically, but now authorities feared that by inviting Breytenbach to speak they were waking up and taking just such a stance. Breytenbach was one of the first Afrikan intellectuals to refuse to toe the government line. He was also one of the first few contemporary African figures to appeal to South Africa's young. Breytenbach, the authorities feared, had the power to incite the nation's white youth to turn against their fathers.

Breytenbach had been reluctant to take part in the reunion, but Brink eventually persuaded him. A capacity crowd, mostly Afrikaners, consisting of Sestigers, churchmen, the wives of several government ministers, students, and security police, assembled to hear him. He used the opportunity to deliver to this mixed audience an impassioned political speech.

"I am convinced that the salvation of this land, if so evangelistic a word is permissible, lies almost entirely in the hands of my black and brown compatriots," he said. "And just as I honor the black man who tries to improve his people's lot, so, I believe, will the black man only respect me to the degree that I am willing to work for the transformation of my own community—and not if I try to tell him what he ought to do."

He went on to flay his audience with the most virulent criticism of South Africa's politics ever voiced by an Afrikaner:

We are a bastard people with a bastard language. Our nature is bastardy. It is good and beautiful that it should be so. . . . Only we have fallen into the trap of the bastard who comes to power. In that part of our blood which comes from Europe was the curse of superiority! We wanted to justify our power. And in order to do that we had to consolidate our supposed tribal identity. . . . We had to entrench our otherness and at the same time hold on to what we had conquered. We made our otherness the norm, the standard—and the ideal. And because the perpetuation of our otherness was *at the expense* of our fellow South Africans—and

16

our South African-ness—we felt menaced. We build walls. . . .
And like all bastards—uncertain of their identity—we began to
cling to the idea of *purity*. That is apartheid. *Apartheid is the law
of the bastard*. This apartheid is the scope of our suicide, our self-
destruction, our death.

His audience was visibly stunned, although most supported
his views. Even Schalk Pienaar, a hostile commentator, conceded
as much in *Die Burger*. "The man's mastery with words is something exceptional," Pienaar wrote. "In addition, his emotional
attack found strong echoes. Our politicians ignore at their own
risk the violence with which such an audience reacts to the premise
that white superiority is a thing of the past. It was 'our people' who
reacted thus."

Clearly, the government had taken on more than it bargained
for when it invited Breytenbach to visit the country. But as Harry
Minetree noted in an article in *Quest* magazine, the BOSS (Bureau
of State Security) agents who questioned Breytenbach after his
speech were still unaware that the poet now thought of himself as
more than a political wordsmith, that he considered himself a
working revolutionary. Three months before leaving for South
Africa, Breytenbach and Johnny Makathini, the head of the African National Congress in Paris and Algiers, had aligned themselves with Barend Schuitema, an Afrikaner exile, and established
Atlas, an underground organization "aimed at launching a South
African revolution." The agents were also unaware that while in
South Africa Breytenbach had met clandestinely with students and
black labor leaders. Had they known, Breytenbach would certainly
have been arrested, rather than allowed to leave for Paris with his
wife on April 2, 1973.

On his return Breytenbach continued to meet with Schuitema
and other antiapartheid radicals. Atlas had by then been dis-
banded because of protests from an antiwhite faction in the London office of the African National Congress which, much to Breytenbach's dismay, had become increasingly Communist. Together
with Schuitema and Donald Moerdijk, a professor at the Sor-
bonne, Breytenbach founded a new organization called Okhela
(the Zulu word for "spark") to replace Atlas. It was his hope that
Okhela would function as an all-white extension of the ANC, and it

was similarly bent on establishing black majority rule in South Africa. But the organization's efforts never went beyond rhetoric.

Though aware that his activities were now being monitored by South African agents, Breytenbach was not intimidated. Nor would he listen to pleas from his brother Cloete, then on an assignment in Paris, to stop his acts of treason. The two brothers, though formerly close, parted in anger. Several weeks later a violent confrontation took place between the poet and his eldest brother, Colonel Jan Breytenbach, who came to Paris to warn him that the government was losing patience with his activities. Breytenbach remained adamant.

It was evident that he would stand his ground—not only from the risks he had already taken but from an extraordinary work of prose he had published the year after his 1973 visit to South Africa. Entitled *A Season in Paradise*, it is a fusion of poetry, narrative, fantasy, and manifesto in which Breytenbach wrote despairingly:

> One would like to believe in a miracle. One would like to believe that it could be possible to write in this country for and about people as people. But the poison of racism flows so deeply in our veins. Even in our language, our beautiful language, our wonderful vehicle, we speak of man and woman, of boy and girl. And when they are not pale enough? Koffir, nigger, coolie, blockhead, "uncle," ayah, kwedin, wog, munt.

Terrence Des Pres, the humanist philosopher, termed the work a "moral-aesthetic revolt rooted in the author's need to embrace artistic freedom and political commitment equally." Des Pres concluded his remarks on the book by saying: "*A Season in Paradise* evokes life in South Africa, its beauty, its obscene dismemberments, with extraordinary liberty and force. And Breytenbach . . . emerges as a prototype of the new writer—a Rimbaud for whom lyrical perception and logic of history combine in dignity and visionary triumph over the terrible world, in this case the terrible world of apartheid."

Then in 1975 Breytenbach, now thirty-six years old, shaved off his beard and flew to Johannesburg with the help of a French antiapartheid organization that supplied an illegal French passport in the name "Christian Galazka." He was homesick and frustrated in Paris, and came back as much to see family and friends as to engage in political activity. But he told one writer he did decide to contact antiapartheid whites and some black spokesmen, such as Steve Biko, in order to channel money from European church groups to black trade unionists in South Africa to "help develop a political infrastructure among anti-apartheid whites and to project to other whites inside South Africa the ideal of an alternative society free of racial barriers." He came into contact with the South African Council of Churches. The council is filled with people whose Christian beliefs make acceptance of apartheid a moral impossibility, but even they recognized that Breytenbach was impatient.

Breytenbach seemed to have a naïve belief that if he was not arrested upon entry, or after he had let his presence in South Africa be known, then in future he might be able to come and go as he pleased. It was as if he thought his presence would be of no interest to South Africa's security forces. He did little to hide from BOSS and spoke openly in Afrikaans. On several occasions he arranged to meet old friends in the foyers of large hotels.

But he underestimated the interest his visit caused. He had only an erratic regard for the delicate condition of activists operating under apartheid. From Paris came the famed writer in disguise, he himself admitted, as a Lord Byron/Walter Mitty mix—hardly the costume for blending in with students dressed in jeans and caftans.

He immediately fell in with informers. Months afterward he would say he should have known better. Breytenbach later hinted that he knew at the time—"I had known even as I arrived that I was blown, that they knew about me" and had ignored the signals "rather in the fashion of a small child closing its eyes hoping that in so doing the hideousness will go away." From the outset he was shadowed by security police. He was squarely in the cross hairs of the South African political rifle. Then, a few days before he was to leave, Breytenbach was arrested, charged with treason for attempting to overthrow the government, and imprisoned. Under South Africa's treason laws all the state had to show was that Breytenbach entertained anti–South African thoughts. They did not have to prove either an overt act or any hostile intent to injure his country. His writings alone could convict him.

The more sophisticated members of the government were un-

comfortable about charging South Africa's most respected Afrikaner writer with treason. They knew the English would join forces
with a significant part of the Afrikaner community in support of
Breytenbach—a grouping that could significantly split the white
bloc. But they were overruled by the police and the prosecutors,
who believed that by humiliating Breytenbach, by revealing the
presumed shallowness of his thought, and by flexing their own
political muscle, the government could use the poet as an example
to potentially rebellious Afrikaner students and dissidents that
those who strayed would be severely punished.

The "proof" they offered at the trial was designed to reveal
that Communists were behind the growing incidents of black unrest. Breytenbach's lawyers, retained for him by his parents, but
who were primarily corporate lawyers with little experience in
either criminal or political trials, and who had no sympathy for
revolution or, as they saw it, terrorism, did not dispute it. They
told Breytenbach that unless a deal could be struck, he might be
sentenced to death. And Breytenbach, much as he may have welcomed a martyr's role, did not want to pay the price of a lifetime
in jail.

During his trial, Breytenbach testified: "I know now that the
manner and the methods by which I tried to work for the growth
of our civilization and our future were wrong, that my behavior
was foolish, and that things I got mixed up in with good intentions
could only lead to harm for other people. I am sorry for all the
stupid, thoughtless things I did which brought me here, and I ask
to be forgiven for them. But I feel, I know, that I still have many
poems in my fingers and paintings in my eye. I hope that one day
if it is given to me to go out into the world again, I will still be able
to make my contribution to the future of our country and its people
through my writing and art. It will be a privilege."

He then apologized to Prime Minister Johannes Vorster for
"Letter from Abroad to Butcher." "It was," he said, "a crass and
insulting poem which I addressed to him. There was and is no
justification for it. I am sorry."

Touching all bases, he even extended thanks to Colonel Kalfie
Broodryk of the South African police, "the chief investigation
officer in charge of my case, and also the officers who worked for
him for the correct and humane way in which they treated me from

20

the beginning of my detention . . . their courteous conduct made these traumatic three months bearable for me." He admitted using his brother Jan's influence to arrange meetings in jail with BOSS during which he gave them information about his accomplices.

After Breytenbach had wound up his apologia, Colonel Broodryk then took his turn: He testified that Breytenbach was a poet, a romantic, a repentant and good man. It sounded like a testimonial.

Breytenbach's friends were stunned by Broodryk's testimony, the poet's torrents of apologies, and the political implications of the trial. No poet of Breytenbach's caliber would ever dream of apologizing for his work. Many assumed he had been drugged, tortured, or brainwashed.

He had not. His lawyers had indeed succeeded in convincing him that he would get off more lightly if he refrained from using his trial to launch a political attack on the government. They also told him that the quality of his treatment in prison—for prison was inevitable—would depend on the extent of his cooperation with the security police. Although the lawyers and judges deny it to this day, most people who witnessed the trial, sensing the complete understanding between the prosecution and defense, realized a deal had been struck, with the poet's cooperation, to get him a lighter sentence in exchange for his political surrender.

The trial ended in a manner unprecedented in South African legal history. Both the public prosecutor and the security policemen in charge of the investigation joined with the defense counsel in asking for the minimum sentence of no more than five years in a minimum-security prison: this in a case under the Terrorism Act, where there is effectively no minimum sentence and life imprisonment is the standard.

The judge, also suspecting there had been a "deal," angrily turned on everyone. Even the prosecutor was visibly shocked when the judge imposed a sentence of nine years' hard labor and refused to allow an appeal. Years later, when journalists sought to examine the court files to make some sense of the case, they found that all the documents relating to it had disappeared.

The verdict was a complete victory for the state. According to Charles Morand, a foreign observer representing the International Commission of Jurists, an organization whose concerns were similar to those I was to represent at the second trial:

> The Breytenbach case constitutes a remarkable success for the government. It has helped impress upon the white community the image of a vast subversive conspiracy. It must be expected that the government will exploit this favorable situation by intensifying the repression. The arrest of other leaders is the first sign. In the political context, which an impartial observer is bound to take into account, the Breytenbach trial, like many of those which preceded it, is to be seen as a lever which enables the white government to legitimate and reinforce its dictatorial powers and to pursue its policy of apartheid.

Morand's report, which was made public shortly after the trial, was correct. The state trumpeted its win. In the annual report of the commissioner of police for 1975–76, the arrest and conviction of Breyten Breytenbach are termed "one of the major successes in the sphere of internal security."

On the afternoon of November 26, 1975, immediately after the sentencing, Breytenbach, beginning his nine-year sentence, was taken from security police headquarters in the ill-famed Compol Building to the maximum-security section of the Pretoria Central Prison, known to its inmates as "Beverly Hills."

The poet had lost nearly everything. He was in shock as a result of both his capitulation and the severity of the sentence. He had not realized the effect such a repudiation would have on him, nor how humiliating the trial would be. He had been manipulated into playing the part the police had wanted him to play, and although he had avoided a life sentence, the reality of the nine years of hard labor that confronted him hit him hard.

As soon as Breytenbach arrived at Beverly Hills, security police and BOSS agents began to question him relentlessly. His friends, shocked and bewildered by his testimony, were not coming to see him. Some friends and political allies had disowned him completely. Isolated and lonely, he began to look forward to his inquisitors' visits. "Any contact with the outside world was a relief to me at that stage," he later explained.

In March 1976, after four months, Yolande, his wife, was allowed to pay him a visit. By permitting her to enter the country, the government had granted him a favor, one he knew would not quickly be repeated. Breytenbach realized he would probably not

22

see Yolande again for years. From that point on he began to plan his escape.

Many months passed. A diary he wrote, later printed, describes the horror, squalor, and madness of the prison world into which he was thrust. The years Breytenbach spent in prison were made even more difficult for him by outside events. Along with the few remaining English liberals and radicals, he was cast aside by the new young black leadership. Steve Biko's all-black student movement shunned the nonracial National Union of South African Students, as well as other biracial attempts to end apartheid. He claimed the biracial groups were merely a salve for the guilty conscience of a handful of liberal whites, who formed them to create the false impression that something was being accomplished. Evoking memories of America's Malcolm X, Biko said, "The biggest mistake the black world ever made was to assume that whoever opposed apartheid was an ally."

In prison Breytenbach began to fear that the jailers would treat him worse than other prisoners, black or white, because he was a "traitor" from the ruling class. He was correct. They threw him into solitary confinement for months on end, isolating him from all other prisoners. The secret police continued to offer him deals in exchange for information, but he insisted he had no information to give them. Breytenbach had too quickly gone from the streets of Paris to South Africa's jails, and despite the serious nature of the trial, he was unprepared for the relentlessness of prison life. The security officers could not break him, but in the year after his detention, they did drive him toward what appeared to be a foolhardy escape attempt. What happened was that in collaboration with a seemingly sympathetic jailer, he wrote personal notes, political harangues, and jailbreak plans to his friends on the outside, not suspecting that the jailer was toying with him and using him to implicate his friends. His letters were turned over to the state, which charged him with subversion and attempting to escape from prison. He was to stand trial once more.

3

BREYTENBACH'S 1977 TRIAL was to be held before the same judge, Albert Boshoff, who had tried the nine young blacks the previous year in what had come to be known as the SASO Nine case.

I met with him in his chambers, a large room behind a courtroom that looked very much like a typical American court-room, a half hour before the second Breytenbach trial began. In his gray suit the judge was a stern, white-haired figure. Over tea and petits fours, he voiced his strong personal feelings against the recent United States Supreme Court decision to abolish the death penalty.

We discussed at some length the SASO Nine case in which the judge had severely sentenced the black student defendants, not because of what they had done but because of their criticism of apartheid. The judge said Biko's Black Consciousness philosophy was "a danger to public safety because it was likely to lead to a mobilization of black opinion against the established white order, in a manner calculated to cause racial confrontation."

With a good deal of satisfaction, Judge Boshoff told me he believed American law would also have permitted prosecution on these grounds, even though it was the defendants' thoughts rather than their actions that were placed on trial. You have your own "clear and present danger test" given to you by Oliver Wendell

Holmes, one of the world's greatest jurists, he reminded me.

I told him I believed he was wrong on the American law. "The SASO 9 indictment," I replied, "would have been dismissed and the case thrown out of court." The United States Supreme Court, in a number of treason cases, distinguished between advocacy and action, between abstract thoughts and inciting others to act. Here no one acted on his words, and I added that many of the charges against Breytenbach were only for words he wrote. There were no overt acts there either.

The judge pointed out that under South Africa's treason statutes abstract discussions in support of Marxist ideology were punishable. I asked, "What about university professors who praise certain socialist ideas off campus?"

"They don't," he said.

The judge seemed amused when he learned the names of the international organizations that had an interest in seeing that Breytenbach had a fair trial, but he asked, in a cordial tone, how he could accommodate me. I told him I would want to see the entire trial, including those parts that might be closed to the public and press, to examine the court exhibits, to talk to lawyers on both sides as well as to witnesses and the defendant, and at the end of the trial, to submit a brief to him. Judge Boshoff, engaged by our talk, agreed to read what I wrote. Then he put on his judicial attire, a white wig and a black robe with a red sash, and we walked back to the courtroom.

I was introduced to the poet by his defense counsel. In a gray suit, his hair already flecked with gray, looking very much like a young college professor, Breytenbach was already seated, handcuffed, in the dock. He smiled, obviously very pleased at my presence, and at the fact that the judge had agreed to take a brief from me. Then he said quietly, and with a sad, accepting expression, "But they will try to hang me. . . ."

The prosecuting attorney walked close to us as he went to his seat at the far counsel table; I thought he was trying to overhear my short conversation with Breytenbach. As I took my seat, I noticed that the world press was represented, as was every major South African newspaper. In an atmosphere of expectancy the trial began.

The state's case was simple and brief. It was built around one star witness and Breytenbach's letters. The witness was a twenty-year-old short, plump prison warden named Pieter Groenwald, who looked as if he were too young to shave. Groenwald testified that Breytenbach had befriended him, affectionately called him "Lucky" (a nickname Groenwald's jailer friends had stuck on him), offered him money for his help in an escape, and asked him to deliver messages to Yolande and six coconspirators who included André Brink and other Afrikaner liberals. Groenwald dramatized his testimony by claiming that he and Breytenbach had used a so-called "Cuban code" (the word "Cuban" was used to imply Communist influence) as Breytenbach tried to revolutionize him.

The jailer then explained how he had encouraged Breytenbach to continue his escape attempt and how he had shared the poet's intimate letters with fellow jailers who despised the prisoner. Breytenbach's letters were full of stunning indiscretions. As Peter Dreyer, a South African writer, noted in his excellent book *Martyrs and Fanatics*, "What was inexcusable was that in correspondence that was going directly into security police files several of the people he was writing to—James Polley, André Brink, Gerry Mare—were South Africans living in South Africa." Later Groenwald submitted those damning letters as evidence. The letters that the poet wrote to his radical friends "proved" that Breytenbach continued to violently oppose the government and hoped, when he escaped, to get help to blow up such symbolic targets as the Afrikaans Language Monument in the township of Paarl.

One particular letter was different from all the rest and most startling. Written to General Mike Geldehum, the head of the security police, Breytenbach offered to become an informer for BOSS. Breytenbach's letter proposed that "I be released and try—in collaboration with your service—to become a member of the South African Communist Party. . . . I am convinced that, in my way, I can also make a contribution, however slight, to the solution of some of the problems crowding in on South Africa. . . . I also have a chance, I believe, to build up contact again with people . . . who for one or another reason try to stay on top of the SCAP's maneuvers and plans."

It is impossible to reconcile the author of the Geldehum letter with the man who wrote of revolution. Marius Schoon, a member of the Communist Party, had shared a flat with Breytenbach in Cape Town years before, and was in a cell in the same prison on charges of sabotage. Writing to him from his cell, Breytenbach said: "My complaints are that the C.P. isn't revolutionary enough. . . . I would like to see the C.P. more strongly socialistic, more-self assured and with more confidence in the bright weapon of Marxism."

Breytenbach's supporters, still shocked by the extraordinary and bewildering evidence of the first trial, were again amazed at what was unfolding at the second. Again, the trial raised more questions about Breytenbach than it answered: Was Breytenbach still ambivalent? Was he prepared to do anything at all, even become an informer, to get out of jail? Was he trying to lie to BOSS, hoping they would believe him, and then planning to leave them after he was released? Or were jail conditions so intolerable that they were driving him mad? The trial's observers and Breytenbach's friends hoped that Breytenbach would testify and clear up the confusion. They were to be bitterly disappointed.

Breytenbach took the stand. He calmly admitted the escape attempt, but then just as calmly denied there was any possibility of achieving the radical changes he wanted. As he testified, it became clear that he was peculiarly unsuited for the role of a revolutionary.

Breytenbach claimed he knew the jailer Groenwald was setting him up and that, through these inconsistent and contradictory letters, he was playing with his jailers and BOSS. He claimed that little in his letters was true. But he could not fully explain why he had endangered the lives of his friends and why he offered to become an informer. After two and a half days of solid testimony, his friends concluded that naïveté and an emotional artistic temperament went with his radical passion; others, including many blacks, were less charitable—they concluded he had at times believed BOSS would save him and that he was prepared to deal to save his life.

But the poet did throw light on how he had suffered in prison. During his testimony he referred to other letters that described his mental deterioration and loneliness in jail. Believing that only international pressure could save him, he kept looking over at me as he tried to describe the conditions that had driven him to try to escape.

I did not believe any part of Breytenbach's story. I believed he was trying to escape and that he had not fully realized he might endanger the lives of his friends while doing so. I believed his politics were best expressed by his apologizing at the first trial, while on the stand, to the Vorster government.

Even as I was extremely sympathetic to the spot he was now in—he later called it trying to "find elbow room in hell"—I felt my dislike for him. His charming style could not obscure the fact that he had been a political disaster. Leading figures in the anti-apartheid movement were punished because of the information the poet gave the police. White leftists, trying to expand their base and attempting against odds to forge links with black compatriots, could not afford the albatross Breytenbach had become.

During a recess Breytenbach's lawyers showed me eloquent letters that had not been produced by the prosecution. For the two years of his incarceration, he had been deliberately kept next to the death cell, where each month a dozen black Africans waited to be hanged. He heard the prisoners singing, stamping their feet with every note as they tried to quiet their fears, and saw each of the more than two hundred men as they left the cell for the gallows. Even in their final moments, blacks are discriminated against: For their last meals white prisoners get a whole roast chicken. The black prisoner gets half a chicken. The way of death is also subject to apartheid. White men get new ropes, while the same ropes are used over and over again to hang blacks, even though many of them are covered in vomit and saliva from the previous hangings.

Black prisoners are told they will be hanged a week before the execution date, and from that time on they sing day and night with "wonderful voices full of grief." Sometimes there would be a younger voice in the group, quavering with fear, and the older voices would sustain it, lift it up. Then there would be, muffled in the distance, the thud of the trap door, the instant of death. But the singing would go on to the end.

Breytenbach said he thought he could tell when a condemned prisoner was told he was to die "because," he wrote, "the quality of his voice changes at once. You can hear that he sings in an entirely different way. I don't know whether you can call it a sort of ecstasy or a despair or a spiritual transport—but it's entirely another tone."

Breytenbach and Stefaans Tsafendas, the Greek immigrant who was declared insane and sentenced to life imprisonment for stabbing Prime Minister Hendrick Verwoerd to death in 1966, were the only long-term white prisoners in the jail. Breytenbach said that Mr. Tsafendas was subjected to a daily ritual of hate for killing "the architect of apartheid." His food was routinely spat in or scattered on the cell floor and his slop bucket overturned. Destined to be kept in solitary for his life, Tsafendas would not talk to anyone during the years of his confinement except at exactly 6 P.M. on Friday, when for ten minutes he would sing two songs, and then be quiet for another week.

Breytenbach's trial lawyers tried to explain away some of their defendant's more radical thoughts by showing that Breytenbach had been given a special kind of treatment previously reserved only for extremely militant blacks. They said Robert Sobukwe, an important black revolutionary whom he had met during his 1973 trip, had told Breytenbach that the government had tried to break him by holding him for nine years in solitary confinement. Now Breytenbach himself was being given similar treatment. No warden or prisoner was permitted to talk to him and no reading materials were furnished to him. He spent twenty-three and a half hours of the day in silence in his dark cell and took his half-hour exercise alone, away from all other prisoners. He was allowed one five-hundred-word letter a month.

As soon as Breytenbach finished testifying, the judge rendered his decision. The verdict was as freakish as the trial. Even though he had admitted the escape attempt, Breytenbach was acquitted on both the escape and the terrorism counts because the judge said he did not believe he was the radical that the secret police claimed he was. Breytenbach was convicted only on the minor charge of smuggling letters out of prison and was returned to jail to serve out the last seven years of his original sentence. If he had sat out this sentence to its end, he would have been eligible for parole in 1980. Now parole was forfeit and the date of his freedom was postponed until 1984 unless the government commuted his sentence—which was highly unlikely. There had not been a commutation of such a sentence for thirty years.

It was impossible and unnecessary to disguise the political nature of the trial. The climate at the time Breytenbach was first arrested and during the eight months before the case was tried was totally different from that which prevailed at the time of the second trial. By then the government crackdown on its internal enemies, black and white, had been so successful that there was no longer any reason to come down hard on the white Afrikaner poet.

Perhaps more importantly, the government was deliberately showing that the courts were a direct arm of the political machinery. It was ending the dreams of many of South Africa's liberals that there still was a branch of the government where justice could be obtained, ending the dreams and hopes of many whites (and a few blacks) who felt that change could come legally and peacefully.

After the trial concluded, an Afrikaner lawyer with government connections told me it had been considered such a special case that it was conducted by a judge who had been specially appointed to try it. The "legal" reasons Judge Boshoff gave for the acquittal were transparent—he had simply changed the conclusion drawn from the previous trial. In 1975, when Breytenbach had been sentenced to nine years, he was found to be a dangerous terrorist. In 1977, when acquitted, he was found to be a harmless poet. In 1975 his poems and paintings were considered sufficiently inflammatory to brand him a revolutionary; now they were merely construed as the illusions of a romantic.

There was more. Breytenbach's underground group, Okhela, which in his first trial was characterized as a Marxist revolutionary organization with an elaborate plan of action and cache of weapons was, in the second trial, found to be largely a figment of Breytenbach's artistic imagination. By branding Breytenbach and his followers fools, the government chose not to punish him but rather to discredit once again whatever remained of the Afrikaner anti-apartheid movement. I had never seen judicial decisions like this in any court of law—they were especially shocking in a country that so often claimed the executive and judicial branches of government were separate.

The government won. Breytenbach had miraculously recreated the disaster of his first trial. Breytenbach's trial got extensive newspaper and television coverage, both at home and abroad. In South Africa most of the white public was satisfied with the trial's result. They felt that Breytenbach's original sentence and jail term had been punishment enough and that any more would just make another martyr in a country that had more than its share. It certainly proved to those Afrikaner and English whites who cared to listen how brutal jail conditions could be.

4

ONLY TWO BLOCKS away from where the Breytenbach trial had taken place, another kind of treason case was getting underway. The defendants were eleven black men and one woman, all members of the banned African National Congress, charged with attacking a police station and killing two policemen.

The government wanted to prove in this case that China and Russia were running terrorist training camps in neighboring black states, and that these camps, in their recruitment of South African blacks, were the cause of the growing black unrest in the country. The charge was as much designed to win the hearts and minds of the United States and other anti-Communist countries and get their support for the repressive white regime as it was to influence the judge that tried the case.

In this case the government was seeking death sentences, and in this case there was absolutely no doubt that they meant to get what they were after.

The trial was held in Pretoria's old Jewish synagogue, now surrounded for security reasons with a dozen police guards and trucks. The temple had been remodeled for the occasion to resemble a courtroom, with spectators sitting in the pews and the judge seated in the center on a sort of elevated throne beside an open cupboard which had once housed a Torah. The holy building now had accommodations for lawyers, stenographers, and witnesses.

There were no Stars of David or any other religious trappings to be seen. The balcony that once seated women was empty. The only trace of spirituality was the green and pink light which reflected on people's faces during the day as the sun moved over a stained-glass window in the center of the ceiling. Outside in the courtyard in the back of the synagogue were makeshift cells that held the prisoners when they were not in the courtroom.

There was a sense of excitement at the synagogue at the first day of the ANC trial. The families of the defendants came to court, proud of their involvement with the banned black resistance movement, happy that the male and female prisoners were still alive. As each man, and the very young woman, entered the court, they walked proudly, looking for their families. Although there had been no formal seating arrangements for the spectators, there was a sense of separation in the place. The blacks, their few white supporters, some black members of the press, defense lawyers, and aides filled up one side of the pews. The security police, courtroom attendants, interpreters, Afrikaners, and prosecutors filled the others. Although the whites held all the dominant positions in that courtroom, they soon dissolved into a sort of colorless backdrop against which the black revolutionaries and their supporters took over the scene.

The trial began sharply on Monday at 10 A.M. The state's key witness, who, it was "announced," had turned state's evidence, was the coal black, slightly built Ian Deway Rwaza, twenty-three years of age. He testified on direct examination for four long days. The prosecutor asked questions in English, which were then translated into Xhosa. The witness replied in Xhosa, which was then translated back into English.

The courtroom acoustics were terrible. The afternoon heat and the endless translations induced sleep in me and most of the other spectators. There was no public address system, no microphones. The proceeding sounded like a private conversation at the end of the room. No doubt the authorities felt they had no responsibility to the public and hoped that the courtroom procedure would be so boring that spectators would lose interest and go away. The authorities were wrong; black spectators filled the seats, while the overflow patiently waited outside.

As Rwaza's answers were translated back into English again, I heard him link each of the twelve defendants to the Soviet Union and China, and tell lurid tales of how sabotage, subversion, bombing, and killing in South Africa were being carried out from bases in Angola. He told of plans to bomb police stations and ammunition dumps in Johannesburg. He deciphered get-away sketches, diagrams, and plans, and identified the owners of vehicles and guns. But as the trial wore on, it became evident that there was no corroborating proof to back his testimony of the training camps in the Soviet Union, China, or neighboring black states.

The cultured voices of the barristers, with their educated English accents, phrased their objections and statements to the court with exquisite style. If I closed my eyes, I could almost imagine myself in the Old Bailey; it sounded far more gracious than any American court I had ever been in, even the United States Supreme Court.

At the start of the fifth day, as the state prosecutor began asking detailed questions about the Russian training schools for Southern African terrorists in Russia and Angola, Rwaza suddenly, without explanation, stopped giving answers. The prosecutor continued to ask questions, but although Rwaza's eyes remained fastened on his interrogator, it seemed as if he had lost the thread of his dialogue. The judge intervened and prodded the witness, but Rwaza stubbornly remained silent.

No one knew quite what to do. The courtroom, cool before the afternoon heat, was still. The seated defense lawyers, exchanging glances, decided not to say anything as the witness sat mute. Minutes dragged. Then the flustered prosecutor, stopped dead in his tracks, was granted a ten-minute recess to talk to Rwaza.

Ten minutes turned into half an hour. Then Rwaza dutifully went back to the makeshift witness box, and the prosecutor seemed confident the trial would now continue on its predetermined path. He asked the first question. As before, it was translated into Xhosa, but as before, Rwaza continued his silence. More time passed. He stopped looking at the prosecution and started to stare down at the wooden floor. Finally, turning slowly to the judge, Rwaza asked—softly and in English—if he could "talk privately to His Lordship." His use of the English language after four days of Xhosa was as startling as his request.

The judge, who for the first time seemed to become interested in the trial, replied in a gentle voice to the witness. "I cannot speak to you privately, but you may speak now while you are in the witness stand and, remembering that you are under oath, say what you want."

The court caught its breath. Rwaza sat up in the witness box. At first haltingly, but then with increasing confidence, he described what had happened to him after his arrest and while he was in detention. The trial seemed suspended as he continued uninterrupted for nearly an hour.

Rwaza described his lot as a political black witness in a South African jail. He spent three months in solitary confinement and was denied contact with family, friends, or even police. When he seemed softened, he was taken to see his three-year-old son, spent an hour alone with him, and then was given money by the police to give to his child. He was told that if he cooperated no harm would come to his son. They never told Rwaza what would happen if he did not cooperate, but he understood that if he did not he certainly would never see the child again.

For the next three months the police came to him every day, asking him for more and more information. Beaten daily, he was also strangled, suffocated, tortured, and kept naked in the cold cell. Rwaza made believable the tales of police brutality in a way the defendants themselves never could. As I heard his testimony, I asked myself, if this was what the government did to its own witnesses, how much worse did it treat its prisoners to force confessions?

Rwaza looked at each of the defendants in turn as he spoke. Although all of them knew his testimony could do nothing to change the outcome of the trial, they also knew they were witnessing a heroic sacrifice that would become part of the history of black Africa. The longer he spoke, the more he felt the defendants' and the spectators' respect for him grow until finally, eyes focused only on the defendants, he became at one with them. Although the state could and would deny Rwaza's accusations, every single person in that makeshift courtroom, black and white, knew they were true.

After Rwaza finished, the judge advised the witness that because he had changed his testimony, he could be charged with perjury. I asked one of the lawyers whether that was likely. He smiled softly and said, "No, I don't think he will be charged for changing his testimony. I don't think he'll ever see a courtroom again. In fact, I don't think we'll ever see him alive again."

And the lawyer was right—after his testimony, Rwaza disappeared without a trace.

During the lunch recess that followed Rwaza's heartrending outburst, the trial judge and I caught sight of each other leaving the court. He knew who I was—he had to approve my credentials before I could enter the courtroom. I walked a few steps with him. He seemed to want to talk, although he did not seem to know what to say. We stood together on the synagogue steps for a few minutes exchanging pleasantries in the hot midday sun, and finally with sadness he said, "It's good that you are here."

The following day the proceedings resumed as if nothing had happened. The parade of black prosecution witnesses and secret-police witnesses continued. It was briefly interrupted when Rwaza's mother entered the old synagogue. A dark, stolid woman, she raised her arm, clenched her fist, and was in turn saluted by the defendants and the courtroom spectators. A Xhosa freedom song, with its clucking sounds, broke out in the balcony. Where years before Jewish hymns and prayers had flooded the holy building, where Jews in skullcaps and talithim had sung of their determination to be free, and to have Moses deliver them from their Egyptian oppressors, now bareheaded blacks sang for their own deliverance. The judge, obviously moved, let the singing finish, waited a few moments, and then called the courtroom to order.

The trial resumed, but now it was a different trial, one whose mood was of defiance and of victory.

Many evenings, after a day in court, I would go to dinner with the defense lawyers for the ANC. Many lived in comfortable, even elegant, homes in Johannesburg, staffed by servants. Many had second homes an hour away from the city. Their life-styles were supported by highly paid law practices which also allowed them to try select political cases such as this one. When I was with them, these cases were not discussed. However, I knew that these lawyers were often caught between a rock and a hard place; for example, in their latest case they found themselves in a no man's land, rejected and distrusted by their African National Congress clients yet horrified by the conditions of apartheid which had led them into court. Whenever the fire came, these lawyers knew they too would have to pay a price for the years of inequity, but although some of their children were leaving the country, they were not.

One of the lawyers, Ernest Wentzel, a short, chubby man, not quite as elegant and certainly not as affluent as most of the others, maintained his distance from most of his Afrikaner compatriots, as well as the more affluent English lawyers who made up the defense team, as they did from him. In 1976 Wentzel had himself spent forty-eight days in solitary confinement for too actively defending men thought to be members of the ANC.

Describing his jailing, he said, "The worst part of solitary came when the jailers said, 'We're going to take your shoelaces and belts from you. We don't want you to harm yourself.' I believed them and started to feel grateful to them. It's when you think of them as human beings that it becomes easy to break." Wentzel also spoke sadly of the day-to-day isolation of his present life. He had lost contact with the blacks he had devoted his life to and became estranged from the whites who, as a result of his work, had grown suspicious of him. I felt a deep admiration for Wentzel and felt closer to him than to any other South African I had met.

Wentzel, speaking as much about his own life as Breytenbach's, said, "You can't fight the Afrikaners without finding support among the blacks. It's too lonely otherwise. A black activist will have his family's and friends' support, but Breytenbach stood alone."

One day at Wentzel's home, with its furniture that looked as if it had been rescued from an American Salvation Army store and bare wooden floors, he showed me the pants of a young black given to him by the boy's mother. The black had supposedly committed suicide by jumping out of the tenth-floor window of the police station at John Vorster Square in Johannesburg.

Wentzel pointed out black India ink markings on the inside leg of the dead prisoner's khaki pants. "The police gave his pants to his mother. They didn't know the Xhosa writing. In Xhosa it says, 'They are going to kill me.' Even though this was shown to the magistrate, he still found that the youth had fallen accidentally."

"Every year," the lawyer went on, "ten to twenty blacks go

37

out that same police station window on the tenth floor of Vorster Square. After the police beat them up, they set the defendants near the open window and let them know that's the only way the torture will end. They'll bring the same man back again and again to that opening."

That tenth-floor window has already earned itself a place in South African literature. In Athol Fugard's *Lesson from Aloes*, the black man, Steve, resisting all torture in the police basement, breaks down and cries inconsolably when placed invitingly before the tenth-floor window. He has the only choice he is allowed while under interrogation—he can give in to torture and inform on his friends or he can save his friends and end his agony by killing himself. Sitting by the window, all alone for thirty minutes twice a day is his peak of humiliation. Hundreds of blacks and Indians have dropped from the tenth-floor window of security police headquarters in Johannesburg.

Ernie Wentzel asked me to join with other lawyers in filing damage suits against the police on behalf of blacks who had died while in detention. There were dozens. All were imprisoned without trial, charge, prosecution, or evidence. All were denied legal representation and access to friends or relatives. In some cases the cause of death was given—"death by suicide and hanging" and "slipped in shower" were the most frequent "causes"—but in most cases the government did not even bother to come up with a cause.

Wentzel felt that if any of the organizations I was representing in South Africa communicated their opposition through letters or calls to the court and prosecutor, or spoke to the families of the murdered men, it would put pressure on the South African government to stop these barbaric practices. South African lawyers who filed suits against the police were exposing themselves and their families to retaliation by the police—including the kind of detention that Wentzel had undergone. But I agreed to do what I could, and after I returned to the United States, several American lawyers established contact with their South African colleagues and joined them in suits. However, I was never able to get sufficient numbers of volunteers or funds to make the program a permanent one.

One case I might have taken up was that of Joseph Mdluli, who within hours of his arrest by the Durban security police in

March 1976 was dead in peculiar circumstances—as a result of "falling over a chair," according to police witnesses. At the subsequent trial four policemen were charged with culpable homicide, but at a press conference in February 1977, the minister of justice, James Thomas Kruger, stated that Mdluli had attempted suicide and that the police had grappled with him to save him. Despite the existence of photographs showing that Mdluli had been badly beaten, the case against the police was eventually dismissed. Kruger felt the verdict was an important one for the police force, for otherwise, he said, "other officers might be inhibited from trying to stop security detainees from committing suicide."

There are many other cases on record. Mapetla Mohapi, the police report says, hanged himself with his trousers in his cell at the Kei Road police station in King William's Town on August 5, 1976. At the inquest the magistrate found that death was "not brought about by any act of commission or omission by any living person."

Luke Maxwembe, aged thirty-two, also supposedly hanged himself with strips of blanket on September 2, 1976, the day of his detention in Cape Town. Wounds on his body which the police were unable to explain indicated swelling and bruising of the right cheekbone, swelling of the scrotum, abrasions to the ankle and shoulder blades. The police were not indicted.

Many other black prisoners have lost their lives in white police stations—all, according to the authorities, as a result of accidents or suicide. The police have in nearly every case defeated any legal attempt to hold them responsible.

5

THE MOST SIGNIFICANT contrast between the trials of Breytenbach and the African National Congress members was not in the testimony or the outcome, but in the demonstration of the distance between the black and white communities. In two weeks there had not been one black spectator at the Breytenbach trial. The trial drew merely the curious and people who wanted to see the "trumped up pseudo-radical" poet severely punished.

At the ANC trial, apart from three dozen clearly identifiable plainclothesmen, there was only one white sympathizer among the two hundred black spectators. She was Helen Joseph, a small, white-haired, sixty-eight-year-old Englishwoman. Joseph had long ago been derided as a crank by most whites, and thus her activity on the behalf of the blacks was tolerated. Very few people spoke to her.

There were other differences between the two trials. The ANC trial had a spirit and fight that was the total opposite of the atmosphere that prevailed at Breytenbach's trial. The Breytenbach trial had an air almost of capitulation to it, probably born of intimidation: every spectator was photographed entering the courtroom—probably for the government to use, if needed, as evidence of contentious political involvement. As a result, many of Breytenbach's friends, particularly the academics, stayed away.

Sometimes I was the only one around at the end of the day to see him climb into the van and be driven back to his cell.

But the ANC trial remained vibrant and full of hope. There was no fear or intimidation. It reminded me of trials I had participated in in the American South in the 1960s. The black defendants' makeshift tin jails seemed much like those hastily thrown together in Mississippi and Alabama.

Moreover, the ANC trial, like the trials in the rural American South, had few white supporters, but all white judges, prosecutors, and courtroom personnel; blacks jammed shoulder to shoulder singing songs of freedom and defiance, while each day the white police tried to provoke incidents among them. The German shepherd dogs, barking with vicious anticipation from inside their small cages in the police vans, brought to mind Selma, Alabama, and Jackson, Mississippi, where they had been used against blacks who were fighting for their rights.

The courtroom spectators at the ANC trial hung on each word, reacted to each answer. At lunch and at each court recess, the defendants, lifting their hands in Black Power salutes, shouted, *"Amandla!* [Power!]." The audience answered, *"Awetui!* [To us!]." Others chanted, *"Amandla ngawethy* [Strength is ours]." One day a black man read the Sermon on the Mount in Xhosa, the rolling passages punctuated by groans, sighs, and amens from some members of the crowd. But silence met a black man who asked his listeners to "turn the other cheek."

At the end of each day, as I stood outside the synagogue, other incidents occurred that took me back to the American South. The blacks began cheering in voices so loud that the prisoners being led to the detention areas in the back heard and replied with an answering chorus. On one of these occasions, when the cheering had gotten particularly loud, helmeted riot police appeared as if from nowhere with a dozen snarling dogs. The police, ostensibly trying to force back the crowd, actually tried to provoke an incident. But the blacks flooding the sidewalk refused to be drawn into a fight. I was standing in a group of about ten blacks in the inner circle facing the courthouse. The German shepherds on short leashes snapped and jumped at the blacks on either side of me, but not at me. They had been trained to attack selectively.

The blacks sang their freedom songs more loudly and allowed themselves to be pushed back only a tiny bit. Dozens of white plainclothesmen spilled out of the synagogue to help the uniformed police, although probably none of them realized that the song's Zulu refrain meant "We shall kill them." Only when the blacks had finished this song did the inner part of the crowd open up, as if a taut rubber band had snapped, and the entire crowd filed slowly and deliberately down the sidewalks and into the street.

Finally, the ANC prisoners were piled into a waiting van. As the van drove away, the blacks on both sides of the street shouted supporting slogans at the passing vehicle. The blacks then streamed down the middle of the street to the buses and cars that would take them back to their townships.

The remainder of the three-week ANC trial went smoothly from the prosecutor's point of view, ending in conviction for all of the twelve defendants, as had been expected. A brief I submitted to the Court and prosecutor arguing both that even under South African conspiracy law there could not be a conviction and that, if there were a conviction, clemency should be granted, was of no use at all. Two defendants were sentenced to death. Five life sentences were handed out, committing the men to the bleak isolation of Robben Island, where the judge told them they would stay for the rest of their natural lives. The others received fifteen years. Once the sentences had been handed out, the judge stood up and left the room. As soon as he was gone, the convicted men started to sing. They kept singing as the police grabbed them, dragged them from the dock, and pulled them away—some by their feet. The Afrikaans press and some international newspapers applauded the South African courts both for proving that militant blacks were controlled by the Russians and for dealing with them appropriately.

6

ONE UNUSUALLY HOT afternoon I took a break from the trials and went walking in a beautiful green park in the middle of Johannesburg. There was a small lake with ducks, and white children tended by black nannies were pushing little wooden boats along the water. There were young people holding hands on the park benches. It was a scene evocative of many small towns the world over.

As I walked along the narrow concrete path that circled the lake, two black women coming toward me stepped off the pavement and stood to one side so I could pass. When next some blacks approached me, I stepped aside to let them pass. They were visibly embarrassed.

Soon I learned to continue walking, letting the blacks step out of the way. With a sixth sense, and without even appearing to see the whites, they always stepped aside. They effaced themselves so effectively that after a few hours I almost failed to notice that there were hundreds of blacks in the park.

The longer I stayed in South Africa, the more invisible the blacks became. For the first few days I was aware of the many black domestics, sprinkled on the green lawns and in the suburban homes, not to mention the thousands of blacks in the city. At first I was angry when I saw police indiscriminately stop them on the street, ask for their passbooks, and jam them into police vans.

But by the end of my first week, I could almost forget as I traveled around Johannesburg by day that it was a city with far more blacks than whites.

Many blacks were then tried each day for passbook violations. In 1976 the commissioner of prisons noted that there were 273,393 sentenced prisoners and 243,965 prisoners awaiting trial for passbook violations. The average daily number of prosecutions is over 1,600.

The infamous passbook laws then in effect governed every aspect of a black's life in South Africa. Without permission duly acknowledged in the passbook, blacks are confined to particular areas, can only hold certain jobs, and cannot effectively function without permission from the state for every move they make. The failure to have a passbook in their possession at all times, or the failure to have a job or a living area properly approved, can result in severe criminal penalties, jail sentences, or transportation to a labor farm for "reeducation."

I decided I wanted to witness some of the passbook trials—a decision that was easier made than carried out.

From the time I entered the recently opened municipal building in which the trials were to take place, it took me half an hour to find the right courtrooms, which were hidden away on the third floor. The South African government tries to discourage both critical whites and the defendants' families from attending. The directory on the first floor that purported to describe the function of every courtroom did not even mention that there was a third floor. And the elevator did not have a third-floor button.

I suppose many black members of the defendants' families never do find the trials. I did so only with the help of clerks in other courtrooms who, while they helped me, refused to help blacks asking similar questions.

The courtroom was partitioned down the middle—one side for blacks, the other for whites. My companion and I were the only whites in the room, other than the judge. The black side was filled to overflowing with hundreds of family members who, probably through conversations with other blacks, had somehow managed to find the right place.

The trials were conducted at a rate faster than one a minute.

44

During the four hours I was there, 320 cases were tried. Not one defendant had a lawyer. Not one defendant pleaded innocent, and not one defendant spoke the same language as the judge. I was told later that when the defendants answered the question "Where do you live?" the court interpreter told the court the defendant pleaded guilty. The defendants left the courtroom as sentenced violators a few minutes after they first came in. The entire procedure, from arrest to sentence, was so fast that many were working their punishment off on white-owned farms before their families knew where they were.

Most of the defendants' families were not in court. But I did see one young wife with two infants watch her husband, her sole support, as he was sentenced to six weeks of labor far from home. Pain creased her face as she sat in the courtroom straining to hear. Before she fully understood what had happened, her husband was taken out of the courtroom to begin serving his sentence.

During a day's trial break I went to Soweto with Elizabeth Glyn, a member of the Black Sash, a white women's organization that today helps organize demonstrations. Glyn, white-haired and sixty-four years of age, taught black children in Soweto their own languages—languages the state schools refused to teach. She and the other women of the Black Sash were involved in numerous black-support activities such as getting lawyers for criminal defendants, locating displaced black families, or giving monies when blacks did not have funds for food—activities which, if done by a male group, would result in severe penalties.

I wanted to see the site of the 1976 uprising—an uprising originally believed to have been triggered by the white man's attempt to stamp out the blacks' language and make black children speak only Afrikaans in their schools. It seemed appropriate that Elizabeth should be my guide.

Less than forty-five miles separate the wide, elegant boulevards of Pretoria from the smoke-clogged streets of the infamous township of Soweto, but the two places might as well be at opposite ends of the globe.

Now, a bit more than a year after the first black protester died in Soweto on June 16, 1976, the government and those who claimed to speak for the township's million inhabitants remained at an impasse, unable to agree even on a basic system of local government, much less on any of the wider political reforms that South African blacks were demanding.

Our car drove through pools of water left by an early morning storm. It was stiflingly hot—it seemed at least twenty degrees warmer than Johannesburg, which was only fifteen miles away. Soweto looked on the surface like many poverty-stricken black towns in the American South, with its broken-down houses, yards littered with trash, its red clay streets, its lack of water supply and sewage disposal facilities. What was different was its ghastly air pollution and its physical setting. Soweto was like a black island, totally exposed on all sides, with streets built wide enough to enable tanks and police to move in and out and surround the township. Indeed, police cars were constantly visible.

The town's separation from any white homes was absolute; it was a jail compound without barbed wire. All the black "locations" in South Africa are selected both for their poverty and their geography. Black towns and the countryside that surrounds them offer very little cover for possible guerrilla warfare, unlike neighboring Zimbabwe. But as Soweto had shown and as the white rulers of South Africa fear, cover is not essential for successful resistance.

And however far the distance between the black cities of America and their affluent white suburbs, the gulf that exists between Soweto and Johannesburg is that much wider. Each white in South Africa gets a document at birth saying he has been "classified as a white person for the purpose of the Population Registration Act of 1950." The certificate, printed in Afrikaans and English, measures only $4\frac{1}{2}$ by $5\frac{1}{2}$ inches, but it is a priceless endowment. It guarantees that no black resident of Soweto will ever own property in Johannesburg, vote there, or hold public office. It guarantees that the white man will continue to rule, omnipotent, in South Africa over a huge majority of oppressed, dispossessed black people.

No one knows exactly how many disenfranchised people, working or hoping to find work in Johannesburg, live in Soweto. As of mid-1986, the official population was 868,354, crammed into 102,000 so-called homes. But these figures are meaningless since they fail to take into account the vast illegal population. Those who are not there legally do their best to avoid official notice, since on discovery they are likely to be "endorsed out"— that is, sent to rot in one of the many rural settlement areas up and down the country.

Steve Biko explained to Judge Boshoff at the 1976 SASO Nine trial how government head counters get their figures wrong:

> Well of course, M'lord, when the census official comes around to my home as a black man, he never really says to me: 'We are counting the people who are here in the country.' It is a typical white approach again. He comes in and he says, 'How many people live here?' Now the first thing you think about is registration. If I have got people squatting in my house I am going to be arrested, so if there are ten people but six are registered, you say: 'Six, baas,' so he writes six and he goes next door. . . . If it was explained to people nicely that the officials were only counting, and would not prosecute, people would give the correct figures, but they never know, they are never told.

It is estimated that today the actual population of Soweto is in excess of 2 million. Obviously, this makes for a lot more than six to a house, and since most of the houses have four rooms or fewer, overcrowding reaches levels simply unthinkable in even the worst slums of Western countries. Perhaps 20 percent of the houses in Soweto have electricity. Seven percent have a bath or shower. Only 1 percent have hot running water. The Ministry of Community Development, obligated by law to provide housing for the residents of Soweto, had not spent any money there for at least two years.

But perhaps even more shocking than the physical hardship is the evident mental anguish of Soweto's inhabitants. The blacks live in desperate fear, not only of the police, but also of the Tsotsi gangs, groups of marauding black kids who terrorize the community with acts of robbery, assault, rape, and even murder. In a recent year the police were notified of 767 killings—the highest homicide rate in the world.

Yet it has been estimated that no more than a quarter of the crimes committed in Soweto are even reported. Bloke Modisane, a black writer, has vividly described in *Blame Me on History* the demoralization and helplessness of the location dweller in the face of unchecked crime:

> Violence and death walk abroad in Sophiatown, striking out in revenge for thrills or caprice. I have lived in my room trembling with fear, wondering when it would be my turn, sweating away the minutes whilst somebody was screaming for help, shouting against the violence which was claiming for death yet another victim. The screams would mount to a final resounding peal, then nothing but the calm of death.

Other writers tell similar stories.

"It is agony for a family to see daybreak with one member not having slept at home," writes Joyce Sikakane in *A Window on Soweto*. "Immediately, one of them is assigned to go and look for the missing person. Should members of a family reach their point of departure to work without recognizing one of the dead bodies they saw lying in the streets, they sigh with relief."

I visited on this trip, and then again years later, the Dube men's hostel in the center of Soweto, not far from the railway station. Seven hundred black men, separated from their families, were crammed into a barracks-like building. Each day they rode for hours on hot, dirty, jammed buses to work in Johannesburg. There were only cold showers in the Dube hostel; there were no cooking facilities, no plaster on the walls, and the floors were made of rough concrete. Most of the windows were broken. Some of the men have lived there for ten, twelve, fifteen years, occasionally visiting their families on weekends. If a resident is one day late in paying his exorbitant rent, he finds someone else in his bed.

The Dube hostel was far noisier than the poor black homes of the South, the American Indians' shacks on the Rosebud Reservation in South Dakota, or the migrant farmers' quarters I saw in Delano, California, and southern Texas. It was very different and far worse than anything I saw in America, not only because the economic level was lower, but because these blacks were more thoroughly hopeless and beaten. I felt that the black South Africans were truly prisoners; their families were ripped apart; the system of apartheid continually deprived them of any sense of dignity. Even most prisoners in most American jails have some rights, some hopes, illusory as they may be, some chance to better their lives.

I spent that night with a black family that, because the daughter was away working as a domestic that week, had an extra single metal-frame bed. They lived nine people in a broken-down four-room house. For that evening I shared their paltry meal, their home, their standard of living.

The following morning as I stood on the red clay of Soweto, I knew I could never join that chorus of voices that condemn the black violence and terrorism in South Africa. The blacks are themselves the victims of daily terror—a relentless pounding that keeps nearly all of them entrapped in a horrible life. While perhaps this may not be described as a calculated policy of genocide on the part of the government, it has destroyed millions of blacks.

Returning to Johannesburg after two days in Soweto, I spent my first evening back with a middle-class businessman whom I had met on the plane from New York.

I went to his home in the "wilds," a large section of hills painstakingly developed into a suburb on the north ridge of the city center. It is an area of mile after mile of solid affluence; of swimming pools, well-tended gardens, highly polished motorcars, deferential blacks in spotless white uniforms, tennis courts, and, as my host told me, a continual round of parties—cocktail parties, bridge parties, Christmas parties, New Year's parties, going-away parties, coming back parties, Sunday morning sherry parties— any excuse for a party. The only party never held in these affluent suburbs is a Thursday night party. Thursday is the maid's night off.

At his home there were three black servants. They helped me off with my jacket and played with the host's children. My host, glad to talk to someone new, spoke nonstop.

"There was a bombing in the mall last night. That's why I don't go downtown to Johannesburg anymore after five. But we don't miss going out: we just spend more time at home with our friends. Not that we go to their houses that often, because it's dangerous to be in cars at night. If you stop at red lights in the center, you'll be attacked, so cars don't stop."

"Don't you want to leave?" I asked. "It seems that Johannesburg is getting very dangerous." To me it felt like an armed camp, police all over the street stopping blacks.

My host seemed defensive.

"Didn't you see the article on today's front page? A Jo'burg doctor who left South Africa for the safety of America went to New York and was then mugged and killed on his way to his office. I've looked at the crime rates. It's more dangerous in New York. How can you live there? I hear you can't go out in Central Park at night."

However, he admitted that some people, particularly Jews, were leaving South Africa because of the increasing black violence.

"Jews have the money to get out and start somewhere new. So most of them are leaving even though they really used to run this country. But I can't leave." He told me about his very successful advertising company. Advertising was a highly lucrative business here because the South African government did not control advertising claims as the United States does. Since many of the consumers were blacks, who bought on the basis of totally fraudulent ads, the South African government seemed not to care. Even their best magazines, newspapers, and television ads spoke of patent medicines that could cure cancer, of cigarettes being essential to your health and virility, of tires being safe for tens of thousands of miles at extraordinary speeds. Such untruthful claims had made this man very rich indeed.

But he described with quiet desperation how he spent his money—with the air of a man who marvels at an amazing good fortune and enjoys it as fast as he can, knowing that somebody will tap him on the shoulder and ask "Where did you get that?"

"I've never been to Soweto, but I know what it's like," he added. "They have everything—we gave them everything—work, a place to live, clothes, food, pocket money, good hospitals. I wish I could have so few worries."

7

AFTER NEARLY TWO weeks I left South Africa. I had spoken at length with a great many people: residents, both black and white; South African reporters; the defense lawyers for both the Breytenbach and ANC trials, and even the presiding judges. Some of those people who had given me information about the trials had asked me not to write about certain subjects we had spoken about and not to quote them. I respected those confidences.

The morning I left, I filed a petition with the South African government for Breytenbach's clemency. I had no reason to believe it would have any effect at all. As events turned out, it may have been of significance. I argued that the first trial was palpably unfair, for there was no proof that Breytenbach was the political terrorist described in the first indictment. Because I believed it would be unwise for an outside lawyer to argue that he had inadequate counsel, I instead pointed out, as a basis for clemency, that inexperienced counsel called no witnesses in his defense, that Breytenbach's acts (as compared to his speech) were insignificant, and that even the prosecutor, Colonel Huntingdon, testified in open court as to Breytenbach's redemption in light of his full and total cooperation.

But on the plane going back to the United States, I did begin to write my report on the Breytenbach, African National Congress, and passbook trials. Once finished, it was furnished to the organizations that had sent me, then forwarded to Kurt Wald-heim, the secretary-general of the United Nations, and then re-leased to the press and subsequently reported by the media both here and in South Africa.

The report, and some newspaper articles I wrote in the *New York Times* and the *New York Review of Books,* stated that the ANC and Breytenbach trials were politically manipulated and were not in any sense fair trials. It included much of the matter that you have just read. My report concluded that the trials were "elegant facades covering one of the most vicious political states in the world. The judges do not mete out the justice their pro-cedures permit. Justice, and these procedures, will soon be a relic of the past. In part, because of these judges and because of the legal system, future violence, more terrible than before, is in-evitable."

The report drew a barrage of outraged criticism from many sides. But the inequities of the country seemed so obvious to my foreign eyes that I was surprised at how many South Africans, even liberals, failed to see them clearly. Alan Paton, still one of the country's leading liberals, condemned the report in no un-certain terms. Paton had in many of his novels written of the legal system as one institution that the South African people could be proud of.

And, while he did not dispute my description of the ANC or passbook trials, he took great issue with my description of the white poet's trial. Addressing my allegation that the government dictated to judges, Dr. Paton wrote, "I can't believe that. It's ob-vious that the judge at the Breytenbach trial who acquitted the defendant was a very understanding man and was not influenced." The South African legal system, he said, can be a just system, one that dispenses justice irrespective of color.

He threatened to withdraw from the International League for Human Rights, one of the organizations that had sent me to South Africa, unless it disowned my report.

The same day that Paton's comments were printed, the liberal Johannesburg *Star,* in its lead editorial, said I had no right to attack South Africa's judges, "men who lived their lives sworn to uphold the law."

"Apart from virtually demolishing his own credibility, Mr.

Garbus' incredible (in the literal sense of the word) reports could seriously reflect on the League itself," it wrote.

The chairman of the Bar Association of Johannesburg was even more vehement. He attacked me both in a personally signed article in the *Star* and then in a report signed by the South African Bar's leaders, where my conclusions were condemned. The Bar Association insisted that their system of justice, based in large part on the English common law, had a unique and internationally famed sense of fairness. The Breytenbach trial was a model of legality. Judge Boshoff was a model for other South African judges. But they were strangely silent on my description of the passbook and ANC trials.

Not everyone in South Africa condemned the Breytenbach trial report. Some of the Afrikaan press supported my conclusions. The English-speaking *Comment and Opinion*, agreeing that the judiciary was political and that the Breytenbach judge bowed to public pressure, said, "We should understand two things. The first is that [Breytenbach's revolutionary group] Okhela does exist and that it intends to overthrow the state. The second is that Breytenbach is not just a dreamer and poet, but a man who is accused of plotting to overthrow the state." They concluded that my report had captured the underlying issues of the Breytenbach trial.

The Johannesburg *Sunday Times* on July 17, 1977, while it attacked my report, conceded that the two Breytenbach trials contained anomalies that could not lightly be explained away.

Not all liberals stood behind Paton. Helen Suzman, the leading liberal member of Parliament, refused to agree with him and called for a review of Breytenbach's earlier conviction and an examination of the "pathetic conditions" under which he was continuing to serve his earlier sentence. "You simply cannot leave a man sitting in virtual solitary confinement next to the gallows," she said.

While this front-page debate went on in South Africa, I received a call from Bethuel Webster, a prestigious New York lawyer and a member of the International Commission of Jurists, one of the international rights organizations. Webster wanted to know where, and from whom, I had got my information, and implied his inquiries were not prompted just by personal interest.

Sensing some kind of trouble brewing, I refused to tell him anything.

Later that same day I learned that representatives of the South African government had contacted the *New York Times*, demanding as their right of reply to have an article and an editorial published in the newspaper. They labeled my report "ludicrous, unprofessional claptrap," and accused the *Times* of "dishonesty" for publishing it, on the grounds that anyone who could make the charges that I had made was obviously a liar. Johan Adler, the deputy consul counsel general of South Africa, submitted lengthy testimonials to both the *Times* and the *New York Review of Books* to point out the distortions in my articles.

Finally, the *Times* did agree to print a letter from Mr. Adler. It, and subsequent longer pieces published in other publications, called me a liar, implied that I was a Communist interested in subverting America's important ally, and insisted that the South African legal system had a "unique history with a reputation for fairness." Adler concluded that "our judges and a vast proportion of our magistrates—could give Mr. Garbus lessons on legal professionalism and judicial objectivity."

The attacks against me in the South African press continued for several weeks until, in early September, they were abruptly pushed off the front page by the dramatic arrest and murder of Steve Biko. Although the thirty-one-year-old founder of the South African Students Organization and leader of the Black Consciousness movement was now internationally known, this did not prevent the police from arresting and then killing him. Biko became another of the government's grisly statistics: another black who died in detention less than a month after his arrest, of brain injuries caused by blows to the head—what the authorities described as an accident.

September passed. Then, on October 27, 1977, a complaint was filed against me with the Committee on Grievances of the Association of the Bar of the City of New York. The South African government had asked that "Martin Garbus be disbarred because he does not maintain the ethical standards of a lawyer admitted to the Bar of New York."

The Bar Association, headed by Cyrus Vance, then a New York lawyer in private practice, later to be secretary of state in the Carter administration, forwarded the complaint to me and advised me by letter that I was required "to submit a statement in duplicate setting forth my position with respect to the allegations in the complaint."

The complaint, signed by P. W. Botha, then the South African minister of justice, was nearly one hundred pages long and two pounds in weight. It had numerous affidavits, letters, and exhibits attached. All the affidavits said the same thing—that the articles about my experiences of South African justice were dishonest and full of lies. The reason the New York Bar Association was called on to mete out due punishment on behalf of a foreign government was that its Grievance Committee has authority over its lawyers who are alleged to be dishonest. And, according to the Grievance Committee's precepts, it was just as reprehensible to lie about South African judges as to cheat widows and children over trust fund monies.

The letter the Bar Association sent me along with the complaint warned me that failure to cooperate with the committee constituted professional misconduct. This was the very same letter they send to lawyers about to be disbarred for committing a felony. The Bar Association's letter was as outrageous as was the analogy they used between me and a dishonest lawyer out to cheat orphans and widows out of trust funds.

Disbarment is a terrible penalty. I was a member of several federal and state bars, but the rules stated that if I were disbarred in New York I could no longer practice law anywhere in the United States. Nearly twenty-three years of study and practice would be wiped out. I had never worked at any other trade or profession, nor had I even thought about it. I was very frightened.

The New York Bar Association rules require that the formal complaint against a respondent must be filed by a lawyer who practices in New York. In my case this was Charles Friedman, a South African who was a member of both the New York and South African bars, and who has earned substantial fees from clients in both countries. Friedman assumed his role with gusto: Charging that my articles were improper in implying that armed guards impeded the fairness of the South African trials, he pointed out that probably more armed police were present at the Chicago Seven conspiracy trial and other American court cases. An American lawyer should first make sure that trials in his own country were fair before criticizing other countries, Friedman said. He then proceeded to take my articles apart, sentence by sentence, refuting virtually every point I had made, and ended by saying that I had made an "unfounded attack on the personal integrity and ethical standards of the judge."

I was stunned by the fact that the Bar Association of the City of New York had not immediately rejected the disbarment application as a form of intimidation by the South African government to prevent me and others who traveled to South Africa from writing about what they saw.

Other lawyers had written books and articles criticizing foreign courts, but to my knowledge no similar proceeding had ever been brought against any other American lawyer in any American bar association. In 1976 Telford Taylor, an international lawyer, wrote a book entitled *Courts of Terror*, in which he criticized the Russian judges and lawyers. Jerome Cohen, a former law professor at Harvard University, has written books critical of the Chinese judicial system, pointing out that the judges could in no sense be considered independent of the political system. Critical, often violent attacks were written by legal scholars during the 1930s on Hitler's legal system. Yet disbarment proceedings were not brought against these authors, just because those countries did not like what was being written about them.

The Grievance Committee could have rejected the complaint because of the First Amendment or because they did not have jurisdiction over articles written about foreign legal proceedings. However, in my case, the association had apparently determined that the South African government transparently acting through Friedman had the right to try to disbar me, and on their behalf they were prepared to act against one of their own members.

Incredulous, I called Oscar Cohen, counsel to the Grievance Committee, to double-check that the application against me was genuine and that the committee would not dismiss it. His chilly formality provided a clear answer.

8

I KNEW ENOUGH about the Bar Association's disbarment procedure to know that it would be long, painful, and expensive. What it involved was for me to rebut in writing what Friedman and the South African government had said, and then several months later there would be a lengthy trial.

Because the trial would be held before lawyer members of the Bar Association, all of whom had practices, it could drag on for six or seven months, and during that time it would be very difficult for me to think about anything else. Given that the Bar Association was, in effect, both prosecuting and judging me, I was not optimistic. It was clear that I needed a lawyer—and quickly.

I saw two choices. One was to retain an established lawyer, respected by the Bar Association, who could persuade the Bar Association to withdraw the proceeding. The other option was to sue the Bar Association in federal court in New York. I could make a First Amendment attack on their right to try me, claim that they were selectively persecuting critics of South Africa, then seek to enjoin the disbarment trial and have the bar rules declared unconstitutional because they sought to limit my free speech rights by imposing a penalty on me because I chose to write about foreign courts.

After consulting with a number of colleagues, I decided to opt for fighting it out within the Bar Association itself. Those who had advised me against this route warned me that the result could be a disaster. Fee estimates for a full-fledged fight within the bar ran from twenty-five thousand to seventy-five thousand dollars, and if I lost, it would mean my financial ruin.

I had been given twenty days to respond to the complaint. Oscar Cohen made it clear to me that it would be difficult to get an extension.

I called a respected partner at one of the most powerful law firms in the country, whose partners included high-up members of the Bar Association. A former politician, he seemed at first eager to represent me. But after studying my documents for a few days, and after discussing the case with his partners, he turned me down. It was the first of several refusals. Among the others I approached were Harold Tyler, a former federal judge, and Floyd Abrams, an attorney with a formidable First Amendment reputation. Each one gave a reason: Tyler said that because I was to try an unrelated case against his office, his client might believe there was a conflict of interest if he represented me, and Abrams, who represented the *Times*, where my article appeared, also said there could be a conflict of interest.

With each refusal the possibility of losing my ability to practice law became more real. Even winning a disbarment proceeding can be ruinous. Not only could the Bar Association proceedings drag out, but also, if either side is dissatisfied with the result, it can appeal to two intermediate courts within New York and finally to the United States Supreme Court. The appellate process would easily take over two years, and where and how I would find a lawyer, let alone get the money to pay him, was going to be a serious problem. Over all loomed the nightmare that I could be prohibited from practicing law.

Time was running out, and my answering papers were due in one week. Then, on December 15, 1977, I called Leonard Boudin. Boudin, a prominent civil liberties lawyer, has also taught at Harvard and has probably been before the Supreme Court more than any other living lawyer, representing such people as Benjamin Spock, Daniel Ellsberg, and the Harrisburg Six in the most significant political trials of the Vietnam War era.

Sitting in his office in his shirt sleeves on a Saturday afternoon, Boudin looked over my complaint. Without hesitation he agreed to take on my case—free of charge. I felt an extraordinary sense of relief, a sudden relaxation of fierce physical tension. I slouched in the chair, the air went out of me, my arms and legs went slack for the first time; I realized that the pressure had exhausted me.

Boudin immediately got an extension and then made arrangements to have his secretary and two associates work through several weekends with him. By late Monday, just forty-eight hours before it was due, he completed the final draft of my answer. On December 22, eight weeks after the complaint had been filed, our brief was ready.

The brief said that Boudin and I, as lawyers, "were deeply concerned both with the independence of the legal profession and freedom of speech," and that we believed this disbarment proceeding was not constitutionally permitted. Referring to Telford Taylor's *Courts of Terror*, the brief said:

> Not even the Soviet Union has had the effrontery to do what was attempted here, to interfere with a lawyer's freedom of speech and to seek sanctions against him as a member of the Bar. This is a form of censorship which obviously exists in both the Soviet Union and South Africa, but may not be exercised in this country, even under the rubric of regulating the conduct of members of the Bar. The thought that a lawyer's standing at the Bar, achieved through many years of practice, can be imperilled by his comments upon a foreign country's political, legal and social system, is antithetical to the First Amendment and is not a legitimate basis for the exercise of supervisory power by bar associations and courts.

As a result, we told the Bar Association, if they did not dismiss the proceedings, we would file a lawsuit against them in federal court in Manhattan. We insisted that the bar had no right even to prosecute me on the basis of the Friedman complaint.

Finally, we pointed out that none of the judges I wrote about had filed complaints against me, but that even libel laws did not permit the South African government to sue me on any group libel theory, a legal concept rejected years ago by the United States

Supreme Court. Even if I had written articles criticizing particular United States judges, those articles could not form the basis for a disbarment application. Any South African judge libeled by my articles was free to sue me in an American court. The brief concluded:

> The officials of the South African government have not instituted a libel action because of the impossibility of success of such an action and because they would have to reveal in such a public inquiry the facts about the denial of human rights in that country.

The brief filed, I took stock of my position. Although I continued to believe all of the "facts" I had quoted were true, I began to have serious doubts not about the accuracy of my conclusions but about details. I had not been in South Africa before, and it might have been that the horror of what I saw had distorted my perspective. I might have been right about the police but wrong about the judges. They might, in fact, have been honest men, laboring in a cesspool.

But while we waited to hear from the Bar Association, events in South Africa were providing corroboration for my charges. In late 1977 an inquest into Steve Biko's death proved to the satisfaction of everyone other than the presiding judge, Magistrate Marthinus Pines, that the cause of Biko's death recorded by the police as "suicide by hanging" was false.

The last days of Biko's life were brought out in the inquest. Arrested on September 6, 1977, Biko was handcuffed, chained to a grille, and subjected to twenty-two hours of interrogation in the course of which he was tortured and beaten, primarily on the head. This damaged his brain fatally. He lapsed into a coma and died six days later.

For the first time, Americans began to appreciate the horror of South Africa. Several international groups asked me to return to South Africa to observe the Biko inquest. I applied for a visa, knowing in advance that it would be refused. It was.

Time and *Newsweek* ran long stories on the Biko inquest for several weeks, and public opinion in America and around the world changed dramatically. There was shock and indignation when James Kruger, South African minister of justice, said,

60

"Biko's death leaves me cold" and that Biko's horrible death proved "every man has a democratic right to die." Prime Minister B. J. Vorster, responding to the world outrage, compounded the disgust when he dismissed it with "The world can do its damnedest."

The evidence at the inquest was overwhelming and undeniable. No disinterested observer—not even, I thought, my accusers in the Bar Association—could reach any conclusion other than that Biko had been beaten to death by the police. The government's twenty-eight affidavits claiming that the police had nothing to do with his death did not change things at all. Sydney Kentridge, the Bikos' family lawyer, confronted the magistrate again and again with evidence to the contrary. Finally, the magistrate, in finding against Kentridge's claim, admitted (in interviews with John Burns of the *New York Times*) that, despite the evidence, he could not "politically conclude" that Biko had been beaten to death.

Abroad, political conclusions were being drawn anyway. Hodding Carter III, then the Carter administration State Department spokesman, released this statement about the Biko inquest findings:

> We are shocked by the verdict in the face of compelling evidence at least that Steven Biko was the victim of flagrant neglect *and* official irresponsibility. . . . It seems inconceivable on the basis of the evidence presented that the inquiry could render a judgment that no one was responsible . . . even if the individual responsibility was not established. Mr. Biko's death clearly resulted from a system that permits gross mistreatment in violation of the most basic human rights.

This was not the only official reaction. Richard Moose, assistant secretary of state for African affairs, was quoted in the *New York Times* as saying:

> There's a particular horror about the kind of violence perpetrated on Biko—to take a helpless man, keep him handcuffed and naked and treat him in that manner . . .

With such corroboration, I called Oscar Cohen, the Bar Association lawyer, and said, "Our government has made complaints similar to mine about South African justice. Doesn't the exposure of South African justice in the Biko case tell you something? Why don't you drop the case against me?" Cohen refused.

During the months awaiting my trial, I continued to practice law. I told very few people about the disbarment proceedings. Some lawyers I had spoken to were surprised at my naïveté for getting myself into this position. Did I really think I could come back and write articles like this and not ultimately face the bar? To many lawyers, criticizing a judge, any judge, is a violation of the "gentlemen's code" that exists within the legal profession. Didn't I know that the South African government and South African business paid large legal fees to law firms powerful in the Bar Association? I stopped discussing my case with anyone.

There were times I felt not so much paranoid as stupid for not having anticipated it all. I tried to come up with the real reason for the proceedings. Years ago, during the Nixon and Watergate days, when the morality of lawyers was under attack, I had written a criticism of white-shoe lawyers and law firms in an anthology put together by Ralph Nader. I particularly criticized Nixon and John Mitchell (who, after leaving public office were members of a prestigious New York law firm), and—ironically enough—I also took a swipe at the New York Bar Association disbarment proceedings.

Claiming that the New York Bar was elitist, I argued that they permitted the establishment law firms to get away with unethical behavior while they too often cracked down on the smaller practitioners. Some years later I wrote an article in the *New York Times* calling for Nixon's disbarment because of his lies and evasions during the Watergate inquiry, and asked why the New York Bar Association was not moving against him as the California Bar had done years earlier.

There was also an incident in 1972, when the well-known investigative journalist Jack Newfield wrote a series of articles in the *Village Voice* attacking New York State judges for corruption, bribe-taking and the fixing of cases. Representing Newfield before the Bar Association, I had stirred up hostile feelings among the attacked judges and within the Bar Association by trying to stop the bar's investigation into Newfield's confidential sources.

But did all of these single factors together lead to the Bar Association's decision to try to disbar me? I don't think so. I believe it was the South African issue, pure and simple.

I had, in my professional life, represented other lawyers facing disbarment. I thought I knew something about the stress it exacted upon my clients, the time it took from their lives, the psychological toll. But it was only when I myself was accused that I fully understood.

Yet through the months of waiting, I could never really come to grips with the disbarment as a reality. Although disbarment is a weapon traditionally used by both left- and right-wing governments to stifle dissent, and although during the fifties it was used in this country against "radical lawyers," it still seemed—in the context of my alleged "misconduct"—absurd and far-fetched. During the time my disbarment was pending, the press was full of stories of how the South Korean government was trying to disbar its political lawyers. Even these proceedings made more sense than what I was going through; at least they were seeking to disbar lawyers for work done in their own courts.

The Grievance Committee had forty days within which to schedule the case for trial. We waited through January but heard nothing. February and then March passed. We called and were told we would soon receive a response to our briefs and that the trial would be held in the fall.

Finally, in April 1978, six months after the proceedings had been started, Leonard Boudin was told that, provided we did not make the matter public, the Bar Association would not press ahead with the case. But Oscar Cohen cautioned Boudin not to tell me "because we still haven't finally decided what to do."

Two years went by, and even though the disbarment proceeding was still officially hanging over my head, we were told nothing and I continued to practice law.

Finally, on the morning of February 7, 1981, an envelope arrived for me from the Bar Association marked "Personal and Confidential." The enclosed letter, also marked "Personal and Confidential," was actually addressed not to me but to Charles Friedman, the South African lawyer who had filed the original complaint against me. Dated January 27, 1981, it said:

> This is to advise you that following an investigation of your complaint against the above named attorney, the matter was submitted to the Committee for disposition.

The Committee has determined that there is no basis for taking action and therefore the matter has been closed.

At first I felt relief, then only anger. Why had it taken three and a half years to make this determination? When had the committee met, and what information did they have before them? Did they decide the South African affidavits were full of lies or had they decided it was not politic to go after me?

More importantly, did the bar's dismissal of the case against me have any precedential value? Or could another proceeding be brought against the next person who chose to write the truth about South Africa?

I called the Grievance Committee but was told I could not look at my file or the minutes of the committee's deliberations. The documents, I was told, were to be forever confidential.

The incident is behind me now, and I have continued to practice law in New York. But the case still stands as a warning to any lawyer who writes unfavorably about South Africa.

In December 1982, the year after the proceedings against me were dropped, Breytenbach's sentence was reduced from nine years to seven and he was released—the first such commutation in thirty years. Public pressure was intensified when the socialist government of François Mitterrand came to power, compelling the South African government to release the poet, attaching no conditions beyond requiring that Breytenbach leave the country. He settled in Paris, reunited with his wife, and began writing again, but no longer in Afrikaans—now only in French.

Since his release Breytenbach has become a prominent South African exile whose literary work has met with general acclaim. He can be found, in Europe and in America, speaking out on apartheid and the political situation in South Africa. The eloquence of his jail writings, together with his recent explanation about his actions that led to both trials, along with his consistent opposition to the apartheid government, have made him an important figure in the South African struggle. In April 1986 when he returned to South Africa to receive the Anisfield Wolf Award, the highest award the African establishment can bestow on a writer, he delivered a scathing attack on those who resisted change in South

Africa. His statements were far more "treasonous" than the earlier statement that led to his arrest and jailings. But the government is now too busy to deal with Afrikaner writers, especially one who is distrusted by significant numbers of both blacks and whites.

But wherever I have heard Breytenbach speak, or read what he has written, I feel angry for the harm he did. He set back the possibility of whites and blacks working together to forge a more humane society as he helped persuade many South African blacks that even committed whites cannot in the end be too easily trusted. Breytenbach panicked and pleaded guilty in the first trial to charges of terrorism, apologizing in the dock for the "ridiculous and stupid things I have done." He was given permission to make that apology by the prosecutor and by Prime Minister Vorster, both of whom approved every word of his statement before it was read in court. Worse, while in jail he wrote to the security police, giving up names and offering his services in exchange for his freedom. Breytenbach has no excuse to offer but his human fallibility. Often called South Africa's Solzhenitsyn because of his brilliance in depicting the horror of the prison world into which he was thrust, he nonetheless remains a political innocent—a better writer than a political analyst. In Brink's book *The Wall of the Plague*, a black activist sneers at a South African writer whom I thought could be Breytenbach, "Nice words you can stuff up your ass, man. It's what you do that counts."

The ANC defendants are still in jail.

As petty and insignificant as my personal experiences were in relation to the future of South Africa's millions of blacks, they have shown the lengths to which that government is prepared to go to stop a lawyer's accurate report of what goes on in that country. The South African government, having attempted to censor me and others who wrote critically about the government, has now further expanded its attempts to stop writing critical of apartheid. It was not surprising when, in 1980, the South African government first extended its ban to local journalists and photographers. But it was not until 1986, when the South African government severely restricted foreign reporters and photographers, that the peoples of the world finally became aware of that government's success in controlling the news.

The tacit support that the New York Bar Association apparently gave to the South African government is tantamount to a betrayal of the very rights and freedom of speech that a legal association is enjoined to preserve. Kafka might have savored the irony; we, however, will be diminished by it.

THE
STATE
OF
CHILE
AGAINST
SALVADOR ALLENDE'S
GOVERNMENT

9

A government that tramples on the rights of its citizens denies the purpose of its existence.

—Henry Kissinger, Santiago, Chile, June 8, 1976

C H I L E   T O D A Y is in most respects exactly the same as when I went there in early April 1974, at the request of a group of American lawyers. It was seven months after the coup which overthrew Salvador Allende. Secretary of State Henry Kissinger was still taking the position that our government could support the Pinochet regime without betraying its commitment to human rights. Soon after it seized power, the junta announced that it would hold its own self-styled, misnamed "Nuremberg trial"—a trial for treason of sixty-five Army officers and two civilian advisers to Allende who were principally responsible for keeping the government in power by following Allende's direct orders.

Here, the Chilean government announced, as they wrongfully referred to the 1946 trial of the major war criminals before the International Military Tribunal at Nuremburg, that Chilean citizens were to be criminally punished for acts that, unlike those of the Nazi accused, were legal when done. Chileans were also to face the death penalty for acts that were previously considered acts of state for which there was no personal responsibility.

The government sought the death penalty for six of the sixty-seven defendants. The junta said that the trial to be held in a military court in Santiago would produce conclusive proof that

Allende's government had been run by Russia and Cuba and that Allende's supporters intended to turn Chile into a Soviet satellite. The first trial would set the pattern for thousands of other trials that would take place throughout the country.

Immediately after the 1973 coup the government suspended the writ of habeas corpus. The most essential part in any legal structure, the great writ, derived from Magna Charta days, requires any government officially holding a prisoner to tell the court why that prisoner is being detained and to produce him in court. That writ has never been suspended in this country except during the Civil War. England's Dr. Johnson was correct when he told Boswell that "Habeas Corpus is the most important advantage our government has over other countries." The effects of its suspension in Chile, leading to the unexplained disappearance of thousands arrested by the police, show clearly how critical habeas corpus is to the freedom of citizens throughout the world.

The planning for my trip began in November 1973, at the junta's first announcement of their "Nuremberg trial." The lawyers' group I would represent had decided to send a delegation to Chile to look at the "secret documents" and "conclusive proof" the Chilean government had, in the hope we might be able to cast a spotlight on the validity of the allegations. The reporting of the trip would also remind the people in Chile who opposed the regime that the outside world had not forgotten them or the thousands who had died since Pinochet seized power.

At the first meeting of the sponsoring lawyers' group, which was convened by New York lawyer Victor Rabinowitz and composed of Orville H. Schell, President of the Bar Association of the City of New York; City Council President Paul O'Dwyer; and practicing lawyers, judges, and law school deans from throughout the nation, we tried to figure out the most effective way to cast that spotlight.

Henry Kissinger and the United States State Department had a commitment to the propaganda success of the upcoming trial. Since Allende's downfall, Kissinger had made it clear he believed that groups such as ours, which might illuminate America's role in the coup and the brutality that then existed, were enemies of democracy. More significantly, we feared that the Chilean government, if it had advance notice of our visit, might try to keep us out, indefinitely detain us, tell terrorists where we were, or leave us to the mercies of the grisly private hit squads which were springing up across the country.

Nevertheless, we felt it was very important for foreign observers to go to Chile to witness the trial and to perhaps play a role in it. We had heard that the military leaders were trying to use the courts to establish that the junta had acted in accordance with the Constitution by overthrowing Allende. They were trying to make the case that the Allende regime had been destroying the rule of law, and that the military had acted responsibly as guardians of the constitution by taking over the government. At the same time they suspended the constitution and kept detaining, jailing, and killing anyone they considered in opposition, in violation of its guarantees.

Back in the United States, we strongly doubted this declaration, but we were hampered by the fact that we had little information. We did not know whether trials were taking place and if so, what they looked like. Other than the reports of Jonathan Kandell of the *New York Times* and a few others, the only information coming out of Chile came from the military dictatorship. The Chilean newspapers obtainable here were of no help. They were based entirely on government handouts and planted stories.

We decided to work out a rotation system so that there would always be two lawyers in Chile for a three-month period starting February 1, 1974. If in that period of time we could not find out about the lead "Nuremberg trial" or any other trials, we could at least try to visit the secret detention centers run by the military that the government claimed did not exist. We knew that most of those arrested were held in the detention centers before they ever underwent the legal process. It was decided to hold off making any public statement of our findings until all the lawyers who had gone down to Chile returned safely.

Our caution was mandated by historical precedent. In previous years outside legal observers in other Latin American countries, primarily Paraguay and Argentina, had disappeared. In Chile right-wing terrorist groups were killing months after the coup.

Various support groups were formed in New York. Letterheads from bar groups in support of fair trials in Chile were printed so that they could be used as credentials to gain entrance to the trials. Letters of introduction were written by New York Supreme Court jurists, including Judges William Booth and Arthur Caro, and internationally known legal scholars wrote to members of Chile's highest court and politicians in the prosecutorial wing of the government. Because no visa was required, we decided to buy our tickets a few days before we were to take the eleventh-hour flight to Santiago. We hoped to be in Chile before the Chileans or the United States government could find some reason to stop us. We succeeded.

As we were leaving the United States, Chile was beginning to slip off the front pages of America's newspapers. When in 1973 the most naked class conflict in the country's history culminated in the military overthrow of Salvador Allende and the scrapping of his peaceful road to socialism, few observers in America or in Chile were surprised: A "creeping coup" had been taking place for months.

But the violence of the coup, culminating in one of the largest bloodbaths in South American history, had shocked even those who had anticipated it. Many of these observers had believed that a military takeover would install civilians who would steer a middle course, consolidating some Allende reforms, modifying or attenuating others, while halting the revolutionary process and defusing the violent upheaval which a revolution would arouse. Even if the military itself did attempt to constitute a Chilean government, there was reason to believe its rule would not be brutal.

As a result, the military's overthrow of Allende's government on September 11, 1973, probably enjoyed the support of roughly half the population. But just five months later, much support had evaporated, with a substantial majority of Chileans in active or passive opposition to the junta's continuation in power.

Some of this opposition was political—and comprised Christian Democrats or traditional conservatives who had been disappointed by the general's failure to extend patronage, and those whose relatives or friends were affected by the repression. But the main reason was that most Chileans were horrified and frightened by continuing wanton killings in a country proud of its long constitutional traditions.

When the armed forces seized power, they talked about the

moral regeneration of Chile: "exorcising the cancer of communism." Four months later the reports of unwarranted torture and killings had grown to horrendous proportions, although the government denied wrongdoing and claimed fair trials were going on. Outsiders could not verify the awesome statistics, but the conservative news media estimated five to ten thousand killed in a country with a population slightly larger than New York City's.

The CIA's estimate then given to Senator Edward Kennedy was that the military had killed twenty-five thousand of its 10 million countrymen—the equivalent of five hundred thousand in the United States. Another one hundred thousand passed through the detention camps, prisons, and torture chambers of the secret police, which, according to Amnesty International, intimidated one out of every ten Chileans into spying on his friends, colleagues, and neighbors. The local chapter of Amnesty International stopped functioning. Chilean officers disappeared. Month after month the junta created an atmosphere for the "Nuremberg trial" by publicly distributing copies of documents that purported to prove that Allende was part of an international Communist conspiracy.

In January 1974, the United States government, which was rumored to have played a clandestine part in the coup, was publicly accepting Justice Enrique Urrutía's view that this right-wing military dictatorship was capable of guaranteeing human safety.

But no one at the top of the Ford administration cared about the arrests and killings. Secretary of State Kissinger publicly rebuked the former U.S. Ambassador to Chile, Edward Korry, for expressing his concern in discussions with Chilean officials. The Office of Humanitarian Affairs of the Department of State, specifically created to deal with human safety and refugee questions, sidestepped the allegations of unlawful detentions, torture, and killings in Chile and concentrated on refugees from Communist and socialist countries.

Kissinger's department would not tell us when the "Nuremberg trial" was actually scheduled to take place. We decided we would go anyway.

On December 12, 1974, the first group of lawyers, including Judges Caro and Booth and Ramsey Clark, the former attorney general of the United States, set off for Santiago. There they met with representatives of the Chilean Christian Democratic Party, a party which before the coup had opposed Allende and which now, within permitted limitations, was critical of the junta it had helped to bring to power.

Even though Caro, Booth, and Clark did not observe the trials (they had not begun), they got in and out of the country safely. This meant a second group could also get in and see the trials once they started. We were aware that the Chilean government had reasons for allowing these visits. The generals, angered by charges that whatever trials took place were rigged and that Chileans were randomly tortured and killed, and perhaps decided to allow American observers to come in and see the "truth" at the most important trial, thus establishing Chile's credibility with the world and in the process, making sure that the flow of funds from the United States would not stop.

On April 8 Ira Lowe, a Washington, D.C., lawyer, and I left as the second group. An experienced international and constitutional lawyer, Lowe had attended Fidel Castro's trial in 1959 of Fulgencio Batista's supporters before ten thousand people in the Havana Stadium.

Although then sympathetic to Castro and the revolution, Lowe was nonetheless critical of Castro's attempts to make a public spectacle of the trial, and played a role in having it moved into a less circuslike atmosphere. The use of show trials, of course, was not uncommon. Practices in different countries vary. While Fidel Castro put Batista's generals on trial, the Sandinistas in 1979 decided not to do the same for leaders of Anastasio Somoza's National Guard. Whereas the Cuban and Chilean proceedings, however they were legally dressed, sprang from a motive of revenge, the Nicaraguans were different. Vilma Núñez, that country's first woman Supreme Court justice, told me in Managua in 1984 that they refused to hold "Nuremberg trials" because they wanted to heal the society, not inflame old enmities.

10

Santiago, the capital of Chile, resembles a traditional European city with large boulevards, parks, ornate hotels and restaurants, and a fashionable residential district. On the other hand, the *poblaciones* ("people's quarters") surrounding the city are similar to those in many other Latin American cities: urban shantytowns with huts constructed of cardboard, unpaved roads, no electricity or plumbing, and no schools or health care. In these areas are also the larger factories which supply goods for Santiago and much of the rest of the country.

In April 1974, nine months after the coup, Santiago was still an occupied city. Army patrols in jeeps and trucks raced through the streets, guns at the ready. Billboards in ominous black and white outside the airport read, *"En cada soldado hay un Chileno; en cada Chileno hay un soldado"* ("In every soldier there is a Chilean; in every Chilean there is a soldier"). Felled trees and sandbags protected guard posts around government buildings and police outposts. At night after the hour of curfew, sporadic machine-gun fire crackled. Morning newspapers—those left after the shutdown of all publications not in line with the new regime—provided daily reports of the number of leftist prisoners killed the night before "while trying to escape."

The first person we spoke to when we arrived in Chile was a taxi driver who spoke English, but he was not talkative. The car he was driving was very large, and its gas consumption was obviously high. And gas was expensive in Chile; like everything else, it shot up in price over the last few months. "It's only to be expected," he sighed. "We're paying for Señor Allende's Russian extravaganza." I asked him whether people were discontented about the high cost of living. "No. They are happy now, because they are living in peace, and law and order has been restored."

On the main road from the airport to Santiago, we were stopped twice by young soldiers belonging to the "special forces"; each time, one of them checked the names of the passengers in the vehicle against a "list of wanted persons" which he ostentatiously flashed in front of our noses.

In Santiago itself our large hotel on Constitution Square was generally guarded at night by a helmeted soldier carrying a submachine gun. The hotel belongs to one of the subsidiaries of the American corporation ITT.

The first visit Ira and I made when we arrived was to the home of Orlando Letelier, formerly Allende's ambassador to the United States and now a prisoner of the junta. His wife Isabel, a short, dark, intensely attractive woman, was waiting for us there.

As one of the most visible opponents of the junta still living in Chile, Isabel Letelier, then under house arrest "for her protection," knew she might be killed any day, either by the government or the paramilitary terrorist groups of the right. But she refused to leave Chile until she could help free her husband from jail on Dawson Island.

At dinner in her apartment in an elegant old Spanish house, we met the wives of other jailed men. They were anxious for information about the outside world, and we talked of Nixon and Vietnam as shots rang out in the Santiago streets. Isabel told us of a dinner party at Joseph Alsop's house in Washington, exactly one year before. Kissinger, coming in late with a tall young woman in hot pants, assured Orlando Letelier that the United States would not interfere with Allende, did not have any people working there, and did not intend to play any role in unseating the winner of the 1972 Chilean election, whoever he might be.

Then Isabel told us the "Nuremberg trial" was to start soon—somewhere on the outskirts of Santiago. On trial, she said, would be a number of Air Force officers who had refused to join in

Pinochet's coup, along with Erich Schnake, a socialist senator, and Carlos Lazo, the vice-president of the Chilean State Bank, and a close adviser to Allende. Both men faced the death penalty.

The sixty-seven defendants were originally known as "Bachelet y Otros" ("Bachelet and the Others") after General Alberto Bachelet, a close friend of Allende and the head of Allende's Consumer Supply Board. The military was furious at General Bachelet; he was one of theirs who went to the other side. The other civilians, including José Espinosa Santis, a financial adviser to Allende, several socialists, and two alleged Communists, were brought into the trial to help show they infected the other military defendants.

As it turned out, Bachelet and Espinosa were never to stand trial. Junta officials announced on March 12, several weeks before we arrived, that General Bachelet had died of a heart attack in a Santiago jail. His family and friends were never permitted to see the body. And, according to Isabel, Espinosa had been shot and killed several months earlier while in custody at an Air Force compound. Military authorities had advised his family that he had been eating in a dining room when a guard accidentally fired his rifle and the bullet hit the prisoner.

Nevertheless, the trial of the others was moving ahead. Rules establishing a formal review procedure of all court decisions by the ruling junta were distributed, Isabel said, in instructions to military commands. Surprisingly, they seemed "judicious." They were part of the government's effort to fit political purges within formally correct judicial procedures.

These procedures were heralded to be a "dramatic" return to a rule of law. The junta claimed that now that the Allende cancer had been removed there could be a return to normal legal procedure. Since the military took power, there had been officially authorized summary executions and then secret executions after court-martial sentences. But this, the junta now said, was part of the past.

During dinner Isabel gave us more information about the continued political repression in Chile. She made sure we knew it would be dangerous to meet with large groups of people while we were in the country. "This dinner is called a meeting and it breaks the law," she said. "You cannot have a meeting of more than four people without permission from the government. I'm sure the police followed you here, and they could, if they wanted to, arrest you. I suggest you leave two by two so that the patrolling police do not stop any of you."

She added that the police were not the only menacing presence on the street. There were also terrorist groups who waited outside buildings for certain people. We were also to be mindful of the 11 P.M. curfew. "It is a serious business," she explained. "You should leave here by ten-thirty and go straight back to your hotel. Last week an Italian tourist was shot dead in Viña del Mar after curfew over a misunderstanding with a policeman who demanded to see her documents."

Isabel's portrait of contemporary Chile pictured a nation of hunted prisoners. She concluded: "Nowadays it is possible for them to snatch you up at home, at work, on the street, in a bus, or in a coffee shop. A person may be arrested because he is a relative or a friend of a political prisoner or a suspect. Arrests are often made on the basis of anonymous denunciation, and then weeks or months pass before the authorities even acknowledge a detention. Every part of the country has been destroyed. They have infiltrated and purged all of the unions, universities, and churches. Informing has become a way of life—the only way of life for many."

It was ten-thirty. We left Isabel's house one at a time. Patrol cars slowed down to pass us as we made our way to the hotel. I experienced for the first time how it felt to be in an occupied country: the always-present platform of trucks at every corner with six soldiers poised at machine guns; the guns that seemed to be aimed at everyone in the street all at once; the soldiers stationed at every block and in the doorways of all large buildings.

The following morning Ira and I decided to walk over to the Ministry of Justice to see if we could get any information about the upcoming trials. All we saw were military men and machinery— the building was ringed with troops and machine-gun placements. We spent three hours speaking to captains, colonels, and, ultimately, to the arrogant, condescending minister of the interior himself, General Oscar Bonilla, a Christian Democrat, who continually asked us about our politics and then refused to talk about the trial. (Bonilla, a politically substantial rival to General Pinochet, would later die in a suspicious plane crash.) We saw no civilians—no one

THE STATE OF CHILE

who could answer the simplest questions about the forms the trials would take. The officers, immaculate in their bemedaled uniforms, sat behind large desks that did not have any papers or books on them. All the law books belonging to the judges and lawyers who previously occupied the rooms were long gone. No one would tell us about the cases or about the specific charges against any of the sixty-seven defendants. The only information we got was that we would not get any information no matter how much we tried.

We then walked to the American embassy. After the uneasiness of the nighttime, Santiago by day had a deceptive surface calm. The streets were crowded, the tourists and international businessmen were reappearing, the weather was delightful. With the men in their double-breasted suits and felt hats, the women in long dresses, and the cars mostly pre–World War II Packards, Chile's capital made me feel as if I had stepped into a 1930s George Raft movie. One quickly grew accustomed to the constant military presence. It was only in the evenings, when nearly everyone except the soldiers had gone indoors and darkness closed in on the veneer of civilization, that a sense of the reality returned.

On our way from the ministry, we passed a newsstand. *El Mercurio*, once one of the freest newspapers in South America and now controlled by the government of President Augusto Pinochet, carried a large black headline announcing the upcoming trial of the traitorous Air Force officers. Alongside it was a red headline which said, "Trial to Be Observed by Foreign Lawyers." The article listed information concerning our arrival in the country and reported where we were staying, although we had not checked in with the government. According to the article, we were not the only foreign lawyers there: Some had supposedly arrived from Switzerland and England, and their names and backgrounds were also listed. It seemed to me to be a notification to "hit teams." The article then went on to say that the trials, when they got underway, would show people both in Chile and abroad that the Chilean system of justice was now working and that all defendants were receiving fair trials.

Later on that week the international edition of *Time* magazine, noting that foreign lawyers were being permitted to observe the trials, concluded that the new government was now fully in control and the country was getting back to normal. "The opening of the major political trial may put to rest the claims of those who say that the rule of law has ended in Chile," it said.

At the American embassy I asked whether they knew exactly where the trial would take place. I also wanted to formally advise them of my hotel. Other Americans in Chile had disappeared even months after the coup and had not yet been found. I wanted to keep in daily contact with our State Department, although I knew that that alone would not guarantee my safety.

After making me wait several hours, the State Department official, who knew who I was before I spoke my name and was clearly not pleased to see me, told me he did not know where the trials were taking place. He refused to take the name of my hotel. He refused to furnish me with a letter of introduction to members of the Chilean Supreme Court. "There is no reason for you to contact us," he said. "You are here on your own."

For the remainder of the day, Ira and I tried to find out from the prosecutor and other Chilean government officials where the trial was being held. We could not. The defense lawyers were not able to provide any information either. They were as much in the dark as we were. It was never clear whether the officials would not or could not give us the facts.

Ignoring the 11 P.M. curfew we met the leading defense lawyer, Roberto Garreton, at his office at midnight that evening. Garreton was representing dozens of people in Santiago and a few more outside of the capital who had been arrested by the junta. When we met him, he was exhausted. Having spent most of the day trying to locate his clients, he asked us to come to his office at that hour because he did not want the military to know he was seeing us. He seemed resigned to the fact that he would not be informed of the trial until the night before it was due to begin. Even though the people he was defending were facing the death penalty, he could not see the criminal file, or even see the charges, or learn who the government witnesses would be, or indeed whether the trial would actually be going ahead until the day he arrived in court. He would start the trial with no time to prepare.

The Chilean Constitution and the military code that supposedly governed the trials required that he be given advance notice so he could line up his witnesses. But lack of notice was not critical because he knew his clients would be sentenced to death no matter what he did. The military judge under the military code had unbridled discretion; he had to reach decisions "according to the dictates of his conscience." So there it would be. We were back to the fourteenth-century English statutory crime of "harboring bad thoughts about the King."

There could be no appeal from the Army tribunals' decision. The tribunals were called *consejos de guerra* (literally, "war councils") rather than courts, so little did they resemble judicial bodies.

Overjoyed that we were there to witness the proceeding, Garreton said only our presence and the possibility of provoking an international reaction could save the defendants' lives after they were sentenced. For the next two days we spent endless hours going from office to office, trying to learn the start date of the trial, running into a bureaucracy that refused to acknowledge openly that they did not want any of us to attend it. Instead, we were told that the government was reluctant to identify the place and time too far in advance because they were afraid there might be violence and demonstrations.

Then, one evening at eleven o'clock, the wife of a defendant called to say that the trial was set for the following morning at nine-thirty at the Air Force Academy, far on the outskirts of the capital. She said the government had announced this would be the first trial of any kind open to outside legal observers and that the trial would comply with all judicial requirements.

There was another message. The location held a symbolism for the Chilean people that most foreign observers missed. The Chilean Air Force had the reputation of being the most brutal among the armed forces. Its personnel had carried out a disproportionate share of the killings and torture after the coup. Trial at the Air Force center effectively meant that the executioners were trying their victims.

Although I tried to contact some of the other lawyers to tell them about the trial, I could not reach them on the telephone, either because they were out when I called or because the Chilean government was redirecting my calls. Of the seven foreign lawyers in Santiago, only Ira Lowe and I attended the first court day.

11

WE TRIED TO GET a taxi to take us to the Air Force Academy, but none would go. The drivers made excuses. Eventually, we called the wife of a defendant, who agreed to drive us.

After twenty minutes we reached the barricaded academy. The semiofficial letterheads we carried gained us entry. Our driver was afraid to tell the guard her name. She turned around and drove away.

The guard told us that if we wanted to watch the trials, we could walk to the auditorium one mile up the dirt road. Sweating, with our jackets draped over our shoulders, we approached to within fifty feet of the building, which was surrounded by tanks, when we were stopped by four soldiers, spotlessly dressed in fatigues, with machine guns over their shoulders. They refused to let us pass. Using hands and gestures, they made it clear we would not be allowed further.

We walked back down the road and encountered a group of Chilean journalists, one of whom I had met the day before. As they approached the courtroom, we slipped in among them and were able to enter—but not before all of us had our pockets emptied and were carefully frisked and finger-searched. The search was clearly meant to discourage visitors from coming back a second time.

A right-wing Chilean defense lawyer, standing with a group in front of us, refused to let continue a finger search that strayed too long over his genitals, and left. A woman defense lawyer endured the violation by an abusive officer whose fingers stayed and stayed on her breasts by clenching her teeth, and tried to ignore the enlisted men enraptured by her humiliation.

When it was my turn to be frisked, I wondered why I was placing myself at such risk. I didn't know if any good would ultimately come of this trip, and I was sure my presence would not affect anyone's fate in the short run. But I felt that I had at least to be a witness.

Most of the four hundred seats in the large auditorium where the trial was held were taken up by the military. There were no members of the public there, the only civilians in attendance being a handful of Chilean journalists and those few family members who had learned that morning where the trial was to be. Family members who arrived late, as I did, had to stand at the back of the hall. Although it was now 11 A.M., the trial had not yet started.

At eleven-twenty, an officer jumped up and brought the courtroom to attention. Everyone in the courtroom stood. Seven military judges entered from the side and sat on a raised platform in front of the auditorium. I was later to learn that only one of them was a lawyer. The other six were high-ranking Army officers. The spectators sat down. The presiding judge, General Juan Soler, whose dark glasses were evocative of Pinochet, motioned to the sentry to open a sliding door. The few relatives, lawyers, and journalists leaned forward, eagerly awaiting the sight of men who had not been seen alive in months. The courtroom silence was cut only by the whir of an electric fan that barely relieved the humid air. Finally, the men entered. As wives and children searched for fathers and husbands and found them, I could sense the relief that flooded the visitors' gallery. Sixty-three of the sixty-seven accused men appeared. No one ever accounted for the other four; they had disappeared without a trace.

For many of the defendants, this was the first time they had seen their families, lawyers, or codefendants in over six months. Many of them knew that this would be the last time they would be seen in public—and might also prove to be one of the last

83

days of their lives. But now, as they entered, looking past their military escorts, they had only one thing on their minds—to see their friends and family. In single file they dutifully filled the first eight rows of wooden seats assigned to them, their eyes running wildly over the assembled spectators.

The defendants looked surprisingly well despite the torture they had experienced. I later learned that for the two weeks prior to trial, they were given medication to reduce swelling and contusions. Spruced up now for this show trial with the help of make-up to add color to their hair and skin, they wore neatly pressed suits, clean shirts and ties, and well-polished shoes. On the surface there was no evidence of their beatings.

The chief Air Force prosecutor, General Orlando Gutiérrez, chunky but resplendent in his brown uniform, began the trial by reading a long statement of charges against all defendants. He made no allegation of illegal overt acts: Nearly all the charges related to speeches and words informally spoken or to everyday acts the defendants carried out while working at their jobs. Justifying the trials by referring to the Allies' trials of German war criminals at Nuremburg, he said the Chilean officers in the dock performed daily acts that destroyed the country. His passion obscured the difference between pulling levers releasing gas and signing bank credit orders. He asked for the death sentence for six Air Force officials, life imprisonment for one civilian, and prison sentences of six months to thirty years for the rest.

Outlining the case, General Gutiérrez began with a thundering attack on Salvador Allende. He said the accused had committed treason by trying to overthrow the true government, by collaborating with foreign and domestic enemies of the Chilean people, by establishing ties with civilian Marxists, and by turning over "military secrets" to the "enemy." The prosecution defined "enemy" as Allende, his cabinet and congress, and a Marxist party that supported the Allende government.

He made these accusations even though the Chilean constitution prohibited the entire procedure. Chile has a deeper and longer commitment to democracy than most nations of the Americas. Its constitution severely limits the government's power and gives the people broad and novel rights.

Specifically, the constitution prohibits torture; requires that no one can be sentenced unless legally tried in accordance with a law passed prior to the act upon which the trial was based; requires that within forty-eight hours after an arrest a judge be advised of the arrest and where the person was being detained; and that no one, whether or not an arrest be made "under the pretext of extraordinary circumstances," can ignore civilian courts even in cases when defendants were charged with treason.

These and other constitutional provisions were all violated when the junta seized power, using as its pretext reference to the "extraordinary circumstances" the constitution specifically forbids. But in initiating the coup, killing the president, and suspending the Congress, the military claimed that the constitution (which it had suspended) supported its actions by not specifically prohibiting them.

When one of the defense attorneys politely pointed out that it was impossible to trace constitutional or statutory authority over the accused to this military court, General Soler shouted him down. When the attorney persisted, Soler barred him from further appearance in court and asked the Bar Association to provide a substitute attorney for his client.

Speaking about the first defendant, Captain Daniel Aycinema, the prosecutor's assistant, with his glasses riding down his nose, read an indictment which supported his allegation that the Allende government was violating the law by reading into the record speeches made by politicians who opposed Allende. This was far from hard evidence, but the presiding judge, a "respected" Christian Democrat selected to prove his loyalty to the junta, permitted it.

When Horacio Carvajal, one of the defense attorneys, argued correctly that only facts could be presented in an indictment and not political statements or opinions, the court cut him off, saying it would not hear his "political arguments." When the lawyer vigorously replied that fairness required that political statements made by Allende's opponents should not be part of the indictments because they were not necessarily true statements of fact, he was ordered to sit down. His cocounsel grabbed his arm and forced him into his seat. But when Carvajal shot up again and began at-

85

tacking the alleged constitutional bases for the seizure of power, the guards beside the judges' bench rushed toward him, grabbed him by the upper arm, and shoved him back in his seat.

Alfredo Echeverría rose quickly to give Carvajal and the shaken defense his support. One of the country's leading defense attorneys, a professor of law at the Catholic University and a member of the Christian Democrats, he quietly, and respectfully, asked for leave to protest the court's action. The judges ordered him to sit down.

The second senior judge, General Juan Fornet, a Christian Democrat and a former adviser to former President Eduardo Frei, also put on the court to test his loyalty, announced that he would now enforce a flat prohibition on "constitutional arguments" by the defense, although he would permit the prosecutor to continue with the political allegations in the indictment.

Echeverría rose again. He said that one of the six Air Force officers serving as judges should be disqualified because he was a government witness to some of the "Marxist" acts that were contained in the indictment. He asked that another judge be removed because he was the father-in-law of an officer who obtained confessions from defendants who claimed they had been tortured.

After a thirty-minute recess, the disqualification petition was denied by General Soler. The government then quickly presented its case without any witnesses, relying solely on the confessions of the defendants to "prove" the accusations. It was a fast, dramatic procedure that complied with summary court-martial procedures in Chilean military law.

The individual trials all took the same shape. Captain Aycinema, the young assistant prosecutor, would announce the name of the defendant, read the confession, and then ask aggressively for the death penalty. His superior, General Gutiérrez, would add a passionate sentence about the Marxist devils who conspired against the government. It took no more than an hour to present each of the most serious cases, those involving the death penalty.

The defense lawyers would then respond with their own views of each case, called the *alegato*, taking perhaps another thirty minutes. They had to make technical arguments because they were afraid to attack the prosecution's case head-on. The defense lawyers claimed their clients were not Marxists but were in fact lovers of Chilean democracy. Gutiérrez would then in three or four short, precise sentences, attack the character of the defendants, argue that the defense should not be believed, and ask that it be rejected. The cases were dispatched by the judges with computer-like efficiency. The total time for the more serious trials was less than two hours. The average was less than an hour. No appeal was permitted.

Despite the speed with which the cases moved, the military code was strictly adhered to. Confessions had been taken from each of the sixty-seven persons charged. They were taken to show the population at large that the trials were necessary and that the defendants were self-confessed traitors who deserved the punishment they were about to receive. The judges, having announced before the trial began that the Allende government was illegal and had acted contrary to the will of the people, now took the position that they had only to prove that these defendants had belonged to the Allende government and had done work on its behalf.

Of that there was no question; thousands of internal documents confirmed it. Ordinary memoranda dealing with agriculture, education, and economic matters that carried the defendants' names were used to claim they were part of the international Communist conspiracy. Acts, indisputably legal (and often insignificant and nonpolitical) when done, were now called crimes. It made the Nuremberg analogy meaningless.

When Echeverría read Article 11 of the Chilean constitution, which said, "No one can be sentenced unless he be legally tried in accordance with a law promulgated prior to the act upon which the trial is based," he was asked to sit down.

Patricio Barrios, the dark, mustached, thirty-two-year-old Air Force captain now facing the death penalty, had been a valedictorian in the auditorium where he was now being tried. His confession was forced by his former beloved teacher, in the classroom where Barrios was once a star student.

After his arrest Barrios was made to stand night and day for twenty-two days wearing a hood that nearly suffocated him, but he refused to implicate any other defendant. However, other confessions placed Barrios at meetings with Senator Schnake and banker Lazos, neatly tying the conspiracy together at the top.

Colonel Bejamino Constanzo, military attaché to General Alberto Schneider (an Allende supporter who it later turned out was killed by CIA-funded Chileans), after being tortured by men he once considered friends, said that he, in the ordinary running of the government, gave military documents to Allende.

Furnishing these papers to the "enemy" Allende, said General Gutiérrez, was an act of treason. But Allende in 1972, was president and was of course fully entitled to all such documents.

Constanzo, because he actually had dealings with Allende, was treated worse than many others. He was tortured and kept in a building originally designed by one of the country's leading architects—his wife.

At first the defendants paid close attention to the proceedings. Then they began to look around the auditorium. During the twenty-minute intermission that first morning, the family members in the courtroom tried to reach the areas where the prisoners were seated. Constanzo saw his wife. He was overjoyed to see her look as well as she did. She had been tortured for two weeks to secure evidence against him. Not having been allowed to see anyone in his eight months in jail, Constanzo did not know she had survived the ordeal.

But the defendants' pathetic attempts to talk to and touch their wives were frustrated by the relentless guards. As the guards quickly led them away, Erich Schnake lingered behind and unobtrusively tried to wait for his wife as she came forward from the back of the courtroom. As they approached each other, the guard saw them and started toward them. Schnake's lawyer, Hernan Montealegre, president of the Human Rights Commission of Santiago, tried to place himself between the guard and Schnake.

But Schnake, recoiling as if he were afraid of being hit, quickly turned away and moved to join the other defendants. Later, as he sat listening to the rest of the morning's testimony, we could see that he had decided he had little to lose by staying to see his wife. At the afternoon recess, ignoring the oncoming guard, Schnake broke away from the other prisoners and reached out to touch hands with his wife for a moment. The moment was all Schnake wanted. Three of the defense lawyers stood around Schnake and his wife, forming a protective wall. The guard hung back for a moment. Then, squaring his shoulders with dignity, the senator let go of his wife's hand and walked back to the other men. The same scene was repeated for several days, until finally the guard let them and other prisoners have more than small touchings with their wives.

Here in Chile, as in South Africa, most of the well-dressed defense lawyers kept a respectful distance from their clients. They sat separate, and spoke to them only when necessary. Politically, nearly all the lawyers were from the right of center, supporters of the junta and former opponents of Allende. There were no Allende supporters on the defense team. Lawyers who openly sympathized with Allende had disappeared, left the country, been killed, or knew that their appearance at the trial would seal their death warrants. Many defense lawyers, such as Roberto Garreton, who took a lead role at the trial, were members of the Christian Democrats, who would oppose Allende, but now opposed the military. They cared deeply for the defendants. Other defense lawyers hated their clients and their clients' politics, and appeared only so that critics of the junta could not claim that the men sentenced to death did not have lawyers.

The first day, court broke for the day punctually at one o'clock. Before the trials began, the seven judges reckoned that, by sitting four hours a day, they could finish sixty-seven trials within a week to ten days. They maintained their schedule.

The last case of the first day involved Eduardo Beccerría, a small olive-skinned Army colonel who, at the time of the coup, was stationed in Antofagasta, a major city nearly one thousand miles north of Santiago. In his confession he admitted to being at meetings in Santiago in 1972 and 1973, months prior to the coup. Later that evening both Juan Hermosilla, his lawyer, and Eduardo's wife told me he hadn't been in Santiago for years; and that he was participating in military exercises near Antarctica at the time he confessed he was in Santiago.

At a private meeting with the presiding judge, the following morning, Hermosilla showed him the military records proving the confession was wrong, but the judge refused to permit him to present it in open court. Hermosilla told me that Beccerría, not involved in politics, had, at Antofagasta, once at a lunch, expressed support for Allende's plan to nationalize the American-owned copper industry, an act approved by the unanimous vote of the Chilean congress.

After the first day in court, as we were driving back to Santiago, one of the defense team said to me that some of the more committed lawyers felt they must use the trial to raise sensitive issues such as torture and totally fabricated confessions, even though they feared it would displease the court and might result in more severe sentences for the defendants and trouble for themselves. Some felt that any arguments on their clients' behalf would almost certainly expose them to reprisals. They were arranging to send their wives and children out of the country before they sought to prove that the confessions presented in court had been obtained by torture.

The lawyers held a meeting that evening to discuss trial strategy, to which I was invited. Before the trial, when some defense lawyers first suggested that the question of torture be raised, others objected, claiming there had been none. Others thought that even if the government admitted it, this would not stop its practice or even hurt the image of the regime. Many of the defendants' wives with whom I had spoken before the trial thought it would be pointless to raise the issue because it would either be denied by the military or go unreported abroad. Some added that even if it were reported, most of the world had grown immune to the killings taking place in Chile and would not react. The only result, they felt, would be to jeopardize the safety of both the lawyers and the defendants, and perhaps even to end what they still hoped would be an "open" trial.

Most of the lawyers and wives in one of the lawyers' offices that night wanted to raise the issue. All now agreed that every confession came only by torture and that without the confessions there could be no prosecution at all. The majority felt the issue had to be raised. But after hours of debate at the evening meeting, a decision on what to do was deferred. The views of most of those in the room changed during the four-hour discussion.

The majority view was that the military would not permit this lead show trial to be jeopardized, that it would not permit all the trials that were to follow to be aborted, and that if the lawyers pressed the torture issue, they and their families would be severely punished. As a consideration, it was pointed out that the trial would continue for several more days, and there was still time to raise the issue. At the end of the meeting I was asked to leave because the lawyers wanted to forward personal communications from their clients to the defendants' wives. I was also asked to take out of the country "confidential" information to be given to anti-Pinochet groups in Washington, D.C. I agreed to do it.

The following morning the telephone woke me up abruptly. It was one of the defense lawyers. He told me that shortly after I left the meeting a group of armed men, either military intelligence or right-wing terrorists, had invaded the lawyers' office and taken away the two paralegals who had been working with the lawyers. He was badly shaken. Obviously, there had been an informer in our group who had told the government of our meeting, and now the paralegals were almost certainly being tortured to force them to give information about the meeting.

The informer could also have disclosed my presence at the meeting. It would have been easy for the government to arrest or detain me (or have me "disappear") on the grounds that I too was actively opposing the Pinochet regime. If the government did this, it would certainly also discourage and limit future legal observers in the country. I tried to reconstruct all that had been said and done. In my mind's eye I saw again the faces of the paralegals and visualized what was now happening to them.

For the next few days every morning when I left my hotel and every evening when I came back, I saw two men seated in the lobby. Later I was told by one of the junta's members that the men were instructed to follow me to protect me against left-wing terrorists. Each night until about 2 A.M., the phone in my hotel room rang dozens of times. Each time I answered, the caller hung up. These calls reminded me of similar ones I had received during Cesar Chavez' Farmworkers' Union meetings at the Stardust Motel in Delano, California; in civil rights offices and hotel rooms in Jackson, Mississippi; and in migrant workers' homes in Florida. The telephone can be an effective instrument of menace, anywhere in the world.

12

N ow afraid that anything we said at our conferences could be reported back to the junta, several lawyers who were already concerned about the safety of those involved in the trials became even more fearful. Hermosilla, who had been assisted each day by a young leftist lawyer and a paralegal, now told both of them to stay away from the trial and disappear. The events of the night before convinced Hermosilla that the junta could also decide to arrest the defense team whether or not they raised the torture issue. Why not raise it? Hermosilla asked, since we have little to lose and possibly a great deal to gain.

So the following morning, as a sort of compromise, Hermosilla and Garreton deliberately told a Chilean journalist that they would shortly raise the question, not of intentional torture but of the maltreatment of defendants and the filthy conditions in which they were held. A discussion of prison conditions was a travesty of the real tortures the prisoners had endured; all of them, the lawyers told me, had been beaten, had had electric shocks applied to their genitals, and were nearly drowned day after day by having their heads pushed in and out of barrels of water.

Garreton had five clients, including Sergeant Mario O'Ryan, one of the six defendants facing a death sentence.

Garreton told the press that O'Ryan told him that he had

been beaten, tortured with electric shocks, and, like Barrios, had had a hood placed over his head while he was questioned. Garreton added that he would not protest the alleged torture to the court, however, because he was unable to speak to O'Ryan until fifteen days after the interrogation and thus would be unable to prove his case.

During the morning recess the presiding judge summoned Garreton and Hermosilla to his chambers and told them that if they even mentioned the prisoners' conditions, they would be arrested for treason and face the death penalty. The issue was not raised again.

But the international press did not let this slip by totally unreported. In an April 18, 1974, *New York Times* article headlined, "Chile Opens First Public Political Trial Since Coup," it was written that "the defense attorneys have charged privately that the confessions were obtained by force." The article quoted Roberto Garreton: "According to my clients they were all tortured by beatings and electricity into signing confessions." Although the press remarked how well the prisoners looked, the *Times* quoted Garreton as saying that "none of the prisoners showed any evidence of mistreatment because weeks had passed since their torture."

The *Times* article caused a furor in the court. The Chilean defense lawyers, advised that the military was furious at the press reports, realized they had not thought out the consequence of seeing these allegations in a foreign newspaper printed six thousand miles away. They felt vulnerable. They needed support not far away but here in Chile, at the trial, and they asked me for help.

Luckily, it was possible for the foreign lawyers present to support Garreton's allegations in the press and at the same time defuse any personal attack against him by the junta. We could do this by telling the international press and the Chilean judges at the trial that, independent of Garreton, we believed that a hearing should be held on the issue of coerced confessions and torture if the judicial proceedings were to be taken at all seriously.

The following morning, as a representative of the foreign lawyers present, I confronted Jaime Cruzat, the civilian legal assistant to the prosecutor, with my "suspicion" that the question of torture was at issue and was not being dealt with.

During the recess Cruzat, who unlike the prosecutor was a lawyer, escorted me to the chief judge. Cruzat acted as interpreter. General Soler, with narrow eyes behind steel-rimmed glasses, and with a tight smile, dismissed the question by saying that it was absurd to think that the prisoners had been tortured. He said my "investigation" had been entirely based on what the defendants had said. When I called for an opportunity for the foreign lawyers to conduct a full investigation of their own, speaking to defendants, prison guards, and those whom the defendants claimed were their torturers, his jaw tightened in anger. He said it was not possible.

"But," he said with his anger rising, "we might also deal with Mr. Garreton and Mr. Hermosilla. It is notable that Mr. Roberto Garreton has made this type of claim to the foreign press and to you while he has not used the paths provided by the law to place those alleged acts before the tribunal."

I told him that all the foreign lawyers believed that Garreton had acted reasonably and properly under the military code, and that the trial procedures were violating not only Chile's laws but international laws as well.

I said that among the fundamental human rights set forth in the Universal Declaration of Human Rights and the International Covenant of Civil and Political Rights, both of which had been ratified by Chile, were the rights not to be subject to arbitrary arrest or detention; the right not to be subject to torture or cruel and degrading treatment or punishment; the right to a fair and public trial before an impartial and independent tribunal; and the right not to be subject to arbitrary interference with one's privacy, freedom of thought, conscience and religion, freedom of opinion, expression, assembly, and association. The foreign lawyers would that day, I told him, hold a press conference defending Garreton and Hermosilla if the court punished them in any way.

He replied that this trial "complied with Chilean and international law."

I said he was wrong. "This court could not try treason offenses against civilians even under Chile's military code. The international legal community will ridicule these legal proceedings." He bristled. I said, "If a state of war were formally declared only after the coup on September 11 in which President Allende died, then you could not say that one existed prior to September 11."

General Soler angrily responded that a state of war existed only "formally" as of the morning of September 11, when troops and tanks began to move on the presidential palace, but that it had existed "informally" for several years before.

He said the Chilean armed forces had been at war since the existence of armed leftist groups inside the country had been detected. Jaime Cruzat, joining the discussion, said, "This meant 1971, when arms shipments from abroad to the MIR (or Revolutionary Left Movement, a left-wing revolutionary underground group that was anathema to many Chileans) were first legally noted."

After Cruzat spoke, both he and Soler waited for my response. I rose, said "This is all nonsense," and left the room to return to the courtroom.

Garreton and Hermosilla were both permitted to finish the trial. Neither suffered any reprisals for his action.

General Soler was not the only government official who made his views plain to us. On the third day of the trial, several high-ranking officers invited Ira and me to lunch at the Air Force Club in downtown Santiago. The club is an elegant building with the splendor of an opera house. Although many of the buildings surrounding it were shell-marked, it stood untouched.

We walked into the lofty foyer and then up a sweeping marble staircase into a dining room. Commandant Luis Rojas, Group Commander Ernesto Florit, Lieutenant Colonel Manuel Contreras, and General Camilo Valenzuela were there to greet us. Over a lavish four-hour meal, the generals told us of their travels throughout the United States: the Grand Canyon, California, Yellowstone National Park, Big Sur—they had all visited these places while they were "training" in Washington, D.C. By the time lunch was over, it was clear that they all knew Washington nearly as well as Ira Lowe, who had lived there for years. They also had firm views on all aspects of American politics. The United States Senate, for example, was "infiltrated by Marxists," Senator Edward Kennedy was "an agent of international communism," and the Ford Foundation was "not only infiltrated but controlled by Marxists, including admitted Communists."

They seemed, for reasons we never understood, to assume

that we supported the junta and saw Allende, as they did, as a red devil. Lieutenant Colonel Contreras, one of the military personnel responsible for the coup and later founder and head of DINA, Chile's dreaded secret police, told us in great detail what Nixon and Kissinger were at that very time denying—that America had poured millions into the effort to disestablish the Allende government; that Kissinger's 40 Committee—a group primarily composed of conservative American businessmen—had paid $250,000 to support an assassination of Allende; and that $50,000 had been given to General Valenzuela (one of our lunch companions) to "dispose of" General Rene Schneider, the constitutionalist army chief. Although Schneider was assassinated in 1970, Valenzuela was acquitted of that charge.

Valenzuela was, however, convicted under Allende of having attempted to kidnap Schneider; that the Chilean military was constantly receiving monies prior to the coup from Colonel Joseph Wimmert, an American attached to the CIA; that many of the high-ranking Chilean officers were trained in the United States and had close connections with America's civilian and military leaders; and they told us of the government and military leaders of Paraguay, who were supported by the United States. They also explained how, with the aid of the CIA, they sent "false floggers"—people with false passports—from Chile, through Paraguay, to the United States. Years later, in Washington, "false floggers" were to kill Isabel Letelier's husband.

The generals candidly discussed how the CIA helped bring down Allende. During the last days of Allende, when food was scarce in the capital, American dollars were given to truckers to stop the transport of food into Santiago. American dollars also controlled nearly all the anti-Allende media. Christian Democratic members of Congress who were supporters of former President Eduardo Frei were given funds in an attempt to get them to turn on and subvert Allende. These facts are denied by Kissinger to this day. Contreras did not offer any denials when I suggested that while the government was demanding the lives of dozens of men at the trial, there was really only one dead man on trial in the courtroom—Allende.

That evening we spoke to people who knew Contreras well. Lieutenant Colonel Manuel Contreras made rules that governed life. He had dismissed a left-leaning judge and imprisoned her at the jail at Tejas Verdes. The outcry was immediate. Since Pinochet and the junta had announced that no changes would be made in the judicial system, two national court officials traveled to San Antonio to demand that Contreras respect the court's procedures for the removal of judges. One of the officials reported that Contreras received them in his office and dismissed their complaints. Standing over the two officials, as was his custom during interviews, Contreras said coldly, "Gentlemen, I am the law," and putting his hand on his pistol, added, "This is the judicial system."

The junta undoubtedly believed that system was operating not only efficiently, but effectively, and that the Bachelet y Otros trial had created an atmosphere favorable to the trial of bigger fish. On the fourth day of the trial, the media blared the military junta's announcement that the highest of the remaining Allende appointees would imminently be transferred to Santiago in preparation for a second set of court-martial proceedings at the Air Force Academy.

These twenty-nine prisoners had been held since the coup on Dawson Island, in the Strait of Magellan, nearly twelve hundred miles south of the capital. They included the former leader of the Communist Party, Luis Corvalán, and five former cabinet ministers: José Cademartori, Fernando Flores, Sergio Bitar, Anibal Palma, and Jorge Tapia. Orlando Letelier and Clodomiro Almeyda, who served as foreign ministers in the Allende government, were also there. José Toha, an important Allende cabinet minister, thought to be in prison, was not mentioned. It was later feared he was killed or committed suicide in March while being held in a military hospital.

Meanwhile, the first group of Air Force trials limped on.

On the seventh day of the hearing, Alfredo Echeverría interrupted the proceeding. He began reading from what appeared to be a long document drawing on Chilean and international law, arguing that the government could not try the defendants in a military court. Something in Echeverría seemed to have snapped. He was clearly out of order. All the judges bridled. General Soler tried to interrupt. Echeverría, gaining momentum, refusing to be stopped, talked over the voice of Soler. His body expanded and filled out his elegant gray suit. The junta, he said, had no right to use military courts even if the country was attached by foreign forces. They could not legally declare, as they had, "a state of internal war," with martial law, curfews, unlimited detention, and warrantless arrests.

Everyone in the courtroom knew Echeverría was placing himself in danger. Until this time, eight months after the coup, no one in Chile had had the courage to say what he was saying now. Had he spoken these words in public outside of court, he would certainly have been killed. The prosecutor, at first flustered, then furious, asked that the defense lawyer be removed from the case. This was done at once. One week later Echeverría was disbarred on the grounds that this speech showed him to be a traitor. But Echeverría got what he wanted—some members of the international press heard and reported his argument.

Some of the defense lawyers refused to give up. Their next strategy was to call character witnesses on the defendants' behalf. They made it clear that the proposed witnesses would not dispute the "facts" of the prosecutor's case. When, surprisingly, General Soler agreed to let their testimony be taken, the first defense witnesses were called. It was a dramatic scene. The witnesses walked from the witness room in the rear of the auditorium to seats slightly below and to the left of the tribunal. They were walking a gauntlet of fire. The courtroom was silent; everyone stared at them—the military judges with undisguised hatred.

For the second time the clockwork rhythm of the trial was broken. Seven character witnesses testified, and they made everyone in the room remember that men with families and rich pasts were here on trial for their lives. "He came from a poor family, and was the first of his family to go to school . . . he was a wonderful father to his six children. . . . He was the kindest man I knew . . . he walked every Sunday in the park with his wife."

I held my breath as I watched the defense witnesses give evidence—a storekeeper who lived near the defendant, a soldier who had served in his unit, a teacher at the university. Even though there was a stenographer in court who took the witnesses' addresses before they testified, the military judge in charge interrupted the testimony of one man to again ask him his address.

His motive was plain. The next day two of the character witnesses were arrested, one never to be seen again. But the poignancy of the testimony caused the judges to stop the parade of witnesses. "That's enough," Soler said. "We must get back to the trial."

But the defense lawyers insisted on their rights under military law. General Soler then agreed to permit additional character witnesses, but, he said, the character witnesses must first meet with the prosecutor before they were to testify for the defense. The following morning the first three character witnesses called by Carvajal, visibly frightened, gave evidence that hurt Barrios. They said Barrios was a Marxist and had met and conspired with the MIR. No other character witnesses appeared.

The first case on the eighth day was against a former sergeant, Carlos Trujillo, who faced a five-year sentence on charges of having been a member of a clandestine leftist cell in the School of Aviation. A lieutenant who testified on the defendant's behalf said that Mr. Trujillo had served as his bodyguard after the coup and that he had complete confidence in him.

Mr. Trujillo's lawyer, Alfonzo Ferrado, a supporter of the military coup and the ruling junta, then launched into an attack on his client's codefendants. He bitterly denounced the former Marxist government, going far beyond the prosecution's opening statements. He agreed that the coup was justified because "a state of internal war" existed in Chile from the moment Allende was elected president in September 1970, and he agreed that the legal proceedings were fair. His client was ultimately acquitted.

Each day after court we read the afternoon Chilean papers. They always mentioned the presence of foreign observers, and quoted us as saying the proceedings were fair and open. They misstated the testimony in court. They printed entirely fictitious quotes, purportedly from the defendants' confessions, alleging that Allende's government was a tool of the Soviets.

The only woman tried, a mid-level cabinet official, María Teresa Wedeles, did not contest her confession in court. But her mother told the reporters that her daughter had been beaten, sexually abused, tortured with electric currents, and had had rats and spiders put on and into her body by the Army. General Soler, in open court, said he would forward the woman's claim of torture to the armed forces to determine if it was true. If not, he said, she would also be tried for perjury.

On April 18, 1974, the entire front page of *El Mercurio* laid down the details of "Plan Z," a plan that was stopped by the military coup only days before it was to go into effect. Plan Z, supposedly created by Allende's cabinet ministers, was a "hit list" that named hundreds of people who were to be killed by the Allende coalition, including liberals, leftists as well as a large number of people with no record of political activity. Now, according to the newspapers, Plan Z was finally being "confessed to" by defendants in court, and—thanks to the junta—was finally being destroyed, even as "Allende supporters plotted in a final desperate last fling to carry it out."

Plan Z was a total fabrication. Even most of Pinochet's supporters never believed it. It was a transparent compilation of rhetoric and hyperbole strung together from confessions and Pinochet's public statements. If one believed the newspapers, it looked as if some new conspiracy was discovered in court every day and proved by testimony, and was then promptly crushed by the very efficient regime. The papers used lurid language— "The Red Marxist Spiders Spreading Tentacles"—and courtroom witnesses, who were never actually called, were said by *El Mercurio* to have given evidence of large gun supplies and mass truck movements that even at that very moment threatened Santiago. *El Mercurio* reported that a forest fire near Valparaiso had been started by Communists because it burned in the shape of a hammer and sickle.

Separating fact from fiction in the new *El Mercurio* was exceedingly difficult. Only years later did we learn that the CIA had, in a one-year period, channeled over $1 million into the newspaper, first to help in the election campaign to stop Allende, then to build support for the coup, and then to support the Pinochet regime.

The reporters who tried to report the true facts about Chile placed themselves in danger. During the second week of the Air Force trials, the Reuters reporter told me that his news service had been threatened with shutdown because the junta did not like his reporting of the trial. Radio Balmaceda, a Christian Democratic radio station, was shut down for commenting on the trials.

Pierre Rieben, a young Swiss newsman, told me the junta had complained to his paper that he was not reporting the trial fairly. Shortly afterward, he failed to appear in court. After several days his friends started to get anxious. The junta claimed his whereabouts were unknown, but years later, in *Le Monde*, he described what had happened:

> Several plainclothes cops came to the place where I was staying Thursday, April 11, around 12:30 in the afternoon. They asked me to accompany them to the Bureau of Investigations, supposedly to clarify my status as a foreign resident in Chile. We had hardly gotten into the car . . . before they began to rough me up a little. Then, as we were driving, they handcuffed me, covered my head, and forced me to crouch down on the floor of the car. . . .
>
> We . . . arrived at what I later learned was the Air Force Academy. Here they continued to rough me up. Still blindfolded, I was then put in a cell. Actually, I was kept blindfolded continually during the week I passed in the hands of Pinochet's thugs. Those people do not like to have their faces seen. I was very quickly subjected to my first interrogation.
>
> The proposition was the following: Tell us what you know and in a few hours you will be at the airport and aboard the first plane out of here. Otherwise your life is not going to be worth very much. What they wanted me to tell them was the names and addresses of my supposed "informers" on the Chilean situation, the activities of the left-wing organizations, and, above all, the activities of the MIR, which seemed to be their *bête noire*.
>
> Given my lack of cooperation, the second interrogation and those that followed took a different turn. I was systematically kicked and pummeled in the stomach and head. But they also used more classical, more refined methods. Electric shocks, for example. The officers strapped me down to a table and attached electrodes to my penis, in my anus, and to my toes. The sessions lasted for half an hour. The pain was excruciating, almost as if they had torn off my genitals and my legs.

After one week Rieben was finally "found" by the junta and immediately put on a plane to Switzerland.

As the trial drew to its end, the government announced it had new evidence of leftist conspiracies. Arrests of thousands of "extremists" in the working-class neighborhoods of Santiago followed immediately. On the last day of the trial, the government said that ten thousand of these "extremists" were massing on the Argentine border to invade Chile. The story disappeared the following day. There was now a new story: that jailed prisoners had obtained arms and were planning other revolutionary acts. After a few days that story too ran out.

13

I HAD HEARD from the defense lawyers at the Air Force Academy that even while these so-called "open Nuremberg trials" were going on, secret trials were being held outside the main population centers secure from the eyes of "outsiders."

The defense lawyers asked me to help file habeas corpus petitions in the Chilean Supreme Court demanding minimal rights for those arrested detainees—the right to consult lawyers, to see a list of the charges, and release from imprisonment pending trial. The petitions we drafted, citing the Chilean Constitution and the Universal Declaration of Human Rights, concluded:

> The relief sought is nothing more than a demand for the ob-servance of basic civil and human rights. To deny these funda-mental rights would place the Republic of Chile outside the in-ternational community. The charter of the United Nations, to which Chile subscribes, imposes upon it and every member state the obligation to guarantee human rights. Article I states that one of the purposes of the United Nations is to achieve inter-national co-operation in promoting and encouraging respect for personal rights and for fundamental freedoms for all. These obligations have both a moral and legal character. The present government is failing to fulfill its obligations.

We tried to answer the claim that all those who opposed Pinochet were in the pay of the Soviet Union. We cited James Madison, who in 1776 said, "Perhaps it is a universal truth that the loss of liberty at home is to be charged to the dangers, real or pretended, from abroad."

Most of these petitions were ineffectual. The magistrates simply did not act upon them. But even when they tried to order the military to answer the petition (as two judges outside of Santiago did), the Army claimed they did not know where those arrested were. According to Ramsey Clark, who months before had been in the Chilean countryside, judges in Osorno province were afraid to sign orders directing the military to produce their prisoners. In that rural province dozens of farmers and farm workers who had disappeared several months before were located only after they had been "tried" and their sentences were announced or, more often, when their bodies were found. Habeas corpus, a proud pillar of Chile's democratic past, was totally ignored.

On March 29, 1974, Senator Edward Kennedy's office learned that two Osorno women had been condemned to death and thirty others sentenced to six to twenty years' imprisonment for treason by military tribunals, simply because they supported Allende during the elections. At least thirty corpses, some dismembered, were washed up on riverbanks in Osorno during the winter, months after relatives had reported they had disappeared.

In these "private" military trials in the countryside, the state-appointed defense lawyers usually were given less than the forty-eight hours' notice required by law to prepare their defense; in many cases they had less than twelve hours.

One of the defense lawyers at the Air Force trials described the trial of a young man named Marcos, whom he was called on by the government to defend one hour before the trial was to begin. "They said unless I was there Monday at noon, the trial would start without a lawyer," he said. The defendant was an eighteen-year-old charged with giving a treasonable political speech, for which the prosecutor sought the death penalty. The lawyer recalled: "The prosecutor read the defendant's confession. Marcos refused to let me raise the question of torture, feeling the tribunal would only get more hostile if I did. I said the confession was untrue. The trial took half an hour, and then the judge said he would call me and give me his verdict. By Thursday I had heard nothing. I called the tribunal and was told that Marcos had been shot on Tuesday." The lawyer said he had to notify Marcos' parents of his death. "They had not heard from him in months and did not even know he had been arrested or charged."

Such stories were not uncommon: Four young students from the University of Chile at Arica were arrested for nothing more than participating in political discussion at the university. One of them, a twenty-three-year-old graduate student named Enzo Villanueva, received an arbitrary nineteen-and-one-half-year sentence after seeing his lawyer for five minutes. Another, twenty-two-year-old Jorge Jaque, was sentenced to thirteen years' imprisonment. Although he suffered from a disease of the joints, his captors denied him medicine and tortured him severely. One hand and the toes of his feet were amputated. The other two students, Miguel Berton and Sergio Vasquez, neither of whom was yet twenty, received sentences of twenty-five and eighteen years respectively, even though the only charge against them was that they were critical of the junta. All four are now dead.

I spoke to a father whose nine-year-old daughter and four-year-old son were tortured to death in front of his eyes. The Army officers wrongly believed he could identify the Marxist sympathizers in their small town.

While I was in Chile, and in the decade since, Catholic priests and other clergy did more than virtually anyone else to help the victims of terror. They emerged as the only group that openly challenged the Chilean regime for its maltreatment of the people and its repression of human rights. Indeed, the church has played a crucial role in the movement for human rights throughout Latin America.

Men like Bishop Pedro Casaldalgia and Cardinal Paulo Evaristo Arns of Brazil, Bishop Juan Gerardi Conedra of Guatemala, and Archbishop Oscar Arnulfo Romero of El Salvador followed a path of church resistance to oppressive governments opened up by Archbishop Helder Cámara of Brazil and Cardinal Raúl Silva of Chile. In the case of Archbishop Romero, in 1980 the path led to death.

Unlike the governments of El Salvador and Guatemala, the

105

junta in Chile has tended to be more circumspect in its treatment of the clergy and in the pressures it applies to them. As Air Force General Gustavo Leigh, one of the four generals who led the coup, put it, the regime had "great respect for the Churches, but like many men, without realizing it, they are vehicles for Marxism." And despite their caution, there have been notable atrocities: Several Chilean priests have been detained and imprisoned for so-called pro-Marxist and antijunta activities, and shortly after the junta seized power, one priest, a Spaniard named Juan Alsina, was assassinated in the hospital where he worked because of his friendship and commitment to the revolutionary poor in one of the *poblaciones.*

In the turbulent months following the coup, and at increasing risk to their immunity, the Catholic priests began to pursue every means available to secure information on missing persons and to arrange for the release of prisoners or publication of the charges against them.

Cardinal Raúl Silva gave moral and financial help to the thousands of Chilean children who had been orphaned by the coup, to families in which the wage earners were in jail or dead, and to those who wanted to emigrate. Much of his time was spent trying to find lawyers to defend the poor, weak, and ignorant.

He was not alone; the Lutheran bishop, Helmut Frenz, organized the Committee of Cooperation for Peace along with Fernando Ariztía, the auxiliary bishop of Santiago and Fernando Salas, a young Jesuit priest. Prominent Jewish and Protestant clergymen supported this committee, which tried to help political prisoners and their families as well as the unemployed. In the few weeks I was there, Bishop Frenz' committee sent 131 writs of habeas corpus to the minister of the interior. Not one received a response.

Meanwhile, Cardinal Silva, the senior Catholic prelate in Chile, who had been a vigorous opponent of Allende but who was increasingly appalled by the continuing violence and killing, released a statement called "Reconciliation in Chile." It said, in part:

> We are concerned by the climate of insecurity and fear, whose roots we believe are found in accusations, false rumors, and the lack of participation and information.

We are worried, finally, in some cases, over the lack of effective legal safeguards for personal security that is evident in arbitrary or excessively long detentions in which neither the persons concerned nor their families know the specific charges against them; in interrogations that use physical and moral pressures; in the limited possibilities for a legal defense; in unequal sentences in different parts of the country; in restrictions of the normal right of appeal.

We understand that particular circumstances can justify the temporary suspension of certain civil rights. But there are rights that affect the very dignity of a human being, and those are absolute and inviolable. The Church must be the voice of all, especially those who do not have a voice.

On April 24, 1974, the day the statement was to appear, the junta commanded front-page headlines in the papers with the "news" that they had uncovered an extremist plot to kill the cardinal. The junta decided he should be given a four-man bodyguard. They apparently also decided that he, along with some of his church colleagues, should go into retreat for a while. There was no mention anywhere of his statement until, a few days later, when the Air Force trial was nearing its end. The papers then published a mild statement over the cardinal's name. It said that a climate of fear existed in Chile, but omitted his judgments upon the practices of the junta. But this was enough for the government to claim proof that the church was part of a "Marxist conspiracy."

The defense lawyers I had met in Santiago felt we might have some effect on local justice if we visited some rural courtrooms or jails. The atmosphere of the courtrooms varied across the country: In some, goats climbed up the front steps and tried to intrude themselves into the proceedings. In others, armed police lined the courtroom entrance to create a sense of menace. Whatever the atmosphere, the judicial results were nearly always the same—speedy injustice by a regime that nearly always claimed the sanctity of the law.

Following the suggestion of the Chilean lawyers, during a two-day break in the trial, I drove to San Fernando, a small farming community one hundred miles south of Santiago. The cool

Chilean autumn weather was turning the wheat fields a rusty hue. Peasants in ponchos drove herds of cattle along the narrow roads past rickety machines harvesting the crops. I did not see soldiers, guns, or tanks. It seemed to be a different country. But under the surface it was not. Like dozens of other quiet communities north and south of the capital, San Fernando was still, in the phrase of the military junta, "extirpating the Marxist cancer."

In San Fernando, a conservative town of 46,000, not a shot was fired on September 11, the day of the coup. But in the five months that followed, more than 700 people were arrested, 30 of whom disappeared and 160 of whom were detained without being charged with a crime. The prisoners smuggled out stories of torture through the priests, and it was they who informed the outside world of the proceedings taking place there: "trials" conducted in secret, presided over by police and military officers, with no notice given and neither clergy nor members of family permitted to attend.

Colonel Carlos Morales, the military governor who heads the San Fernando Military School, had the power to raise or lower the sentences handed down at these trials.

A hard-line anti-Marxist, he often raised the sentence dramatically. For example, even in a rural community such as this, where revolvers and shotguns go unregistered by both leftists and conservatives, he raised the sentences of persons caught with guns after the coup who were not outspoken anti-Marxists like himself from two hundred days to ten years. But no lawyer in this area dared to raise the defense of brutality or illegality against Morales. One lawyer explained it would be difficult to prove the prisoners were physically mistreated. But, he added, "It does strike me as strange that all without exception signed written confessions that they were involved in terrorist activities." One result of all this repression was a frightened populace, even in a town noted for its anti-Allende feelings.

The trials I saw and those that go on today, ten years later, are illegal. One need not be a scholar of Chilean law to know that the trials we witnessed were not governed by either preestablished principles or procedures uniformly applied in Chile in the effort to determine the truth. It was impossible to trace power from the Chilean Constitution to the court proceedings we saw.

Perhaps that was why, posted outside one courtroom, there was a rain-spotted carbon copy of a memo saying that no attorney should criticize the jurisdiction of the court or the procedure it uses. Because there had been no legal officer to guide the court, to instruct it in procedural and substantive law, the trials had been a pantomime, where soldiers played the parts of prosecutor, judge, and jury.

I spent another day in the adjoining shantytowns of Violeta Parra, El Montijo, La Legua, and Villa Resbaladon in Santiago's vast dusty western slum area. In the morning of the day I was there Army troops blocked off paved roads and dirty alleys leading out of the shantytowns in order to catch people in their prefabricated wooden houses before the end of the curfew. By 6:30 A.M. they had knocked on the door of each house in the town and ordered all males over eighteen to assemble in the neighborhood soccer field. By 7:30 A.M. about 16,000 men had gathered there and were lined up alphabetically. I saw the soldiers check their identification cards against criminal and political records. When the raid ended at five o'clock that afternoon, about 550 men were ordered into buses and taken to police headquarters because their records showed either previous convictions or cases pending against them for suspect political activity.

When the military searched a home in the town of Las Barrancas, the wife complained it was the third such search and she begged them to leave her in peace. As the soldiers departed, they called to her little boy, "So long, you won't be seeing us around anymore." The child, surprised, inquired, "You mean you found my daddy on the roof?" The police came back, took the father from the roof, and shot him in front of his family and neighbors.

Wherever I went, it was clear the entire legal system was a shambles. Only weeks before the coup Justice Urrutía, the crusty septuagenarian president of the Supreme Court, virtually legitimized a future military uprising by expounding the thesis that the Allende government, though legally elected, had "lost its legality by acting on the margin of the law." A few days after the coup Justice Urrutía had welcomed the junta members to the Supreme Court chambers and declared, "This Supreme Court, which I have the honor of presiding over, receives your visit with satisfaction and optimism, and appreciates its historical and juridical value."

President Pinochet responded by reasserting the junta's intention to preserve the autonomy of the judicial branch—in marked contrast to its dissolution of Congress and its disbanding of political parties.

"Dr. Urrutía and the Supreme Court have set the tone for relations between the judicial branch and the junta," a court of appeals judge said. "There has been an unstated desire throughout the court system to try not to clash with the executive power."

Justice Urrutía said that human rights were "fully respected in our country."

14

As I MOVED around the country, sometimes with Ira, sometimes without him, I saw prisoners, various jails, and the still bloodstained National Stadium, which housed more than ten thousand of the junta's prisoners. Throughout Latin America, stadiums play a double role: In peacetime they are sports arenas, and in times of war they turn into prisons. Many prisoners were kept in the stadium for weeks. Then most of them were killed.

I also went to the smaller Santiago stadium where, some months before, the Chilean folk singer Victor Jara, in defiance of the guards, had tried to keep up the prisoners' spirits by singing. The guards took him to a table where the maximum number of people in the stadium could see what was going to happen. First they told him to continue to sing. When they kicked him and punched him, he rose, playing his guitar for the thousands of prisoners who were soon to be killed. The guards broke his guitar, but he went on singing. In full view of the prisoners, they then broke first his hands and then with an ax, cut his hands off at the wrists. He lifted his maimed arms in the air, and swaying back and forth, kept on singing as they beat him to death.

Interviews had been arranged for me by the military with prisoners who, as could be expected, denied any experience or knowledge of torture. But there were, as we walked through the jails, brief opportunities to communicate with other prisoners.

This was first done by signaling—for example, a prisoner pointing to his arm in a sling. Another prisoner let his arm hang limp while making a slicing sign to indicate that it had been broken.

The men got bolder as we walked along, some lifting shirts to show me the sides of their bodies where they had been burned by electric shocks. They told us under their breath where they had been tortured—jails and places I had never heard of before. They displayed great courage in trying to let us know what had happened.

In Santiago, at the risk of her own safety, Isabel Letelier arranged for us to meet men and women who had already served out their sentences. Early one morning they came to our hotel. They jammed into our room, spilling over from the bed to the floor. Showing us what had been done to their own bodies, they also told stories of alleged suicide cases who, when their bodies were finally found, had had their hands and genitals cut off.

One of the women who shared her story with us was Mrs. Virginia Ayress. She said that her daughter, Luz de las Nieves, had been tortured in Santiago's women's jail. There she was handcuffed and blindfolded and raped ferociously by three or four men. They introduced sticks into her vagina, her mother told us. "They tied her up and separated her legs and made rats walks over her, making them enter her vagina. . . . They applied electric current to her tongue, ears, and vagina. They hit her head, especially behind the ears. They hit her stomach. They hung her up, sometimes by the legs and sometimes by the arms. They terrorized her because she traveled to Cuba on a scholarship to study cinema in Cuba in 1971."

Cases such as that of Luz de las Nieves Ayress are not made public. But Chile, for all its narrow length, is a small country, of small cities and towns (except Santiago), and most of the population of 10 million knows of many unreported incidents. The Army, although its size is secret, is probably no larger than the student body of a medium-sized state university in the United States. The whole Air Force has less than ten thousand men. Words of arrests, some executions, and above all of the dismissals of leftists on a large scale from jobs in factories, mines, and in the bureaucracy, gets around.

Most of the time I was in Chile I felt extraordinarily helpless—a powerless witness to a great tragedy. Despite the climate of unchecked violence and lawlessness, there was one small instance in which I believe I had an immediate effect. And my transformation from an observer to a more active involvement exhilarated me.

On Saturday, April 13, a small item appeared in *El Mercurio* announcing that four persons had been condemned to death by a council of war at a secret trial in Linares. They had supposedly been guilty of engaging in "paramilitary training."

Linares is 175 miles from Santiago, but one of the lawyers with whom I had been working managed to find out the name of the defendants' lawyer, Alejandro Carlos Cortazar. I went to see him, and he told me that if a foreign lawyer could contact the commander of the military zone in Linares, indicating international interest in the case, the defendants' lives might be spared. I decided to go.

No one knew how quickly the commander of the military zone would act on the sentence. Under the code of military justice, the command was to execute the prisoners immediately without appeal. It was clear to me that at a minimum the trials in Linares suffered from the same legal defect as the trial at the Air Force Academy—they involved a retroactive application of penal laws. The defendants were accused of having taken part in training with military weapons during the Allende period, but what they did was legal at the time they did it. I immediately wrote a legal appeal to the commander of the military zone, had it translated into Spanish, and typed it onto the letterhead of one of our support groups. I took the letter to regimental headquarters and asked the guard to deliver it to the colonel immediately. Sensing the urgency of the matter, he took it to the colonel's house. Since nothing more could be done on that day, I returned to Santiago to wait for developments.

Cortazar became more optimistic with each day of delay. Weeks later, on May 22, after I had returned to the United States, I was advised that the colonel had commuted all four death sentences to prison terms. Cortazar later wrote to me that the commutation "to some extent" set a precedent for defendants throughout Chile and certainly within the Linares zone. It was a wonderful feeling that my visit had, in a small way, helped to save lives.

After returning to Santiago from Linares, I returned a phone call from the Air Force Academy. The young prosecutor, Captain Daniel Aycinema, whose number I called, told me I was "invited" to a meeting with Chief Justice Urrutía. I was surprised. He had not seen any of the dozens of other foreign lawyers who wanted to talk with him. The defense lawyers urged me to go, thinking only good could come of the meeting. Elegant in a white linen suit, the aged justice bounded to the door to greet me. His very large room, with large windows on three sides, filled with law books, was like hundreds of other judges' chambers. After offering tea, he got quickly to the point. "What did you think of the trials?" he asked. "We are following the rule of law, although it is very difficult."

"Not as I understand it. You are ridiculing the rules of law. The military is judge and jury. The men on trial were never real enemies of the state."

"But they are traitors. You punish your traitors in the same ways. You prosecuted the Rosenbergs, Hiss, Debs, and others because they worked for the Communists. Had Allende been in your country, you would have prosecuted him."

"The men on trial never worked for a foreign power. They never advocated violence against the state. They worked within the system. You believe they worked for Communists because they had some ideas similar to those given birth elsewhere. In my country we do not have treason prosecutions based solely on confessions. The Fifth Amendment prohibits it. In our country treason law requires independent evidence of action and two independent witnesses. Your law also requires it, but you have chosen to ignore it here."

"We had to adopt these procedures," he replied. "We could not get two witnesses in each case. It would take too much time. That is a luxury of other systems."

"We believe free speech and free pursuit of ideas is to be given the widest latitude and that speech alone cannot be the basis for a treason prosecution."

Judge Urrutía interrupted me: "You know that is not true. We know that both governments do prosecute speech anytime they want."

Trying to get away from the political discussion and the discussion of the trial, Justice Urrutía agreed that the most important human rights provision in any constitution is the writ of habeas corpus. The Chilean Constitution was similar to ours, which provides that "the privilege of the writ of habeas corpus shall not be suspended, unless when in cases of rebellion or invasion, the public safety may require it."

The judge said he believed Pinochet was correct in suspending it. We both started up again. I replied, "The suspension of habeas corpus by the executive is the beginning of fascism. Not merely liberty of movement is involved; habeas establishes freedom from terror. Habeas corpus forces the jailer to cite an offense known to the law. This compels recourse to law, takes the matter away from the police or military and puts it in control of courts and lawyers."

"We can have law without making the military and the courts enemies," he said.

I replied: "No, suspension of habeas corpus is the end of the rule of law. It has never been suspended in this century in the United States. Even if free speech is prohibited, people will talk. Censorship can be evaded; prosecutions against ideas may break down; but a prison wall is there. Only habeas corpus can penetrate it. When imprisonment is possible without explanation or redress, every form of liberty is impaired. A man in jail cannot go to church or discuss or publish or assemble or enjoy property or go to the polls. I might consider parting with all the other rights in the international documents if we could erect a worldwide barrier against a knock on the door at three A.M."

He continued. "Abraham Lincoln, your great president, suspended habeas corpus during your civil war. Because he could not get your Congress to pass laws locking up people, he just arrested and jailed them. That is exactly the situation we have here today."

There was nothing to be gained by arguing with him. Even before we talked, I knew of Judge Urrutía's actions since Pinochet came to power. After approving the suspension of habeas corpus, he had presided over the dismissal of forty lower-court judges appointed during the Allende years. Although this number represents a small fraction of all judges in the courts of Chile, these dismissals sent a clear message to the judge's colleagues.

Perhaps the most significant of Justice Urrutía's habeas

corpus decisions that he told me about came in a case involving a fifteen-year-old boy who was arrested and had been detained incommunicado without formal charges for months.

A court of appeals had approved a writ of habeas corpus, and ordered the Interior Ministry to make know the charges against the boy or release him.

In an appeal to Justice Urrutía and the Supreme Court, the interior minister, General Oscar Bonilla, acknowledged that no formal charges existed against the boy, but alleged that he had been a member of the Communist Party since the age of eleven and that he was being held "as a preventive measure" in "defense of the state."

Justice Urrutía, who wrote the opinion, upheld the interior minister and ruled that under the state of siege declared by the junta the authorities had the right to detain minors for whatever reason and for as long as they deemed necessary.

The court opinion went even further in declaring that "the motives for the decree of arrest are the executive concern of the authorities; that the Courts should not interfere."

It was getting late. He was getting tired. Neither of us was getting anywhere. We both then tried to make small talk. It was forced. If his purpose in our meeting was to persuade me that the trials were fair, Urrutía knew he had failed. I spoke about other treason trials I'd observed in other countries. But I went on to say that I had never seen such a transparent trial as I had witnessed now. It made a mockery out of the law.

His face crimsoned. Then he spoke about the force of international law. "Other countries or international organizations can't tell Chile how best to treat its own problem—especially the United States. You have not dealt well with the Left. It runs your foreign policy. Why are you here?"

"Many of the men at this trial, because of their love of Chile, will face death, beatings, jail, phony trials, and long confinements in terrible places. The world will not forget them. Many of them could have sided with the Army when they saw the coup coming. They chose not to. They could have taken up weapons to beat back the coup. They chose not to. The world will know of them and their trial. That is why I am here."

He looked up, stared at me for a moment, extended his hand,

and said "Good-bye." I asked if he would read a legal brief we'd prepared expressing our view of the trials. He took it as he sat down to his work. I felt exhilarated. The defense lawyers later told me I had spoken in a way that they could not have.

The next day I was back in court. Captain Aycinema did not ask how the visit with Urrutía went. For the remainder of the trial, he refused to talk to me.

I had become locked into the rhythm of the trial at the Air Force Academy with familiarity. The defendants' lives became ever more important to me. Their lawyers had told them who Ira and I were, and over the two weeks a strangely close relationship had been established. When I arrived, I knew almost nothing about the men in the dock, but by the time the trials were in their second week, I had met some of their wives and children, and had a good idea of what many of them stood for and how they had lived their lives.

They exchanged glances with us; at several particularly absurd allegations by the prosecutor, Erich Schnake's eyes met mine. Beccerría, small and pale, fidgeted in his seat, and worried for his wife, who had already been arrested and tortured on four separate occasions. Barrios, who had admitted meeting MIR members, knew he had no chance of avoiding the death penalty. He never expected to see his two-year-old child again.

I also better understood their prosecutors, the generals, and those under them who always defended the oligarchy. They viewed the better-educated younger officers, who frequently came from the lower classes, as threats to established order and old military values. I also understood why the generals saw the defendants, particularly General Bachelet, as traitors; like Breytenbach (and, as we will see, Andrei Sakharov), they were offered privilege and turned it down. The prosecutors and generals in Chile, South Africa, and the Soviet Union saw their opponents not only as traitors to the country but also as traitors to their class.

Two weeks after we arrived, I decided to leave. I felt the best way to perhaps save these defendants' lives was to help focus public attention in the United States and Europe on the trial before the verdicts would come down. First Ira and I decided to hold a press conference at the Santiago airport. We believed the junta would not arrest us and risk an international incident after all the publicity favorable to them. I also thought that if we could round up the free-lance journalists who had been furnishing information to the international press, we could provide them with our own version of the trial.

There was not much time before our flight, but I made half a dozen calls from the hotel room. Then I quickly walked over to the Reuters office. The bureau chief thought a press conference was a fine idea if it could be set up quickly and quietly, and he walked back to the hotel with me. But as I entered the hotel lobby, two men in the lobby started to come toward us. The Reuters man immediately walked away, out of the hotel. One of the two men told me in clear English, "There will not be a press conference." There was nothing I could do. If we disobeyed, they could arrest Ira and me and we might join the ranks of the disappeared. Or they could kick us out of the country, probably with the testimony of the tortured paralegal proving we were guilty of acts against the state. I went to my room, packed my bags, and went to the airport. We did not hold our press conference, and I was relieved to leave without incident.

On the LanChile plane leaving Chile, we saw the latest edition of the international edition of *Time*. It repeated the thrust of its earlier reportage—that the trials were being opened to the public by a regime intent on proving that the allegations of torture made against them were false. The article also contained denials by American officials that the United States had been involved with the overthrow of Allende. As we looked out over the cloud-shrouded Andes, I was terribly depressed. I feared we had been outwitted, that the junta had gained more from our trip than we had.

I hoped we could change that when we arrived in the United States.

15

WHEN WE CAME BACK to the United States at the end
of April, the first thing we did was to hold a press conference.
It was attended mostly by wire service stringers and a few New
York radio and newspaper reporters. Ira and I distributed briefs
critical of the legal procedures that we had submitted to Judge
Urrutía and the military court at the Air Force Academy. We
discussed both in the briefs and at the press conference Chile's
constitution, its treason and conspiracy laws, the military code,
and the junta's claim that if a Communist worked with an individual as a peacefully elected government official, then the individual was tainted and was also a Communist. When a reporter
asked whether the procedures used during the trials were in accord with Chilean military law, I answered that they were. But
I also pointed out that not only were the military courts the wrong
places to try such charges, but the charges themselves were without legal merit.

After the press conference I learned that this questioner was
not with the press, but was an official of the Chilean government.
My answer, taken out of context, led to a misinterpretation of our
report. The following day, the *Washington Star*, one of the many
newspapers that reported the press conference, ran a headline on
page 1: "Chile holds open trials. American lawyers describe pro-

ceedings as in accord with law." Other papers throughout the country ran nearly identical stories: A front page article in the *Los Angeles Times* was headlined "Chilean Trial Passes Observers' Test." The news story, quoting liberally from an interview we gave a Chilean reporter on our first days there, said we "gave cautious approval to the procedure in Chile's first open court-martial since the military seized power last September." In the original article I had been quoted as saying that I "hoped the Air Force trials would be a 'showcase' and set a precedent for open military court proceedings as well as establishing legal guidelines for the treatment of detained persons." But the quote did not include my follow-up statement that my hopes had not been fulfilled. Other papers, setting forth parts of the Chilean interview, had similarly inaccurate headlines and selective reportage.

Commenting on the Santiago trials, the Sunday, May 5, 1974, *New York Times* relied in part on a Chilean government press release. It said, "Defense attorneys have been given free rein to raise broad legal issues and call large numbers of witnesses."

The reception of my Chilean report and the way the facts had been twisted were as suprising to me as the reception of my South African report would later be. Letters were written by members of the committee that sponsored Ira and me to the editors of the major newspapers that carried the stories. Some were published, but they were never able to "catch up" to the inaccurate story. The editors of *Newsday*, the Long Island newspaper, invited me out to speak to them, and I described the details of my trip.

It was not until the following month, on June 14, that *Newsday* tried to set the record straight. An editorial entitled "Unfortunate Silence in Chile," said:

Late in March the British government announced the suspension of military aid to Chile because of its "desire to see democracy restored and human rights fully respected." Canada opened its doors to Chilean refugees. A few days later the United States rammed through a 22-million-dollar loan from the Inter-American Development Bank to increase Chilean food production. The U.S. has never breathed a word of protest against the right-wing junta's brutality although it often made no secret of its distaste for the previous left-wing government and blocked development loans to it. The U.S. makes much of the Soviet Union's restriction on free immigration by Jews to Israel. Does it really have nothing to say against the Chilean government that purges its political opponents as Stalin did in the 1930s?

Had our efforts in Chile been worthwhile? What more could we do to win back what we had lost? Many of the lawyers who had visited Chile, including Ira Lowe and me, testified before congressional committees in 1974, 1975, and 1976, when military aid to Chile was under consideration. I also spoke at colleges, fundraisers, and other meetings in the United States, and at international human rights conventions in Rome, Copenhagen, and Mexico.

But I felt that we might have done more harm than good. By going to Chile, by allowing the Pinochet government to claim that our very presence was proof that Chile had held free, open, legally proper trials, and then by participating in press conferences where we were misquoted, I felt we had legitimized a fraudulent legal process. I believed we might have done more good by totally ignoring the trials.

Ira Lowe demurred. He reminded me of the complaint that the lawyer-observers, including himself, had issued to the press in Cuba, when, shortly after the successful 1959 revolution, Castro decided to hold the anti-Batista trials before ten thousand people in the national stadium. "At first Castro dismissed our statement, but then he did move the trial," Ira said. He added, "The Chilean government will ultimately feel it has to respond to our charges."

He was correct. Two weeks after I gave testimony before Congress, I saw a letter which had been sent to Congress by Walter Heitman, Chile's ambassador to the United States, replying to our version of the trials. Shortly after the coup, Heitman had publicly denied the military had killed anyone, saying, "I never saw any bodies." Now, denying our claim that the Chilean court system had been suspended, he insisted, "No, it has never been suspended. The judiciary system is the same as before, we have the same judges, the same Supreme Court. That's why we say there is no dictatorship and complete freedom. A free judiciary system means we have freedom."

Ambassador Heitman's letter to Congress called us Communists and put forward his government's argument:

> As you know, Marxist propaganda has been very active world wide in trying to mask the tremendous defeat imposed on communism by the Chilean people. Their endeavor appears to be to induce public opinion into looking at the Chilean events as a major setback for democracy. To this end . . . they keep up a constant flow of false news and misleading reports on the alleged violence in Chile.

> Supporters of Marxism will attach no meaning to the fact that foreign observers are free to come to Chile and see for themselves under no restrictions whatsoever, how our nation is handling its problems and recovering from the outrages of Communist rule. We are not concealing our actions from public criticism from abroad.

> We hope that the openness of our society to international public scrutiny will be appreciated by fair observers in this country, particularly the distinguished members of the U.S. Congress, as a trait that is characteristic to the Chilean deeply rooted democratic tradition.

> I would like to assure you that not only do we not resent constructive criticism coming from our friends, but that we welcome it and are prepared to give it careful consideration. . . .

> Within the context, I feel my duty to express to you my concern over the fact that some statements and inferences made in the course of the Public Hearings on the present status of Human Rights in Chile, may be caused by parties involved in the aforementioned campaign against my country. Therefore, I would like to offer you any information you may wish to have on Chile, including comprehensive statements on particular points of interest to your Subcommittee.

Obviously stung by our reports, the Chilean government also considered it necessary to pay for a series of half-page advertisements in the *New York Times* and the *Washington Post*. They claimed we were not experts in Chilean law and that the trials followed legal forms. After our visit they stopped many legal observers and foreign lawyers from coming into the country.

16

O N J U L Y 3 1 , 1 9 7 4 , three months after I left Chile, the judges delivered the verdict in the longest trial in Chile's history. Garreton called me in New York. "Although you may not think it is a victory, it is!" He read me the sentences. "Death sentences for five defendants, including the two civilians, socialist Senator Erich Schnake and the former head of the State Bank, Carlos Lazo; Patricio Barrios; and two Air Force officers. Prison sentences ranging from three hundred days to life imprisonment were ordered for the remainder of the defendants. Three defendants were acquitted." "But," said Garreton confidently, "no one will die. Nor will they be severely brutalized in jail as they might have been, because the government is concerned that you and others like you will come back."

I was angry. I thought he was looking for solace when the facts did not justify it. I did not believe the defendants would live out their sentences. I knew how horrible the jails were and that Pinochet was going to be around, with American aid, for many years. The American government had not attempted, in any way, to interfere with the verdicts before they were handed down.

But Garreton's optimism was well founded. International outrage at the procedures of the first Chilean "Nuremberg trial" made it impossible for the junta to execute any of the convicted defendants. By the end of the year Schnake and Lazo were exiled—and the other death sentences were commuted. Soon after, Chile released, and then deported, Orlando Letelier and other high-ranking officials. Perhaps more important, the criticism of this trial stopped other proceedings that the junta had planned. All this was a direct result of French, Italian, German, and English criticism, European countries with which Chile needed to do business.

The United States government, on the other hand, had done nothing. It criticized neither the trials nor the sentences.

Nonetheless, Orlando Letelier told me later that he felt that the exposure we gave to the trial saved people's lives. Barrios, exiled five years later, agreed, and said that even those who were still in Chilean jails were living under better prison conditions than they otherwise might have.

Two years later, in 1976, I thought again about what Letelier had said to me when I learned he had been killed instantly when a bomb exploded in the floor of his car in Washington, D.C., blowing off both his legs. Ronni Moffit, an associate who was seated in the car with him, was also killed.

Indicted by the United States attorney at the trial of Letelier and Moffit's killers was the man who gave the order. He was none other than Lieutenant Colonel Contreras, one of my hosts at the Air Force Club luncheon. One of the more powerful and truly evil members of the Pinochet regime, besides issuing the directive, Contreras had written to various governments, primarily that of Paraguay, to facilitate the secret movements of Letelier's killers, had passports forged, and directed the Chilean government to give false information to the American prosecutors of Letelier's killers.

The Nixon and Ford administrations vigorously supported Pinochet. But the election of Jimmy Carter led to a new policy. After Carter was elected, he banned aid to Chile because the Chilean government repeatedly frustrated America's attempts to get the Chileans to send Contreras here to stand trial for the Letelier killing.

Carter's presidency, for all its ambiguities, was consistent and clear in letting the South American military dictatorships feel the hostility of the United States. But relations between the Pinochet regime and Washington again changed immediately and improved dramatically when Ronald Reagan was elected president in 1980.

I planned to return to Chile at the beginning of 1981. Isabel Letelier, then living in Washington, had visited Chile for ten days in 1978 amidst great fanfare—she felt too public to be harmed. "Of course, I was afraid," she said. "But I live with that fear here also. They can kill us in either country if they want to."

I canceled my trip after President Reagan relieved Ambassador Robert E. White of his duties as United States ambassador to El Salvador to signal a new policy in Central and South America. He sought to nominate Ernest Lefever to the job, a man who as this country's new assistant secretary of state for human rights and humanitarian affairs said he did not "believe in human rights." Signs such as these indicated that it was now open season on domestic and foreign human rights activists. I felt I could no longer go to South America with confidence that my own government would or could physically protect me. There were mass arrests and killings when Reagan withdrew support from human rights activists in Argentina. Ernest Miglione, a key rights activist in Argentina, was arrested in Rio de Janeiro in 1983, one week after testifying before the United Nations Human Rights Commission in Geneva. It was more dangerous than when Richard M. Nixon was president. Then at least some of the world's attention was focused on Chile.

My fears were confirmed on January 4, 1981, when two Americans, a forty-two-year-old lawyer named Michael P. Hammer of Potomac, Maryland, and thirty-six-year-old David Peachman of Seattle, Washington, were killed in the coffee shop of the Sheraton Hotel in San Salvador. Because they were not official American representatives, they thought they would be safe. So too did the four American nuns who were killed in El Salvador later that year.

The Reagan administration continued to do nothing. In 1980 Reagan announced that the United States Navy would invite the Chilean Navy to participate in joint maneuvers in the South Pacific. It was no surprise when, a few months later, the president announced the resumption of all relations with Chile.

But I did return to Chile in 1984. Isabel Letelier and others had gone back and forth safely—the Pinochet government was forced because of international economic pressure to at least curb its death squads. I saw that much of our administration's propaganda about Chile thriving under Pinochet was wrong. The economic conditions of the vast majority of Chileans were miserable and had deteriorated considerably.

I spent a day with some of the defense lawyers I had met. Garreton and Hermosilla still practiced, nearly exclusively representing political defendants. They had the same offices, but the offices were now worn and seedy. Most of the other lawyers no longer practiced. There were safer ways to make a living. So far as I was able to determine, none of the defendants were in Chile.

But very little else had changed. The streets were still patrolled. Rural towns were still constantly raided. Hundreds disappeared without a trace. The newspapers still wrote about the red menace. Plots were constantly uncovered, the bloody hands of the governments of the Soviet Union, Cuba, and Nicaragua were supposedly backing every group critical of the government. But the church, even in the aftermath of Pope John Paul's injunction against liberation priests, remained a strong critic of Pinochet and other Latin American dictators.

The legal system still did not function—political rights were faring even worse than economic rights. When asked in 1985 when the state of emergency would end, Pinochet replied, "Our rules are valid for as long as it takes to scrub minds clean." Even the most determined, such as Isabel Letelier, had conceded defeat in trying to work for change within Chile. She moved permanently to Washington, the city where her husband was killed and where she continues her work against Pinochet.

The state of emergency in Chile still exists. The American media have remarked on this as a routine matter every six months or so since 1973. On November 7, 1984, the two lead headlines of the day were that Reagan was reelected by a landslide and that Pinochet was cracking down in a manner reminiscent of 1973. These events were not unrelated. Shantytowns were being raided by police, and the stadiums were again being used to hold and torture prisoners. Pinochet again said there would be no elections during his lifetime or the lifetime of his successor. His new constitution, hailed by him as the beginning of democracy, merely institutionalizes the dictatorship. That constitution, drafted without the participation of independent lawyers, provides for neither political parties nor for civilian trials for any crimes that could be characterized as having any political element.

In late 1984, after Reagan's reelection, Pinochet's government approved a new antiterrorism law that would apply to acts "committed in order to create disruption or serious fear in the population." The law does not specify what actions constitute crimes. But it is essentially aimed at political association. It makes all members (or presumed members) of any so-called terrorist organization guilty of an act allegedly carried out (or planned, or conceived) by one member. As the church's human rights office has emphasized, the law is designed to maintain a climate of fear, since even suspicion is grounds for arrest.

Lifting the formal state of siege for periods of time in 1985 and 1986 changed little. In Chile prisoners continue simply to disappear. The regime thus avoids trials that can be criticized and become focal points for world-wide agitation. The absence of trials also precludes the need for bothersome foreign observers like me and undercuts the effectiveness of international watchdog organizations. Chileans are kept continually aware of the danger they risk in defying the government. There are other new antiterrorist laws codifying the excesses I saw a few months after the coup. These laws permit detention without warrants, warrantless searches of homes, and the suspension of the right of habeas corpus.

Even though Pinochet has manipulated the rule of law for over ten years, some small legal concessions have been obtained from the junta—that there have not been more can be traced, in large part, to the policy of the United States government. Although a recent Amnesty International report confirms that Chilean courts still continue to tolerate secret detention centers, some courts have started to act more aggressively to protect detainees' rights in other areas.

First the judiciary tried to take antiterrorist jurisdiction away from the military courts and put it back in the civil courts. On October 28, 1983, ten years after the coup, a judicial body established for the first time the existence of a secret detention center. Authorities had arrested eleven students the previous day and held them incommunicado. Their lawyers immediately submitted a complaint to the courts. The same day the magistrate of the Seventh Criminal Court instructed Judge Haroldo Brito to investigate allegations of secret detention at the Calle La Habaña 476 in Viña del Mar, where the students were thought to be held.

When the judge arrived, occupants of the building denied it was a torture or detention center and turned him away. Returning the next day in the company of plain-clothes police, he was able to enter and to confirm that the building was, at the very least, a detention center. He also determined that the students were there, though he was not allowed to see them. A few hours later, however, five of the students were released and six were transferred to prison.

The court then ruled that the secret police have no power to arrest and detain people in secret locations, that individuals can be detained only in public places or in prisons. Although the government disputed the legality of the court's ruling, it announced on November 25 its intention to introduce a law requiring that the location of detention centers be made public.

Instead, the government introduced a draft antiterrorist law that legalized secret detention centers. The president of Chile's Supreme Court, Judge Rafael Retamal, attacked the law, saying it would not only reduce the powers of the civilian courts but also demonstrate "a lack of confidence in the effectiveness of ordinary justice." The government withdrew its legislation.

Allende called Chile a "silent Vietnam." We still do not know either the full extent of the CIA's war against Allende or of the Reagan administration's present financial support of Pinochet. Neither serves America's real interest. It is a pity that Reagan, even as he now proclaims his opposition to the "tyranny of the right" as well as the left, continues to support the worst elements in South and Central America. Many of our leaders have such poor memories of the deaths they contribute to. Or perhaps, as was said of the Bourbon king, they have forgotten nothing and learned nothing.

Ronald Reagan's 1980 campaign rhetoric was unmistakable not only in Chile but also in Haiti, South Korea, and El Salvador; and in all four countries human rights abuses soared in the period between his election and inauguration. And among the many telegrams Reagan received on January 20, 1985 when he was sworn in for a second term, one offered the congratulations of Augusto

Pinochet. At the very moment, perhaps, that hands in Washington were opening that message, a raid was being conducted by thirty Chilean secret agents on an apartment in Santiago where for the previous few months a loose coalition of democratic socialist parties known as the Bloque Socialista had been meeting. In similar raids all over Chile, dozens of dissidents were rounded up, tortured, and interrogated. Reagan's new term gave Pinochet clear sailing for the next four years. Right-wing death squads that kidnap and torture human rights activists and labor leaders today have free rein again. The state of emergency in 1987 is, in fact, permanent.

When representatives of the Reagan government presented a resolution at the 1986 United Nations Human Rights Commission in Geneva condemning violent acts of repression by Pinochet, it seemed to be the administration's strongest stand against the Chilean regime. But its timing led to doubts about the depth of the administration's commitment to human rights in Chile. The resolution was offered the same week that Reagan sought to get support in the House for his $100 million aid package for the Nicaraguan contras. It became clear that the government's policy in Chile takes two steps backward for every step forward. After criticizing Pinochet it allowed the World Bank and International Monetary Fund to loan Chile money, despite congressional legislation instructing U.S. representatives in international banks to oppose such loans.

Ironically, Pinochet's iron fist has strengthened those in Chile who today argue that violence is the only way to end his dictatorship. Communist gains among students and slum dwellers have been striking, and leftist guerrillas have become active once again. A radical younger generation—people who have never held jobs and have little prospect of finding them in General Pinochet's deindustrialized Chile—has grown up in the shantytowns that ring Chile's cities; and it is increasingly convinced that Nicaragua is the model to follow.

Disenchanted with Chile's lack of progress toward democracy and prosperity, they are attracted to revolutionary groups that make the Chilean Communist Party seem moderate by comparison. Nonetheless, given Chile's long democratic tradition and a strong political center, the prospects for democracy in Chile are historically better than either in the Philippines or Haiti. But unless the United States pressures the Chilean armed forces to oust General Pinochet, it will find that it has either encouraged the violent revolution it wishes to prevent or strengthened the continuing dictatorship.

THE
SOVIET UNION
AGAINST
ANDREI SAKHAROV
AND
ANATOLY SHCHARANSKY

17

A man may hope for nothing, yet nonetheless speak because he cannot remain silent.

—Andrei Sakharov

In late 1976 I was asked by the National Conference on Soviet Jewry to go to the Soviet Union and appear on behalf of Amner Zavurov, a Georgian Jew facing five years in jail because he wanted to emigrate to Israel. He was representative of the growing number of "refuseniks," Jews who had asked permission to emigrate to Israel but who had been "refused" and then punished. The National Conference representative described the conditions of Zavurov's family and others like his. In addition to prison, many of them feared other punishment in the form of personal reprisals. Two recently accused refuseniks had already lost their jobs, and two others had been expelled from institutions of higher learning. Two of the wives had also got the sack. Earning wretched livings from odd jobs, several of them could not find full-time employment because there is only one employer—the state. One of the families' children had been expelled from schools. They were easy, unprotected targets for harassment and threats by KGB agents.

I was eager to go. I wanted to see exactly how in the détente period the Soviet legal system operated when that country's critics were put on trial. Although I knew it was unlikely that I would be permitted in court, I knew I could submit briefs on behalf of Zavurov and let the local officials know that at least some outsider was looking in at the system. If it didn't mean that he would be treated more leniently—past experiences with American lawyers showed that it could make the Soviets at least adhere to the Soviet criminal code and constitution—it might discourage totally arbitrary behavior.

Jews who wish to emigrate could be charged with treason. Soviet law, unlike ours, makes it a treasonable offense, punishable by death, to try to "escape the country." In this regard, the founders of the Soviet system were anticipating the "brain drain" problem, that is, the eventuality that the elite and educated classes who benefit most from the system might wish to leave the country to find a better life. Many Russians feel that people like the Sakharovs and Shcharanskys use their state-sponsored educations, and the privileges that follow from it, at the expense of the average Russian—and that the educated elite bears a responsibility to give something back to the society. The Russian law that categorizes refuseniks as "traitors" does reflect the views of many Russians who would like to see the rule more strictly enforced. Present international law establishes free and unrestricted emigration as a "right." The Helsinki Accords commit the Soviet Union to a free emigration policy. But this has no effect on Russian policy, its law, or the attitude of most Russians I spoke to.

The National Conference showed me letters from refuseniks and their families that were deeply moving. Many were written from jail, where they had been imprisoned on false charges ranging from hooliganism (anti-Soviet conduct) and parasitism (not having a job) to anti-Soviet slander, and in severe cases, treason.

Because refuseniks know that if they persist in trying to emigrate from Russia their wives and children may go hungry and homeless, many give up any thought of leaving. But even when they do give up, few are accepted back into the mainstream of Russian life. In the late 1970s, the Soviet response to the Jewish emigration movement hardened, the National Conference thought it critical to show both the Jews in the USSR and the Soviet government the extent of outside world interest in the unimpaired right of free emigration.

Amner Zavurov, the man I was to try to represent, had been arrested and convicted of anti-Soviet activity. His case, then on appeal, had become a cause célèbre within both Russia and the United States. The appeal was now being handled by the Moscow prosecutor's office even though the original trial had taken place in Tashkent.

Zavurov was caught in a Catch-22 prosecution for not having the internal passport that authorities had taken from him when they gave him permission to emigrate to Israel.

In early 1976 Zavurov, claiming an example was being made of him, sent a petition to Leonid I. Brezhnev. Describing the background of his case, the petition said:

> On the 23rd of August, 1975, we and our families received visas for going to Israel for permanent settlement. On October 3rd the director of the emigration offices of Tashkent, Col. Yusopov, took away our visas, but did not tell us the reason for it or the date to which our departure was postponed. Our families found ourselves in a very poor state—without visas and without work. Almost a year ago when we received the exit visa the Presidium of the Supreme Soviet decreed that we would be deprived of our Soviet citizenships. We therefore ask you to issue us documents stating that we have citizenship as without such documents we cannot find even temporary jobs and apartments for our families that include small children. As the result of the absence of such documents, we could not register the birth of the baby that was born in our family on the 8th of July, 1976.

Finally, in 1976, Zavurov and his wife were told they were going to Israel. They surrendered their passports and then were arrested at the airport for not having a passport. Denied the lawyers of his choice, Zavurov refused the court-appointed lawyer. He was sentenced on January 13, 1977, the week before I came, to three years in prison for being without an internal passport, being without a job, and for disorderly conduct.

I was asked to go to the prosecutor's office in Moscow and, because Zavurov did not have counsel, ask to be designated as his lawyer on the appeal, file a legal brief, and argue for clemency. In the short time before my departure, members of the National Conference and I wrote a brief arguing Zavurov's rights under Soviet and international law, and, through the conference, I received a written request from Zavurov's parents to represent him.

Also prior to my trip, I began to contact Russia's leading dissidents. I made an appointment in Moscow with Andrei D. Sakharov, the winner of the 1975 Nobel Peace Prize and Russia's leading dissident. I also contacted Anatoly Shcharansky, the leading Jewish activist, and leaders of the Helsinki Watch Group, a group of prominent Soviet citizens attempting to compel the government to pay more attention to individual rights. Finally, my wife Ruth and I left the United States on January 19, 1977, the day after Jimmy Carter was inaugurated.

The process of détente and the concomitant leveling off of the deployment of offensive nuclear weaponry were still in their fragile first stages. With the election of a new president, whose ideas on foreign policy were not fully worked out, it was not clear whether détente would continue. One aspect of the Carter foreign policy— an emphasis, even a priority, on other nations' attitudes toward human rights—would surely affect our relationship with the Soviet Union.

The country's "commitment to human rights must be absolute," President Carter said in his inaugural speech, promising it would become "a central concern" of the new administration. But whether his concern would be even-handed was another matter. While the United States often mutes its criticism of our friends in Central and South America, South Korea, the Philippines, and South Africa, we rarely lose an opportunity to criticize human rights violations in Russia. And in early 1978 the situation in the Soviet Union was worse than it had been in a decade. Not since the days of Stalin and the short period in the 1960s after Khrushchev's fall had the Soviet government, through the security police, the KGB, acted as aggressively toward Soviet dissidents as it was doing now.

During this Russian trip I had an opportunity to see from close up the clash between the superpowers and the victims of that fight. On the Aeroflot plane to Moscow I read Carter's inauguration speech that spoke so forcefully of his concept of international human rights. The political realities would present serious obstacles to the implementation of that concept. Although Carter's speech seemed deliberately timed to increase Soviet-American tensions, it nonetheless held out great hope to the Russian dissidents and seemed to raise their expectations. They and other emergent dissident groups in Asia, Africa, and Eastern Europe felt that with Carter's election and the activities of organizations like Amnesty International and the Russian Helsinki Group, a world-wide crusade for human rights might be on the horizon.

It also seemed as if the concept of international human rights had been accepted formally by the Soviet Union and thirty-four other Western nations in Part III of the 1975 Helsinki Accords. The Russians had consented to Part III as a quid pro quo for Part I, which the Soviet Union sought. Part I ratified the boundaries of post–World War II Europe in the absence of a peace treaty that— from the standpoint of international law—was impossible to negotiate because of the partition of Germany.

Most observers believe that the Soviet Union had expected the Western nations to sign all three parts of the Helsinki Accords, and then to pay scant attention to its human rights provisions. Instead, human rights activists in Soviet-bloc nations and throughout the world formed human rights committees citing the Helsinki agreements and other international documents as their charter.

But whatever they expected of the Helsinki Accords, it is clear that the Soviet establishment saw the emergence of a Moscow chapter of Amnesty International and the creation of a Helsinki Watch Group in various Russian cities as unacceptable challenges to its power.

Ruth and I arrived in Moscow on the morning of January 20, 1977, brief in hand. Although customs officers confiscated a copy of Hedrick Smith's *The Russians* from another American passenger, they did not find the two dozen blank cassette tapes Ruth had brought for people we were to see.

I had wanted to go to Russia all my life. Born of Jews from the Pale of Settlement in Czarist Russia (today part of Poland), I had been told stories as a child of the battle of Leningrad, of the heroes of Stalingrad and Kiev, of Russia's 20 million World War II dead and its extraordinary devastation. I felt for Russia a mass of mixed emotions: respect for the original promise of the revolution and much of its fulfillment, on the one hand, and respect for the lives destroyed in the violent thirties and in the gulags on the other.

The night we arrived in Moscow, there was a heavy snow. Driving down dark boulevards past giant monuments, we saw the enormous Kremlin and the circular dome of St. Basil's. A few blocks away was the Hotel Rossiya, a mass of glass and aluminum, Europe's biggest hotel, where we were to stay.

As soon as we had checked into one of the thirty-two hundred comfortable rooms, I called my contact at a Moscow phone number. "We've been waiting for you," he said. "I shall come and see you." Within the hour I opened my hotel door to Lev Berlin, a young Hasidic Jew with earlocks, dressed all in black. Forty feet behind him walked a short man, who I soon learned was Anatoly Shcharansky. He was in a heated argument with a woman who was sitting behind the desk at the elevator, surveying each person who came and entered the rooms on that floor.

"Why do you want to go there? Why do you want to bother to talk to Americans? Who are they?" were just some of the questions he later told us she asked. He was also told, "We're going to get you, you'll be in jail soon."

I had heard about Shcharansky for several years. A Russian Jew, twenty-nine years of age and balding, a chess master and computer expert with a moon face seemingly too large for his short, muscular body, Shcharansky was now recklessly gambling with his life. Daring the Soviets to jail him, yet becoming so prominent a public figure that the threat of jail would cause an international outcry, he as first hoped he would become such a thorn in their sides that he would be expelled.

But now, after years of speaking out against the Soviet Government, he knew that before that were to happen he would first have to serve years in Soviet jails and isolation cells undergoing psychological and physical pressures. And that he might well be killed in the streets or die in prison.

The three of us spoke of world events, starved as they both were for outside news. Anatoly Shcharansky laughingly said that his birthday had been a few days before, the same day as Carter's inauguration, so he knew that the year ahead would be good.

He talked emotionally about the new wave of anti-Semitism that was raging through the Soviet Union. Since the end of 1976 more Jews were being arrested and given harsher sentences, and more anti-Jewish articles were appearing in the press. Those arrested were uniformly charged with hooliganism, defined in the criminal code as "intentional actions violating public order in a coarse manner and expressing a clear disrespect toward society." This was a euphemism for pro-Jewish demonstrations, punished by jail for one year. More severe is the charge of "malicious hooliganism," that is, "the same actions distinguished in their content by exceptional cynicism or special impudence." For this the sentence was five years. Although most of Shcharansky's friends had been arrested, he had not. He stayed away from demonstrations, preferring to play a different role.

Tomorrow, he excitedly told me, there was to be a Moscow television showing of *Buyers of Souls*. The movie, supposedly exposing the international Zionist conspiracy in Russia, showed the faces of Anatoly and his friends and implied they were "agents of world Zionism and secret services." Anatoly had filed a lawsuit claiming that the inflammatory and blatantly anti-Semitic film would incite Russians to riot against Jews, and that he and his friends would be killed in the streets. The film showed a meeting between Shcharansky (a "soldier of Zionism") and Israeli authorities (his Israeli "spies"). It also showed an allegedly illegal meeting between Anatoly and several American congressmen. Anatoly's petition, filed in the Peoples Court of the Dzerzhinsky Region of Moscow, demanded "a denial of the slanderous information defaming my honor and dignity published in the same way by which this information was distributed."

We talked about the difficulties he would have under American law in stopping such a film. He was surprised when I said I believed that even such a film as this should be free to be shown in America. He listened to my explanation, and rather than arguing over it, said he'd like to think the issue over and talk about it later.

When he returned to the subject, he showed me a Soviet illustrated magazine that said before World War II "Zionists" had conspired to set up a pro-Nazi Zionist state. The paper charged Israel with having kidnapped and prosecuted Adolf Eichmann to keep him from disclosing that story. "Would you permit that in America?" he asked. He was clearly amazed and discouraged by my positive answer.

He told me more of his past. He spoke quietly, in fluent English. A high-level engineer and one of the leaders of the Russian

Jewish movement, Anatoly had, since 1974, been threatened with arrest dozens of times, had actually been arrested twice, and was once jailed for seven months.

Married in 1974, he and his Soviet-born wife, Avital, believed they would be reunited that very year in Israel. Instead, while she was permitted to leave for Israel on their wedding day, Anatoly was kept in the Soviet Union. He was never told why. After the government refused to act on his visa application, he and other Jews began holding public demonstrations asking to leave. He and five or ten others would walk out to the middle of Red Square wearing placards. As soon as they were spotted by the KGB, they were quickly put into automobiles and taken for interrogation. Sometimes the foreign press saw the demonstrations, but most often not.

Although Anatoly was continually arrested and harassed, he never received the long and hard prison term some of the others did. Unlike the dissidents, many of whom wanted to change the government but not to leave, he tried not to criticize the government. While he appreciated the rapid economic revival of the past six decades and what it had brought—the end of extreme poverty, a constantly rising standard of living, full employment, free education, and the availability of medical care, he nevertheless felt oppressed by the many limitations on his freedom and he did want to leave.

Anatoly gradually became one of the leading voices of the "*Aliyiah*," or "Return to Israel," movement. A consummate public relations man, scrupulously accurate with the facts, he took it upon himself to keep up contacts with Westerners and serve as their window to the Soviet world. As such, he was a critical link in the chain that Soviet authorities found so threatening, a chain of communication that ran from the dissidents through Western correspondents to world-wide publications and back into the Soviet Union again via foreign radio stations such as the BBC and the Voice of America. Anatoly thus believed, unlike Sakharov, that, "Western pressure is the only possible way of saving the movement. Forget about détente."

Nonetheless, Shcharansky had been part of the Russian dissident group formed in May 1976 to monitor Russian compliance with the 1975 Helsinki Accords. This group proved to be an important development for both the Russian Jews and the dissidents because through it, people like Sakharov and Shcharansky came to understand and be sympathetic to each other, although they had separate sets of concerns.

Shcharansky and most of the Jews only wanted out; they did not believe the system would ever work adequately for them. Sakharov, on the other hand, passionately attached to Russia, desperately wanted to stay and make function a system from which he still substantially benefited.

Differences in ideology meant differences in action. The Jews did not want to submit petitions for reformist changes and did not want to speak out for Ukrainian statehood. Non-Jewish dissidents did not want to praise Israel and its policies. Some of them were as anti-Semitic as they were anti-Soviet. The Ukrainian separatists had a long history of brutality against Jews. The Pentacostals, the largest dissident faith in the Soviet Union, did not want ties to any Jewish movement. As a result, many Jews refused to work with, or ally themselves generally with, the dissidents. Shcharansky felt differently, and although many Jews attacked him, he was a key link between the Jews who wanted to leave and the Russians of the Helsinki Group who wanted to stay and liberalize the society.

So even if the Helsinki Accords did not better the lives of most Russians, they had the unanticipated effect of making Jews work more closely with other dissidents. The Helsinki Accords gave renewed vitality to the Jews because in them the signatory countries, Russia included, had agreed to ease emigration procedures. They also became a rallying point for non-Jews who wished to remain because the accords purported to guarantee their human rights.

In the hotel room as we started to talk about the progress of the Helsinki Group and the Zavurov case, Lev (who had himself been arrested several times) turned the radio on loud so our voices could not be heard by the omnipresent listening devices in each of the hotel's many rooms. Shcharansky shrugged and, when the noise of the radio began to interfere with our talk, turned it down, saying, "It doesn't matter anyway. They'll know what we're doing. They tape the Helsinki Group meetings as well. There's also probably an informer in the group." Months later, after he was arrested, it turned out Shcharansky was right. Lipavsky, who rented the apartment that Shcharansky lived in, admitted at a state-sponsored press conference in Moscow that he was a KGB double agent.

I asked Shcharansky why the government continued to put up with him.

"What else can they do now?" he answered. "To take more direct measures against us would be to return to the days of Stalin, and that they don't want. They're interested in Western opinion and in détente and in good economic relations, and most of the present leaders are the very men who survived Stalin. World opinion is what keeps us going, what keeps us alive."

Anatoly finally walked across the room and angrily switched the radio off altogether. "We have a right to talk about these things; Amner Zavurov has a right to have a lawyer who will look after him," he said loudly. "Neither Zavurov nor his lawyer was in the courtroom throughout the whole of Zavurov's trial. The lawyer they gave him didn't help him at all."

With Anatoly we made a list of all the people we should see in connection with Zavurov's case. Prior to my leaving the United States, letters requesting appointments had been written by Jerry Goodman of the Committee to Free Soviet Jewry to Vidor Fedorchik, Tashkent minister of the interior; Boris Kachanov, the head of the KGB in Tashkent; and Colonel Andrei Yuabov, chief of police in Uzbekistan, as well as to various officials in Moscow. Anatoly and Lev added a few more names.

Lev thought a translator might not be necessary at the prosecutor's office because one of the lawyers there spoke fluent English. Anatoly thought I might need help because we did not know if the English-speaking lawyer would be there and he offered to go with me. He rejected Lev's suggestion that someone else should go because it would be dangerous for him to be there. "If Martin can go, I can go," Anatoly remarked.

Then Anatoly, Lev, and I left the hotel. Anatoly looked comical, with his round face peering out from under a fur cap and his chunky body lost in an overcoat too big for him, like a little boy in his father's clothes. We began a tour of monstrous, drab, graying Soviet office buildings that have a kind of instantly aged look common to all Soviet architecture. Our first stop was with Boris Shumilin, the minister of the interior in Moscow. We were told he would not see us, so after leaving my hotel phone number in case he changed his mind, we moved on.

We next went to the office of the Moscow prosecutor in charge of the Zavurov case. Lev waited outside. Anatoly told the receptionist who I was, showed the written authorization from Zavurov's parents, and asked to see the lawyer in charge of the case. Told she was out, I started to leave. But Anatoly, speaking to me in English, said we were being given a run-around—that the lawyer was there, for he had overheard the switchboard operator putting a call through to her. Shcharansky told the receptionist, "We shall sit down in the entrance hall and wait," and we did.

Twenty minutes later we were brought into the office of a lawyer who said he would listen to what we had to say about the case. Anatoly, hearing the lawyer's name, explained to me that this was a local lawyer, involved in Moscow prosecutions only, who could not help us in the Zavurov case.

So we went back and waited another ten minutes. Anatoly said he hoped my wife, Ruth, who would be meeting us later at Sakharov's house, was safe. It had not occurred to me that she could be in danger. We were sent to another lawyer. Anatoly said he also was the wrong lawyer. Finally, after one hour, we were told we could meet with Sobrina Ivanov, the lawyer in charge of Zavurov's appeal.

As Anatoly and I entered her small, neat white office, Sobrina Ivanov, a middle-aged woman in a gray suit, ignored me and started to talk to Anatoly.

"What right do you have to help them? This time you're going too far. You're creating trouble and you're going to get into trouble. This American lawyer is going to get into trouble. You should stay as far away from these people as you can." Ivanov's voice, getting louder and angrier, had little impact on Shcharansky. In a slow, respectful voice, he started to translate the questions he thought I should be putting to the Moscow prosecutor. The more she yelled and berated him, the more he explained that, under the Soviet Constitution, I had a right to ask about Zavurov. Her level of rage rose until she could no longer deal with him.

Ivanov called in a superior, the head of the entire Moscow office. He was a fat man with a harsh voice and large pouches surrounding his sharp little eyes. At first he yelled at Shcharansky, then she joined in. Then they yelled in unison. Even though the language was foreign to me, it sounded as if Ivanov and her male superior were echoes of each other's voices. When it ended, he again, relentlessly, placed my questions to them.

The chaos of the voices in the small room made it sound as if a riot were taking place. After ten more minutes of yelling, followed by Anatoly placing another question, followed by more yelling, it became clear that Anatoly was not to be daunted, so the prosecutor finally agreed to let Anatoly go ahead and translate the questions for me.

I had brought with me my English translation of the Soviet Constitution. Adopted soon after the 1917 revolution and subsequently modified, this constitution is one of the best in the world, in many ways better than our own.

The Soviet Constitution proclaims the right of privacy, prohibits governmental intrusion into citizens' homes, and speaks of a rosy future for all Russian citizens. Article 35 says that men and women have equal rights, all have the right to work, the right to leisure, health, protection, old-age maintenance, and education. According to Article 50, citizens of the USSR are guaranteed freedom of speech, of the press, and of assembly, meetings, street processions, and administrations. The "right of conscience" and "freedom of religion" are similarly proclaimed.

And in order to ensure that the freedoms of speech and press are meaningful, the government is required to put at the "disposal of the working people and their organizations, printing presses, stocks of paper, public buildings, streets, communication facilities and other material requisites for the exercise of these rights." The reality is, of course, something else. Section 70-190 of the Code of Criminal Procedure, which governs court proceedings, seems to twist totally the true meaning of the constitution:

> Agitation or propaganda carried on for the purpose of subverting or weakening the Soviet regime or of committing particular, especially dangerous crimes against the state, or the circulation, for the same purpose, of slanderous fabrications which defame the Soviet state and social system, or the circulation or preparation or keeping, for the same purpose, of literature of such con-

tent, shall be punished by deprivation of freedom for a term of six months to seven years, with or without additional exile for a term of two to five years, or by exile for a term of two to five years.

Penalties governing the circulation of printed or oral materials defamatory to the "Soviet state and social system" and the organization of, and participation in, group activities "which grossly violate public order" are similarly harsh.

The discretion the Code of Criminal Procedure gives the authorities is very much like the old treason laws that were interpreted to permit punishment of anyone who thought ill of the king or contemplated the death of the republic. Under Henry VIII of England absolutely any expression of belief could be considered treasonable, even though the nation was bound within a frame of formal law. It is also very much like the provisions applied to Eugene Debs in this country in 1918 when he was sentenced to ten years imprisonment for opposing America's involvement in World War I, a time when constitutional prohibitions against the overbroad application of espionage and treason laws were overlooked.

I told Ivanov that Zavurov's constitutional rights were being ignored. She then began to explain her view of the Soviet legal system. It was the same rationale I read a few years earlier, in 1975, when Yuri Andropov, head of the KGB said: "Any citizen of the Soviet Union whose interests coincide with the interests of society enjoys the whole range of our democratic freedoms. It is another matter if these interests in certain instances do not coincide. Here we say straight out: priority must be given to the interests of society as a whole, of all working people, and we consider the principle fully just. . . ."

Through Shcharansky I told Ivanov that one of Khrushchev's lieutenants, Leonid Ilichev, made the same point more bluntly and succinctly twenty years earlier when he stated: "We have complete freedom to struggle for communism. We do not have, and cannot have, freedom to struggle against communism." What happened, I asked Ivanov, to those who struggle against communism and how did the principles of the constitution apply to them? Wasn't the Soviet law, as it is applied to political defendants, purely a government weapon?

Ivanov answered by referring to the section of the Soviet Constitution that grants every defendant the right to his own lawyer and the right to a public trial. "In the United States," she said, "the defendants are too poor to have their own lawyer."

"The lawyer," Anatoly said, referring to me, "wanted to know what the charges against Zavurov were. How can you take his internal passport away and then charge him with not having a passport? Why didn't he have a lawyer of his own choosing? Where is he now? Why can't his family see him in jail?" And as Anatoly translated for me, it was clear to Ivanov as well as to me that he was making better and more detailed arguments than I could. As he did, Anatoly became more and more argumentative. She could not answer most of the questions, claiming they were in a file in a different office. I left the brief I had brought from New York, but she refused to agree to submit it on Zavurov's behalf to the appellate court. Her frustration and exasperation ended as she almost spat out the words, "Shcharansky, you will be going to jail for a long time." We told her quietly that I would come back in several days to see if she had answers to our questions.

After the meeting Anatoly was elated. It was, he said, one of the best confrontations an American lawyer and he had succeeded in having with the authorities. Usually, he said, foreign lawyers, senators, congressmen, and others coming to the Soviet Union go to higher-level legal officials. These officials, used to the questions and answers and more aware of the public relations aspect of their jobs, handle everything amicably, leading many foreigners to believe that things will be taken care of and that the bureaucracy is humane and responsive to the people. More often than not, the foreigner only sees public relations personnel on the legal staff. American politicians and lawyers, often impressed by the titles of those that receive them, generally tell their American listeners how courteously they were treated and how much good they were able to do. Only after many months would these same politicians and lawyers, not having heard anything further from Soviet officials, realize that they had been politely stonewalled. Anatoly was pleased I had seen a truer picture.

Shcharansky asked how American defense lawyers operated. After I described our adversary system to him, he chuckled. "Soviet lawyers don't understand fighting the prosecutor and the courts. Their job, in most cases, is not to defend. It is to persuade the political defendant that the state is correct in bringing the charge, for he is truly guilty. His job, after he speaks to the defendant, is to tell the court if his client can be rehabilitated."

I clearly saw the razor's edge on which Anatoly commonly walked every day of his life. Unprepared for the scorn and contempt hurled at him by the Soviet lawyers, I had not understood the basis for the fear Lev had expressed earlier in the hotel room about Anatoly's going with me. Whatever danger I had been in then, it was clearly nothing compared to the danger to Anatoly. He was the primary object of their fury. Lev, who stood outside the building waiting for us, asked Anatoly what had happened. When he heard the report of the meeting, he was appalled. Shcharansky was not only out on a limb, he was sawing it off. He was doomed and he knew it.

18

As we stepped away from the Moscow prosecutor's office, a light snow began to fall through the clear, crisp air. Anatoly looked back and waved to a man who had come out after us. "That's my tail," he said. "I've recently been honored by having one to myself. This man's been my tail before. He's not a bad fellow. But they're mad at me this week, so they let me see him. I'll make it easy for him."

With a smile that showed his pragmatic acceptance that his "tail" too had to live, Shcharansky walked over and told him where we were going, and with whom. The four of us then continued down the street, the tail about twenty feet behind. We spent the rest of the day going to other offices on behalf of Zavurov and other refuseniks for whom Anatoly asked me to appear. The "tail" doggedly followed.

Each meeting, at least those where we succeeded in seeing the person in charge, was similar to the one we had had with Ivanov. When we could not see the person in charge, we left our names, saying we would be back the following day. Other Russian citizens meeting in these offices, who saw and heard what we were doing, were shocked by the row we were making. Anatoly told me it was unthinkable for most Soviet citizens to go to government offices and argue. These offices were hallowed places for the filing of petitions and other bureaucratic procedures, most of which ultimately went unanswered.

Shcharansky and other dissidents are obsessed by the law. The Brezhnev constitution which came into law in 1977 is an exemplary document. Here, in one of the world's most obsessively legalistic states, the people are daily confronted by the contradiction between the legal protection afforded to the friends of the state and the denial of it to its "enemies." I saw Shcharansky and others insist and demand that the laws be applied. The relentless dissident, Vladimir Bukovsky, even while in psychiatric prisons, endlessly bombarded bureaucrats with petitions covering every sort of grievance. When they answered, he accepted it as his right; when they did not, he was furiously righteous.

As we sat waiting in one government office after another, Anatoly and I spoke about his own situation. As he saw it, the government had three choices: They could leave him alone, let him go to Israel, or arrest him. But he could no longer leave the government alone. Not wanting to stay in Russia, he reasoned that by being a visible and consistent irritant to it, he would force the government to make a choice. Meanwhile, he did not feel any single act of his could be of any particular consequence.

"But," I said, "since the government knows you want to leave, isn't it reasonable to assume they'll arrest you?"

"There's no way of knowing. They operate more irrationally than that," he said. Lev, walking down the street, disagreed with Anatoly.

Anatoly, after making it clear that things were not nearly as bad as the American press reported them, went on to explain how the Soviet authorities operated: "The pattern of persecution is usually inconsistent and unpredictable, largely because of sheer bureaucratic inefficiency," he said. "Those who are not put away are openly harassed in their homes and on the street. Political killings are rare in the Soviet Union, but the KGB is employing thugs to dispose of troublesome artists and intellectuals. Last year a poet, Konstantin Bogatyrev, was mugged on a Moscow street. As he lay with a skull fracture in a hospital, KGB agents came in and told doctors to 'fix him so he will come out an idiot.' When the physicians refused, the agents threatened them."

One evening Anatoly suggested that Ruth and I come to a going-away party for Vladimir Gorki, a Baptist dissident, who had just received an exit visa. We went to an apartment on the outskirts of Moscow. The party turned out to be a meeting of the Helsinki Watch Group. Of the fifteen people in the Helsinki Group we met that evening, all but three are now in jail in the Soviet Union, serving sentences ranging from five to twenty years.

At the time it formed, the Helsinki Group members knew the Soviet government was hostile to the public organization of dissident groups. They had seen others suffer the consequences. In 1969 fifteen people had signed petitions as members of the Action Group, a forerunner of the Helsinki Group, and sent them to the United Nations Commission on Human Rights, outlining a broad range of abuses and requesting the United Nations to intervene. Claiming that "the defense of human rights is the sacred duty of this organization," the petitions referred to numerous recent political trials, including those of Andrei Sinyavsky, Yuli Daniel, Aleksandr I. Ginzburg, and Bukovsky. They also mentioned "the trials of Soviet Jews whose desire is to emigrate to Israel—an issue that has yet to assume wide-scale dimensions."

Although the Action Group never truly functioned as an organization, within a half year nearly all the signatories had been harassed and arrested. As the KGB picked up one member after another, the list of signatures on the group's appeals grew smaller, until the appeals were no longer issued at all.

In subsequent years other dissidents would remember the example of the Action Group. Groups formed, tried to avoid the problems of the past, but more often than not, failed. Now the members of the Helsinki Group believed that because of the recent international accords and a liberalizing trend within the Soviet Union, they might have a more substantial effect. They thought their organization might be harder to smash. They were soon to learn they were terribly mistaken.

That evening in a small, cluttered living room, twelve group members jammed around a table meant to seat six and talked about the fear of new crackdowns resulting from the January 8 Moscow subway bombing in which two people had been killed. Weeks before I came to Russia, the KGB had blamed the bombing on the dissident movement, claiming it had turned violent. But those in the room were sure the bomb was a KGB set-up. Anyway, arrests were sure to follow. Some of those in the room were again starting to contemplate the threat which constantly hovered over their lives—prison camp.

Midway through the conversation, Vladimir Albrecht came into the room. He had been secretary of Russia's Amnesty International chapter since its 1974 inception. He said he had been questioned for four hours that afternoon by Soviet state security officials as a "suspect" in connection with the bomb explosion. He warned that everyone would be called in. The room became quiet, the enthusiasm and communality of before suddenly gone. Resignation showed on the drawn faces. For the last six months the pressure on these people had been enormous, and it was now increasing. I wondered if they would now pull back. Could they?

After some moments the conversation resumed. Optimistic statements were made. They saw my presence as a positive sign. Clearly, the KGB knew I was with them, yet the meeting was still going on. And group representatives were still meeting with Western journalists too.

They then told Anatoly and me that word of our "success" at the prosecutor's office had gotten around and that other people wanted us to visit government offices on behalf of other dissidents. Feeling in the room ran high as they told us how "heroic" we had been. During Stalin's time, and even in more recent years, these men and women meeting together could have been arrested for "intent to commit treason" or for failure to inform on the other people in the room. In our Anglo-American legal system, language such as "intent to commit treason" would be unconstitutional. Soviet law, unencumbered by judicial or meaningful executive review, does not permit constitutional attacks on any of its sections.

Such strictly imaginary crimes were defined in Stalin's time by a catch-all provision, Article 58 of the penal code, which punished any conduct the government decided it did not like. All the government had to do was to prosecute a defendant for acts, words, or intent that it considered "anti-Soviet." The government continues today to prosecute particular acts it does not like, but which violate no specific law, under Article 58. As the Soviet writer Nadezhda Mandelstam observed in *Hope Against Hope*, "In this country they don't wait until laws are passed before putting them into effect." Anyone who made a stand against the state either by accident or decision sooner or later could expect to be arrested.

Merely describing Soviet society critically could lead to jail even if the state decided not to charge the defendant with treason, as was the case in the famous 1966 trial and conviction of Abram Tertz and Yuli Daniel for their writings. Similarly, Bukovsky's ten-year conviction was for nothing more serious than his role in a Moscow demonstration. Ironically, the 1967 demonstration had been staged for the repeal of Article 70 of the criminal code regarding, among other things, the freedom of assembly on the ground that the code violated the freedom of expression protected under the Soviet Constitution.

Arrested and brought to trial, Bukovsky spoke of what he saw as the profound contradictions between the Soviet Constitution and Article 70 in his defense:

> Why does the Soviet Constitution contain a guarantee of the freedom of street processions and demonstrations? Why was this article included? For May Day and the anniversary of the Revolution? But there was no need for an article of the Constitution to legitimize demonstrations organized by the state—it is obvious that no one is going to disperse those demonstrations. We don't need the freedom to be "for" something if there is no freedom to be "against" it. We know that the protest demonstration is a mighty weapon in the hands of the workers; it is their inalienable right in all democratic countries. Where is that right denied? In front of me is a copy of *Pravda* for August 19, 1967. A trial was held in Madrid of the participants in a May Day demonstration. They were charged under a new law, recently promulgated in Spain, which prescribed prison sentences of from eighteen months to three years for May Day demonstrators. I note the touching unanimity between the legislation of Fascist Spain and the Soviet Union. . . .
>
> Freedom of speech and a free press is primarily the freedom to criticize; no one is ever forbidden to praise the government. If you include articles on freedom of speech and freedom of the press in the Constitution, then you must tolerate criticism. What do they call countries where it is forbidden to criticize the government

152

and protest actions? Capitalist, perhaps? No; we know that in bourgeois countries there are legal Communist parties whose aim is the subversion of the capitalist system. . . .

Bukovsky concluded:

> I am absolutely unrepentant at having organized this demonstration. I think it achieved its object, and when I am free again I will organize more demonstrations.

Bukovsky went from jail to a psychiatric prison to the West. He, along with other dissidents I met, knew how severely they could be punished—what many of them didn't know was precisely how far they could go before they were stopped. The government's action was totally arbitrary. The law did not matter. Valentin Turchin, a brilliant computer expert and one of the founders of the Helsinki Group, agreed that he and others could more safely speak out in 1977 than in 1947 because even if they were arrested, the penalties imposed on dissidents were lighter and because the more brutal labor camps in the Arctic and Siberia during Stalin's era had been phased out. Andrei Amalrik, the dissident historian, has explained how the changed conditions affected him. "Stalin would have executed me for the fact that my books have been published abroad. His wretched successors dare only embezzle a part of my money."

Like Lev and Anatoly, the people seated at the crammed dining table wanted to know what was going on in the outside world. They got news only sporadically, by hearing the foreign broadcasts. Someone estimated that about one-fourth of the urban population listens to foreign broadcasts. Everyone in the room agreed this was an overstatement based perhaps more on wish than on reality. Although Leonid Brezhnev declared that the broadcasts "poison the atmosphere," he had then not made any move to step up jamming. It is often said that if the dissidents in Moscow want to reach the people in Kiev, they hold a press conference in Moscow, and the BBC and the Voice of America cover it and relay the message to the rest of Russia. Radio communication, in fact, can often be more efficient than the network of the

153

secret police. Lev Berlin said, "When I was detained after the sit-in at the Supreme Soviet, the minister of the interior said to me, 'I heard on the BBC that some of you people were beaten up, but I have no information about it yet in my office.' "

One of the remarkable aspects of the recent Soviet dissident movement has been that its members have virtually never struck back, that it has nearly always been nonviolent. Turchin, Shcharansky, and Sakharov abhor terrorism and the claim that they were terrorists. This feeling was shared by all the people I met. Why this is so is not entirely clear. It may be because they think nonviolent dissent offers the only hope of success. It may be because the country, through previous experiences of terrorism, revolutions, and wars, has had a surfeit of violence, or because the system is so effective in its repression that people are afraid to pay a price for a terrorism they know will not work. Or it may be that some of them believe that the Soviet system will ultimately achieve its goals in part through the use of law.

Turchin, answering my question about the apparent apathy of most Soviet citizens, pointed out a cultural difference between Russians and peoples of other Eastern European countries.

"What happens in Hungary or Czechoslovakia is not at all relevant to what happens here. We're not concerned with political freedom. Russians do not feel deprived because they don't have the right to talk or write and express themselves. In any event, we don't throw bombs here—it's not so clear who the enemy is. The people who control our lives are bureaucrats. They are often invisible. Many of our people aspire to be bureaucrats. In South Africa all the blacks know that the whites are the enemy. And we, again unlike the blacks of South Africa, don't want abrupt change. It would mean violence. The lives of a great many people here have improved in recent years. They don't want to lose what they've gained."

Lev, however, was clear who his enemies were, and even hinted that one day he might be prepared to use violence against them. He observed: "Since 1968 it's hard to believe Sakharov's idea of peaceful democratic change is right. I think even he is giving up. Maybe the only way for us to get free is to have this government totally overthrown. Maybe Solzhenitsyn is closer to the truth: The people need a goal to strive for. Western democracy

154

is not understandable; the glories of the czar are. Once the present government is overthrown, then you look at what you want."

The talk turned to the West. Turchin rejected Bukovsky's previous accusations that the dissidents are naïve in thinking the West can help them. He said: "We must continue to talk to the West. It would be correct to think we were naïve if we said things would change immediately or within the foreseeable future. We know it doesn't go like that. But even if we do not see immediate results, it is still necessary to try! If we didn't try, we wouldn't know that it didn't work. It is only through activism that things can change gradually for the better."

Despite Turchin's optimism, there was a good deal of anger at the West, both for its seeming indifference to the Russian dissidents, and for its perceived desire to use the dissidents' plight for its own purposes.

Vladimir Bukovsky, in his 1979 book *To Build a Castle*, expressed a point of view that many in the room shared. As his Soviet jailers put him on a plane for the West in exchange for the release of Luis Corvalán, the Chilean Communist, he acknowledged to his jailers that he knew his handcuffs were American-made.

"The handcuffs are American, by the way," said the agent who took them off, and he showed me the trademark. As if I didn't know without his help that almost from the very beginning of this regime, the West had been supplying us with handcuffs. Did he think he was disillusioning me? I had never entertained any illusions about the West. Hundreds of desperate petitions addressed, for example, to the UN, had never been answered. Wasn't this sufficient indication? ...

As for the so-called policy of détente—the Helsinki agreements and so on—we could feel on our backs in Vladimir Prison who gained from it. It wasn't the first time that the West's "friendly relations" with the Soviet Union had been built on our bones. The most repulsive thing of all was that the West tried to justify itself with all sorts of intricate doctrines and theories. . . . Sometimes these self-justifications are the same. But violence relentlessly revenges itself on those who support it. Those who think that the frontier between freedom and unfreedom corresponds with the state frontiers of the Soviet Union are cruelly mistaken.

Toward the end of what had become a five-hour going-away party, a short man with dark-framed glasses and a shock of red hair pulled me into the kitchen to talk privately. He was Yuri Orlov, a fifty-two-year-old physicist, then the head of the Helsinki Group. Orlov, a blunt man who, along with Shcharansky and Sakharov, had long been a thorn to the Communist regime, bridged the gaps between the dissidents and the refuseniks.

Born in 1924 to a working-class family, he operated a lathe as a young man, then served in the Red Army during World War II. After the war he graduated from Moscow State University with a degree in physics. He joined the Communist Party and for four years work at Moscow's Institute of Theoretical and Experimental Physics.

But in 1956, when public dissent was very rare, Orlov offered to a party meeting a proposal for democratic reforms in the government and the party. He was promptly expelled from the party and dismissed from his job.

Moving to Armenia, he found work again in physics, earned a doctorate, and was elected a corresponding member of Armenia's Academy of Sciences. In 1972 he was transferred back to Moscow to work in the prestigious Institute of Earth Magnetism of the Soviet Academy of Sciences. As a theoretical physicist, he specialized in subatomic particles.

A year after his transfer, Soviet scientists were recruited by the authorities to sign a letter condemning Andrei D. Sakharov, another physicist, for his dissident activities. Orlov instead composed a letter defending Sakharov. He was fired a second time and when I met him was forced to support himself by tutoring physics students.

Orlov asked if I would take out to the West some sixty pages of information concerning certain prisoners and prison camps, written in Russian. "The government has been releasing false information about these prisoners and the camps. These are diaries and writings, some smuggled out from the camps. Others are letters written to their families."

His dark brown eyes stared steadily at me as he intoned quietly, "We trust you. We want some of the information to be given widespread publication. Can you take it out of the country for us?" We both knew that if I were caught, there could be penalties for him and perhaps for me. When I agreed to do it, he surprised me by giving me a long, warm embrace. We decided I should deliver the documents to an American congressman, Dante Fascell, who was chairman of the Joint Congressional Committee on Compliance with the Helsinki Accords. He took the papers out from under his shirt and gave them to me, and together we returned to the living room.

The people gathered in that room were a fine example of how the Helsinki Accords had succeeded in bringing together the various strands of dissidence. Shcharansky pointed out a man whose feelings about Jews "were the same as Hitler's." Yet here he was, at a farewell party with Jews. Yuri Orlov acknowledged that many in the room were fascists and extreme right-wingers, "but for the first time we have united in the Helsinki monitoring committee all kinds of dissidents, and we have achieved some degree of coordination. Helsinki gives us a banner under which we can all stand."

Ruth and I left the party early in the morning, with the Helsinki group documents on our bodies.

19

OVER THE NEXT few days we met a broad representation of the opposition movement. Some were fighting the terrible past; others, the present; and yet others, the future. Many of the younger people, to whom Stalin is only an ancient name in a history book, are no longer fighting that memory. But Nadezhda Mandelstam was one of the ones who still was.

The diminutive seventy-seven-year-old widow of the poet Osip Emilyevich Mandelstam had fought the Soviets for most of her life. She was then living in a single room in Moscow. If the country had changed, she was not aware of it. Nadezhda's optimistic memoir, *Hope Against Hope* (also translated as *Nadezhda Against Herself*) and the later disillusioned *Hope Abandoned* (also translated as *Nadezhda Abandoned*), were smuggled out of Russia in manuscript form and were published to universal acclaim throughout the world.

Our conversation was minimal—she was, when we saw her, in her last years; a tiny living reminder of those who survived the worst of Stalin's regime. Her husband died in 1938 after years in exile and Stalin's camps. She might have appreciated the irony when, after her death in 1979, when her friends came to take her body for burial, the police barred the door and refused to let them in. The police took her body from the apartment themselves, claiming she must be buried by the state in an anonymous grave. But by demonstrating and writing, her friends fought back against this spiteful final act of vengeance and won. They were finally given Nadezhda's body, which they buried privately. In Stalin's time even the fate of that body would have been certain. It is a strange measure of progress that Stalin's heirs had been content merely to defame her in life and harass her in death. Many of Russia's bureaucrats are still locked in old sectarian struggles— had they left her death alone, it would have passed unnoticed. Unable to possess her spirit, the government tried to possess her body instead and lost.

This story reminded me of the manner in which the South African government in 1975 treated the death of Bram Fischer, the white Afrikaner lawyer who spent his last ten years in prison because of his fight against apartheid. Dying for months of cancer, he asked to be allowed to go home to his wife and children for the last few weeks. The government refused, but then shortly before his death, it relented and permitted him to go home for a few days. But at the last minute they made him return to die in jail. After his death the government refused to allow his wife to bury or cremate him, claiming that because he had died a prisoner the state was entitled to his body. They buried him in an unmarked grave within prison walls.

After a round of office calls with Shcharansky to other pros-ecutors' offices on behalf of other jailed dissidents, we met Vladimir Slepak, another one of the better-known Jews trying to leave Rus-sia. While Shcharansky ran around in daily exuberant battle and Sakharov attempted to address the higher issues, Slepak, unem-ployed, calmly waited in his eighth-floor apartment on Gorky Street, just a few blocks from the Kremlin and directly opposite the police station whose officers daily watched him and photographed his visitors.

With his large brown eyes, patriarchal Russian face, and large peasant body, Slepak waited to see who would break first, he or the government, as they stared across the street at each other. When Jimmy Carter, as the candidate for the presidency in 1976, had publicly expressed his sympathies for Slepak by commending his courage and hoping he would be permitted to emigrate, Vladimir had been estatic. He thought he'd soon be in Israel—until the Russian press agency Tass made the accusation that Carter's statement proved Slepak was a CIA agent.

Vladimir was the son of an old Bolshevik, Solomon Slepak, who fought in the Far East after the 1917 revolution and helped the Bolsheviks win power there. Solomon was a member of the Presidium of the Comintern, the international Communist organization used by Stalin to support the revolution abroad. In the early 1920s he slipped into China on a forged United States passport to make contact with the Chinese Communists. When his son, whom he named after Lenin, applied to emigrate in 1970, the old man broke relations with him, calling him an "enemy of the people." They had had no contact since.

Vladimir's face had an open, spiritual quality, a voice by turns shy and charged with feeling and conviction. Warm, accessible, and giving, Vladimir, who was now fifty, had been at the center of the Jewish emigration campaign for many years. His apartment, within easy walking distance of several major tourist hotels, had become a stopping point for visiting American congressmen and foreign journalists interested in helping and talking with dissidents.

We spent part of a long day at the apartment which he and his wife shared with two other couples. Sitting on his balcony, we watched a heavy snow fall on Gorky Street. I watched him. Well known to most people as a refusenik, he had been unable to work for years, since his immigration application to Israel had been denied. With his wife he spent his days virtually imprisoned in the apartment, reluctant to risk confrontation on the street.

When we at last seated ourselves in the communal kitchen/ living room of the apartment, his natural ebullience seemed tempered by fear. He was becoming fully aware, perhaps for the first time, that he would never see his children, who were in Israel, again, and not only would he not go there, but he might soon be arrested. As we sat on rickety kitchen chairs, surrounded by artifacts from Israel—a brass menorah in a glass cupboard, a beautifully illustrated version of the Old Testament—we exchanged pictures of our children. He tried to hide his disappointment when we told him our oldest daughter could not speak "Jewish" and had not

160

been bas mitzvahed, but he brightened visibly when Ruth said it would be different with Elizabeth, our youngest child.

Slepak confirmed what other dissidents have told me, that the variety of political thought within and outside of the government is far more extensive than it appears from outside the Soviet Union. Literature, theater, and film are more creative and truthful, and the press more critical, than many Americans imagine.

As the blue gray day darkened to evening, Slepak, his voice breaking, said, "There are fewer and fewer of us who will stand up to the government. When I go into the courtyard, the other tenants nearly attack me. I'm like a prisoner, but without the rights of a prisoner. But I can take it. I won't give in."

His later actions, months after I had returned to the United States, showed his frustrations. In a deliberately inflammatory act on June 4, 1978, he unfurled a three-foot banner off his balcony, directly facing KGB headquarters, with large letters proclaiming "Let Us Out to Join Our Son in Israel." The police broke into the apartment, tore the banner into three pieces, let them float down to the street, and charged the Slepaks with hooliganism. He was sentenced to five years of internal exile in Siberia.

After leaving Vladimir Slepak staring out across the brilliant streetlights of Gorky Street, we drove in a cab through the heavy snow to the home of the Sakharovs.

Although Andrei Sakharov had originally agreed to see us several days earlier, he had put the meeting off. He was depressed much of the time and not in the mood to see strangers. But when I told him I thought he should personally write to President Carter and that I would deliver the letter for him, he asked us to come over as soon as we could.

20

EVEN BEFORE we were seated in his kitchen, Sakharov began to speak about the subway bombing. Twice he had issued public statements warning that the KGB might use the explosion as a pretext for new repression against dissidents. But sensationalist hints by the Soviet government that the nonviolent dissenters might be turning in frustration to terrorism were receiving more attention in the Western press than Sakharov's denials that any such thing could possibly occur. He was depressed by his ineffectiveness. He agreed with my speculation that the bombing might have been part of the Soviet response to the dissidents now that Carter was intimating, if not the end of détente, then at least a tougher line on the Soviets than his predecessors.

By United States standards, Sakharov's seventh-floor Moscow apartment would be considered painfully modest. By Russian standards, for a man who once received the recognition he did within the USSR, it was a deliberate deprivation. A narrow entrance corridor led to a tiny bathroom, a toilet, a minuscule kitchen; two other small, book-cluttered rooms served variously as bedrooms, living space, and study areas. Yet if there was an epicenter to the Soviet Union's fragmented human rights movement, it was this dingy apartment. Here he counseled and gave needed sanctuary to his colleagues.

Tall, stoop-shouldered, quick to smile, his gray hair forming a fringe around his bald crown, fifty-seven-year old Sakharov looked more like a genial, shabby professor holding gentle court at home than a man in the process of defying the world's most powerful Communist state. Indeed, the odds then of winning his challenge seemed so impossible that he called himself, with self-deprecating humor, Andrei Blazhenny—an apt Russian description that connotes both sanity and madness, both blissfulness and silliness.

The son of a Moscow physics teacher and textbook author, Sakharov recalled his early family life as "cultured and close." From childhood, he said "I lived in an atmosphere of decency, mutual help and tact, a liking for work, and respect for the mastery of one's chosen profession." Young Andrei lost no time in mastering his: By 1942, having graduated with honors in physics from Moscow State University, he went to work in the war industry as an engineer. After World War II he studied with the theoretical physicist (and later Nobel laureate) Igor Tamm. Soon he was at work on the Kremlin's number-one-priority project: development of the Soviet Union's hydrogen bomb.

Called the father of the Russian hydrogen bomb, Sakharov had been the youngest scientist ever admitted to the prestigious USSR Academy of Sciences. Although he had "money . . . title . . . and everything which my work enabled me to have," he also had "a very tragic feeling" with an "awful sense of powerlessness." In 1958, having been awarded the Stalin and Lenin prizes for science and having been named three times a "Hero of Socialist Labor," he publicly opposed further Russian nuclear tests. He had seen the genetic damage done by nuclear testing and strongly felt "the continuation of tests and all attempts to legalize nuclear weapons and their tests are contrary to humanity and international law."

This was a dramatic statement, ultimately leading to total estrangement from his previous prestigious life as one of the country's most brilliant physicists. Expanding this first tentative step on his pilgrimage of consciousness, Sakharov, in 1961, pleaded with Nikita Khrushchev to reverse the decision to break a worldwide moratorium on atmospheric testing. Khrushchev, who in his memoirs would call Sakharov "a crystal of morality," was unmoved by the appeal.

When another of his efforts in 1962 failed to halt a test blast, Sakharov pressed a nuclear weapons official to consider a limited ban (on air, sea, and space testing) that would avoid contamination. How much Sakharov's initiative helped is not known, but that formula became the basis of the Partial Test Ban Treaty signed in Moscow in 1963.

Sakharov identified himself as a loyal socialist when in 1968 he wrote his seminal essay, "Progress, Coexistence, and Intellectual Freedom," in which he argued that only a convergence of the capitalist West and the socialist East could avoid the destruction of mankind. His words were an appeal primarily to the leaders of his own country to take what seemed to be necessary steps to rescue Russia from her own suffocating past. But he also spoke forcefully of the United States and the West:

> In Vietnam, the forces of reaction, lacking hope for an expression of national will in their favor, are using the force of military pressure. They are violating all legal and moral norms and are carrying out flagrant crimes against humanity. An entire people is being sacrificed to the proclaimed goal of stopping the "Communist tide."
>
> They strive to conceal from the American people considerations of personal and party prestige, the cynicism and cruelty, the hopelessness and ineffectiveness of the anti-Communist tasks of American policy in Vietnam, as well as the harm this war is doing to the true goals of the American people, which coincide with the universal task of bolstering peaceful existence.

Throughout the years he spoke of his concern for the "rights of man," prophesying an ultimate détente that would lead to a world atmosphere in which individual rights on an international level would be recognized, and enforced.

> The goal of international policy is to insure universal fulfillment of the "Declaration of the Rights of Man" and to prevent a sharpening of international tensions and a strengthening of militant and nationalist tendencies.

164

His book and statement made him a celebrity abroad, but at home, where his book circulated in samizdat, the underground press, he became an outsider. His security clearance was abruptly withdrawn.

He was by now well down the path that was to lead first to his isolation in Moscow and later, in 1981, to internal exile in the city of Gorky, 250 miles away. By 1972, hounded by the KGB and now frequently attacked by the press as anti-Soviet, he signed a document protesting Russia's treatment of minorities as "A Member of the Human Rights Committee, A. Sakharov, physicist." At a press conference in August 21, 1973, Sakharov opposed Nixon's efforts toward détente with the USSR because he believed it could only lead to more internal repression. He said that internal repression should be substantially and visibly reduced before Nixon should agree to relax international tensions. In 1975, frustrated by his failure to affect Soviet policy, he wrote *My Country and the World*, which marked the beginning of his attempts to save the world from nuclear catastrophe by appealing to the West. The Nobel Committee, in awarding him their Peace Prize in 1975, called him "the Conscience of the World."

I also looked forward to meeting Sakharov's wife, Yelena B. Bonner, now his primary support. Sakharov's involvement with the dissidents rapidly accelerated after he met Yelena in 1970 while attending a trial of other dissidents. While he was frail and stooped, she seemed robust and taller than her actual height. Yelena, broad-shouldered, dark-eyed, recovering from a cataract operation, served tea as we discussed Chile, China, and my first visit to Moscow. Half Jewish, Yelena Bonner was a political firebrand. Her father, George, had been taken away and shot for apparently no reason at all during the purges in the thirties; her mother, Ruth, was sentenced to eleven harrowing years in the bleak concentration camp of Karagard in the barren steppes of Siberia.

Because Sakharov refused to keep quiet and resisted the Soviet Union's inducements either to stop criticizing the government or leave the country, the government had started to brutalize members of his family. His step-children were kicked out of school and their careers wrecked. When Bonner applied for permission to leave the country to get medical treatment for her eyes, she was refused. Soviet authorities claimed Russia's medical facilities were sufficient—that Yelena need not get privileged treatment denied to all other Soviet citizens. Even the refuseniks I spoke to believed that in this instance the Soviet authorities were correct. Finally, however, the Soviet Union relented and she received permission to go to Switzerland for the operation.

The state had nearly succeeded in cutting Sakharov off from the outside world. His phones were disconnected, and foreign journalists who came to see him were harassed and interrogated. Although the Soviet Union does not have, as South Africa does, legal banning orders, the Russian government easily achieves the same result. South Africa's banning orders isolate the individual (most often by sending them into impoverished areas hundreds of miles from home) by prohibiting others from visiting the banned person, setting curfews, and prohibiting the banned person from attending public functions. The Soviet Union merely identifies the person as a troublemaker. If citizens try to help, or even visit, a troublemaker, they know they can be arrested and sent to jail under laws for conspiring with enemies of the state.

Knowing that the Sakharovs were having trouble communicating with Westerners, I showed them Carter's speech. I told Sakharov I thought he could find material in it that would help him form the basis for a public statement, and I repeated that if he wrote a letter to the president, I would deliver it personally.

Sitting hunched inside his sweater in the chilly apartment, Sakharov thought for a while and then said there was little to lose and everything to gain, and he would do it.

He wanted to bring to Carter's attention his version of the truth of the subway bombing (that it was done by agent provocateurs to discredit the dissidents) and the significance of the KGB's overreaction to it. No one, he believed, either in Russia or the rest of the world, knew those facts. Although I read the Western press and had the Soviet press translated for me, I could not draw any firm conclusions. He would tell Carter, he said, how he feared that by using the bombing as an excuse, the entire dissident movement might be crushed. But perhaps more importantly, once he got word to Carter, some of his countrymen might, through the Voice of America and the Western press, also dissociate the bombers from the dissidents.

As Sakharov rose to his task, he became quite animated. Yelena beamed and brought out some cakes to eat with our tea. Then she took my wife Ruth into an adjoining room, where they sat together on a tattered couch and discussed the magnificent collection in the Hermitage Museum in Leningrad.

Sakharov had been visibly very upset when I told him the statement he had made on the subway bombings had not been printed in the United States. "Then I must make sure this letter has an impact," he said. Sakharov compared those subway bombings to the Reichstag fire of 1933 and the Kirov assassination of 1934—two classic cases of state police provocation during the Hitler-Stalin era. In his letter, originally written in Russian at his kitchen table, then translated roughly into English by Yelena and transcribed by my wife, he wrote:

> Our situation is difficult, almost unbearable not only in the USSR, but also in all the countries of Eastern Europe. Now, on the eve of the Belgrade Meeting, with the struggle for human rights rising in Eastern Europe and the USSR, the authorities are stepping up their repression and their attempts to discredit dissidents. They are unwilling to make any concessions to the human rights most essential to any society (freedom of belief and information, freedom of conscience, freedom to choose one's country of residence, etc.). They cannot accept the honest competition of ideas. The persecution of the members of the Helsinki Watch Groups in Moscow and the Ukraine, and especially the provocation in the Moscow subway, which we have to compare to the 1933 Reichstag fire and the 1934 murder of Kirov, require emphatic condemnation.

Desperately wanting to answer the Soviet claim that his supporters were responsible for the bombing and were turning violent, he wanted to make the point that the movement he spoke for was now, and would continue to be, a nonviolent one. Realizing that his lines of communication were being shut down and fearing this might be one of the last chances to talk to the world, he tried to bring to the attention of the press specific mistreated prisoners who needed exposure:

> I have a serious problem with communications. My telephone to the West is completely blocked. No calls reach me and . . . I'm always closely watched. This question of communications is basic to my public activity and the entire human rights movement in this country. . . .
>
> It is very important that the President of the United States continue his efforts to obtain the release of those people who are already known to Americans and that those efforts not be in vain. . . .
>
> I give you a list of those in need of immediate release, but it is very important to remember there are many others in equally difficult situations. This is the main list. There are very many others who need the same support, and we haven't got the moral strength to cross out any of the names. . . .

The letter to President Carter mentioned fifteen current Soviet victims. Few of the names were known in the West, so I suggested it might be important to focus on particular cases so the letter might get specific results. Sakharov thought any one of those cases would arouse any thoughtful person in the West: Pyotr Ruban, for example, sentenced to eight years in a labor camp and five more in internal exile for making a wooden Statue of Liberty in honor of the bicentennial; Dr. Mikhail Shtern, given eight years on crudely fabricated charges of soliciting bribes for medical treatment after his two sons left for Israel; Semyon Gluzman, a psychiatrist sent to a labor camp for defending the sanity of a dissenter who was kept in a psychiatric ward.

The writing of the letter went slowly because Sakharov was taking great care to get every word right. The curtainless windows showed the black evening's approach beyond the continued heavy snowfall. I mused on his position as he sat in this small, barely furnished apartment, treated as a parasite by most Soviet citizens, nearly alone, despised by the government he battled, this awesome monolithic state that would most surely outlive him.

And then, on behalf of all religious peoples in Eastern Europe, he wrote to Carter:

Do you know the truth about the situation of religion in the USSR—the humiliation of official churches and the merciless repression (arrests; fines; religious parents deprived of their children; even murder, as in the cases of the Baptist Biblenko) of those sects—Baptists, Uniates, Pentecostals, the True Orthodox Church, and others—who seek independence of the government. The Vins case is the best-known example. Terror is also used against other groups of dissidents. During the past year we have known of the murders of dissidents—that of the poet and translator Konstantin Bogatyrev is well known—which have not been investigated at all.

As the letter was being translated, Sakharov and I talked. He seemed to have decided that change would occur in Russia only when there was firm pressure from the outside. Yet over the years he had come to have a deep understanding of the West—its follies, crimes, and shameful acts and attitudes—and he had become skeptical that the West could save Russia from herself.

I began to understand the depth of Sakharov's despair. He had moved a long way down a very sad path—away from a country that, for all the enmity and abuse it had heaped on him, he still loved. The Soviet people, who had "demonstrated the vitality of the socialist course," were *his* people. The country which had "done more for the people, culturally, socially, morally, than any other system"—this was *his* country.

For Sakharov, Stalin's death in 1953 started a period of intense elation. He felt new hope. He remained faithful to that dream for a long time. During the "Khrushchev thaw years," between 1954 and 1958, writers and dissidents alike were encouraged to believe that censorship might be lifted and that the revolution's promise might yet, after great cost, be fulfilled.

A measure of the relaxation in the 1950s was the drop in prison camp populations from something approaching a high of 10.5 million to about 1.5 million. Then, in 1960 discussions began to replace the 1936 Stalin constitution. At the same time, new statutes and glosses on the text indicated a greater concern for individual rights.

The legal and political reforms of the Khrushchev period

were of particular and great importance. The powers of the security police were reduced, and the criminal code was completely revised to provide more specific definitions of crimes and less fragile procedural safeguards. The principle of "guilt by analogy"—a type of constructive treason—the notion that one could be guilty of a crime not specifically defined in the criminal code but merely similar to a specific offense—was abolished. Also abolished was the law permitting the imprisonment of innocent relatives of "enemies of the people."

But Khrushchev, to pacify the hard-liners, put liberalization into reverse in certain areas. Between 1958 and 1964 he conducted a new campaign of harassment and persecution against Christianity and other religions. It was this action that provoked the emergence of the first religious dissent movement—among the Baptists, a group that through active proselytizing grew from their prerevolutionary membership of 100,000 to their present official membership of 550,000. In 1960 and 1961 Khrushchev launched a thinly disguised long-term policy of assimilating all national minorities into the Russian nation. The minorities resisted, claiming Khrushchev was destroying their unique cultures. This action gives rise to one of the more significant nationalist dissent movements, which still exists, based in the Ukraine, an area that has nearly always considered itself independent.

But from 1964 to 1968 the backlash to the thaw became increasingly severe. The ouster of Khrushchev, the failures of liberalization, and the arrests and trials of authors Yuli Daniel and Andrei Sinyavsky in 1968, heralded both a new repression and the emergence of a mature human rights movement. With additional support from the United Nations, which proclaimed 1968 to be International Human Rights Year, the new movement's hundreds of members began to issue the *Chronicle of Human Events*, a samizdat journal which has published more than sixty issues to date. In 1977 the Soviet authorities issued a new constitution, incorporating many of the changes made in the statutory law.

In the vast Soviet Union with its 257 million population, Sakharov estimated there were approximately two thousand dissidents and another ten thousand who were religious prisoners. What I thought remarkable was how low his estimates were compared to the population of the country and comparative figures for other countries. Of course, it may be that many criminal prisoners in the Russian system should have been considered by Sakharov to be political prisoners. Andrew Young, when he was our United Nations ambassador, made a similar point about many of the five hundred thousand minority-group arrests made each year in the United States.

Most of the political prisoners and dissidents are either despised or regarded with suspicion and indifference by the rest of the population. On the whole, the dissidents have never succeeded in becoming more than a nuisance within the Soviet Union, although their international effect has been significant. I believe this is primarily because the vast majority of Soviet citizens are fundamentally satisfied with their lives, although critics argue it is solely because that majority is kept in tight rein by an oppressive police state.

As Sakharov and I talked more about the changes in post-Stalin Russia, he was burningly aware that if atrocity had ended with the dictator, degradation had not. Where Sakharov once believed in the fundamental decency and rightness of socialism as the only way to the future for all the world, he no longer appeared so certain. He accepted as "probably true" that more political prisoners died in a single Siberian camp in a single year under Stalin than in all the czar's jails in the nineteenth century; he also accepted as true Stalin's contribution in bequeathing to his successors a superpower, with extraordinary economic achievements, after he himself had inherited a country that was the primary casualty of World War I. Sakharov made a point of mentioning that although Russia was still a Third World country, its people received extraordinary benefits: a sophisticated educational system, pensions, medical coverage, and income guarantees.

"Improvement there has been since Stalin's day, but it is desperately slow; it will be. There will not be sudden revolutions. There must not be. The West," he said, "must not call or ask Soviet youth to make foolish sacrifices. The people of the Soviet Union are wholly dependent on the state. Its power is enormous. It can swallow them without choking. And we have already had more than enough sacrifices and victims."

21

LETTER IN HAND, Ruth and I left the Sakharovs' apartment and returned to our hotel. As we packed, getting ready to leave Moscow for Leningrad, Ruth noticed that our room had been searched and that several sweaters and a watch were missing. She reported it to the woman at the desk beside the elevator—the same woman who had been at the desk four days before when Shcharansky came. The woman angrily replied: "It's probably the people you invited into your rooms who took your things. There've been a lot of people in there. I'll try to find your sweaters if you give me the names of the people who visited you."

Ruth pointed out that the clothes had been there that morning and we hadn't had visitors for several days. She suggested it might have been either the chamber maid or someone who had gained entry to search through our belongings. The desk woman repeated that before she would report the theft, she wanted the names of all our visitors. Rather than continue what was turning into an argument, Ruth walked away. She tried to find someone else to tell. But after spending some twenty minutes walking through the Hotel Rossiya's endless corridors, many of them cul de sacs leading to luxurious private dining rooms closed to tourists, she gave up. We left Moscow without our missing things.

Our spirits revived somewhat at the sight of beautiful Leningrad, with its narrow cobbled streets and humpbacked bridges crossing the canals. There I met other dissidents and refuseniks. They had also heard of our "success" at the Moscow prosecutor's office and for them I agreed to visit more government officials and carry letters back to the United States.

These men and women had been referred to me by Sakharov. They were people growing desperate after months of writing and going to bureaucrats to find out whether fathers and sons were still alive, and if so where they were. I was reminded of the opening words of *Requiem*. Years had passed sinced Anna Akhmatova, perhaps the greatest Russian poet of this century, wrote her epic poem, recreating the horror of the Stalin years:

> In the fearful years of the Yezhov terror I spent seventeen months in prison queues in Leningrad. One day somebody "identified" me. Beside me, in the queue, there was a woman with blue lips. She had, of course, never heard of me; but she suddenly came out of that trance so common to us all and whispered in my ear (everybody spoke in whispers there): "Can you describe this?" And I said: "Yes, I can." And then something like the shadow of a smile crossed what had once been her face.

These words resonated even more to me following a conversation Ruth and I had with Vera, our English-speaking guide, while visiting the Hermitage Museum. I had asked her about Sakharov. "He's disgraceful," she replied curtly. "Everyone knows he is a millionaire. He has two cars, a palatial mansion, and eats whatever he wants." Her face became distorted with anger as she spoke about him.

"Sakharov's fine," Vera continued. "All this business about the government picking on him is false. He still has his pension. He's still a member of the academy."

Our departure time came upon us fast. It had been a full and exhausting ten days. Ruth and I decided it would be better if she carried the Helsinki documents and the letter to President Carter. We reasoned that I might face a tougher time going through customs. The Helsinki documents were in her bag, the Sakharov letter in an envelope on her body.

As I packed, I was elated to learn that Ivanov, Zavurov's

prosecutor, had forwarded my brief to the Tashkent prosecutor and court that would decide whether to reduce his sentence.

Nonetheless, we were apprehensive about leaving Russia, a concern which increased dramatically when, after waiting an hour at the airport, we were told the plane was going to be delayed while we went through customs again. This time a certain group of passengers, including my wife and me, was selected to go through another search. After the search we were told that the plane was going to be so late that we would not be left at the airport to wait but would instead be taken to a hotel in Leningrad. As we left the airport, I saw most of the other passengers remaining there. We had been singled out.

Being driven back to Leningrad in a private, semiofficial car filled us both with fear. Although deep down I didn't believe anything would be done to us, Ruth was terrified. We waited in a small two-bed room set aside for us on the fifth floor of the Leningrad Hotel. The phone sitting between the beds was the focus of our attention. Ruth and I wanted to pick it up. We felt a need to talk to our children, for we were afraid we might not be able to do so for a while. At least we wanted to tell them we would be later than planned getting in and not to wait up for us.

I also wanted to telephone someone to let them know where I was and what seemed to be happening. But I did not want to be melodramatic and, in any event, I didn't know whom to call. Previous overseas experiences in Chile, Bangladesh, and Pakistan had discouraged me from thinking of calling the United States consulate or embassy offices. The American government could not easily take a stand in my favor, since meetings with dissidents and carrying out documents did technically violate Russian law (the letters, with information on jails and prisoners, could be said to contain secret information). I knew that Ruth and I, like Sakharov and Shcharansky, were small parts of a much larger picture.

But I could not accept the reality that filing a brief urging clemency for Zavurov, carrying private letters from Sakharov to Carter, and documents from Orlov to Congressman Dante Fascell, could put me alongside Orlov in a Soviet jail. But just a few months later, when Robert Toth, the *Los Angeles Times* Moscow correspondent who had had extensive contact with Shcharansky

and Sakharov, was detained on suspicion of disclosing state secrets, interrogated, and nearly jailed only for allegedly repeating
critical statements in his articles, I realized how close we had come
to being charged with anti-Soviet activities and espionage.

We paced the small room. We had no baggage and no books.
The radio did not work. When I thought to leave the room to go
to the lobby for a drink I found the door locked. When I knocked, a
plainclothesman promptly opened the door. He politely asked what
I wanted and then, signaling to his partner by the elevator, ordered
me some beverages.

But finally, after six hours, we were taken back to the airport,
put on a different plane, whisked through customs, and flown back
to the United States.

22

BACK HOME, I immediately called the State Department to make arrangements to fulfill my promise to Sakharov by delivering his letter to President Carter and the Helsinki documents to Congress.

At first Philip C. Habib at the State Department did not want the letter publicly delivered. He said the president did not want to receive a letter from a private Soviet citizen. It was clear, in speaking to Habib, that the new administration had not placed human rights on its agenda. The phrase does not appear in the chapter on foreign policy in Jimmy Carter's 1975 memoir, *Why Not the Best?* Nor was the issue prominent in his presidential campaign. In fact, he was moving in the opposite direction. He criticized not only the Helsinki agreements, but the whole philosophy of intervention. "Our people have now learned," he told the Foreign Policy Association in June 1976, "the folly of our trying to inject our power into the internal affairs of other nations." However, he had a general feeling, as he wrote in his memoir, that "our government's foreign policy is not exemplified in any commitment to moral principles," that foreign policy must rest on the same moral standards "which are characteristic of the individual citizens," and that "there is only one nation in the world which is capable of true leadership among the community of nations, and that is the United States."

We negotiated over three days on the phone. I then met Habib and two of his associates. Habib continued to want the private delivery of the letter to him. He did not want the media to believe that the letter went directly to President Carter, as Sakharov wished, because the administration was not prepared to deal with the consequences of such a public event. I told Habib that if he did not take the issue public, I would hold a press conference and state that the administration refused to publicly accept the letter that Sakharov wished me to personally deliver to the president.

Ultimately, we compromised—Habib refused to allow Carter to accept the letter publicly from me—but it became front-page news when the letter was delivered by me to Habib, who accepted it on the president's behalf. I knew that when confronted by new departures, bureaucracies feel that risks outweigh opportunities. Without a dramatic public event, the letter would not get the result Sakharov wanted.

Sakharov's letter was in the president's hands less than two weeks after his January 1977 inauguration. It was hard, if not impossible, for him now to ignore Sakharov's letter after making such an issue of President Gerald Ford's refusal (at Kissinger's recommendation) to meet with Nobel Prize–winner, Alexander I. Solzhenitsyn. I was also aware, and troubled by the fact, that directing the human rights issue solely at the Soviet Union might play some small role in reviving cold war hostilities. I hoped the president, if he took a vigorous human rights position, would articulate his human rights concerns against all countries.

But because President Carter's State Department, still new to the job and unsure how to react, would not tell whether Carter would respond to the letter or even acknowledge it, I had to decide whether to release it to the press. Sakharov and I had not discussed whether it should be made public, and I did not know if doing so would help or hurt Sakharov and his cause. I spoke to as many people about it as I could, in Washington, New York, and Boston. Several who opposed the release said I had no right to publish the letter without Sakharov's express permission. Others said that unless it was released, it would have little or no effect, and anyway, Sakharov, already committed to risking his life, knew full well that once the letter had left his or my hand, he had no control over it.

Although I tried to contact Sakharov by telephoning him and by contacting people in Russia who could act as messengers, I was unable to reach him. I finally decided to release the letter.

The letter was printed verbatim in the *New York Times*, the *Los Angeles Times*, *Newsweek*, and *Time*, and had an extraordinary and dramatic effect, far greater than I had anticipated.

Russian exiles who were horrified at what later happened to Sakharov, Orlov, and Shcharansky said the writing and release of the letter provided the pretext for the Soviet government to denounce American meddling in Russia's internal affairs and to reject the idea of détente so long as the United States was making Soviet human rights a priority issue. I was personally attacked by the New York editor of a magazine of dissident voices and by Russian emigré groups and their supporters for releasing the letter without written authority and for not having consulted with them first. They claimed it led to the subsequent crackdown against dissidents.

Ruth and I were both terribly upset. Most emigré leaders spoke as if they had a pipeline to Sakharov's thoughts. Many of them knew Sakharov and Bonner far better than I did; many had been corresponding with him for years. I was thrust for a while into the complex world of the emigrés.

But there were greater forces at work. The president's attempts to arm Western Europe and make friends with China, while at the same time rejecting détente and criticizing the Soviet Union's human rights record, were the major reasons for the 1977 clampdown on the human rights activists in Russia. Winning his battle against Secretary of State Cyrus R. Vance, who wanted to make more détente attempts, Zbigniew Brzezinski took a harder line toward the Soviet Union that provoked it into more intransigence on the human rights issue.

In the months following Carter's inauguration, I saw people I had met in Russia become hostages of the new superpower clash. In a small way I had helped put them in the center of the conflict. I felt responsible for not discussing more fully with them the possible consequences. But even if I could have prevented the damage to their lives, I'm not sure they could or would have acted differently.

On February 5, 1977, President Carter, in a remarkable act for an American president, wrote a personal reply to Sakharov. Cyrus Vance seriously questioned it. In "going over the heads" of the Soviet leadership in one of his first acts in office by directly contacting one of the government's leading opponents, Carter was throwing down a challenge at the very beginning of his presidency. He wrote to Sakharov:

> I received your letter of January 21, and I want to express my appreciation to you for bringing your thoughts to my personal attention.
>
> Human rights are a central concern of my administration. In my inaugural address I stated: "Because we are free, we can never be indifferent to the fate of freedom elsewhere." You may rest assured that the American people and our government will continue our firm commitment to promote respect for human rights not only in our country but also abroad.
>
> We shall use our good offices to seek the release of prisoners of conscience, and we will continue our efforts to shape a world responsive to human aspirations in which nations of differing cultures and histories can live side by side in peace and justice.
>
> I am always glad to hear from you, and I wish you well.

Elated, Sakharov released the text of the president's letter to Western journalists in Moscow and that same day, through the United States embassy, sent out his reply to Carter:

> Your letter is a great honor for me and is support for the unified human rights movement in the USSR and the countries of Eastern Europe, of which we consider ourselves a part. In your letter, as earlier in your inaugural speech and other public statements, you have confirmed the adherence of the new American administration to the principles of human rights throughout the world. Your efforts to assist in freeing prisoners of conscience are particularly significant. . . .

Seizing on the human rights issue presented to him at the very beginning of his presidency by Sakharov, Jimmy Carter and his "personal" diplomacy strongly identified with that issue for several years. Whether his administration's identification with human rights would have happened without the Sakharov exchange at the beginning of his presidency is hard to say; other controversies might have taken over. But he had moved the Sakharov dialogue to the front pages of the world's press. Anti-Soviet Americans also focused on it obsessively. It assuaged those who thought that a former peanut farmer could not stand up to the Russians.

The Soviet Union acted immediately. Several hours after the U.S. embassy in Moscow had delivered Carter's letter to Sakharov, Ambassador Anatoly F. Dobrynin in Washington telephoned to ask for an appointment with Arthur Hartman, the acting secretary of state. At their meeting he delivered what a State Department spokesman called an expression of the Soviet government's "displeasure" at the administration's statements on human rights in the Soviet Union. The Soviet news agency Tass, which reported Mr. Dobrynin's visit, said the ambassador had informed Mr. Hartman that the Soviet Union "resolutely rejects attempts to interfere, under a thought-up pretext of defending human rights, in its internal affairs. Such actions," Tass said, "would complicate relations and make the solution of problems more difficult."

On February 6, 1977, KGB agents raided the apartment of a close supporter of Sakharov, dissident poet Mikola Rudenko. They destroyed the contents of Rudenko's flat and stripped his wife naked to humiliate her. Rudenko and Oleksa Tykhy, a Helsinki Group member from the city of Donetsk, were then taken to Ukrainian prisons.

Next they went after Yuri Orlov, one of the Soviet citizens most closely identified with Sakharov. Orlov, the physicist who had given me letters to smuggle out of Russia, anticipating a crackdown after the release of Sakharov's letter, had gone into hiding in late January. He was taken into custody on February 10, 1977, just a day after he had surfaced. Ironically, he had surfaced to tell Western reporters that the United States, by declaring its support of another dissident, Aleksandr Ginzburg, had made the situation safer. Ginzburg, better known than Orlov in the West, had been arrested a week earlier for assisting families of political prisoners with money provided by Alexander Solzhenitsyn.

The United States statement on Ginzburg, made a few days earlier, said the Soviet Union had been informed that the United

States was "watching with concern" the dissidents' treatment. "I think after the State Department statement on Ginzburg, I will not be arrested now," Orlov said. But Orlov totally misjudged the Soviet reaction to that statement.

As a result, in mid-February eight policemen arrived at the apartment of one of Mr. Orlov's dissident colleagues, Ludmilla Alexeyeva. "We're looking for someone who thinks as you do," she quoted one of them as saying. They spotted Orlov in the apartment and seized him.

The new arrests, a few days after Carter's reply to Sakharov, were a clear message to the president to stay out of what the Soviet Government considered its internal affairs, and a sign to Sakharov and the dissidents that they had nothing to gain by looking to Washington for moral support.

But Sakharov, having nowhere else to turn, would not let go. He waited for Carter's public reaction to the Orlov arrest. None came. The new president was learning that he had made a serious mistake. A few days after Orlov's arrest, on February 13, 1977, the Soviet newspaper *Pravda* published the reasoning for the government's new campaign against dissidents. Without mentioning the president by name, the editorial conveyed a sense of growing annoyance with the continued debate over the issue of human rights and détente; the dissidents the West was so concerned about were their pawns in the assault on communism and the USSR, it said. "These unconcealed enemies of socialism are just a handful of individuals who do not represent anyone or anything and are far removed from the Soviet people. What is more, they exist only because they are supported, paid and praised by the West."

This was obviously to be the official line. In a speech on March 22, Leonid Brezhnev personally denounced "outright attempts by official American agencies to interfere in the internal affairs of the Soviet Union." He said the Soviet Union "will never tolerate interference . . . by any country under any pretext," but especially not under cover of "a clamor being raised about so-called 'dissidents' and about the 'violation of human rights' in socialist countries."

Back at home the American papers were also full of the Carter-Sakharov exchange—and not everything written about it here was favorable either. In the *Washington Post* on February 24,

Joseph Kraft wrote that the president "seems not to have fully assessed . . . the scope (of) the issue of human rights in the Communist world" and was "unprepared for a vigorous response" from the Soviets to his actions and statements. "The human rights factor," Kraft wrote, "is far too important to be handled on a one-shot, tit-for-tat basis without a thorough exploration of effects and side-effects on such issues as arms control. . . . A President is probably better off burnishing the (American) record from time to time on an impersonal basis than being a compulsive talker."

In the *New York Times*, James Reston agreed. Carter's letter, he wrote, "has sent a polite shudder through the entire diplomatic fraternity. The best they can say . . . is that maybe it was an innocent mistake of inexperience." Cyrus Vance, years later in his published memoirs, agreed.

Not everyone felt Carter had blundered. Arthur Schlesinger, Jr., writing in the *Wall Street Journal* on March 4 said Carter's stance, while at first possibly "foolish," "must be judged thus far . . . a considerable and very serious success. . . . His letter to Sakharov obviously expressed real personal concern. It also registered public sentiment in the United States and elsewhere. For human rights is evidently one of those ideas whose day has finally arrived." But the historian and one-time Kennedy adviser quickly cautioned that the letter to Sakharov was not "part of a thought-out policy," that the policy should not "seem just one more stick with which to beat the Russians" and that "official sermons to the world may encourage us in the delusion that we are morally superior to everybody else."

While the superpowers argued, Sakharov waited, hoping that some human benefits would still emerge from the furor. On February 23, just over two weeks after receiving Carter's reply, Sakharov spoke of his frustration in an interview with *France-Soir*.

Q. What has changed for you personally and for the struggle after the Carter letter?

A. Concretely—nothing. For myself, personally—nothing. For the struggle, I imagine that it is a matter of time. Those moral criteria which, as President Carter stated in his letter, will be the basis of the activities of the new Administration are very important not only for the movement, but in the long term. When the

President of a great country speaks of it, interest in human rights can only grow, and that is very good.

But I would like to see actual, rapid solutions to those questions where speed is essential. I wrote in reply to the President to ask him to intercede immediately to effect the transfer of Sergei Kovalev, who is gravely ill. But Kovalev is still in Camp 35 and still on a hunger strike. Only an immediate transfer to a hospital can save his life. In my letter, I also asked . . . that the four members of the Helsinki Watch Group in the USSR . . . be released so that the group could continue its important work. However, all four are in prison. I am certain that these three specific issues can be resolved without affecting the SALT negotiations and must be dealt with as soon as possible.

Unfortunately, since this has not occurred, I cannot say that anything has changed after the President's letter to me.

Q. What can the West do?

A. It seems to me that I cannot give advice—any more than anyone could living in our country or in Eastern Europe. Western leaders, Western public figures, are simply better informed than we are. They don't live under pressure, under the yoke of repressions, without a free press, without postal or telephone connections. We can't give advice. We speak out—and loudly—about what is going on here, and just to speak the truth here is very difficult in itself. By speaking out, we are defending peace and the future. But as to drawing conclusions about what should be done—that the West must decide for itself.

This reply was more politic than accurate; Sakharov did feel strongly that America, by having raised the banner of human rights, whether it be in the Soviet Union or in Central America, had an obligation to the people it had singled out for attention. A few days later Sakharov told an ABC news correspondent:

If specific actions do not follow general statements, if the public in America and in Europe—legislatures, business people, scientific and cultural organizations in charge of contacts, and labor unions—do not support these statements and the principles expressed in them, then not only will these people in prison not be freed, but a further intensification of repression may occur.

183

Even as he spoke, Sakharov was being proved prophetically right. The repression was being intensified.

Meanwhile, in Washington, America's visible failure to protect the men whom the Carter administration had encouraged was calling the administration's human rights policies into question. Carter, trying hard to follow through on what he had started, issued public statements. "The United States," he emphasized, "has a responsibility and a legal right to express its disapproval of violations of human rights."

In an address to the United Nations General Assembly, the president asserted that "no member of the United Nations can claim that mistreatment of its citizens is solely its own business. Equally, no member can avoid its responsibilities to review and to speak when torture or unwarranted deprivation of freedom occurs in any part of the world." Next, in growing frustration and helplessness, he denounced the Communist government in Czechoslovakia for harassing intellectuals fighting for liberal reforms, invited Vladimir Bukovsky to the White House, and publicly condemned human rights abuses in Cuba, Uganda, and South Korea.

Few other Western countries followed Carter's lead. Andrei Amalrik, the Russian dissident then living in Paris, tried on February 14, 1977, to see President Giscard d'Estaing to persuade him to speak out on Sakharov's behalf. He failed.

Before long, Carter stopped publicly responding to the Soviet government. But the Soviet dissidents did not have the option of withdrawing from the littered battlefield. In March 1977, they issued a statement to the Western press, saying that they intended to keep "collecting information about violations despite pressure from authorities, including the arrest of four members last month."

Then the dissidents, along with Western newsmen, gathered in the same two-room apartment of Yuri Orlov that Ruth and I had visited months before, and declared publicly that they would not be intimidated by an official campaign to discredit their activities. No one knew where Orlov was, or if he was alive. An air of sadness hung over the room. Only six of the eleven founding members of the Helsinki Group were still active; others had either been arrested or had been given exit visas. The group announced two new members, Yuri Mnyukh and Naum Meiman. They said that

Ludmilla Alexeyeva, a member who had emigrated the previous month, would become a liaison with supporters in the West. They said as a result of the crackdown they were receiving a growing number of human rights complaints from every corner of the Soviet Union. And they would make sure that the West heard them too.

23

CLEARLY IN CONTROL, the Soviet government now began to shape their new, harder policy toward the dissidents by using Shcharansky as a symbol. He was arrested on March 15, 1977, and soon the engineer's activities became a test case, a trumped-up example of the corruption of dissidents by American funding.

Shcharansky was taken to the notorious Lefortovo Prison in Beforty, Moscow, where he was held and interrogated for sixteen months without being charged. This was extraordinary, even in Russia, for Soviet law requires that a person be charged within six months after his arrest.

It seemed they were waiting for a signal from the United States. It was January 1978. Kissinger was gone and Zbigniew Brzezinski was in office. The Soviets were not sure whether détente was alive or dead. Knowing that a trial would inflame international hostility, they waited to see what would happen if they did not set a trial date. By mid-1978 the Soviets evidently decided there were to be no significant moves by the United States, and they stopped wavering and set a date for Shcharansky to go on trial—July 12.

President Carter immediately told the Soviet foreign minister, Andrei Gromyko, that to put Shcharansky on trial would hurt every aspect of American-Soviet relations. Secretary of State Cyrus Vance then echoed these sentiments to Russian Ambassador

Dobrynin in private conversations. America warned that a trial might cause a severe reaction in both houses of Congress, jeopardizing ratification of a strategic arms limitation agreement currently before them.

The Russians soon made it clear that their intention was to turn the treason trial into a showcase to prove to the world not only Shcharansky's guilt, but also that it was the United States that was funding the entire Russian opposition and thereby deliberately subverting the possibility of détente.

The Soviet government's harshness was a remarkable change from the earlier 1970s pattern of dealing with dissidents. The Russians had apparently learned a lesson from the extraordinary three-day trial in February 1966 of Andrei Sinyavsky and Yuli Daniel, the well-known writers who published their "subversive" fiction writings abroad. That trial was a major public relations event. It was the first time in the history of the Soviet Union that writers had been put on trial solely for what they had written. Many Soviet writers have been imprisoned, banished, executed, or driven into silence, but never before had there been an open trial in which the principal evidence against them was their literary work, a work of fiction that satirized Russian bureaucrats. Despite an elaborate prosecution, the state failed to make a respectable argument that a charge could be hung on anything as ephemeral as the authors' words.

The defendants—young, fervent, and articulate—testified, representing thousands of voices. They referred to Western writers such as Dickens, Dante, and Shakespeare, and their use of similar words; they argued that international concepts of law barred a government from putting political meaning in literary allusion and then prosecuting the author for what the government thought the words meant. The defendants' friends in the crowded courtroom outnumbered the KGB officials. The courtroom observers laughed at the state's ignorance of both literary techniques and literature itself.

In briefs PEN, Amnesty, and other international rights organizations submitted, they pointed to Sir Edward Coke's statement (the great source of writing on bedrock human rights) that mere words cannot be treason. Although the fine-sounding briefs, with quotes from the Magna Charta and early American treason trials, had little immediate effect, the public relations aspect of the trial boomeranged on the Russians.

Nearly verbatim transcripts, completed by dissidents who came to court each day, soon circulated through the West. The length of the sentences—seven years for Sinyavsky and five for Daniel—provoked a storm of protest in the outside world for several years, unprecedented in its intensity and in the degree of unanimity between Communist and non-Communist alike. The results of the trial also gave rise to the first widespread and organized protests in Russia itself; ten years after Khrushchev's "thaw speech," this was the beginning of large-scale dissidence and samizdat.

The legal arguments submitted in the Sinyavsky-Daniel case formed a basis upon which lawyers in other Eastern European countries wrote similar briefs on behalf of these and later dissidents. The international literary community of the left as well as the right supported the authors. The Soviets never repeated their mistake by again having such a trial.

Because the Sinyavsky-Daniel trial received such great publicity in the West, and even some attention in Russia, the Soviets adopted, until Shcharansky's trial in 1977, the practice of classifying dissenters as psychiatric cases, thereby avoiding further public trials.

The 1977 charges again Shcharansky were not the usual charges traditionally lodged against Jews who insisted on their right to emigrate. He could have been charged with espionage, which under the Soviet law (as well as American law) is committed by the mere act of collecting confidential information, even if there is no transmission to a foreign power. Instead, he was charged with treason and a violation of Article 64A of the Code of Criminal Procedures, for being an agent of the CIA, and with violation of Article 70A, because of his so-called anti-Soviet agitation.

The language of the Soviet treason statute (like the anti-Soviet agitation section) is so broad that it encompasses speech and thought as well as acts. The statute says treason is "an act intentionally committed by a citizen of the U.S.S.R. to the detriment of the state independence . . . or a conspiracy for seizing power." The Soviet Constitution further says:

> To defend the country is the sacred duty of every citizen of the U.S.S.R. Treason to the motherland—violation of the oath of allegiance, desertion to the enemy, impairing the military power of the state—espionage—is punishable with all the severity of the law as the most heinous of crimes.

Treason then is a catch-all formula designed to carry out the state economic and social goals of punishing any act against the state. There is no overt act required, no witnesses are required—circumstantial evidence and confessions are enough.

Immediately after Shcharansky's arrest we were told he would also be charged with that section of the criminal code which punishes by death the treasonous act of "taking flight" abroad. That this provision violates the Universal Declaration of Human Rights which says that "everyone has the right to leave any country including his own" is, for the Soviets and other socialist countries, beside the point: They have an interest in preventing their educated elite from leaving. Ultimately, Shcharansky was not charged for wanting to leave. As it turned out, the Soviets produced evidence for the more substantial "anti-Soviet" and treason charge.

The "evidence" of Shcharansky's anti-Soviet activity consisted of letters and telegrams of protest to the government with requests and demands for visas to Israel, and meetings with senators and foreign tourists in Moscow and other "agents of Zionism." The accusation of slandering the Soviet state was in response to Shcharansky's involvement with the Helsinki Group. Charging him with interfering with the internal affairs of the Soviet Union, the prosecution referred to papers he distributed to radio stations and publishing houses, including the BBC and the Voice of America. The accusation also stated that as a result of Shcharansky's activities the Jackson Amendment had been accepted by the United States Congress and had done considerable material harm to the Soviet Union.

As soon as his trial was announced, I, along with other attorneys from the United States and foreign countries, sought permission to go to the Soviet Union and help Shcharansky prepare his case.

The Soviet government refused to grant our request. Instead, they selected lawyers for him, all of whom he rejected. He knew they would not argue the defenses he wanted, so he asked for permission to represent himself. He publicly acknowledged that in Stalin's time they would not have bothered with such trivialities. The fact that he could enter a not-guilty plea was a luxury not shared by previous generations.

At first the judge refused the request, making it clear to Anatoly that if he persisted in contesting the case, the penalty would be more severe. But after hours of wrangling, the judge gave in and allowed Shcharansky to represent himself. He fought the judges and prosecutor every step of the way in a five-day trial. Although no verbatim transcript of the trial is even now available (Russian law does not require a transcript being made), persons who attended court every day put together a report of the trial. It, along with a similar "transcript" of the Sinyavsky-Daniel trial, is one of the more remarkable documents of our time. It is testimony of how an individual, alone and without hope, can battle day after day solely for history in a court where the verdict has long been arrived at.

The state's case was originally based solely on what Shcharansky had said. It was a pure speech case. When that proved to be manifest, the Soviet Union shifted tactics.

The Soviet prosecutor then claimed in court that Shcharansky was a paid CIA agent, a charge rarely, if ever, leveled at a dissident in a Russian court. President Carter, in an unusual action, immediately and publicly replied at a press conference:

> I have inquired deeply within the State Department and within the CIA, as to whether or not Mr. Shcharansky has ever had any known relationship in a subversive way, or otherwise, with the CIA. The answer is "no." We have double-checked this, and I have been hesitant to make the public announcement, but now I am completely convinced that, contrary to the allegations that have been reported to the press, Mr. Shcharansky has never had any sort of relationship, to our knowledge, with the CIA.

Carter's answer was not a full answer. He did not say that Shcharansky had "no connection with any intelligence organization of the United States or any allied power." He also relied totally on the CIA's investigation for him and the State Department—the White House did none of its own. I am not confident today that I know all the facts.

The day after Carter's announcement the Soviets produced their star witness, Aleksandr Lipavsky, who had shared a flat with Shcharansky. He testified that Shcharansky had received monies from the CIA and had furnished the CIA and Western newsmen with confidential information. The "confidential information" was more often than not available to the general public.

Further facts were developed adding to the espionage case against Shcharansky. Shcharansky had particularly close contact with the *Los Angeles Times* Moscow correspondent Robert Toth. Eager to demonstrate that the Russians were denying exit visas to Russian Jews in civilian jobs on the false grounds that they possessed military secrets, Shcharansky furnished Toth with lists of names and workplaces of those who had been refused permission to emigrate. Toth subsequently reported in the *Times*: "Jews who worked on three 'oceanographic research vessels' . . . had been denied permission to emigrate on the grounds that they 'learned their secrets at their former workplaces.' This suggested that the research vessels were actually spy ships." As Jack Nelson of the *Washington Post* wrote: "Unfortunately for Shcharansky—and for Toth—this speculation was absolutely correct. 'What Shcharansky did, in effect, was give Toth a list of secret defense plants,' a U.S. official said. And Toth printed the list."

Making matters worse for Shcharansky was the fallout from a trip to Moscow by Lieutenant General Samuel Wilson, then the head of the Defense Intelligence Agency, which had been compiling a catalog of Soviet military installations as a result of the Shcharansky-Toth collaboration. Major Robert Watters, at that time a U.S. military attaché in Moscow (and thus by definition an authorized spy), asked Toth and another American journalist to meet Wilson. Watters subsequently sent Toth a note saying that Wilson considered his analyses to be excellent. The note was retrieved by someone Nelson called "a drunken janitor" known as Mashina Sasha, or Masha's Sasha, after his wife. Sasha promptly turned Watter's note over to the KGB, which just as promptly called in Toth for questioning, at the end of which Toth according to the KGB admitted that Shcharansky had provided him with the names of the refuseniks and their workplaces. Toth denied having done so.

Years later Nicholas Daniloff was arrested in Moscow in August 1986 and jailed on spying charges similar to those the Soviet government made against Toth. With this testimony in the Shcharansky trial, it became crystal clear that even if Lipavsky and the other witnesses were not to be believed, the Soviets wanted the Shcharansky case to send a message to the American people and the world that opposition was treason and President Carter's intervention was tantamount to an attempt at subversion. If the Western world did not believe that the dissidents had been paid, knowing accomplices of the CIA, then certainly many Russians and their allies did.

On the last day of the trial, six days after it began, Shcharansky, now thirty years old and a pawn in the game of big-power politics, was sentenced to a thirteen-year sentence, three in prison and ten in a strict-regime labor camp in remote Tataria.

After the trial, on September 10, 1977, Yuri Andropov, then the head of the KGB, in a speech at a special meeting of Soviet and KGB officials, attacked Carter's defense of Shcharansky. He also defined the limits of free speech in the Soviet Union.

> This is why Western propaganda makes so much fuss about "human rights" and about the so-called "dissidents." . . . Soviet citizens have the right to criticize and to make proposals. This right is guaranteed by Article 49 of the Constitution, which forbids repression of criticism. . . . But it is an entirely different matter when a few individuals transform criticism into anti-Soviet activity, violate the law, and supply Western propaganda centers with false information, disseminate false rumours, try to organize antisocial actions. . . . These renegades have no support from the Soviet people. This is why they never try to make open speeches in factories or on collective farms or in other state organizations. They know very well they would be thrown out of such meetings. The existence of dissidents in the Soviet Union is only possible because of publicity campaigns in the foreign press, and support for them through diplomatic, secret and other special services who pay "dissidents" generously in foreign currency and by other

means. There is no difference between the payment which secret services make to their own agents and to dissidents. . . .

But Andropov's attack was more subtle than those of other Russian leaders. Not all dissidents were, like Shcharansky, paid agents of the CIA, he said. Many of them

. . . do not understand the real truth. These people are given advice and explanations to help them to understand reality. . . . By the way, it must be said that the number of people who are now sentenced for anti-Soviet activity is much lower than in previous periods of Soviet history. There are just a few. . . . This is the real picture of the so-called problem of "dissent."

Speaking to French and West German television correspondents on July 12, 1978, President Carter responded by condemning Shcharansky's and Orlov's trials as an attack on every human being who lives in the world who believes in basic freedoms and is willing to speak out for those freedoms or fight for them.

For a while nothing was heard of Shcharansky or of Orlov or Slepak. Their families could not see them. Then, on October 13, 1980, a British group working on behalf of Soviet Jews received news of Shcharansky. Claiming he was actually resisting his captors, the group said that he had suffered a fall at the prison that rendered him unconscious. He was taken to the hospital, suffering from back and stomach pains, and was receiving antibiotics. He now weighed ninety pounds, at least seventy pounds less than when I had seen him last. Having been in isolation for months at a time, engaged in numerous fasts, he was also reported to have been continually beaten in prison.

That was five years ago.

Today Vladimir Slepak, who spent those same years in exile in eastern Russia, where, he said, it is so isolated that "they don't speak Russian," is back in Moscow. But his life has changed. Even as he lives today in the same apartment where I last saw him, the authorities have refused to issue him a *dopusk*, a form which would officially allow him to live in the city. He has been told if he starts trouble or begins seeing Westerners, he will be kicked out of Moscow. The wandering and suffering of people like the Mandelstams a generation before him thus may become his—going from city to city without a right to live in any of them, until exhausted and seeking only peace, they settle "voluntarily" in some Godforsaken place where no one will bother them.

Amner Zavurov, whose case originally brought me to Moscow, was released from jail four years ago, but got into trouble again because he started to see Western journalists in Tashkent. After being sent with his family to exile in Asiatic Russia he emigrated to Israel in 1984. Many Jewish activities in Tashkent, once the center of Jewish militancy, have been quashed.

Yuri Orlov, who has not drawn as much public attention as the others, has been less lucky. Sentenced to seven years in one of the worst Siberian labor camps, and five years in exile, he was due to be released from prison in February 1984. His sentence was then indefinitely extended. But on October 5, 1986, Orlov was sent to the United States as part of the trade for the American journalist Nicholas Daniloff. As with the Toth-Shcharansky connection, the Soviet Union linked Russian dissidents and American journalists as both working against the Soviet Union.

Andrei Sakharov's turn was next. He was arrested on January 22, 1980. Snatched by a limousine from a Moscow street on his way to a seminar, he was taken to the prosecutor's office. There, Aleksandr Rekunkov, the first deputy prosecutor, read Sakharov a decree of the Presidium of the Supreme Soviet, signed by Brezhnev, stripping him of his state honors. Without a trial and in clear violation of the Soviet Constitution, he was banished to Gorky, a major industrial city 250 miles east of Moscow. He, like Shcharansky, was punished because he sought to exercise his right of free speech.

Once in Gorky, Sakharov learned of further restrictions. He and Yelena Bonner would share a four-room apartment with a middle-aged woman whose function was not hard to guess. Thus, under official supervision, forbidden to leave the city, denied contact with foreigners, he was effectively isolated. Because of the presence of military factories, the town is officially closed to all foreigners.

Yet soon after Sakharov was thought to have been totally silenced, Yelena appeared in Moscow to read his statement deploring the Soviet Union's activities in Afghanistan. The government's reaction was fast. Two days later two men pretending to be drunken workers came to the Sakharov apartment with a pistol. Sakharov described the event. "They threatened to make an Afghanistan out of my apartment and wreak complete havoc. They said, 'Don't think you're going to be here for long. There's a place in a psychiatric hospital thirty kilometers from Gorky that's ready for you.' "

A local prosecutor then told Sakharov not to make any more statements. If there were to be further violations, Sakharov was told, his place and conditions of exile could be changed and sanctions could also be applied to his wife. Even so, he continued to smuggle out letters and articles to the West. Then, in early 1986, yielding to intense international pressure, the Soviets released Yelena Bonner for six months' medical treatment in the West and then allowed Sakharov to return to Moscow.

Nonetheless, the Russian dissident movement has received nearly fatal blows. It has not until very recently been as weak for at least two decades. The Moscow and Leningrad groups are broken up—their leaders either in external exile in the Russian East, in jails, or exiled to the West. No new Shcharansky or Sakharov (or, in fact, Solzhenitsyn) has yet emerged within the Soviet Union to lead the movement. It is still too early to tell if Mikhail S. Gorbachev's proposed sweeping changes will create a country in which dissent can flourish.

Attempts in the West to prevent convictions and severe punishment for the dissidents by publicizing the Orlov, Zavurov, Slepak, and Shcharansky trials, failed. But they may have played a large role in creating the new climate for Russian reform.

Surprisingly though, and, perversely, perhaps because of these successes, Yuri Andropov, who had he lived longer might have helped Gorbachev move the human rights dialogue along, wrote a letter to French Communist leader Georges Marchais hinting at Soviet willingness to release Anatoly Shcharansky. When Anatoly's mother, living in Russia, wrote directly to Andropov, she received a personal answer, not rejecting her appeal but instead telling her to write to the Supreme Soviet. She then met with KGB officials and was told her son would be released if he admitted guilt. Anatoly's mother, in a letter to her son, explained that he supposedly held the keys to his release and asked whether he would admit his guilt.

He wrote to his family explaining why he had to refuse. He

reminded them of the story of the scientist Galileo Galilei, who adhered to the monumental truth that the earth moved around the sun but allowed himself to succumb to pressure from the Inquisition and renounced his stand. At the very end of his life, it is said that he tried to take back his lie by uttering his famous words, "And yet it moves!" Many have used the example of Galileo's accommodation to authority, Shcharansky said, to justify their lives of concealment and fear.

"In addition to Newton's Law on the universal gravity of objects," Shcharansky continued, "there is also a law of the universal gravity of souls, of the bond between them, and the influence of one soul on the other. And it operates in this manner, such that with each word that we speak, and with each step that we take, we touch other souls and have an impact upon them.

"So why should I put this sin on my soul? If I already succeeded once in breaking with the difficult two-faced approach called for by this intolerable situation, closing the gap between thought and word, how is it now possible to take even one step backwards towards the previous status?"

From 1977 to 1986 Shcharansky's wife, aided by dozens of international groups, worked relentlessly on Shcharansky's behalf. Worldwide rallies were held, heads of state were visited, and legal briefs by me and others flowed into Russia. Shcharansky became an international figure as his letters to his wife, mother, and friends documented those terrible jail years as well as his refusal to be broken by his Soviet captors.

Finally, on February 11, 1986, Anatoly Shcharansky walked across the green metal span of the Glienicke Bridge in Berlin. He and three Germans accused of spying for the West were exchanged for five Soviet spies. It ended four months of negotiation. The West originally insisted that Andrei Sakharov be made part of the exchange. But the Russians refused, claiming that Sakharov still knew scientific secrets, although he had been out of the Soviet scientific community for years. The Soviets would be glad to be rid of Shcharansky, who had now become a public relations liability. But they too needed their symbolic victory as they released him.

A Soviet condition for Shcharansky's release was that the "spy exchange" take place over the "bridge of spies," the same bridge where Francis Gary Powers, the American pilot of a U-2 reconnaissance plane downed over the Soviet Union, was exchanged for convicted spy Colonel Rudolf Abel. In this way the Soviet Union was able to get its point across to the world that Shcharansky was convicted of spying for the CIA. Shcharansky may soon tell us how far he went in his opposition to his government.

President Reagan hailed the Shcharansky release as a victory for his policy. He claimed that in dealing with the Soviet Union on human rights issues a less combative approach is a more effective way of achieving not propaganda victories but real results. In March 1986 the president made good on his position, refusing to meet with Yelena Bonner.

When I last saw Shcharansky, he told me of his friends on trial and in labor camps. "Many of them have been rehabilitated." With sureness and sadness he said, "I won't let that happen to me." He didn't.

I've often wondered how men can knowingly walk into terrible prisons leaving family, friends, and material comfort behind. And what are the tools for survival? Everyone has a different version of what keeps him alive. It is not surprising that Shcharansky and Breytenbach describe their jail experiences differently.

The attitudes they took during their trials are similar to the attitudes they took in prison. Breytenbach had said he survived because he tried to live within his own body as if another person were inhabiting it. "In prison, if you want to survive you have to give, you have to let go. The more you cling to what you think is essentially yours, the more hold they have on you because they can exploit that." He says he looked deeply inside himself and was surprised to find there wasn't very much to look at. "When I did that, I think I let go of a sense of importance in myself, a sense of the importance of my own ideas, a sense of intellectual—and even more difficult to do—moral superiority."

Shcharansky, on the other hand, describes his fight in jail as a constant struggle to remain intellectually and morally superior to his captors. "I argued with them, refused to back down on anything. I went on hunger strikes to protest not only my treatment but also the treatment of others."

Shcharansky survived those years in Soviet camps and isolation cells, undergoing extreme physical and psychological pressure. He refused to crack. He remained in jail, as he was with me on the Moscow streets and in the prosecutor's office, a free man. I have met many political defendants in courtrooms and jails throughout the world. He is the freest man I ever met.

THE
UNITED STATES

24

Have we steered away from the self-righteous and strident, remembering that our record is not unblemished? . . . All these initiatives to further human rights abroad would have a hollow ring if we were not prepared to improve our own performance at home.

—Secretary of State Cyrus Vance
April 30, 1977

THE FIRST AMENDMENT, as interpreted by our courts, provides Americans with a far broader protection of free speech than obtains not only in South Africa, Chile, and the Soviet Union, but also in any other Western democracy. Yet other democracies are not seen as more restrictive than the United States. Most other democratic countries do not guarantee the right to advocate the overthrow of the government. Should we?

Clearly totalitarian countries, whether they be of the left or the right, do not permit such speech. Yet our tolerance of free political speech is also too limited. One result is that our ability to speak out on behalf of foreign dissidents is less effective than it ought to be.

When President Reagan and the Congress in 1984 criticized the Soviet treatment of Andrei Sakharov, the Soviets responded by pointing out that President Nixon's prosecutions of Indians in South Dakota at Wounded Knee were far worse than anything the Russians were accused of doing to Sakharov. Four Soviet Nobel Prize winners submitted an appeal to President Reagan that echoed the style of Western petitions on behalf of Sahkarov.

The Indian prosecutions, the Soviet appeal said, are "a typical example of politically motivated persecutions of Americans who are fighting for human rights, against tyranny and lawlessness, against the predatory practices of the government and the monopolies." Although the Soviet Union's appeal was wrongheaded, it did show the difficulty of countries in glass houses throwing stones.

But why is free speech so important, more important perhaps than other rights which are less abstract and are more capable of precise definition and regulation? Why should other countries in international agreements even pay lip service to a concept of free speech that permits extremist rhetoric?

Speech is given a unique primacy in our Bill of Rights and must also be accorded a preferred position in any global bill of rights. Any discussion of a global bill of rights must of necessity focus on the issue of how much speech can a society allow. By looking at what we do here we can help formulate a free speech theory we can adopt in the international documents.

We failed to meet that test at Wounded Knee in 1973. As one of the defense lawyers representing Indians at the Wounded Knee trials, I saw the federal government adopt a legal rationale that was nearly as indefensible as the legal theory constructed by the Chileans in their "Nuremberg trials." Using legal theories repudiated by our Constitution when we rejected English sedition law, federal authorities put on trial the spokesmen for the American Indian Movement. We treated political dissidents as traitors, and because of the fear of the local officials and the FBI, the United States Army was called out, in force, on the incredible pretext that a Communist stronghold was being established in this tiny, isolated South Dakota hamlet occupied by seventy Indians—a theory endorsed by the Nixon White House.

It all began on the evening of February 27, 1973, when several hundred Indians traveled to Wounded Knee, South Dakota, to make a symbolic stand against their mistreatment by local officials, the Bureau of Indian Affairs, and other federal government agencies. Soon after they issued a statement decrying the callousness of state and local governments, they were surrounded by the FBI, U.S. marshals, and BIA police.

A massive quasi-military operation was immediately mounted.

The excuse offered for this exercise was the Indians' brief detention of a few hostages. When Senators George McGovern and James Abourezk arrived at Wounded Knee a few days later, on March 1, to deplore the Indians' seizure of white hostages, they were told by Father Paul Manhardt, a Catholic priest, that those who wished to depart had already gone; those who stayed had done so voluntarily, not only to protect their property but because the village of Wounded Knee was their home. "We as a group of hostages decided to stay on to save the Indians and our own property," said Wilbur Riegert, who was eighty-two years old. "Had we not, those troops would have come down here and killed all of those people."

Ninety-six Indians with two dozen rifles remained. According to an Army intelligence report of March 4, 1973:

> The Indians do not appear intent upon inflicting harm upon the legitimate residents of Wounded Knee, nor upon the federal law enforcement agents operating in this area, even though small arms fire has been exchanged between opposing forces. Because of its isolated geographical location, the seizure and holding of Wounded Knee poses no threat to the Nation, to the State of South Dakota or the Pine Ridge Reservation itself.

This sensible assessment was ignored both by FBI head Clarence Kelley and by General George Crater of the United States Army, who wished to try out the Army's "Garden Plot" operation, designed in 1968 for use against civil disorders such as protests against the Vietnam War. Kelley ordered that men and weapons be sent, along with additional weapons to local law enforcement. This overreaction was thought essential as a result of an FBI report entitled "Disorder by American Indians and Supporters at Wounded Knee." The report stated that "individuals reportedly in or en route to Wounded Knee included not only Indians but representatives of such revolutionary-type organizations as the Vietnam Veterans Against the War, the Students for a Democratic Society, violence-prone Weathermen associates, the Marxist-Leninist Maoist Venceremos Organization, as well as representatives from a black extremist group."

Richard Wilson, the Bureau of Indian Affairs spokesman, announced by proclamation:

> What has happened at Wounded Knee is all part of a long-range plan of the Communist Party . . . there is no doubt that Wounded Knee is a major communist thrust. The supporters of AIM (the Indian organization) come in all shades and the National Council of Churches are very vocal because the liberal press and the TV news media is right at their elbow. No newsreporter or TV cameraman has ever won a war, but they can destroy a nation by the propaganda of lies and hate that they broadcast for every Crackpot, Screwball and Communist-front organization who wants to take a swat at our American way of life, take a blast at the U.S. Constitution, spit at the American flag, burn it, wear it as a poncho or hang it upside down.

At the very beginning the FBI agents were told by Kelley to "shoot to kill." It was the first time such orders had ever been given to the FBI when they were not on a manhunt.

When the Indians continued to refuse to leave Wounded Knee, Kelley of the FBI and Army Lieutenant Colonel Volney Warner announced, on March 4, 1973, that they would cut off food and other supplies and then move armed personnel in. For seventy-one days the FBI, BIA police, the United States Army, and U.S. marshals poured bullets into the tiny hamlet at Wounded Knee. On several separate days over twenty thousand pounds of ammunition were fired. Two Indians were killed; another eighteen Indians and three whites were wounded.

When the Indians surrendered, Indian leaders Dennis Banks and Russell Means and many of their supporters were prosecuted. The charges, brought in state and federal courts, ranged from petty crimes to serious felonies—from assaults to murder charges to conspiracy to attempt to rebel against the government. The defendants, faced with life sentences, tried to show that the military and local police started the violence and that it was illegal to use troops. They claimed that in order to mount this force Richard Nixon; General Alexander Haig, the White House chief of staff; Richard Kleindienst, then head of the Department of Justice; and our military commanders approved, in violation of the Constitution, the "further and continued and unceased" use of military forces to quell a "civilian disorder" that could "threaten the country."

Banks and Means offered evidence at the criminal trials in Lincoln, Nebraska, and St. Paul, Minnesota, showing that military officials, aware that they were breaking the law, which prohibited the use of the Army against American civilians, disguised men and equipment so that no one could know that the military was being used to quell a civilian disturbance. The Army deployed enough equipment to kill every Indian, as well as every white in South Dakota.

General Creighton Abrams, at Haig's direction, ordered Lieutenant Colonel Warner, Colonel Jack C. Potter, and twenty other Army officers to Wounded Knee, with their troops, to take charge of the onslaught, and directed that these men wear civilian clothes. Warner was then chief of staff at the Eighty-second Airborne Division, a full fighting division with special training in putting down civil disturbances; Potter was chief of logistics for the Sixth Army.

Lieutenant Colonel Warner, Colonel Potter, FBI men, and U.S. marshals at the scene testified that General Haig, as the White House representative, played the lead role violating the law and disguising the military forces. Because of this, Judge Fred J. Nichol in St. Paul and Judge Warren Urbom in Lincoln, Nebraska, ultimately found that nearly all of the Indians were not guilty.

The law, both judges said, is clear. Congress passed a statute in 1878 stating that no part of the armed forces could be used "to execute the domestic laws," except as expressly authorized by the Constitution or the Congress, and only after the issuance of a proclamation.

Federal troops have been seen in the South in our time. But that was a very different situation. In the 1950s and 1960s federal troops were called out in southern states when the federal government sought to enforce federal court orders requiring the end of segregated schools. First Dwight Eisenhower in Arkansas and then John Kennedy in Mississippi called out troops to protect blacks trying to enroll in white schools. But until Wounded Knee we had not, in the twentieth century, seen federal troops used in this country to apply force to attack local dissidents.

Other presidents have tried to blur the distinction between

the proper use of federal troops and state guardsmen. Most recently, in 1986, President Reagan tried to federalize Arizona's Air National Guard for service in Honduras. Because it was clear to Governor Bruce Babbitt that his state guardsmen were to be used to shuttle supplies for the Nicaraguan Contras, Babbitt refused. Three other governors refused similar requests.

The reason for the law prohibiting the use of troops to enforce "domestic laws" is simple. Before the Congress, the president, or military commanders can use their awesome powers to call out helicopters, tanks, and troops to be used aggressively against American citizens, the elected representatives of the people must first decide if the use of national force is necessary. No American court, Congress, or president had authorized the use of the Army since the statute was passed, over one hundred years ago. This restrictive law is analogous to the provision of the Chilean Constitution violated by Pinochet that requires the Chilean legislators to approve the use of troops against the Chilean people.

Because it was illegal for troops to be at Wounded Knee, officials of the Justice Department, the executive branch, the Army, and the FBI at the Nebraska and Minnesota trials at first denied that any military equipment or personnel were involved. The Department of Justice produced dozens of civilian witnesses who testified that no military uniforms were to be seen at Wounded Knee. But the defense lawyers subpoenaed, over the government's objections, Army records that proved troop and equipment deployment.

After being confronted with these Army records, Colonel Potter and Lieutenant Colonel Warner changed their testimony, admitting that military equipment was dropped off at various points miles away from Wounded Knee, taken out of marked military vehicles, transferred to civilian vehicles, and then driven to the scene by military men wearing civilian clothes. Warner and Potter admitted that they were in Wounded Knee for sixty-five of the seventy-one days in civilian clothes. They each admitted that never before in their years of service had they worn civilian clothes at "work." For the first time in their respective careers they had been ordered by their superior, General Creighton Abrams, to dress in mufti.

Judge Urbom, a Republican appointee to the federal trial bench, easily disposed of the Justice Department lawyer's argument that General Haig's failure to ask Congress for permission was only a technical oversight which should be excused:

> Congress provided that the President could use the military personnel in quelling civil disorders if he got a proclamation, but the President did not do so with respect to Wounded Knee. Congress could have passed and may yet pass legislation to permit the use of a limited or unlimited number of Army or Air Force personnel to assist law enforcement officers to execute their duties in a civil disorder without presidential order. But it has not done so. The people could have amended or could yet amend the Constitution to permit use of the military services under whatever circumstances they declare. But they have not done so. I am bound to follow the law as it is, not as it will or could become.

Both Judge Urbom and Judge Nichol upheld the rule of law against the vigorous opposition of Richard Nixon's Department of Justice. Both federal judges determined that the Army at Wounded Knee illegally used sixteen armored personnel carriers, 400,000 rounds of ammunition, 100 protective vests, a Phantom jet, 3 helicopters, 120 sniper rifles, 20 grenade launchers, and a host of other equipment. Lieutenant Colonel Warner, after strenuous, painstaking cross-examination, finally admitted having put two hundred men of the Eighty-second Airborne Division on twenty-four-hour alert; he admitted ordering in chemical warfare officers to teach civil law-enforcement officers how to use military grenade launchers; he admitted that the gas grenades were military equipment. Judge Nichol and Judge Urbom found that FBI men produced by John Mitchell, Nixon's attorney general, lied at the trial.

Against whom was this force mobilized? The few protesters of Wounded Knee never had more than twenty-four rifles. Most of the bullets from these guns could not reach the Army bunkers that surrounded Wounded Knee. Roger Ironcloud, a Vietnam veteran who was at Wounded Knee for all seventy-one days, said, "We took more bullets in seventy-one days than I took in two years in Vietnam. The Army fired at everything that moved."

Our top military and civilian leaders treated the Indians' stand at Wounded Knee as if a foreign enemy had invaded our shores. Lieutenant Colonel Warner admitted the use of the Rules of Engagement, which are part of the military contingency plan for foreign wars, and admitted that he compelled the FBI men and the U.S. marshals to follow those rules.

The Wounded Knee military action was part of a larger program. The Indians, with many other Americans, were for years targets of the FBI's COINTELPRO project, a program that systematically engaged in illegal surveillance and the wholesale violation of constitutional rights. The military action was seen as one small further step. Richard Nixon and Alexander Haig had come to believe that the Wounded Knee Indians in this country equalled a foreign threat to the government. Dissenters were viewed as foreign agents and dissent as treason.

So unfamiliar was I with the culture and history of the Indian conflict when I first took on the case, that the trial in Nebraska was in many ways as foreign an experience for me as was my representing members of the Basque separatist movement in Spain in 1975 or representing Indian labor leaders jailed by Indira Gandhi. There was as much hatred and violence by the white farmers and local officials of South Dakota against the Indians as there was by the whites against the blacks in South Africa. More than simply coincidence, this hatred and feeling that those dissenting are different and foreign helps the government to label dissenters as traitors.

The profound racism of South Dakota was new to me. When, during the preliminary examination of jurors, I asked my Indian client, six-foot, 220-pound Wallace Little, to stand, the potential jurors pulled back from him in fear. The women were most frightened. Once they had seen him stand, they could hardly take their eyes off him. It was not his size alone that scared them. They half expected him to go wild in the courtroom. The hatred of many of the white citizens of Nebraska, North Dakota, and South Dakota for the Indians is deep, palpable, and immovable, just as is the hatred of many southerners for the blacks.

The legal system reflects this. Although Indians are a sizable population in South Dakota, and most defendants in local criminal cases are Indian, even today Indians rarely sit on juries. Lengthy hearings by the United States Commission on Civil Rights concluded late in 1977 that it is "very difficult" for an Indian to obtain a fair trial and nearly impossible if he has "traditional lifestyles." Long hair is taken to be a symbol of dissent and, frequently, treason. Like the black, the Indian is different and therefore dangerous.

The FBI officials' conduct at Wounded Knee was unique in its arrogance. There were 562 men arrested, but of the 185 indicted, only 16 were convicted. In 1974 the conviction rate for indictments disposed of by the federal courts having jurisdiction in South Dakota was 78.2 percent. The conviction rate for Wounded Knee cases was 7.7 percent. The FBI's use of perjured testimony was widespread. It ultimately formed the basis for the dismissal of nearly all the Wounded Knee cases. In 1981 Amnesty International, after a lengthy investigation, issued a "Proposal for a Commission on Inquiry into the Effect of Domestic Intelligence Activities on Criminal Trials in the United States," which concluded that the FBI officials at Wounded Knee "abused their power by producing false evidence and infiltrating the defense teams of people indicted on serious charges."

FBI officials, even after the acquittals, justified their harsh action on the ground that the Red menace now had armed support in the Midwest, that treason was afoot. They believed Richard Wilson of the Bureau of Indian Affairs, who said that Wounded Knee is all part of a long-range plan of the Communist Party. The FBI gave him "facts" to back up his accusation. Louis Moves Camp, a government informer, claimed he was present when Dennis Banks and Russell Means met with representatives of Russia and China on an Indian reservation in North Dakota. Moves Camp also testified he saw the deliberate "execution-style" killing of whites by Indians. When Judge Nichol asked the United States attorneys why they offered Moves Camp's absurd testimony, they replied that FBI officials had no reason to believe the witness was lying. This was pure falsehood.

Judge Nichol gave an outraged denunciation of the FBI as well as the United States attorney's office when the defense proved, through television tapes, that at the exact time that Moves Camp claimed the meetings and killings took place, he was in California at a political rally. At Wounded Knee, when the specter of dissent was raised, the authorities overreacted by trampling on the law.

The prosecutors were, to use the words of William Blackstone, the great English scholar, "engines of the state, not of law." What James Wilson told our Constitutional Convention in 1778 is as true today as it was then: "Crimes against the state! And against the officers of the state! History informs us that more wrong may be done on this subject than on any other whatsoever."

Early in the Wounded Knee cases, the defense lawyers argued that the government's misconduct in South Dakota was as great as the government's misconduct that led to the dismissal of the case against another "traitor," Daniel Ellsberg.

At first Judge Fred Nichol, presiding over the main Wounded Knee trial, disagreed with the Ellsberg analogy and denied all of the defendants' pretrial motions to dismiss the case. But he changed his mind when faced with the proof at trial that the government deliberately offered Moves Camp's perjured testimony, withheld and destroyed documents critical to the defense, illegally used military personnel at Wounded Knee, and then covered up that use. Judge Nichol said: "The fact that incidents of misconduct formed a pattern throughout the course of the trial leads me to believe that this case was not prosecuted in good faith or in the spirit of justice. The waters of justice have been polluted and dismissal, I believe, is the appropriate cure for the pollution in this case."

Dennis Pryor, Amnesty's observer at the Wounded Knee trials, a leading London barrister, concluded the FBI agents dishonestly manipulated the criminal process, because, he said, the FBI believed the Indians were traitors. Pryor pointed out that because of the "extraordinary number of unresolved homicides on the reservation and incidents of terror and violence which have become almost commonplace, the sentiment prevails that life is cheap on the Pine Ridge Reservation." Pryor continued, "A contrast is seen between the Wamblee incident where three Indians were killed and shooting was allowed to continue over four days and the incident on June 26, 1975, when two FBI agents were shot and nearly 300 combat-clad agents, along with the trappings and armaments of a modern army, were brought in to 'control the situation' and fire on the 'killers.' "

Rather than deal with the social problems that lead to despair on the reservations, the Department of Justice lawyer resurrected antiquated statutes of questionable validity and used them to prosecute both those they believed had taken part in the uprising and those who only spoke out against Washington officials. Defendants were shot at and attacked because of what they said rather than what they did. According to Arthur Flemming, chairman of the Civil Rights Commission, the usual processes of law were totally ignored during the Wounded Knee prosecutions. The commission, in a 1976 report, concluded that the Indians "cannot count on equal protection of the law at the hands of the FBI or the BIA police. Most Indians justifiably fear that the FBI is 'out to get them' because of the involvement at Wounded Knee and other crisis situations." Ken Tilsen, a defense lawyer at Wounded Knee, summed up his conclusions in a paper given in 1984 at the University of Minnesota Law School. "The FBI is a national political police organization dedicated to punishing those it perceives to be its enemies. The claim of equal justice under the law as enforced by the FBI for those whose political outlook differs from the FBI is a mockery."

Unfortunately, prosecutions such as these have a long history in this country. The exercise of the right of free speech in this country must be considered against both the background of the Constitution and legislation which protects society against conduct that traditionally falls outside of the area of protected expression. The precedents derive from English law.

In 1352 Parliament enacted an elaborate statute that described treason (in part) as "compassing" or "imagining the death of the King, defiling the King's wife, levying war against the King, adhering to his enemies," and sundry other categories. The preamble of the statute establishes that the purpose of the law was to narrow the definition of treason and to limit the crown's then unbridled discretion. But, of course, the king still had more than enough room to punish anyone critical of his family and reign.

John Stubbs, the author of an attack on the prospective marriage of Queen Elizabeth (I) to a Frenchman, was tried in 1579, together with his printer and publisher, in a proceeding that common pleas Judge Robert Monson denounced as illegal. In response to that denunciation, Monson himself was sent to Fleet Prison. When he refused to recant, he was removed from the bench. After the jailer had chopped off Stubbs' right hand, he lifted his hat with his left hand, cried out before the marketplace at Westminster, "God save the Queen," and was carried off insensible. When the cauterizing iron was then applied to the publisher's bleeding stump, he, looking at his severed hand as he was led away, cried out: "I have left there the hand of a true Englishman."

Although the Stuarts at times spared critics of the government some of the extreme punishment reserved for traitors, the marks they bore upon their bodies served as an impressive public advertisement of the dangers of dissent—perhaps an even more efficacious warning to the populace than the spectacle of a public killing. With his nose slit or his ears cut off, the dissenter would serve as a living witness to the infallible power of authority. William Prynne, for example, lost his ears for his mild reproach of what he considered to be Charles I's too tolerant attitude toward the theater and disregard for Puritanism.

The eighteenth century, the "Age of Revolution," eased the intensity by which the concept of treason was applied to criticism of the ruler, but at the same time a new concept of treason emerged, one that spoke of injury to the nation rather than injury exclusively to the ruler who personally embodied the nation.

This expanded definition permitted heads of state of punish dissidents on a greater, more brutal scale. The leaders saw it as their role to use treason laws to protect against the destruction of a people or state, or even a people's revolution, as was then taking place here and in France. Doing so was seen as both a larger and less specific offense. As the intensity and degree of abstraction of treason or counterrevolutionary activity increased, the nature of the offenses increased as the nature of the offenses broadened.

Our forefathers, at the center of the developments of the day, were mindful that "if the crime of treason be indeterminate," as James Madison said, "this alone is sufficient to make any government degenerate into arbitrary power." They therefore attempted to delimit the classification and punishment of dissenters as traitors, and retained only two of the categories set forth in the 1352 law of Parliament—levying war against the sovereign and adhering to its enemies.

Thus, Richard Nixon's Department of Justice could not charge the main defendants, Russell Means and Dennis Banks, outspoken critics of the government's handling of Indian affairs, with treason, for the mere criticism of the government is not treason in American law. Rather, in a treason case the government must prove commission of an overt act against the United States in support of an enemy of the state. But because the Wounded Knee Indians could not be shown to have levied war against our nation or to have helped an enemy of it, the Justice Department had to look elsewhere for a law to prosecute them.

They found it. Under the Federal Rebellion Statute, passed in 1848 during the time of revolutionary uprisings in Mexico and Europe, if a defendant in a speech "incites" rebellion, he can be jailed for ten years. Worse, if he advocates overthrow of the government in a pamphlet, he can be jailed for twenty years. Constitutional arguments made at the time that the statute restricts free speech failed; and the statute became, as a consequence, a precursor of the twentieth century's broader treason laws.

And yet by attacking the Indians for, among other things, "advocating" the overthrow of the government under this statute, the prosecutors were proceeding under an unconstitutional concept. Indeed, it is hard to believe that James Madison, author of the First Amendment, would have agreed expression could be made punishable if only the label were shifted from treason to advocacy or some other tag. In fact, in the journal of the Constitutional Convention kept by Madison himself, he is recorded as saying that the language of the treason clause "was too narrow," that it should be made clear how broad the protection envisioned by the drafters of the clause really was.

There is an opposing argument, namely that the First Amendment defines the limits of free speech and can be interpreted to permit the prosecution of treasonous words. But the mention of Madison naturally suggests the question why the First Amendment was thought necessary if criticism in a political context was understood to be protected by the restrictive implications of the treason clause. The answer is that the treason clause was thought of as a political guarantee, whereas the tradition in the First Amendment is a statement relating solely to expression.

The Bill of Rights was added to the Constitution out of an abundance of caution, as an additional concession to the substantial opposition to it based on fear of the implications that might lurk in the new document. Many thought the entire Bill of Rights was unnecessary because the Constitution already protected all the rights in the Bill. When Patrick Henry voiced fears of the use of charges other than treason to suppress political criticism, George Nicholas, a delegate to the Constitutional Convention, tried to allay those fears by citing the careful definition of treason and declaring, "This security does away with the objection that the most grievous oppressions might happen under color of punishing crimes against the general government."

Although many aspects of American treason law are unclear, our courts, unlike many other foreign courts, have tried to set forth criteria as they seek to protect speech and still punish overt acts that could destroy the state. Dealing with this issue in the 1945 Cramer case, the United States Supreme Court said, "A citizen may take actions which do aid and comfort the enemy— making a speech critical of the government or opposing its measures, profiteering, striking in defense plants or essential work, and the hundred other things which impair our cohesion and diminish our strength—but if there is no adherence to the enemy in this, if there is no intent to betray, there is no treason."

Nonetheless, it is difficult to understand what "intent to betray" means. It is no more precise than the Soviet's test of "agitation or propaganda carried out with the purpose of overthrowing the Soviet regime," or the South African test of punishing one who endangers the "life of the Republic." And at Wounded Knee, these legal ambiguities were also in evidence.

The history of the treason clause of the Constitution makes it clear that the framers rejected the English doctrine of constructive treason which converted written or spoken words into overt acts punishable by the criminal law. Speech alone calling for revolution or rebellion cannot be a criminal act. The treason clause explicitly prohibits criminal prosecution unless based on criminal actions.

Of course, even if Banks and Means had committed treason, the government had no right to move in troops. Article IV, Section 4 of the Constitution states: "The United States shall guarantee to every state in this Union a republican form of government. . . ." Only when that guarantee is threatened may the federal government intervene on its own initiative. The Department of Justice's claim that Banks and Means and their handful of followers imperiled South Dakota's republican form of government was preposterous. That they should have singled them out for leading a rebellion was equally preposterous.

Nonetheless, the use by the Justice Department of legal precedents such as the Federal Rebellion Statute to indict the men at Wounded Knee was also supplemented by other statutes passed early in this century to stifle dissent and to punish speech during the era of the First World War and the "Red scare" immediately following it. That Chilean Supreme Court Justice Urrutía would refer to these very same precedents when he argued that Pinochet was justified in charging Allende's ministers with treason is a telling irony.

25

U PON AMERICA'S declaration of war in 1917, constitutional definitions of the treason clause notwithstanding, the Congress enacted new legislation to stifle dissent. The result, the Espionage Act of 1917, by virtue of the interpretation the statute was given by the courts, resurrected the rejected doctrine of constructive treason and converted written or spoken language into overt acts punishable by criminal law. Now a new series of crimes was created. A citizen could henceforth be punished for being "disloyal" by criticizing the government.

The act made it a federal crime, punishable by death, to "willfully make or convey false reports or false statements with intent to interfere with the operation or success of the [armed forces of the United States] or to promote the success of its enemies," to "willfully cause or attempt to cause insubordination, disloyalty, mutiny, or refusal of duty," or to "willfully obstruct . . . recruiting or enlistment." The next year Congress went even further, adding more offenses, including "uttering, printing, writing, or publishing any disloyal, profane, scurrilous, or abusive language, or language intended to cause contempt, scorn or disrepute as regards the form of government of the United States, the Constitution, the flag, the uniform of the Army or Navy, or any language intended to incite resistance to the United States or promote the cause of its enemies."

Mere speech without any criminal act accompanying it could now result in strong punishment. The statute's political reasoning, like that of the prosecutors' theories in the South African, Chilean, and Soviet Union cases, is that the people are run by the state and that their rulers know what is best for them. But the opening phrase of our Constitution, "We the People," emphasizes a concept totally at variance with this argument. Our courts should then have held that these prosecutions violated the treason clause as well as the First Amendment.

Yet the judicial decisions upholding convictions under the Espionage Act showed the reluctance of courts to rule against public feeling of the day. As a result, over two thousand criminal prosecutions under the act were affirmed by the lower appellate courts. But many thought that the Supreme Court, led by Justice Oliver Wendell Holmes, would reverse these convictions.

Unfortunately, the Court's opinions, and primarily the opinions of Holmes, did just the opposite. Not only were most of the convictions for opponents of government policy sustained by the Court, but its 1919 decisions on the landmark case *Schenck* v. *United States* also severely proscribed freedom of speech for this century.

The defendant, Charles Schenck, was a socialist who published fifteen thousand pamphlets to draftees criticizing the draft. Claiming the draft violated the Constitution, Schenck argued that it should be resisted by legal means. Schenck was indicted under the Espionage Act, tried, and convicted. He faced twenty years in jail even though there was no proof that a single person refused to fight because of the statements made in the pamphlets. He appealed and lost.

Writing for the majority, Justice Holmes rejected the claim that expression was entitled to special judicial protection. He said, as he affirmed the conviction, that expression could be criminally punished when the words caused a "clear and present danger to the state"—a legal standard that sounds as if it gives broad protection to the government's critics, but is in fact so vague that it gave juries and judges the latitude to punish whatever speech they did not like. Justice Holmes was not content to rest upon the express words of the protesters. He looked to innuendo, insinuation, and intimidation to support the conviction. He completely ignored the

Constitution's treason clause requirement of an overt, physical act when he said that speech was an overt act.

Justice Holmes' ruling permitted juries to punish speech on the basis of a potential future danger. Henceforth, there could be a conviction even if the act urged by the speaker never occurred. And if it did occur, a jury could rationalize its decision by deciding, without proof, that the act was caused by the speech. Although Holmes said that the clear-and-present-danger test would give the maximum protection that critics of the government were entitled to, he soon learned that the test could be used to punish speech that even he thought should be protected. He should have known juries in times of social unrest are not usually protective of individual rights.

The presumption of innocence is absent from this and all the World War I "Red scare" cases. The defendants were punished because they were socialists—just as the law was similarly applied in South Africa's Suppression of Communism Act which punishes by life imprisonment anyone who advocates "the establishment of a despotic system of government based on the dictatorship of the proletariat."

The enduring metaphor of the *Schenck* case comes in the celebrated sentence "The most stringent protection of free speech would not protect a man in falsely shouting fire in a theatre and causing a panic." These powerful words have affected free speech law and thinking ever since.

But the false shouting of "fire" in a theater and the printing of controversial pamphlets are two totally different events, with different values to be protected. There is no *social* value to creating a panic in a theater, but there ought to be no question of the right of an audience to hear words critical of the government. A metaphor like Holmes' compels the mind by direct appeal to the sensuous imagination: the horrifying image of panic-stricken theatergoers, rushing for the exits in darkness and confusion, the weak falling under the stampede of the strong—a nightmare. Holmes' metaphor replaces thought and sets the passions in motion. The man falsely screaming "fire" provokes anger, indignation, and an urge for revenge. It is easy to see how readily these emotions transfer to a political defendant, already despised by the juries and judges for his political views. Envision the imaginary theater at home as the theater of war, the miscreant shouting "fire" as the forces of dissent, and see how an entire civilization can fall.

Ever since Holmes' decision, images of flames, metaphors casting language as pyrotechnics and incendiarism, and dissent as inflammation run through the epic of free speech cases. Holmes used the fire image again in later cases. In upholding a 1920 felony conviction based on a newspaper article which "deplored the draft riots in Oklahoma," Holmes said the prosecution was proper because the paper might be circulated in quarters "where a little breath would be enough to kindle a flame."

Holmes' votes with the majorities in two subsequent cases of convictions further showed the danger of the *Schenck* test. One involved the author of critical articles on the constitutionality of the draft and the purposes of the war, and the other, so well known that it was referred to by Chile's Chief Justice Urrutía, sent Eugene Debs to prison for a speech at a socialist rally in which he very mildly condemned the war as a contest between competing capitalist classes. Debs' most provocative statement, "You need to know you are fit for something better than slavery and cannon fodder," resulted in a ten-year prison sentence. Many American citizens did not believe Debs was guilty, for while in prison in 1920, Debs received 919,799 votes as the socialist candidate for president. George McGovern might as well have been sent to prison for his criticism of the Vietnam War.

Holmes, in his letters to his friend Harold Laski, set forth a simplistic speech theory when he said, "We should deal with the act of speech as we deal with any overt act we don't like." When Holmes made it clear he thought "Debs's ideas were not of value" and could not understand why anyone paid attention to them, Laski replied, "The Espionage Act tends to mean the prosecution of all one's opponents who are unimportant enough not to arouse public opinion." And when Holmes said to Laski, "The federal judges seem to me (again between ourselves) to have got hysterical about the war," he should have included himself.

These Holmes decisions came, in the words of his contemporary Harvard law professor Zechariah Chafee, Jr., as "a great shock to forward-looking men and women who had consoled themselves through the war-time trials with the hope that the Espionage Act would be unvalidated when it reached the Supreme Court." "They were especially grieved," Chafee went on in his classic work *Free Speech in the United States*, that "the opinions which dashed this hope were written by the Justice who for their eyes had long taken on heroic dimensions."

Holmes has his defenders. Many scholars still applaud the clear-and-present-danger test and today claim that if Holmes had urged a test giving speech absolute protection he would not have persuaded a single colleague on the court and many more men would have gone to prison. After all, a judge who is trying to establish a doctrine which the Supreme Court will promulgate as law cannot act like a solitary philosopher. He has to convince at least four other men in a specific group and convince them very quickly. Holmes' supporters likened his critics to the mother who, after her son's life is saved, yells at the lifeguard for not bringing back the boy's raft.

But he need not have tried to establish a new doctrine. The true task incumbent upon him was simply to remind his brethren of fundamental principles established long before. Recently published exchanges of correspondence between the great American jurist Learned Hand and Holmes show that Holmes was both very much committed to the preservation of the status quo and truly hostile to critics of authority. Holmes must have known that his "innuendo" approach rendered impossible any objective examination of the government's case against dissenters. Under Holmes' approach the jury is invited to guess at both the dissenters' motives and the probability of danger. Conviction without the necessity of proof that the country is in immediate danger is a near certainty.

Holmes and Justice Louis Brandeis (who also participated in the *Schenck* decision), while remaining faithful to the clear-and-present-danger test, increasingly became disturbed by the broad indictments the Justice Department lawyers brought. As a result, Holmes began to try to cut back and narrow the prohibitions of expression under the test he had created. This is a wonderful irony.

The following year Holmes dissented in *Abrams* v. *United States*, a case that earlier might have seen him vote for conviction. In that case the espionage convictions of mainly Russian-born and Jewish defendants for aiding the Germans was based on a leaflet. The defendants had showered English and Yiddish leaflets from a window of a loft building upon the streets of Manhattan's Lower

East Side denouncing American intervention in the Russian Revolution and calling for a general strike to prevent weapons shipments to anti-Soviet forces. For this, defendant Jacob Abrams received a monstrously excessive twenty-year sentence.

The majority of the Court said the advocacy of actions such as a general strike would affect the war effort against Germany even though "intent to injure," as required by the Espionage Act, was not present. The defense argued that there was no intent to affect the war against Germany. The Court imputed to Abrams and his friends the knowledge that strikes in munitions factories would cripple the war effort against Germany as well as operations in Russia.

Abrams' lawyers, citing the treason clause's prohibition of punishment for mere expression in speech, argued that the state cannot punish speech by calling it something different, espionage. This argument, which gets to the heart of the issue, was neatly sidestepped by Holmes' dissent:

> Congress certainly cannot forbid all effort to change the mind of the country. Now nobody can suppose that the surreptitious publishing of a silly leaflet by an unknown man . . . would present any immediate danger, that its opinions would hinder the success of the government or have any appreciable tendency to do so. . . . When men have realized that time has upset many fighting faiths, they may come to believe . . . that the ultimate good desired is better reached by free trade in ideas—that the best test of truth is the power of thought to get itself accepted in the competition of the market, and that truth is the only ground on which their wishes safely can be carried out. That at any rate is the theory of our Constitution.

Holmes' words supporting the marketplace of ideas have been called by Professor Frank Murphy, a liberal scholar, the "most eloquent and moving defense of free speech since Milton's *Areopagitica.*" But what Holmes may have been doing was masterfully concealing his evasions with a powerful rhetoric fully capable of playing to the hysterical fears of the day.

One cynical interpretation of Holmes' dissent might be that speech is protected only as long as it is ineffective. One cannot ignore Holmes' description of the materials he would protect—the "silly pamphlet published by an unknown man," the poor and puny anonymities "too insignificant to turn the color of legal litmus paper."

Most civil libertarians applauded, however, as they saw Holmes shift. Judge Hand did not. He foresaw that the Holmes dissent would not stem the tide. Hand was correct; the clear-and-present-danger test justified further judicial and legislative excess. After World War I and the Russian Revolution, when various forms of American radicalism blossomed, there followed a period of hysterical reaction, usually referred to as the "Red scare."

State legislatures enacted new sedition, criminal anarchy, and syndicalism laws; thirty-two states forbade the flying of a red flag; and the New York legislature expelled five socialists. Socialist Victor Berger was twice denied a seat he won in the United States House of Representatives; the federal government deported many aliens for their beliefs; and in 1920 Attorney General Alexander Palmer (assisted by a young federal agent named J. Edgar Hoover) conducted the infamous Palmer raids, scooping up twenty-one hundred men and women, primarily Finnish, German, and Russian, whom he designated as traitors.

Harvard alumni and Justice Department officials sought to have Professor Chafee fired for writing in a law review article that the *Schenck* decision's clear-and-present-danger test of the previous year wrongfully gave docile juries unbridled discretion in times of crisis. Charges that he was "unfit as a law school professor" were rejected, but only after a hearing at the Harvard Club. The feeling on behalf of some government officials then was in many regards similar to that in Chile under Pinochet: The socialists, and Communists with their treasonous ideology, were enemies of the people who should be removed from the body politic.

Extraordinarily harsh sentences were handed out during the World War I espionage trials. Our federal judges condemned eleven persons to prison for ten years, six for fifteen years, and twenty-four for twenty years. Federal Judge Frank Van Valkenburgh, in 1924, summed up the Espionage Act's effect in a dissent when he said that freedom of speech now means only the protection of "criticism which is friendly to the government, friendly to the war, friendly to the policies of the government."

After World War I Holmes, along with Justice Brandeis, continued to press for an interpretation of the clear-and-present-danger test that would keep the test but also permit greater freedom of expression than the test actually allowed. Yet Holmes never succeeded in formulating a new standard, nor did he reject the test he established.

Twenty years after Holmes left the bench, the Supreme Court was still harping on the fire image in affirming speech convictions. The "little breath" that "could kindle a flame" had by the 1950s become "the inflammable nature of world conditions." This time fire imagery was summoned to justify the government's acting preventively, striking before the iron was hot, rather than waiting until an overt act was committed.

The government's case in this instance, a watershed for the clear-and-present-danger test, was the famous *Dennis* case in which eleven Communists were successfully prosecuted in 1951 under the Smith Act of 1940 for, according to the Supreme Court majority, subscribing to and organizing to teach others Marxist-Leninist thought. The Smith legislation had created new crimes, making anyone punishable who "knowingly or willfully advocates . . . or teaches the duty . . . or propriety of overthrowing . . . the government of the United States by force or violence."

The case ran from January 20 to September 23, 1949. Witnesses gave seventeen thousand pages of testimony. Judge Harold Medina held five defense lawyers in contempt. The Supreme Court in 1951 affirmed the convictions with five opinions. Four of the opinions gave differing interpretations of the clear-and-present-danger test. Justice Felix Frankfurter, in the fifth opinion, rejecting the clear-and-present-danger test, articulated a new free speech balancing test and found as he applied his criteria that the interest in national security overrode the *Dennis* defendants' free speech rights. Justices Hugo Black and William O. Douglas voted to free the defendants.

Black, rejecting the clear-and-present-danger test, said:

These [defendants] were not charged with . . . overt acts of any kind designed to overthrow the Government. They were not even charged with saying anything or with writing anything designed to overthrow the Government. The charge was that they agreed to assemble and to talk and to publish certain ideas at a later date.

The indictment is that they conspired to organize The Communist Party and to use speech or newspapers and other publications in the future to teach and advocate the forcible overthrow of the Government. No matter how it is worded, this is a virulent form of prior censorship of speech and press which I believe the First Amendment forbids.

"Undoubtedly," Black wrote, "a governmental policy of unfettered communication of ideas does entail dangers that the Founders of the Nation realized; however, the benefits derived from free expression are worth the risk." Very few nations are willing to take this risk. Black believed that our government must take risks that South Africa, Chile, and Russia are not prepared to take. Black's conclusion, that the benefits for a country of free discourse outweigh the dangers, was rejected by Justice Boshoff of South Africa, Justice Urrutía of Chile, and the prosecutors of Amner Zavurov in my arguments with them.

Justice Douglas, agreeing with Black's opinion in *Dennis*, said, "What these petitioners did was to [teach and] organize people to teach the Marxist-Leninist doctrine obtained chiefly in four books: Stalin's *Foundations of Leninism* (1924); Marx and Engels' *Manifesto of the Communist Party* (1848); Lenin's *The State and Revolution* (1917); and the *History of the Communist Party of the Soviet Union* (1939)." He went on to point out that the majority opinion of the Court "does not disallow these texts nor condemn them to the fire, as the communists do literature offensive to their creed. But if the books themselves are not outlawed, if they can lawfully remain on library shelves, by what reasoning does their use in a classroom constitute a crime?"

It seems clear that the Smith Act prosecutions violate the treason clause although no Court has said so. Perhaps the best explanation for this is that, as by Holmes in the Abrams case, the treason clause has been simply avoided, rather than rejected for reasons of principle. Holmes, supposedly writing on a clean slate, pushed the law and all free speech analysis down a certain path with his *Schenck* decision in 1919. But the Smith Act, since it creates a crime against "the established order of government," falls squarely within the historic domain of treason. And what the act makes criminal is expression, and not physical acts injurious to the state.

In fact, as Justices Black and Douglas pointed out in their dissents in *Dennis*, the defendants were convicted without a shred of evidence of acts of espionage or any other overt act injurious to the government. In this context the Smith Act could and should have been held void because of the "overt act" limitation—the historic mode of confining government discretion over dissident expression—of the treason clause of the Constitution.

As Justice Douglas wrote in his dissent, the "First Amendment reflects the philosophy of Jefferson 'that it is time enough for the rightful purposes of civil government, for its officers to interfere when principles break out into overt acts against peace and good order.'" Rather than relying on oblique "reflections" of the First Amendment, Douglas could have flatly asserted that the treason clause requires an overt act of "levying war or adhering to an enemy" of the United States.

The five different *Dennis* opinions showed that the clear-and-present-danger test was so subjective and capable of differing interpretations as to be nearly meaningless and, as a result, unfair. But the *Dennis* affirmance unleashed the prosecutors. They claimed the majority view of the clear-and-present-danger test was sufficiently precise. Immediately, dozens of grand juries were impaneled.

As a result of the *Dennis* decision, the government indicted an additional 141 people under the Smith Act and convicted 89 of them for having, as Black put it, views that were not safe. Six years later, however, another case, *Yates* v. *United States*, reversed the convictions of fourteen defendants charged with the same crimes as the *Dennis* defendants, and put an end to most of these prosecutions. Justice John Marshall Harlan, now writing for four members of the Court, said that the Constitution fully protects "advocacy of ideas," a view that Holmes never truly agreed with. "The essential distinction," said Harlan, "is that those to whom the advocacy is addressed must be urged to *do* something, now or in the future, rather than merely to *believe* in something." A law can prohibit "advocacy of action," but not "advocacy of ideas," he said.

The distinction between "advocacy of action" and "advocacy of ideas" was claimed by Harlan to have far-reaching free speech implications. But its effect is limited. Since "advocacy of action" includes advocacy of future action, the formula omits the element of "present" and therefore cuts off speech at a later point than the clear-and-present-danger test. To this extent it is positive. But it is still a temporal distinction between various kinds of "expression," a distinction that remains blurred and difficult to apply.

Years later, in 1961, when the Supreme Court upheld the membership clause of the Smith Act, making it a felony to be a member of an organization that advocates the overthrow of the government by force or violence, Justice Douglas, dissenting, said, "When we allow a petitioner to be sentenced to prison for six years for being a 'member' of the Communist Party, we make a sharp break with traditional concepts of First Amendment rights and make serious Mark Twain's light-hearted comment that 'it is by the goodness of God that in our country we have three unspeakably precious things: freedom of speech, freedom of conscience and the prudence never to practice either of them.' Not one single illegal act is charged. Nothing but beliefs is on trial in this case. They are unpopular and to most of us revolting. But they are nonetheless ideas or dogmas or faiths within the broad framework of the First Amendment. . . . [This] formula returns man to the dark days when government determined what behavior was dangerous and then policed the dissendents for tell-tale signs of advocacy."

Fortunately, with the *Yates* case, prosecutions under the Smith Act collapsed. Of the eighty-nine persons convicted under the Smith Act, in the end only twenty-nine served prison terms. The campaign to prosecute the advocates of revolution under the Smith Act was over.

But there are pressures again today in both federal and state legislatures for new legislation reminiscent of the Smith Act providing for severe punishments for dissenters. Caspar Weinberger, the Secretary of Defense, asked in 1985 for "execution by a firing squad" when treasonous words were "used to injure the United States." Formal legislation adopting his suggestion was sent to both houses of Congress. Senator Jesse Helms of North Carolina suggested a federal strike force to stop those who "advocate" civilian disturbances and threaten national security—which in effect proposes to give the president the right to use troops without a proclamation and in violation of the clear-and-present-danger standard of the United States Supreme Court decisions. If Weinberger, Helms, and their supporters get the laws they seek, government officials and military men such as those involved in Wounded Knee will, in the name of stopping treasonable behavior and in the name of national security, be able to call out troops against the next rebellious group—be they blacks or Baptists or Democrats or feminists—in Atlanta, Selma, Chicago, or New York.

26

THERE IS, in free speech cases, as in almost all areas of the law, a difference between rights in law and rights in practice. Because the legal standards in speech cases are particularly vague, judges have broader-than-usual discretion. Lower courts tend to be more restrictive of the rights of the individual than appellate courts, and most cases, of course, are decided at lower-court levels.

While the rules governing many business transactions are set out in minute detail, political defendants for most of this century have had to cope with the imprecise clear-and-present-danger standard and First Amendment tests that balance individual rights against interest in national security.

Thus, in periods of extreme and popularly based peacetime repression, the courts have provided inadequate protection. They have not held that free speech means the freedom to advocate even peaceful revolution. Thus, they never reached the next and harder question, separating out advocacy of revolution and violence from the overt act.

As a result, a criminal prosecution often becomes Kafkaesque—the authorities, trying to prove the danger of a pamphlet or spoken word, exaggerate it enormously, telling the public that the defendant has far more power and influence than he really has. For public relations and political reasons, the defendant may go along with the government's overstatement of his importance. During the year-long Black Panther Twenty-one trial in New York, for instance, only the jury failed to share the joint view of the government and the defendants that the men on trial could lead this country to revolution.

In recent years, however, because the inadequacies of the various First Amendment tests have become clear, the Warren and Burger Supreme Courts have been searching for a new speech formulation. Yet they too have not drawn on the historic background of the treason clause as a basis for a new rule.

The clear-and-present-danger rule may have been dealt a fatal blow by the Warren Court in *Brandenburg* v. *Ohio*, a 1969 case reversing the conviction of a Ku Klux Klan leader under an Ohio statute that permitted a conviction for "advocating the duty, necessity, or propriety of crime, sabotage, violence, or unlawful methods of terrorism as a means of accomplishing industrial or political reform." The Court held the statute unconstitutional because it felt this law punished "mere advocacy."

Justice Douglas, in his concurring opinion, took direct aim at Holmes' use of the fire-in-the-theater metaphor. "Though I doubt if the 'clear and present danger' test is congenial to the First Amendment in time of declared war, I am certain it is not reconcilable with the First Amendment in days of peace." The justice continued:

[I] see no place in the regime of the First Amendment for any "clear and present danger" test, whether as strict and tight as some would make it or [as] free-wheeling as the Court in *Dennis* rephrased it. When one reads the opinions closely and sees when and how the "clear and present danger" test has been applied, great misgivings are aroused. First, the threats were often loud but always puny and made serious only by judges so wedded to the *status quo* that critical analysis made them nervous. Second, the test was so twisted and perverted in *Dennis* as to make the trial of those teachers of Marxism an all-out political trial which was part of the parcel of the cold war that has eroded substantial parts of the First Amendment. The line between what is permissible and not subject to control and what may be made impermissible and subject to regulation is the line between ideas and overt acts. The example usually given by those who would punish speech is the case of one who falsely shouts fire in a crowded theatre. This is, however, a classic case where speech is brigaded with action.

The Warren Court's response to the legal problems that Holmes first dealt with in the earlier *Schenck* and *Abrams* cases was that advocacy of the use of force or violence is permitted *if* the illegal action is not "incitement to imminent" lawless action.

Libertarians hailed the use of the word "imminent" as less restrictive of political speech. The Burger Court since then has cited *Brandenburg* several times with approval. In *Hess* v. *Indiana* (1973), an activist remarked during an antiwar demonstration to people blocking the street, "We'll take the fucking street later." The Court reversed his conviction, feeling that later meant days later and not that afternoon. Hence, the Court said, the danger was not imminent.

But even this rule permits courts to punish speech based on semantics and a speculation that it will, in the future, cause harm. At the present time, because of *Brandenburg*, the speculative probability of harm is no longer the central criterion for speech limitations. The precise language of the speaker is now the major consideration. Some scholars see this as a great stride forward; others, as mere rhetoric. To judges and juries caught up in the temper of the times, it is irrelevant.

The failure of the Court and the citizens to accept revolutionary talk as part of the democratic process creates an atmosphere where persons branded as traitors can be brutalized. I saw this most clearly when in 1984 Leonard Weinglass and I represented Kathie Boudin in a criminal case in New York State.

Boudin, an alleged leader of the Weather Underground, was a passenger in a fleeing car during an attempted $1.6 million robbery that saw three Brinks guards killed. Boudin did not have a gun at any time and never fired a gun at any time. Normally, she would have been charged as an accomplice and could have expected a jail sentence of less than five years. Instead, she was charged as a first-degree murderer facing life imprisonment.

Many of Boudin's constitutional rights were violated. These violations began when she was first jailed, prior to the trial. Although even convicted mass murderers are never placed in solitary unless they commit an infraction in jail, Boudin was kept alone in

an overheated cell for months. No one at the New York federal
detention center where she was kept was ever denied the right to
see an infant child or close family members, but she was. Although
the jail had metal detectors, prison authorities claimed they could
not detect guns in the child's blanket.

When these and other facts were brought to federal Judge
Kevin Duffy's attention, he was furious. He ordered her jail conditions changed immediately, saying:

> Liberty for all Americans, no matter to what philosophy they
> may adhere, is . . . to be enforced in a totally nondiscriminatory
> manner. Adherence to these principles both by individuals and by
> government officials cannot be avoided because of mass hysteria
> over the alleged revolutionary ideas of an individual nor from
> the craven fear of criticism from the mass media. It is embarras-
> sing for this court to have to remind the United States Depart-
> ment of Justice and its representatives of these fundamental prin-
> ciples; yet it appears necessary to do so in this matter.

During the trial the political climate surrounding the case
made her defense very difficult. Although few of the potential
jurors knew the facts of the crime, nearly all thought they knew
Kathie's political beliefs. And they hated her for them. During the
extensive pretrial examinations, the jurors made it clear they would
convict her of murder in the first degree, irrespective of evidence
that, in any other case, would result in a jury acquittal on the
murder charge.

Our legal system tried to deal with the jurors' bias, but could
not. The case was set for trial in Rockland County, New York, the
place of the killings. Ninety-two percent of the two thousand potential jurors in Rockland County admitted they knew little of the
case but would convict her anyway.

The jurors' reactions were understandable. They are not
trained in the law. When asked typical questions during the selection process, prospective jurors often do not respond with any
understanding of the issues they must decide in order to render a
verdict. Notwithstanding this fact, once civil trials begin, most
jurors try hard to put aside prejudices. But these attempts are not
made in many criminal trials, and they are strongly resisted in
criminal cases with political overtones. Rockland County residents

were outraged by the triple killings. Boudin's supposed politics were on the front pages of the Rockland papers for months on end. Some jurors thought she was a Soviet agent; others thought a Cuban agent; others held it against her that she was married to a black man (she was not). Rockland children told their parents and teachers dreams about their community being invaded by Russians coming in to help Boudin escape from jail and of big black men coming in to invade the courthouse, jail, and schools.

Faced with these facts, the New York appeals court found that she could not get a fair trial and moved the case farther upstate to Goshen. But the results there were the same. The press continued to distort her politics, exaggerate the size of her political group, and write nonsense about "immediate," "future," and "violent" threats to the nation. Potential jurors were so terrified that they refused to be questioned unless they were promised secrecy. Local pharmacists testified that potential jurors bought out all the sunglasses in town in order to disguise themselves. The judge permitted them to be examined without letting anyone, including the defense lawyers, know their names or addresses. Jurors again spoke of Russians and big black men. Many Goshen residents were terrified when a helicopter flew over the courthouse while jury selection was in process.

Again, after months of extensive juror examination, the New York appeals court, deciding she could not get a fair trial in Goshen, moved her case to yet another city, White Plains.

This third time, after four months of questioning an additional five thousand jurors, the results were the same. Hundreds of thousands of dollars had been spent over a period of two years, and the case was still not on trial. The appeals court was now exhausted and exasperated. This time the court refused to change the case to another city, perhaps New York City, where more sophisticated jurors would be less likely to be influenced by the press. The Court rejected our argument that White Plains jurors were as biased as Rockland and Orange County jurors. As a result we were to be stuck with a jury that would certainly convict her on each and every charge in the indictment. Boudin had no option but to plead guilty to three first-degree murder charges and to try to get the best sentence she could. But Boudin, now thirty-eight years old, was sentenced to a jail term of not less than twenty years, with a maximum of life imprisonment. She cannot be released on parole prior to serving twenty years. Given her political history, she will probably spend the rest of her life in jail.

Because of the heinousness of the crime, very few civil liberties groups would speak out for the substantial legal rights that were being violated. It is not uncommon for many civil libertarians, as they balance the competing needs of this democracy, to argue that the right of free political expression must bow to the need for a society free of disturbances. But the historic background of the treason clause shows that the Constitution assigns a higher value to the free and nonviolent play of controversy over public issues than to the prevention of the dangers to the country that arise from such controversy. Especially does it underline the importance of preventing use of the criminal law as an instrument of competition for political power. As a result many present federal and state laws that impose criminal punishments on speech should be declared invalid. As Sir Edward Coke said, "words may make an Heretick, but not a Traytor."

A broader use of the treason clause can give us a new expression test—that dissident expression can be stopped only when there is also a treasonous act. The minimum function of an overt act in a treason prosecution is that it must show sufficient action by the accused, in its setting, to sustain a finding that the accused actually "levied war or adhered to an enemy." A real enemy, not merely some person or group holding an unorthodox philosophy. Political speech cannot meet that test. Urging peaceful revolution and peaceful resistance is not criminal. The overthrow of a government by legal means is not a crime.

Stopping crime at its inception, before it matures to the point of injury to person and property, should be the limiting test for expression. Activities injurious to government such as destruction of public property, assassinations of and assaults on public officials, and acts of sabotage are made illegal by a host of ordinary state and federal criminal laws. For example, we are not talking about pure speech when a member of an alleged revolutionary group tells a fellow member to place a bomb in the cellar of a government building. The law in this area must be invoked only by determinate acts. Mental events must remain beyond its reach.

Espionage prosecutions are proper only when they are limited to activities (not words) by persons on behalf of an enemy to obtain state secrets—they are not properly used when they punish expression. Zechariah Chafee, Jr., the Harvard law professor who had come under fire for his criticism of the clear-and-present-danger test, examining espionage prosecutions since 1917, said:

> [T]he courts treated opinions as statements of fact and then condemned them as false because they differed from the President's speech or the resolution of Congress declaring war. . . . [I]t became criminal to advocate heavier taxation instead of bond issues, to state that conscription was unconstitutional . . . to say that war was contrary to the teachings of Christianity. Men have been punished for criticizing the Red Cross and the Y.M.C.A. . . .

Public speech must be absolutely protected. Justice Black, a self-described First Amendment absolutist, says: "I learned a long time ago that there are affirmative and negative words. The beginning of the First Amendment is that 'Congress shall make no law.' I understand that it is rather old-fashioned and shows a slight naïveté to say that 'no law' means no law." He then goes on to say that strong arguments have been made almost convincing him "that it is very foolish of me to think 'no law' means no law. But when I get down to the really basic reason why I believe that 'no law' means no law, [it comes to this:] I took an obligation to support and defend the Constitution as I understand it. And being a rather backward country fellow, I understand it to mean what the words say."

But the problem with Black's expression here is not that the words "no law" are ambiguous. The ambiguity is in "freedom of speech and of the press," which lacked the precision necessary to override restrictive interpretations of the First Amendment. Black's critics argue that the freedom which Congress was forbidden to abridge was not some absolute concept which had never existed on earth. It was the freedom the founding fathers believed they had—what they wanted before the Revolution and had acquired through independence. But Black has argued that the writers of the Constitution were not giving their countrymen less rights than the founders wanted for themselves. The Constitution must be read to protect speech sufficient to lead to another revolution if new rulers became despotic.

Black himself did not follow his own absolutist logic in all cases involving speech. He took a narrow view of free speech problems posed by picketing and demonstrators. When asked to comment on Holmes' example of the man falsely shouting "fire" in a crowded theater, Black replied, "That is a wonderful aphorism about shouting 'fire' in a crowded theater. But you do not have to shout 'fire' to get arrested. If a person creates a disorder in a theater, they would get him there not because of what he hollered but because he hollered." It is the disruptive act that is being punished, not the content of the speech.

But this much can be made "absolute." Public speech—speech on public issues, speech connected with self-government—must be wholly immune from regulation. The bailiffs can wait until specific lawless action is imminent.

The First Amendment means, as Professor Alexander Meiklejohn has written, "that certain evils, which, in principle, Congress has a right to prevent, must be endured if the only way of avoiding them is by abridging that freedom of speech upon which the entire structure of our free institution rests." "Certain evils" means the criminal act (the planned bombing or assassination in support of revolutionaries) that may not be caught in time.

Meiklejohn's balancing speech test is similar to that behind the free speech argument that no one can be jailed or sued for criticism of public officials. Although innocent people may be hurt, the greater value is the complete freedom to exchange ideas about matters of public importance. There should be no criminal libel, and no civil libel, if it is a public official who claims harm.

Indeed, it would be fair to conclude that civil libel lawsuits such as these have been as effective as prosecutions for criminal libel or "espionage" in stopping expression. They reach wider groups of people, are filed by private lawyers unhampered by the limits put on state prosecutors, and speech and conduct tests are less stringent than the criminal law requires. It is in the Generals William Westmoreland and Ariel Sharon cases that we first saw the private use of the libel suit by elected public officials and governmental agencies as a substitute for criminal prosecutions of speech. "Treasonous speech" has now become a new and highly charged body of law.

27

TWENTY-THREE YEARS ago, in the watershed case of *New York Times* v. *Sullivan*, the Supreme Court held that to prove libel, a public official must establish that the statements about him had been published with "actual malice," that is, with knowledge that they were either false or printed in reckless disregard of the truth. But the Sullivan rule has failed to give government critics the freedom the First Amendment promises. There has been an explosion of lawsuits against the media; juries have awarded large damages (since 1980 there have been more than twenty cases in which damages exceeded $1 million); and the high legal costs incurred by defendants have been a warning to others, inducing self-censorship and reducing the flow of information to the public.

Actions brought by public officials are not attempts by individuals to win restitution for personal wrongs. They are attempts to vindicate their political position and their conduct in office—to rewrite history and to punish their enemies. The recent libel suits filed by Generals Sharon and Westmoreland prove that point. The Founding Fathers never intended the civil courts in this country to be used to prohibit political debate by punishing critics of government.

People outside the publishing and legal professions have little idea how difficult it is for critics of the government to establish and report the exact truth in matters of controversy. Frequently, the government denies access to information. Critics and reporters often try to locate the ultimate truth in a welter of controversial facts and charges, often without knowing all the facts.

The very men and women who write articles that expose wrongdoing or criticize the powerful are the ones most likely to provoke brutal, acrimonious litigation. The only way a critic or news organization can be sure it will not be sued is not to discuss controversial news. The operative word is "controversial." Thus, the chief effect of the recent flood of libel judgments has not been greater accuracy but greater timidity. Free speech has been curtailed; the flow of information to the public has been diminished.

The most serious impact of this trend has fallen on investigative journalism, which has decreased in recent years. Most investigative reporting is antiestablishment. It is no surprise that expensive libel suits are often backed by conservative elements, which tend to support the power structure. Indeed, the media have become a prime target of the right—witness, for example, Senator Jesse Helms' call for a conservative takeover of CBS.

Libel suits inhibit journalists and critics by making them excessively cautious about having the facts. Obviously, they should base their reporting on the facts, but sometimes all the facts are not available because a government or a corporation refuses to divulge them. In such cases journalists should be free to make inferences about public issues. During the Nixon administration, official statements on the progress of the Vietnam War drove the press to smoke out the facts that turned the public against the war. Similarly, the speculations and hunches of *Washington Post* newspaper reporters, often based on a frail basis of facts, led to the Watergate exposés. If Nixon, Mitchell, and Haldeman were under attack today, they might successfully use libel suits to stop the investigations and punish today's Woodwards and Bernsteins.

Critics and whistle blowers and muckrakers must frequently rely on evidence that would not hold up in court, and that is proper. Take, for example, Carl Bernstein and Bob Woodward's *All the President's Men*, their book describing the events that led to Watergate, and Strobe Talbott's *Deadly Gambits*, which describes the secret arms negotiation talks in the Reagan administration. Those books were pieced together by authors who were not at critical meetings; their conclusions were often based on fragmentary information and confidential sources. Authors should be permitted to draw even wrong conclusions without the threat of a libel suit hanging over them.

As our Supreme Court recognized in 1943 in *Board of Education* v. *Barnette*, "compulsory unification of opinion achieves only the unanimity of the graveyard." The genius of the Constitution is its recognition that more speech is the cure for misleading speech. All that government may demand is that the dialogue be expanded, not that the offending remark be stopped or that the publisher be shut down.

But without that protection self-censorship arrives insidiously. The criterion for deciding to print a controversial article becomes not whether the company could successfully defend a libel suit, but whether the plaintiff could keep it alive and force the company to bear the expense and burden of frivolous litigation. If the latter seems likely, the natural tendency is not to publish. Although publishers routinely deny that they kill articles because of the risk of libel, the chilling truth is well known to writers, editor, and lawyers who work with the media. Publishers who once asked whether the target of an article could win a lawsuit now simply ask "Will he sue?"

The reality—and threat—of being sued for libel has left social critics and much of American journalism in a state of siege. A St. Louis NAACP chapter that was critical of a housing project because of racial implications and criticized private developers and city officials was shut down by a dozen lawsuits. A black political caucus in Alabama that claimed a white judge was a racist was financially broken. Environmentalists in Oregon were silenced by libel suits filed by developers. Perhaps most vulnerable to court rulings and the attitudes of libel juries are the nation's smaller publications and local television and radio stations. They play a vital role in exposing private and governmental incompetence and corruption, but they can easily be driven into bankruptcy if they are forced to defend even a single libel action.

In 1979, for instance, the *Point Reyes Light*, a 3,100-circulation weekly newspaper in northern California, published a series of articles based on an investigation of Synanon, the drug rehabilitation center. The series brought the paper a Pulitzer Prize but led to four libel suits seeking a total of more than $1 billion. The cost of legal fees drove them into bankruptcy.

Public attitudes about the rights of a free press have had a major impact in suits against the press. According to a poll by the National Opinion Research Center in 1985, 13.7 percent of the people had "a great deal of confidence in the press"—down from 29 percent in 1976. Such negative feelings have their greatest impact in the jury room. Under the law juries have almost complete discretion in deciding the merits of a libel case and in determining how much money to award an injured party. And emotions and politics rule, both in the jury room and in the chambers of many appellate and trial judges.

The public official comes into court claiming that his reputation has been ruined because of words printed by an editor or author. He may be, like Senator Paul Laxalt, an extraordinarily successful politician who gets over 70 percent of the vote. The local jury, part of his constituency, sees the trial as a fight between a popular political figure and the bad press. In some cases the words printed are clearly false, and that is what jurors want to know about. They find it hard to believe that freedom of the press is in peril because one critic is found guilty of libel and punished for his sin. How else, they ask, can the press be prevented from printing falsehoods? It comes as little surprise when juries find for the plaintiff—90 percent of the time.

When judges and juries make an award of thousands of dollars against a newspaper in punitive damages, they usually assume that the award will deter the paper from printing falsehoods. And such judgments, or the threat of them, may indeed cause the media to go to even greater lengths to check their facts. That option may not, however, be feasible for financially hard-pressed publications or local broadcasters, since it typically involves hiring larger staffs and paying high fees to have lawyers screen articles for potentially libelous statements. The atmosphere created by large damage awards has also changed the focus of investigation by many journalists and writers. Since, under current law, it is less dangerous to print controversial material about public officials than about private citizens, publishers are rapidly becoming disenchanted with hard-hitting books and articles about private citizens.

Twenty-three years ago when the Warren Court decided *New York Times* v. *Sullivan*, it was clear that the libel law as it then existed was not working. Because of the uproar over civil rights and the response of the southern states, public officials threatened to use juries and judges to hold the press hostage. Today, though the nation has changed in so many ways, there is a certain similarity in the conditions confronting the press. Once again we see huge awards levied against the media, and once again we see the Supreme Court preparing to confront the issue.

The legal fraternity has not been shy about offering solutions. One proposal, for example, seeks a law that would make an appropriate correction in an offending newspaper acceptable as a substitute for damages. Of course, it is difficult to decide was is "appropriate" or "acceptable." Other suggestions focus on the role of the jury. One would eliminate awards of punitive damages (as apart from and in addition to compensatory damages) on the basis that the Founding Fathers never envisioned that a jury or judge could punish and perhaps render such a large award as to drive a publisher out of business. Another would eliminate compensatory awards for "mental anguish" on the basis that objective evidence of such damage is seldom available.

The framers of the Constitution never intended to permit public officials to use libel suits to punish a press that writes about their public role in public affairs. This does not mean every aspect of a public figure's life can be written about free from the threat of suits for libel. Public figures should be able to sue if the material written about them is purely private. Deciding what is public and what is private is of course no easy matter, but the courts have already tried to define these issues in various areas of the law.

But if criticism of a public official can be found to be libelous, then no citizen can safely utter anything but praise about the government or its representatives. As Justice Black wrote in his opinion in *Times* v. *Sullivan*: "This Nation, I suspect, can live in peace without libel suits based on public discussion of public affairs and public officials. But I doubt that a country can live in freedom where its people can be made to suffer physically or financially for criticizing their government, its action or its officials."

When I testified before the House Judiciary Committee in July 1985 that public citizens should be free to say anything they wanted about their elected representatives, many of the congressmen were aghast. They became more thoughtful only when Representative Robert Kastenmeier of Wisconsin pointed out that a congressman, by virtue of congressional immunity, can say anything he pleases in Congress about a citizen without the fear of libel. Why, Kastenmeier asked, should a citizen have fewer free speech rights than the people he elected? Congressman Howard Berman of California then pointed out that Senator Joseph McCarthy could libel anyone from the floor of Congress, but if a critic made similar libelous accusations against McCarthy, the Wisconsin senator could file and win a multimillion dollar suit.

There is good logic, history, and authority that allows us to interpret the First Amendment language, as Black has said, to mean there shall be no civil or criminal limitations upon political speech. The treason law furthers our constitutional protections because it permits speech against the government to be punished only when it is combined with an act. Yet because the Supreme Court has been so long caught in the clear-and-present-danger quagmire, many thorny questions have not been asked.

What, after all, constitutes an overt act? Is the drawing of a detailed plan for a revolutionary uprising an overt act punishable under treason statutes? Must the police wait until the revolutionary group commits acts of violence before an arrest can be made? Or must the police wait until the group is supplied with the means for revolution? Is the test for criminal arrest different from the standard for a court's grant of permission to get evidence by eavesdropping for a future arrest? Can you safely broaden the area of surveillance as a quid pro quo for requiring law-enforcement officers not to act until the last possible moment?

Black's formula to limit government power over speech until lawless action is imminent reaches the same ultimate end as does the adoption of the treason clause. It is Black—who repudiated the clear-and-present-danger test—rather than Holmes who is in tune with democracy. History has vindicated the Black approach, for it has helped protest personal liberties in an era of encroaching public power.

Nonetheless, it is clear that our legal system, any legal system, whatever tests are adopted, cannot truly stop all wrongful expression in times of crisis. It is difficult to say when antidemocratic acts of a group go to the essence of the democratic process and would destroy the democracy that permits these acts, or when these acts will merely modify the government. And of course most treason trials come when the nation is seen to be in crisis. Yet the supression of critics of this and other governments intensifies hostility, drives the opposition underground, and encourages the solution of problems by force rather than by reason. It helps create fear, hatred, prejudice, and hysteria.

And what have we gained through the Supreme Court's refusal to follow the treason law's logic? Starting with World War I, we have prosecuted and imprisoned advocates of causes found hateful by authority. During that war we prosecuted socialists like Schenck, and prosecuted Communists after World War II, and Dr. Benjamin Spock and draft card burners during the Vietnam War. But have we indeed caught any spies, terrorists, or saboteurs by such advocacy-based enforcement activities? The answer is no.

For this reason free speech should be argued as much on the levels of wisdom and policy as on the level of constitutional prohibitions. A democratic society must tolerate, and even encourage, opinions which attack its elected officials and institutions. The citizens of the United States are fit to govern themselves only if they have faced squarely and fearlessly everything that can be said in favor of their institutions and everything that can be said against them.

Groups that would abolish democratic institutions if they came to power do not operate in a political vacuum. Those groups should be protected. They should be seen as a treasure rather than as a liability. They show the country is healthy, not sick. They advance ideas. These groups often represent real grievances that must be heard; it is a commonplace that the accepted laws and institutions of today were the notions of subversive heretics of yesterday.

These distinctions are not easily arrived at. In our own time we have seen the test of "clear and present danger" which was used to justify exceptions to the First Amendment replaced by a new test, "national security."

The outcome of the Pentagon Papers case (*United States* v. *The New York Times*), the Supreme Court's six-to-three decision permitting the *Times* to go forward with publication of the secret history of the American war in Vietnam, was hailed in 1973 as a great victory for free speech. The release of the Pentagon Papers, and the debate that followed, as much as any other single event, led to America's review of its involvement in Vietnam. But the publication nearly did not occur. And when it did, days elapsed while the *New York Times* and the *Washington Post* were enjoined from further publication. By establishing a national security exception to the First Amendment, this case marked the beginning of the Supreme Court's sweeping aside of constitutional free speech protections when the executive branch asserted that national security was at stake.

For two years Daniel Ellsberg, a former policy analyst who first supported the Vietnam War and then opposed it, went around the country in an attempt to get at least some of the papers published. He saw six congressmen, the representatives of three television networks, and the editors of several newspapers. All refused to give the public the papers. No one would release the documents. Everybody, from Senators William Fulbright and Wayne Morse to CBS' "60 Minutes" producers, were afraid of the espionage statutes. Publishers and government officials believed that the law would be broken by the release of the papers. Those who felt the papers were too hot to handle claimed the Rosenberg case and the defendants' ultimate death penalties were a fearful precedent that must govern their acts.

For two years prior to publication, a set of the entire Pentagon Papers was in my closet. For those two years I feared being named a codefendant at the treason or espionage trial that was sure to come. The war raged on. Finally, when the *Times*' Neil Sheehan took a set of the papers to his editors, they agreed to let the *Times*' lawyers look at the papers to get their own legal evaluation.

The lawyers for the *New York Times*, Herbert Brownell and Louis Loeb, advised the editors not to publish, warning that publication could set in motion successful legal action by the Department of Justice under the Espionage Act.

Brownell claimed to be an espionage law expert. He had been attorney general of the United States in 1953, and had persuaded President Eisenhower not to pardon the Rosenbergs by saying he had secret intelligence communications that proved their guilt. His expertise seemed to carry the day with the *Times* officials.

But Sheehan and other writers at the *Times* won out. The

Times rejected Brownell and Loeb's advice. They resigned from the case, new lawyers were hired, and the *Times* won the legal action.

Until the government sought a court order prohibiting publication of the Pentagon Papers, it had been generally assumed that, at least as to such prior restraints, the First Amendment meant just what it said—Congress could pass "no law" prohibiting free speech.

Judge Murray I. Gurfein, a courageous district judge and a new Nixon appointee, did what the Constitution demanded. First, he refused to accept the government's claims at face value; he made the Justice Department offer proof of their claims that publication would endanger lives, alienate our allies, and cripple the war effort. In secret sessions before Judge Gurfein, the government's chief witness, Vice-Admiral Francis J. Blouin, deputy chief of naval operations, on direct examination testified it would be a "disaster" to continue to publish the Pentagon Papers. Impressive in demeanor, candid in response to questions under cross-examination, Blouin made it clear that in virtually all respects his testimony was based on the general ground that "there is an awful lot of stuff in [the Pentagon Study] that I would prefer to see sleep awhile longer."

Judge Gurfein ultimately ruled that the courts simply lacked all authority to prevent a newspaper from publishing information in its possession. The government immediately appealed, first to the federal appellate court in New York and then to the highest court in Washington. Although Judge Gurfein's clear, forthright conclusion carried the day, his underlying legal theory did not. The federal appellate court judges who heard the government's appeal, and a majority of the Supreme Court, while permitting the publication of the Pentagon Papers, ruled that the government could enlist judicial aid in suppressing publication of information conceded to be important to public debate on a major issue of the day.

Acknowledging, at least by implication, the government's inherent right to enjoin the press in national security cases, the courts differed with the government only on the appropriate legal standard and whether it had proved its case.

Justices Potter Stewart and Byron White, who signed the decisive opinion in the Supreme Court, and agreed that the government could not stop publication of the Pentagon Papers, nevertheless said there was a national security exception to the First Amendment's absolute ban on prior restraint. Their holding foreshadowed a string of Supreme Court decisions that used the term "national security" to impair constitutional rights. The opinion appeared to establish a tough standard, requiring the government to prove that publication would "surely" result in "direct, immediate, and irreparable" harm to the nation. Future cases were to show, however, that the government would allege facts that appeared to meet that standard and that the courts would show great deference to such assertions.

Because the Court has become more conservative in make-up since its decision in the Pentagon Papers case, it is important to look at the opinions supporting the government's position. Of the three dissents, the most influential and harshest of these was Justice Harry A. Blackmun's.

After complaining of this "hurried decision of profound constitutional issues" without sufficiently careful deliberation, Blackmun noted, "the First Amendment, after all, is only part of an entire Constitution. Article II of the great document vests in the Executive Branch primary power over the conduct of foreign affairs and places in that branch the ultimate responsibility of the Constitution . . . I cannot subscribe to a doctrine of unlimited absolutism for the First Amendment at the cost of downgrading other provisions."

Blackmun, in one of his worst moments, went on to echo the sentencing speech of Judge Irving Kaufman, who condemned Julius and Ethel Rosenberg to death for espionage: "I hope," Blackmun said,

> that damage has not already been done. If, however, damage has been done, and if, with the Court's action today, these newspapers proceed to publish the critical documents and there results therefrom "the death of soldiers, the destruction of alliances, the greatly increased difficulty of negotiation with our enemies, the inability of our diplomats to negotiate," to which list I might add the factors of prolongation of the war and further delay in the freeing of United States prisoners, then the Nation's people will know where the responsibility for these sad consequences rests.

Seldom, if ever, in the nation's history has a Supreme Court Justice predicted the press would become a pariah by exercising its freedom to publish. History has proved him wrong.

Two days before the Supreme Court decision permitting the papers to be published, John Mitchell, then the attorney general of the United States, and Robert Mardian, a Justice Department lawyer (who later became a celebrated Watergate defendant), after discussion with President Nixon, sought to punish Ellsberg by filing criminal charges that could have jailed him for the rest of his life. The specter of treason again caused the authorities to go overboard. The burglarizing of Daniel Ellsberg's psychiatrist's office by the CIA-equipped, presidentially inspired special unit was only the final assault upon the judicial process in a case littered with despicable conduct. The authorities also destroyed logs, tapes, records, and documents that the judge ordered to be turned over to the defense.

But the best example of the arrogant ruthlessness with which Ellsburg was pursued by Mitchell and Nixon was an episode which occurred during the pendency of the trial. Judge Matthew Byrne, the judge presiding at the criminal trial, was invited twice to the summer house of President Nixon at San Clemente, where John Ehrlichman, a special assistant to the president, broached to him the possibility of an appointment to the directorship of the FBI. That Judge Byrne admitted to the meeting only after the defense team learned about the offer from a reporter covering the trial and publicly pointed out that Nixon was trying to bribe Byrne with the offer, shows the judge's insensitivity to the impropriety. Finally and defensively, Judge Byrne exercised his discretion and dismissed the case because of government misconduct in the prosecution of the case.

Vice-Admiral Blouin, recently asked what specific harm the publication of the papers might have caused, commented, "Looking at them today, I don't think there was any great loss in substance." Charles Nesson, a Harvard law professor who was a member of the defense team, claims the publication lent credibility to and finally crystallized the growing consensus that the Vietnam War was wrong. Former Secretary of State Cyrus R. Vance, reviewing the Nixon era, said publication helped end the war and that none of the dire consequences foreseen by the government or the three dissenting members of the Court came to pass.

Lawyers in the Reagan administration's Department of Justice, like their Nixon administration counterparts, have also wrongfully tried to use espionage statutes to suppress information critical of the government.

Samuel Loring Morison, a disgruntled U.S. Navy employee, was prosecuted in October 1985 for a violation of the Espionage Act as well as for stealing government property because he gave *Jane's Fighting Ships*, a British publication, three U.S. satellite photographs of a Soviet aircraft carrier and because he gave that publication information about explosions in a Soviet shipyard. This was the same statute that was used against Ellsberg. The information Morison disclosed had been published in other magazines even before *Jane's* received it. Edwin Meese III, Reagan's attorney general, contended that Morison was guilty of espionage even though he acknowledged that part of Morison's motive was "to expose obvious wrongdoing in high official circles" and further may have been to "point out that the Soviets are better prepared than we are."

Morison was convicted in a Baltimore federal court and sentenced to four years in prison. It is most likely that the conviction will be upheld by the appeals court. Yet Morison's prosecution for releasing photos to an ally of the United States boggles the mind. It would seem that the government is reaching as far as it can to make an example. Morison was the first person found guilty under the 1917 espionage law for leaking documents to a friendly party. The Department of Justice succeeded in persuading federal judge Joseph H. Young to interpret the federal criminal law to create a working version of the British Official Secrets Act, the law that makes it a crime to disclose any government information to anyone without proper authorization. In so doing Judge Young rejected the defense's argument that "espionage rules cannot be used to prosecute leakers." His verdict gives the government the final judicial, unreviewable right to impose its own definition of what information injures the nation.

Although the Baltimore case involved only Morison and not the publisher, the administration has made it clear the Espionage

Act can be used to go after those who publish leaks "relating to the national defense." According to Stephen S. Trott, the assistant attorney general in charge of the Justice Department's Criminal Division, the administration intends to prosecute, under the espionage laws, anyone who participates in giving information to the public.

Publishers of books on arms control, defense spending, nuclear weapon debates, "Star Wars," and nearly every area of foreign policy, have reason to be concerned. Anytime they publish information not based on officially approved sources, they now face the threat of prosecution. The publishers of books in the future like Strobe Talbott's *Deadly Gambits*, William Shawcross's *Sideshow*, or Jimmy Carter's *Keeping Faith* could face prosecution. So too could the bookstores that sell the books, the printers that print them, and all those involved in the distribution of such publications. For under the Reagan administration's theory, all of those people may be involved in "willfully" transmitting information that could endanger the United States.

Indeed, although espionage laws since their inception in 1917 have been aimed solely at passing secrets to a foreign enemy, bills now pending in the House and Senate can be interpreted to expand the definition of espionage. They would require the imposition of the death penalty for passing to any third party any document that creates a "grave risk of substantial danger to the national security," and for mandatory life sentences for those convicted of receiving and publishing such documents. This includes nonclassified as well as classified material. The legislation would permit the government to decide after the fact if the documents leaked to the press could lead to such danger.

The Reagan administration has for years been submitting legislation to go after whistle blowers who complain about such things as defense overruns, as well as against the press that reports the complaints. The Justice Department under Presidents Nixon and Reagan has argued that publishing leaks and secrets amounted to giving it to the enemy, but until now Congress and the courts have rejected those conclusions.

But it is different today. The recent espionage incidents have created a new atmosphere as previously rejected bills are being resubmitted. The chilling effect of these pending statutes is awesome. According to members of the various Senate and House committees, there is a good chance this new legislation will be passed. As a legislative aide before the Senate committee that has the espionage legislation put it, "Morison is scaring everyone to death. If the appeals courts affirms the conviction, they don't need any new laws to go after the press."

Justice Department officials claim the Reagan administration did not seek out the Morison case as part of their attacks on the press. But this claim is false. The sole criminal prosecution for leaking documents since 1917 was against Daniel Ellsberg for disclosing the Pentagon Papers. Morison was the second, but the first such prosecution to be successful. There is a reason why from 1973, the year of the Ellsberg prosecution, until 1985 there were no prosecutions in this country for the unauthorized disclosure of information. It is not that there were no leaks in the Ford and Carter administrations or the first Reagan administration, or that they did not want "leak" prosecutions. But there were barriers to such prosecutions—barriers between the CIA, the FBI, and the armed forces on one side, and the Justice Department on the other—that made the cost of criminal prosecution, in terms of damage to the press and to the First Amendment, often outweigh the benefits of a successful prosecution.

Then in 1983 the Department of Justice circulated a document known as the Willard Report. Prepared by Richard Willard, Counsel to the Office of Intelligence Policy and Review, at the direction of William P. Clark, assistant to the president for national security affairs, it marked the surrender of the Justice Department. Seeking to convict those "journalists who seem to believe that quoting from 'highly classified' documents is an appropriate means of entertaining as well as informing the public," the report says that "the person who receives classified information is no less responsible than the person who takes it."

The Willard Report acknowledged that present legislation had never been interpreted by courts to cover leaks to the press and that a conviction was unlikely when a reporter could claim that he did not intend to injure the United States and therefore was protected by the First Amendment. The Willard Report acknowledged the strong pressure on the administration to prosecute those who published the Pentagon Papers—a pressure the Nixon administration resisted.

But Judge Young, adopting every argument urged by the Reagan administration, set a precedent for all future prosecutions when he ruled that it was conceivable that Congress, during the McCarthy period in the 1950s, "would have considered a person who leaked national security information to the press to be a 'saboteur.' " Under this rule a newspaper reporter receiving information would be considered a saboteur.

Morison claimed that the statute required the government to prove he had intended to injure the United States. Rather, he claimed his intent in sending the pictures to *Jane's* had been simply to alert the American public to Russia's naval strength. Had *Jane's* been a defendant in the case, this is a defense the publisher might have urged.

But Judge Young refused to allow Morison to produce character witnesses to prove that he was a devoted American opposed to the Soviet Union and concerned about Soviet power. Under the government's theory of prosecution, accepted by Judge Young, anyone who "willfully" transmits or receives such photographs is guilty of espionage "no matter what his motives." A leak is therefore a crime, whether inspired by policy or profit or patriotism.

Judge Young also refused Morison's request to charge the jury that the potential damage to the United States be "reasonably foreseeable, not remote or speculative." When Judge Young ruled that the prosecution did not have to prove that the disclosed information injured the United States (he permitted the jury to speculate if "any" potential damage could flow from the release of the information), he made future prosecutions and convictions very easy. A conviction is now appropriate even if no vital secret is lost.

William E. Colby, a former CIA director, conceding that the Morison case makes the job of the press more difficult, said, "We've got to do something to pull up our socks here and put a little discipline back in the Government." The Reagan administration tried to do just that when it fired Assistant Undersecretary of Defense Michael Pillsbury for allegedly giving reporters details of an administration plan to provide Stinger missiles to antigovernment rebels in Angola and Afghanistan.

The political climate after the Ellsberg case and Watergate made it difficult both to interpret the old laws in the way the administration wanted and to have a federal judge make discretionary rulings free from daily coverage and criticism by the press. Even if there was a conviction, it would have to run the gauntlet of a federal appeals court and then the Warren Court. Now, with a judiciary heavily influenced at all levels by Reagan appointees, the press and the public have reason to view skeptically those at the Department of Justice who claim the Morison case does not set a precedent.

While an official secrets act may be appropriate for Britain, it has no place in the United States. Britain recognizes no supreme law, no "unalienable" rights. Neither the Magna Charta nor any other document guarantees the rights of ordinary people against an act of Parliament. The British system is founded on the legislature's absolute power. Our Constitution rejects giving either the executive or legislative branch of government absolute power.

While sentencing Morison to two years in jail, Judge Young said he was aware that no one had been sentenced before under this statute for leaking. In the wake of this case, publishers will not be able to claim they did not know the law applied to them. The Morison prosecution, a test case seized upon by the administration, will have an awesome, chilling effect.

The administration moved quickly to capitalize on the conviction. In May 1986 CIA director William Casey met with Deputy Attorney General D. Lowell Jensen, who had directed the Morison prosecution. Casey wanted five news organizations, the *Washington Post*, the *Washington Times*, the *New York Times*, *Time*, and *Newsweek*, to be considered for prosecution under the espionage statutes for printing details about our intelligence-gathering operations.

Casey later met with *Washington Post* executive editor Benjamin Bradlee and told him he was considering asking the Justice Department to take the *Post* to court for, among other things, reporting on messages intercepted by our government between Tripoli and the East Berlin's "People's Bureau" (as Libya calls its diplomatic missions). Casey made it clear to Bradlee that he was also concerned with a story that Bob Woodward was writing dealing with Ronald Pelton, the National Security Agency employee then charged with espionage (and since convicted). The story set to run two days after the Casey meeting was "postponed," although Bradlee claimed he was unpersuaded that the story threatened national security.

A few days later, on May 19, 1986, Casey said he asked the Justice Department to consider prosecuting the National Broadcasting Company on charges of broadcasting a report containing classified information discussing Pelton's activities that was based upon much the same information included in the original Woodward story. Later Casey threatened to stop Random House from publishing a book by Seymour Hersh on the 1983 Korean airliner shoot-down that was critical of the United States. He also threatened to prosecute the Viking Press for reprinting a book originally published in England that claimed the Korean plane was on an intelligence mission for our CIA.

But these threats of prosecution will not stop the publication of books by authors officially approved by the administration. Nor will it deter continued leaks favorable to the administration from coming out. As Vermont Senator Patrick J. Leahy, a Democrat who is chairman of the Select Committee on Intelligence, said in a 1986 speech: "I believe nearly all leaks of sensitive information come from the executive branch. This tendency to conduct policy debate or advance political interests through leaking classified information existed in the Ford and Carter administrations. But in my nearly twelve years in Congress I have never seen it on the scale practiced by government officials under the present administration."

The future Kissingers and Kirkpatricks will have their say. Their opponents will not. For every editor who gets "unauthorized" information relating to present foreign policy is put at risk if he prints the story. He will have to speculate if his author is in or out of favor with the administration. It may well be that the administration in power at the time of the signing of a book contract will not be the administration in power when the book finally appears— books safe at the time they were signed up may become unsafe when published. And now that the Morison decision has been upheld by the appellate court, the attorney general is free to decide which of the publishers who publish leaks will be tolerated and which shall be presented as criminals.

President Reagan admonishes that those who exercise First Amendment rights have a "responsibility to be right." The Burger Court, as it was constituted in the Pentagon Papers case, rejected that concept and the government's spurious claim that national security required the *New York Times* not to publish the documents received from Ellsberg. It is not likely that the new Rehnquist Court will be as protective of the press, for it may affirm both Morison's conviction and press prosecutions such as those threatened by Casey.

At the same time, President Reagan today insists on his right to conduct, free from the press interference, a "disinformation" policy aimed at spreading self-created false stories.

We can expect Edwin Meese's Justice Department and the CIA to orchestrate intensive attacks on the press in order to guarantee its control over the flow of information. Reagan officials threatened the news media with a Defense Department investigation if they even "speculated" on the details of the space shuttle flight scheduled on January 23, 1986. (If the press had scrutinized NASA more closely the deaths of six astronauts and Chrisa McAuliffe in January 1986 might not have occurred.) And when the *Washington Post* published an analysis of Libyan misconduct based on information in the public record, Defense Secretary Caspar Weinberger vehemently accused the newspaper of endangering national security and of giving aid and comfort to the enemy.

In another case Lieutenant General John T. Chain, Jr., director of the State Department's Bureau of Politico-Military Affairs, ordered his staff not to talk to Leslie Gelb, national security correspondent of the *New York Times*. Gelb had written an article—based on information that had already appeared in the foreign press—that revealed contingency plans to deploy nuclear depth charges in the territory of eight allied countries, none of which had been consulted by the government about the plan. According to Chain, the piece contained "classified information the release of which is harmful and damaging to the United States" and which served to "aid our potential adversary." Although acknowledging that the information Gelb reported had been disclosed previously in the foreign press, Secretary of State George Shultz said that the article had caused "a considerable amount of damage" to U.S. interests. Although Gelb was then prohibited from attending future press briefings, he was never criminally prosecuted.

Invariably, when those in power want to stop speech critical of the government or its representatives, and invoke the threat to national security, or label that which they seek to censor as treason, what they are doing implies that they know better than their fellow citizens where the nation's and the people's interests lie. It is a paternalistic and antidemocratic impulse.

"Liberty," said Judge Learned Hand, "lies in the hearts of men and women, and when it dies there, no constitution, no law, no court that can save it." The responsibility for keeping liberty alive by refusing to accept concealment and suppression rests with each of us.

28

"**N**ATIONAL SECURITY" in this and other countries often becomes a magic phrase used to justify laws that ban political speech. There is no simple rule for determining how to balance the claim of national security against the individual's rights of free speech and to a fair hearing and the rights of the people to wide-open debate on public policies. The vicious assumption underlying the national security argument is that the nation is perpetually in a de facto state of war—so "balancing" is often illegitmate from the start. South Africa in Breytenbach's trial, the Chileans in the "Nuremberg trial," and the Soviet Union in the Shcharansky trial simply ignored both free speech and the individual's due process rights as they rushed toward conviction.

The starting point is to take such rights seriously, and American jurisprudence does. In a series of cases, our government has formulated various concepts to limit dissent and punish dissenters; "treason" has been replaced by "national security," but the fundamental rights in jeopardy remain the same. "National security" has crept into legislative chambers, for it has recently captured the mind of President Reagan and his lieutenants. It was used by the Reagan administration during the Iran arms senatorial hearings as a justification for having withheld information from the Congress and the public. After the scandal broke, William Casey continued to claim that national security interests required his testimony be given only in closed session. Edwin Meese claimed it justified his delaying the FBI's investigation of Contra aid. It has also in previous years infiltrated the courts, where the concept threatens to sabotage the vital core of the First Amendment.

Ever since societies have been organized, authority has attempted to suppress scandalous discussions about itself on the grounds that such discussions can ultimately disturb the peace. Authority is partially correct. Dissent does call into question official orthodoxy, and critics put themselves on an equal footing with the authority criticized. But when scandalmongers and disaffected persons have questioned their superiors' view, the authorities have claimed that dissenters themselves created conditions of unrest rather than acknowledging that, more often than not, it was the authorities who had created the conditions that lead to unrest.

But our Supreme Court, when first faced with national security claims by the executive branch, held firm, refusing to find in "national security" a bogeyman to sweep away all rights. Even during the Korean War the court rejected President Truman's seizure of the steel mills despite claims that our military forces required uninterrupted steel production. It mitigated some of the harsh anti-Communist actions of the McCarthy era, and later it struck down a federal statute that barred Communists from working in defense plants. In these cases the Supreme Court did not assume that national security claims were spurious; it tried, rather, to accommodate them without releasing the government from constitutional limitations.

If one argues that all national security claims are frivolous, it is easy to conclude that all efforts to expand state power should be resisted. Similarly, if one accepts all claims of national security at face value, then it is a short step to the sacrifice of individual rights. But if one acknowledges the legitimacy of both values, then it is necessary to reconcile the competing interests to enable the judiciary to act consistently in terms of national security while protecting the individual rights of citizens.

One problem is that leak cases are often hard to solve. Even in the Ellsberg case it took the government a while to learn who Xeroxed the papers. But even when a suspect is identified, there are numerous political obstructions to criminal prosecution. First, criminal prosecutions serve to confirm the accuracy and sensitivity of the disclosed information. For this reason the Justice Departments of various administrations have not wanted certain cases prosecuted, in order to maintain doubt as to the accuracy of the disclosed information.

Second, criminal prosecutions require the government to prove the disclosures were damaging to the national security, which then requires further public disclosure of classified information. This proof, prosecutors know, is essential to the jury rendering a verdict of guilty.

Third, criminal trials are normally conducted before a jury and are open to the public. Defendants can threaten to require disclosure of sensitive information in the course of the trial—the government calls this "graymail," a situation that can lead to the dropping of cases after they have been started, resulting in a publicized defeat for the Justice Department.

As a result, the Department of Justice has sometimes determined that the damage to national security brought about in the course of a criminal proceeding would outweigh the benefits of a prosecution. On the other hand, the agencies from which the disclosures came—the CIA, the FBI, and the armed forces—have often bitterly disagreed. The ensuing departmental infighting has been brutal. Finally, in the last years of the Carter administration, Attorney General Griffin Bell, reacting to pressures primarily from the CIA, agreed to prepare legislation to try to deal with these problems, and then to start new prosecutions. But the new legislation has failed to solve these issues so peculiar to a free and open society.

Reagan, in prosecuting Morison, of course, was following paths laid down by some of his Democratic and Republican predecessors. This same pattern of suppression was present when the Nixon administration resorted to the courts to stop a book critical of the CIA under the guise of seeking to prevent publication of national security information. It sought to enjoin Victor Marchetti, a former CIA official, from publishing *The CIA and the Cult of Intelligence*, his book that described both the agency's dirty tricks and its institutional paranoia. The district court and the court of appeals, using the logic of "clear and present danger," upheld the government's right to censor the book, and the Supreme Court was so little troubled that it declined twice to hear the case.

Following the Pentagon Papers and Marchetti cases, Attorney General Bell continued the practice of enlisting the aid of the courts in restraining publication of information on national security grounds. When in 1979 Bell learned that *Progressive* magazine was about to publish an article by Howard Morland purporting to describe how to build a hydrogen bomb, Department of Justice lawyers sought an injunction. The publication of Morland's article would shatter the prevailing illusion that the design of the bomb was as impenetrable as the ark of the covenant.

In the *Progressive* case the prosecution's arguments were a product of seeds planted in the Pentagon Papers decision. But the lawyers from the Justice Department also displayed contempt for the high standard of proof established in that case. Although their factual affidavits showed that any harm from publication was tenuous, speculative, and remote, their legal theory, based on Holmes' clear-and-present-danger argument, was that publication would result in severe damage to the nation.

Only the publication of the very same material in another magazine, and the government lawyers' embarrassment when it was revealed that a researcher for the American Civil Liberties Union had found the same information on the public shelves of a government library, prevented the case from reaching the Supreme Court, probably with disastrous results. The case was, however, a severe setback to the First Amendment prohibition on prior restraint. Indeed, for weeks *Progressive* was enjoined from publishing Morland's article.

These cases clearly endanger the power of the press to publish and of the public to receive information. Whenever Justice Department lawyers are sufficiently upset, they can allege grave and irreparable damage to national security and almost certainly persuade a judge to delay publication until the government has an opportunity to prove its case.

The expansion of censorship under the Carter administration was directed at publications that did not even raise national security issues. In 1978 Bell brought suit against Frank Snepp, a former CIA employee who had published the shabby details of the agency's last days in Vietnam. Bell did not allege that Snepp had published classified information, as in the *Marchetti* case, but that he was bound by an employment contract prohibiting him from publishing his manuscript without his first submitting it for government review.

In its most shocking national security decision to date, a decision which exhibits disdain for the right to speak and to be informed, the Supreme Court decided the case without the benefit of briefing or oral argument. In a footnote of breathtaking brevity, the Supreme Court barred Snepp from publishing his book:

> We agree with the Court of Appeals that Snepp's agreement is an "entirely appropriate" exercise of the CIA Director's statutory mandate to protec[t] intelligence sources and methods from unauthorized disclosure. . . . Moreover, this Court's cases make clear that—even in the absence of an express agreement—the CIA could have acted to protect substantial government interests by imposing reasonable restrictions on employee activities that in other contexts might be protected by the First Amendment. . . . The government has a compelling interest in protecting both the secrecy of information important to our national security and the appearance of confidentiality so essential to the effective operation of our foreign intelligence services. . . . The agreement that Snepp signed is a reasonable means for protecting this vital interest.

The Court's decision also upheld a crippling fine of $140,000 against Snepp. It also held that before Snepp may again publicly criticize the CIA he must obtain the permission of the very officials he seeks to criticize. The Court did not deal with the argument that when books sympathetic to the authorities at the CIA disclose classified information (for example Henry Kissinger's book) the Justice Department does nothing.

It was wonderful irony in 1985 when Stansfield Turner, former CIA director who supervised Snepp's prepublication review and testified against Snepp, himself became involved in a long dispute with his former agency over whether his own book contained classified information. Ultimately, Turner acquiesced in the suppression of parts of his book.

In the *Marchetti, Progressive,* and *Snepp* cases, as with *Schenck, Abrams, Dennis,* and *Yates,* dissenters were trying to show that our elected officials were wrong. Attacking official judgment as corrupt or deceptive, they tried to show that the official view of reality was obscured by orthodoxy. This the First Amendment not only permits but encourages.

Properly fearful of the breadth of the *Snepp* decision, Benjamin Civiletti in the closing days of the Carter administration sought to limit government discretion to censor former officials by establishing criteria specifying when an injunction would be proper. William French Smith, Reagan's first attorney general, had no such qualms. He revoked the Civiletti restraints, and then issued an order vastly expanding the censorship system.

The Reagan administration's distrust of the Freedom of Information Act was evident from its first days in power. Passed in 1966, the act—which has come to symbolize openness in government—permits citizens to request documents detailing government activities. It resulted in news articles revealing, among other instances of governmental wrongdoing, the My Lai massacre, the FBI's harassment of domestic political groups, and the CIA's surveillance on American college campuses. It also made possible such diverse books as Allen Weinstein's *Perjury: The Hiss-Chambers Case*; Andrew Boyle's *The Fourth Man* (which in turn led to the identification of Anthony Blunt as a one-time Soviet spy), and William Shawcross' *Sideshow: Kissinger, Nixon, and the Destruction of Cambodia.* Shawcross, a British writer, has called the act "a tribute to the self-confidence of American society."

Contending that the FOIA had weakened law-enforcement and intelligence agencies and had become burdensome to implement, the administration made securement of amendments to limit the scope of the act a high priority. One proposal, not adopted by Congress, sought a total exemption of the CIA from the provisions of the act, even though the agency had won every case in which it sought not to disclose properly classified information.

Unable to obtain congressional approval of its major amendments, the administration resorted to a different tactic. Under the FOIA, classified information is denied the public unless it can be shown in court that the material, according to the prevailing guidelines, was improperly classified in the first place. By changing the classification guidelines so that almost anything can be labeled top-secret if the administration does not wish to divulge it—something the president may do without congressional approval—the government avoided the risk that the courts would order the release of such documents.

President Reagan's "secrecy order," as it came to be known, prepared under William French Smith's direction, was issued on March 11, 1983—late on a Friday afternoon, to avoid public attention and debate. The most radical portion of Reagan's "up to my keister" directive requires government agencies to establish procedures to assure that all present and former officials who have access to special intelligence information, and perhaps all who have access to any classified information, must agree as a condition of employment to submit for government review anything they write that is based on their government experience.

The regulations implementing this executive order cover every senior official in the Departments of State and Defense, all members of the National Security Council staff, many senior White House officials, and all senior military and foreign services officers. Anything that is written—a book, a news column, the text of a speech, or a TV or radio commentary—must be submitted even if it obviously does not include classified information. The government can describe anything as classified, even after the fact. For example, in the Morison case the government admitted that when Morison released the pictures they had not been classified as top secret or described as documents that "could injure the United States." Morison knew that some of the pictures had already been published elsewhere and no prosecution had ensued. Nonetheless, Morison was prosecuted and convicted.

Because judicial review is a long and cumbersome process, the government will ordinarily be able to impose its view of what "injures the United States," since authors will rarely subject themselves to long publication delays through litigation. If an individual fails to submit a publication for clearance, he or she forfeits all profits from the publication, even if the manuscript contains no classified information.

This provision could make it extremely difficult for former officials to function as newspaper columnists, radio or TV commentators, or political figures, since anything they write will be delayed while it is being cleared. The CIA has the only currently functioning censorship procedure, having reviewed more than eight hundred manuscripts of its former officials. Although the CIA did not have to consult other agencies and was ordinarily dealing with former agents whom it considered friendly, it nevertheless has often required the deletion of material a writer did not believe to be classified, and it has forced protracted negotiations before agreeing to permit other material to be published.

The practice of classifying many documents that need not be kept secret came under attack from both Secretary of State Shultz and Attorney General Meese when espionage prosecutions against Ronald Pelton, the Walker family, and FBI agent Richard Miller were filed. They conceded we need to change our system for classifying even those very few secrets that should be protected.

We must distinguish between those secrets we need during wartime and those secrets (if any) we need during peacetime. When the secrecy system was put into place just after World War II, it was directed at ferreting out Communists and other "subversives" seeking to enter the government in order to spy for the Soviet Union. We used our wartime yardstick as we equated the cold war with a hot war. The focus was on the initial clearance process and on learning about the political beliefs and associations of the applicants. In recent years, however, almost all spies, like the Walker family, seem to be motivated by money and are recruited after they are given clearances. It's time to take a fresh look at the entire process.

There is a developing consensus within the government that one feature of our security system above all others has contributed to the crisis: Too many people have access to classified material. As Delaware Senator William V. Roth, Jr., said recently, "It is easier to get a security clearance than an American Express card." But before we can cut down on the number of security clearances, we have to address a second feature: excessive classification. When everything is classified, everyone must have a clearance, even to do the most ordinary work. Even if the test is that we permanently classify only when information released can create a real danger to the United States we may do ourselves a disservice.

There should be a different standard. We can use a danger standard, but it must be strictly construed. The data that should be allowed withheld should be minuscule. Even this small bit of data should automatically be made available to the public after a short period of proscription (perhaps six months) unless a court determined its release posed a danger. Very little should be withheld beyond five years.

Reagan's Department of Justice, which shares blame for the overclassifying of information, recognizes that the effort to protect everything has hampered the government's ability to protect anything. As Attorney General Meese has said, "A lot of things which shouldn't be classified are, and therefore there is a kind of ho-hum attitude toward the protection of national security information."

Nor is the Department of State immune from indulging in excessive protection. Secretary of State Shultz has even interfered with the free speech of scientists who may come into contact with their counterparts abroad. With no basis in law the State Department wrongfully relies on the Export Control Act to censor unclassified scientific papers and to deter American scientists from discussing unclassified research with foreign colleagues. A court challenge to this action has not yet been filed, but that may be coming, since the administration had begun to threaten American scientists with termination of research support for those who did not comply.

Indeed, Shultz's State Department has used secrecy, censorship, and propaganda to protect itself from other forms of public scrutiny and criticism. Witness the way his employees armed themselves with the McCarran-Walter Act—passed over President Truman's veto in 1952, during the McCarthy paranoia—to ban controversial foreign speakers from visiting this country. The banned individuals have included Nobel Prize–winning authors such as Gabriel García Márquez; antinuclear advocates; Hiroshima victims who wanted to attend a disarmament session at the United Nations; human rights activists such as the Argentinian dissident Ernest Miglione; Hortensia Allende, the widow of Salvador Allende; and the Reverend Ian Paisley and Owen Carron, spokesmen for, respectively, the radical Protestant and Roman Catholic groups in Northern Ireland.

The Reagan administration seems obsessed with the risks of information, with its potential for leading the public to its wrong conclusion. While carrying out this policy of information "lockout," other agencies of Reagan's administration engaged in information "lockup." For nearly three years, beginning in 1981, the United States Information Agency covertly compiled a "blacklist" containing the names of eighty to one hundred people, including Walter Cronkite, Coretta Scott King, James Baldwin, and Ralph Nader, who were deemed unfit to represent America in an overseas speakers' program.

The CIA's efforts to blanket its own activities in secrecy have been unrelenting. Of course, the agency's recent success in hiding its five-year involvement with the Nicaraguan Contras was as much due to Congressional indifference as to the agency's duplicity. William Casey curbed the Central Intelligence Agency's contacts with the media and the public as soon as he became its director in February 1981. In his widely quoted 1984 letter to Casey on the mining of Nicaraguan ports, Senator Barry Goldwater, former chairman of the Senate Intelligence Committee, asked, "Bill, how can we back [the President's] policy when we don't know what the hell he is doing?" Since the Iran arms controversy we now know the policies were executed without Congress's knowledge or backing.

Federal employees and academic researchers who want information about domestic and foreign policy have also fared worse under the restricted Freedom of Information Act. Through changes in the FOIA guidelines on fees, the Justice Department made it possible for agencies to restrict the flow of information further by charging exorbitant sums for material, sometimes in advance of receipt. And the administration lobbied intensively to persuade Congress to narrow the scope of the act when that could not be achieved by executive decree alone. The across-the-board rejection of the values of information is unprecedented. So is the ease with which those values have been overcome. The wall of secrecy that allowed Lieutenant Colonel Oliver L. North to work as an agent independent of Congress had been created many years before the first discussions between Iran and the United States concerning swapping arms for hostages.

The extension of the censoring mentality has also resulted in the suppression of art. By labeling fine award-winning Canadian films on nuclear war and acid rain "political propaganda," Shultz's State Department tried to restrict their distribution and impact in the United States. Conversely, by arbitrarily refusing to certify award-winning American films on toxic-waste disposal and on the My Lai massacre as educational, scientific, or cultural—certifications which would have exempted them from foreign import duties—the administration made their dissemination abroad prohibitively expensive. As former Assistant Attorney General Jonathan C. Rose has admitted, "Freedom of information is not cost free; it is not an absolute good."

Rudely "book-ending" 1984 were the Justice Department's attempts in January to obtain a court injunction banning the publication of a judge's opinion that criticized the professional behavior of its own lawyers, and the CIA's attempt in November to invoke the power of the Federal Communications Commission to punish a major television network because of a broadcast that criticized the agency's activities.

Perhaps more than any other Reagan action, the president's blackout of independent press coverage of the Grenada invasion—his exclusion of the press from the island, the creation of his own media (government reporters, photographers, and cameramen), and the resulting misinformation, which prompted Deputy Press Secretary Les Janka to resign—was a radical departure from this country's tradition. "The very purpose of the First Amendment," said Supreme Court Justice Robert Jackson in 1949, "is to foreclose public authority from assuming a guardianship of the public mind through regulating the press [and] speech. . . . In this field every person must be his own watchman for truth, because the forefathers did not trust any government to separate the true from the false for us."

Given the national security power claimed by the executive branch and in some instances sanctioned by the courts, and the present clear-and-present-danger test, a foreign affairs crisis that triggered domestic dissent could lead to a substantial further curtailment of civil liberties and free public debate.

Imagine (if the Iran-Contra scandal had not come to light) a massive escalation of military involvement in Central America followed by public demonstrations and the organization of groups promoting opposition to American policy. The high-riding Reagan administration would have attacked its critics. Not surprisingly, Patrick Buchanan, President Reagan's former director of communication, claimed in 1987 after North's activities came to light, that Reagan's and North's critics, including the press, were undermining the country. Imagine what Reagan and his spokesman would have said and done if the Iran mess had not weakened the Reagan presidency. The attorney general might well have decided that some of the groups organizing the opposition were guilty of treason for aiding this country's enemies or were "agents of the foreign power" (as described in espionage legislation), since they would be working in solidarity with unfriendly political movements in Central America.

Although the precise definition of "agent of a foreign power" is amorphous and vague, precedent holds that "foreign power" includes foreign political movements that the Congress and the Department of Justice do not recognize as legitimate. If Attorney General Meese were to decide that there was a sufficient link between an American political group and a foreign political movement, he could authorize the FBI to conduct warrantless physical searches of the offices of the organizations and the homes of its leaders. These surreptitious searches could involve the photographing of records, including membership lists, the privacy rights of political groups notwithstanding. Other forms of surveillance might also be authorized, including infiltration of the alleged organizations with informers. The targeted groups could not know that they were subject to surveillance and hence would be unable to challenge the investigation or the Justice Department's use of the information.

Other specific actions of government individuals and agencies would be visible but very difficult to challenge successfully.

The State Department might seek to prevent Americans, including congressmen, from traveling to Central America to meet with opposition figures and to make statements in opposition to American policy. Relying on the 1981 *Agee* decision in which the Supreme Court punished a former CIA agent by canceling his passport on the unfounded claim that his revelations had incited murder, the Secretary of State could try to lift the passports of those whose travel was found detrimental to the national interest.

If a newspaper gained access to a classified government document describing U.S. military plans for expanded operations in the region, Attorney General Meese might seek an injunction against publication by arguing that the Pentagon Papers standard was met. At best there would be a delay while the court decided the case; at worst the first permanent injunction against publication of politically relevant information would be entered.

Since these actions would be public, they would be challenged in the courts. But given the recent tendency of the Supreme Court to broaden the power of the president and erode constitutional protections in national security cases, the likelihood of a successful defense would be small.

Prospects for action in Congress are no better. Experience indicates that there is little or no chance to enact national security legislation that the president or the intelligence agencies oppose. Many members of Congress are simply unwilling to take the responsibility for passing such laws.

Accordingly, in the absence of events comparable to Watergate and Vietnam, the only hope for reform is election of a president and Congress committed to legislation designed to avoid violations of personal rights in the name of national security.

Such a commitment to individual rights is rare but not unprecedented. Unfortunately, once an individual is designated by the FBI or the CIA as a traitor, entrapment, illegal surveillance, and other acts hitherto suspect or scorned are easily justified. But a committed president could support legislation that specified proper standards for counterintelligence and that prohibited all warrantless searches. Such a president would also support laws to terminate the president's powers to deny passports for political activity and to censor manuscripts written by former officials. Griffin Bell, Carter's attorney general, did support legislation to require warrants for electronic surveillance in national security cases.

Even if a president were willing to take these actions, it would be difficult to overcome bureaucratic or congressional opposition without strong public support. This in turn requires public understanding of the great powers now claimed by the president and what their impact on American liberty could be, especially in a foreign affairs crisis.

We must return to the basic principle that guided the founders of this nation. Claims of threats to the "national security," like claims of treason, must be scrutinized with skepticism. Even when these claims are valid, they must be met in ways that protect constitutional rights. Anything less makes a mockery of the assertion that the government is conducting its national security policy in order to maintain an environment in which liberty in America can continue to flourish.

Elected authority is not entitled to maintain secrecy simply because secrecy is necessary to enhance its reputation. "All silencing of discussions" wrote John Stuart Mill, "is an assumption of infallibility!" But too often our officials evince no respect for Mill's view. "You've just got to trust us," Richard Helms, the former director of the CIA told Congress when they wanted to know what happened in Chile in 1973. The ideals that Mill discussed, that Helms rejects, are the ideals our forefathers thought they were enshrining.

29

THERE IS NO REASON to believe that officials in any country will, in the future, be more fair to men and women who threaten their power than they have been in the past. It is not reasonable to expect the personal ethics of government officials to improve over time, especially when they are dealing with either real or supposed enemies of the state. Consequently, concern for traitors and dissidents must be focused on the large issue of better human rights for all persons through an internationally accepted bill of rights.

Over the years, I and other witnesses have testified before congressional hearings in an attempt to stop American aid to repellent foreign regimes that ignore fundamental rights and to help make Congress more conscious of personal rights in this and foreign countries. On this issue Congress, and not the courts, must lead the way.

The origin of the recent United States human rights policy lies with our 1970s Congress rather than in the often empty idealism expressed by our presidents. Citizens' outrage over what we had recently done in Chile and Vietnam was the springboard for this policy. It is built on the rhetoric of the past, but the policy is very new.

What is known as international human rights is built around two ideas: first, that citizens should be protected by international law and international norms against violations of their rights by their own governments; and second, that governments in shaping policies toward other governments should try to protect citizens of other countries. Both ideas are relatively new. They gained acceptance only in the era following World War II, to a significant extent because of the experience of that war. The United Nations Charter, adopted in 1945, embodies both human rights ideas.

Subsequently, a substantial number of international agreements have legally obligated governments to respect the rights of their own citizens. These include the Universal Declaration of Human Rights (1948); the Convention on the Prevention and Punishment of the Crime of Genocide (1948); the European Convention for the Protection of Human Rights and Fundamental Freedoms (1953); the Standard Minimum Rules for the Treatment of Prisoners (1955); the International Covenant of Economic, Social, and Cultural Rights (1966); the International Covenant on Civil and Political Rights (1966); and the Helsinki Accords (1975). Among them these agreements spell out, often in considerable detail, all the rights to which Americans are entitled under the United States Constitution. But the rights set forth in these international agreements go beyond even those, as in the case of the asserted "right of everyone to . . . a decent living for themselves and their families" in the Covenant on Economic, Social, and Cultural Rights.

Although many of these agreements were signed by other nations half a lifetime ago, the United States is a party to very few of them. And it is only recently that we became a signatory of one of mankind's most basic documents—the Genocide Convention.

Passed by the United Nations to declare mass killing of ethnic, racial, or religious groups an international crime, the value of the 1948 Genocide Convention is that it legitimizes the international scrutiny of genocide policies, granting the victims a right to trial either where the crime occurs or by an international tribunal. It thus broadens and enforces the Nuremberg War Crimes doctrine.

The word "genocide," meaning the annihilation of an entire people or group, was coined in 1944 by Raphael Lemkin, a Polish jurist, to characterize the Nazis' slaughter of 6 million Jews. It has come to denote any mass murder, like the killings of the Ottoman Empire's Armenian minority in 1915.

But the Genocide Convention languished unratified in the United States Senate for nearly four decades. The leaders of the nation that helped sponsor the Nuremberg Trials should be profoundly embarrassed. For decades the Soviet Union piously censured the United States for failing to ratify the convention. Most recently, at the 1984 Madrid meeting of the Helsinki signatories, Moscow challenged American advocacy of human rights by noting that we had failed to ratify the Genocide Convention and other human rights treaties such as the 1966 International Covenant on Civil and Political Rights.

Ninety-two other countries have signed it. The year of the Madrid meeting Senator William Proxmire correctly, if sadly, observed: "There is not a single proposal that has been before the Senate as long." This is not because it has not had its backers. Every administration except the Reagan administration in the last quarter of a century has endorsed ratification, including Richard M. Nixon's. In 1971, following his urgent appeal, the Senate Foreign Relations Committee voted ten to four for the treaty, but further action then stalled. The late Chief Justice Earl Warren, urging ratification on the Senate, observed that "we, as a nation, should have been the first to ratify the Genocide Convention. Instead, we may well be near the last."

Finally, on February 18, 1986, the full Senate approved the ban against genocide, thirty-seven years after President Truman first submitted it, and twenty years after Raphael Lemkin died disillusioned and alone in poverty in a New York hotel. After President Reagan signed it into law, Elie Wiesel, chairman of the United States Holocaust Memorial Council, said, "I know that a law on genocide will not stop future attempts to commit genocide. But at least we as a moral nation, whose memories are alive, have made this statement: We are against genocide, and we cannot tolerate a world in which genocide is being perpetrated."

The reasons why this country, nearly alone, refused for so long to pass the Genocide Convention are fascinating. Much of the American opposition has been indirect, carried over from old battles over domestic civil rights, where states' rights were argued to be paramount over federal jurisdiction. In this same way, opponents of the ban saw domestic or national rights to be paramount over the rights of the rest of the world to make demands on us. The

World Court, known formally as the International Court of Justice, is the tribunal that would hear claims under the Genocide Act. This court, formed in 1945 as the judicial organ of the United Nations, has been repeatedly attacked by the American right wing in much the same way that they previously attacked the power of the United States Supreme Court. Senators Jesse Helms of North Carolina and Orrin Hatch of Utah claimed for years that the World Court, whose judges were a bunch of foreigners dominated by the Soviet Union, would try to tell American states how to treat their own citizens.

It is similar to the attack Helms and others make on the United Nations now that we often find ourselves exercising our veto power so often in the Security Council—a body we applauded when the Soviet Union was constantly invoking its veto in the early days of the United Nations.

The most recent flagrant violation of such international understandings was Reagan's refusal in January 1985 to defend the suit Nicaragua brought in the World Court in April of the previous year for this country's mining of Nicaraguan harbors.

The administration's position—that the court lacked jurisdiction—was immediately criticized by many lawyers in this country and abroad. For example, Robert Owen, a former State Department legal adviser, said that Reagan's decision gave the "impression that we will stick with the court if we think we are going to win. But if not, we will pick up our marbles and go home."

When the Reagan administration said that it would no longer take any part in the Nicaraguan case, it was the first time the United States had defied an order of the court and walked out of its proceedings. Sadly predictable was Reagan's announcement on October 8, 1985, that the United States was ending its thirty-nine-year recognition of the World Court's authority in political cases.

Our decision to ignore and ridicule the court, claiming it is dominated by enemies of freedom, has helped to impair one of the fairest, most respected, and thus most important international institutions.

Moreover, our hypocrisy with respect to the World Court is transparent. In 1946 Secretary of State John Foster Dulles in a persuasive speech pointed out that United States acceptance of the World Court was important because if the U.S., which has the material power to impose its will widely in the world, agrees to submit to the impartial adjudication of its legal controversies, that will inaugurate a new and profoundly significant international advance. Conversely, a failure to take that step would be interpreted as an election on our part to rely on power rather than reason.

And when Iran, in 1980, refused the United States' request to have the hostage case submitted to the World Court (Iran then used the argument that the United States is now making, namely that the issue is a political one that does not belong in the court), our attorney general, Benjamin Civilletti, said:

Anyone who had been a trial advocate in any court would approach this court with respect and awe. In a real sense, this court represents the highest legal aspirations of civilized man.

The World Court often fulfilled Civilletti's prophecy, rendering decisions of both great moral and legal significance. One of the court's greatest moments was its 1971 decision roundly condemning South Africa's apartheid policies. The court, upholding the Security Council's termination of South Africa's stewardship over Namibia and directing that the way be paved for Namibia's independence, held that South Africa's racial policies violated the basic rights of blacks.

The court has also, in a number of decisions, found in favor of the United States. In 1980 the court gave this country an unequivocal political victory by holding that the Iranians had absolutely no right to hold American diplomats as hostages. Needless to say, our president and other elected officials applauded the World Court's actions as moral and unbiased.

Sadly, America is not unique in distancing itself from the World Court. Many other countries, including France, West Germany, China, and the Soviet Union have also refused to accept the court's jurisdiction.

But America is nearly unique in refusing to sign the 1949 Geneva Convention on the humane treatment of combatants and civilians during the war. Over one hundred nations have signed the treaty and more than forty have ratified it. Signing obligates a nation to act in accordance with the treaty, but only formal ratification gives it legal force. The Carter administration, when it signed the treaty in 1977, agreed that a decision on ratification would await the approval of the Joint Chiefs of Staff. On July 8, 1985, the Joint Chiefs recommended to President Reagan that we not ratify the agreement.

Britain, West Germany, Italy, and dozens of other countries are moving toward ratification. One reason Secretary of State Cyrus Vance very much wanted the agreement ratified was that it would strengthen the right to search for and be given information about Americans missing in action in Vietnam. Another was powerful pressure from the International Committee of the Red Cross. The Reagan administration, fearful of placing the United States in a position where other governments could render decisions on our conduct, claimed the ratification of the treaty could lead to dangerous precedents.

Most countries of the world, including countries that fall far short of the United States in respecting the rights of their own citizens, have committed themselves to be bound by international agreements and institutions. Though it obviously diminishes the significance of these agreements and institutions for countries that say they are bound by them not to implement them, the international agreements and institutions retain a great importance.

This has more to do with the fact that they are international than with their precise language or legal status. Their importance lies principally in serving as part of the apparatus that legitimizes the idea that the way a government treats its own citizens is of international concern. Though abuses of individual rights are still practiced as widely as ever, it is now accepted that governments that murder, kidnap, or torture their citizens, or imprison or exile them for their views, are transgressing international legal norms.

The question of this country's greater "involvement" in personal rights in foreign countries was in large part an outgrowth of the easing of cold war tensions, the American civil rights movement, and the changing perception of what the United States role ought to be in Asia after the Vietnam War. Human rights was not an altogether credible issue for a state engaged in indiscriminate slaughter in Southeast Asia; and it lay dormant in Washington even after American forces left Vietnam.

Henry Kissinger's diplomacy made a virtue of what he described as the deideologization of foreign relations. A policy aiming at the manipulation of the balance of power contained a bias in favor of the governments that could deliver their nations without having to worry about political opposition or a free press. The realization that the United States had directly abetted many human rights violations prompted hearings in 1973 by the House Committee on International Affairs examining, systematically, the role of our government in both the protection, and violation, of human rights in foreign countries.

Their resulting report, "Human Rights in the World Community: A Call for U.S. Leadership," signed by two hundred members of Congress, observed that

> the human rights factor is not accorded the high priority it deserves in our country's foreign policy. . . . Proponents of pure power politics too often dismiss it as a factor in diplomacy. Unfortunately, the prevailing attitude has led the United States into embracing governments which practice torture and unabashedly violate almost every human guarantee pronounced by the world community.

The report proposed a higher priority for human rights in the conduct of foreign affairs, and called for the termination or reduction of foreign aid to governments that exhibit a consistent pattern of gross violations of internationally recognized standards of human rights. The language was carefully chosen: "Gross violations" means violations such as torture, prolonged detention without trial, cruel and inhuman or degrading treatment, denial of fair trial, and flagrant denials to an individual's life, liberty, and security.

The report also underlined that America's effectiveness in raising human rights issues would be enhanced if the governments concerned knew economic assistance would be suspended if more traditional diplomacy failed to bring results.

In 1974 the Senate debated a series of proposals linking military aid to human rights. These proposals led to the enactment that year in the Foreign Assistance Act of the original version of Section 502B, which provided that it was the sense of Congress that, "except in extraordinary circumstances, the President shall substantially reduce or terminate financial aid to any government which engages in a consistent pattern of gross violations of internationally recognized human rights."

In 1975 Congress enacted legislation prohibiting all economic assistance to any country whose government engaged in a "consistent pattern of gross violations of internationally recognized human rights" unless the aid directly benefited the needy; and the following year the language of 502B was amended even further by Congress to require an absolute cutoff in military aid to governments engaging in gross abuses of rights. This new law, however, was vetoed by President Gerald Ford. A new, watered-down version was then adopted by Congress and signed into law by Ford, permitting military aid under specified circumstances and requiring a joint resolution of Congress to end military aid to a given country.

By 1978, however, with President Jimmy Carter in the White House, who could be counted on not to veto tougher legislation, Congress adopted the version of 502B in the form that prevails today. As in the case of the earlier version of the legislation, the essential language bars "security assistance . . . for any country the government of which engages in a consistent pattern of gross violations of internationally recognized human rights." As in earlier versions, the legislation contains an exception for "extraordinary circumstances." However, in circumstances in which an administration is intent on maintaining aid to such a government, rather than imposing the onus on Congress to bar aid by a joint resolution, the 1978 law requires that military aid must stop "unless the President certifies in writing to the Speaker of the House of Representatives and the chairman of the Committee on Foreign Relations of the Senate that extraordinary circumstances exist warranting provision of such assistance."

New York Senator Jacob Javits and the other authors of this amendment to the Foreign Assistance Act felt that the United States for too long had ignored the human rights impact of its economic development programs and that in certain nations the administration was using development assistance more for political purposes—such as to prolong the staying power of regimes—than to provide help for the needy. Iowa Congressman Thomas Harkin, a sponsor of the bill, said: "While we may not be able to force other governments to embrace human rights principles, we ought not to encourage those governments through economic aid to use secret police, detention without charges and torture to perpetuate their power."

This new act marked the first time in our history, or the history of any other country, that human rights was tied to foreign aid. The new law also set up a mechanism to enforce the legislative goals. The 1975 Foreign Assistance Act required the executive branch to provide the Congress with human rights reports on aid-recipient countries. Congress could end aid if it disagreed with the executive branch's justification that the aid was benefiting the needy. The legislation thus passed into law the policy that a government's respect for human rights would be a basic factor in economic assistance decisions and that grave and systematic violations of human rights could constitute grounds for restrictions unless the aid benefited the poor. In certain instances, even if aid did benefit the poor, it could be suspended on human rights grounds.

As a result, Congress passed new laws banning aid to specific countries. For example, in 1979 Congress, in large part because of memoranda, affidavits, and briefs submitted by international human rights groups, restricted Export-Import Bank credits to South Africa because of that country's apartheid policy. A trade embargo was also imposed on Uganda when it ousted its Asian minority, and Russia was denied wheat by the Congress because of its Afghanistan adventure.

In contrast to the Ford administration's selective execution of the Foreign Assistance Act, the Carter administration made human rights a key ingredient in its foreign policy and tried to apply the law's provisions as even-handedly as competing considerations would permit. Pat Derian, the assistant secretary of state for human rights and humanitarian affairs during the Carter administration, actively solicited the views of individuals and international organizations.

Even so, Carter's record was far from satisfactory. There was notorious conflict between his two foreign-policy lieutenants, Cyrus Vance and Zbigniew Brzezinski. As secretary of state, the soft-spoken, patient, and moderate Vance exemplified the essential decency and emphasis on human rights that Carter pledged at the time he received the Sakharov letter. As national security adviser, the energetic, ambitious, intensely anti-Soviet Brzezinski refused to penalize anyone who could help us in the struggle against communism. Brzezinski ultimately won out. As a result, during Carter's four years in office—a period covering the perpetration of atrocities in Argentina, Guatemala, and the former Portuguese colony of East Timor—only a relatively small number of governments were condemned for having "engaged in a consistent pattern of gross violations." Security assistance was cut off from only four countries.

But on the whole, the United States record under Carter did improve. In part as a result of United States pressure, many Chileans jailed by the junta at the time of the coup, including ten Bachelet y Otros defendants, were released and exiled in 1977. In 1985 when I last met some of them in Washington, they told me that pressure exerted through formal governmental channels by the Carter people had helped lead to their release.

Since 1978 the United States has opposed nearly one hundred World Bank loans to countries that engaged in serious and persistent violations of human rights, including Argentina, the Central African Republic, Ethiopia, Korea, the Philippines, Uruguay, and Chile. The United States told other countries that if they attempted to obtain loans, the United States would stop them. A half-dozen loans were withdrawn from consideration as a result.

But after Reagan took office in 1980, the United States withdrew financial aid from UNESCO, the World Bank, and the International Monetary Fund, three of the chief sources of funds for the undeveloped countries. At the same time, in the name of the war against communism, that administration increased aid to several regimes that violated their citizens' rights.

When the newly elected civilian Argentine government courageously announced it would fulfill its campaign promises and would try the generals who had so ravaged that nation in 1983 by torturing and killing more than nine thousand of their countrymen, President Reagan sat on his hands while other world leaders applauded. This message was not lost on Chile.

One of the debates within the Carter administration after the receipt of the Sakharov letter was exactly how to define the bundle of rights that constitute the basic human rights that all could agree should be protected. Everyone concurred that "human rights" included basic civil liberties as we know them—freedom of speech, privacy, and due process as well as the right to be free from any physical violation through torture. What the Carter administration could not agree on was whether basic human rights also included economic freedom and security, or as Secretary of State Vance has called it, "the right to the minimum economic necessities of life." Thirty years before, President Franklin Roosevelt himself acknowledged its legitimacy when listing among his "Four Freedoms" the "freedom from want." Yet today the Congress has not accepted this category in any enactment.

Our failure to adopt President Roosevelt's and Secretary of State Vance's positions isolates us from the Third World, a world concerned as much with the need for bread as with free speech. It permits administrations less liberal than Carter's to disregard the rights issue under the slimmest pretext. We have already seen this happen.

Jeane Kirkpatrick, President Reagan's former ambassador to the United Nations, articulated her standard in a 1979 *Commentary Magazine* article "Dictatorships & Double Standards" when she said we should support governments that are "authoritarian" but not governments that are "totalitarian" even though neither furnishes its citizens with minimal rights. This is doublespeak. Her distinction that we should support authoritarian governments such as Chile's because they do not totally control the minds of their citizens, but not totalitarian governments such as Nicaragua's, because they totally control the minds and bodies of their people, is without meaning.

Kirkpatrick's assumption was that Marxist dictatorships were totalitarian, while anti-Marxist dictatorships were authoritarian and hence less noxious. But if "pluralism"—the existence of autonomous institutions—is proof of authoritarianism, then Marxist states in Eastern Europe, Poland and Hungary, for example, are plainly authoritarian and not totalitarian. If state torture and murder are proof of totalitarianism, then Pinochet's Chile, pre-Alfonsín Argentina, and the shah's Iran are more totalitarian than Poland or Nicaragua. And, of course, there is the anomaly of China—considered a totalitarian regime by the Reagan administration, yet spared obloquy for compelling geopolitical reasons.

President Reagan continued that viciously simple distinction when he claimed at the beginning of his presidency that we should support Argentina and Chile because they were "authoritarian" rather than "totalitarian." Starving children in Argentina, like the blacks of South Africa, were constantly confronted with the wealth of those who benefited from their government's policy. At night, in Buenos Aires, as in the outskirts of Johannesburg, drivers, afraid in their cars, kept their windows tightly closed and sped dangerously through red lights so that gangs of poor, angry blacks waiting at the corners would not jump them. But more importantly, in Argentina immediately after Reagan's election, and in reaction to it the killings of the junta's real and imagined enemies dramatically increased.

Most people engaged in the struggle for human rights in Argentina believe that the disappeared may be accounted for by the junta's men, who regularly tossed people out of planes over the Campo de Mayo with their stomachs split open. If new President Raúl Alfonsín investigates deeply into the financial and military support system for the Argentine generals, he will find substantial American responsibility for some of these atrocities.

The United States has for years persisted in turning a blind eye to these practices. It is doubtful whether the new Reagan commitment to also oppose tyrannies of the right is meaningful—it was articulated when he was trying to get broader support for his aid package to the contras fighting the left-wing regime in Nicaragua. It is hard to forget that Michael Novak, the Reagan administration's delegate to the thirty-seventh and thirty-eighth sessions of the United Nations Human Rights Commission in Geneva, Switzerland, cast the sole vote in 1981 against the condemnation of Argentina's military government for its role in effecting the "disappearances" of thousands of civilians, including nuns, schoolgirls, and small children, who were abducted, tortured, and murdered by government death squads. And as late as 1984, President Reagan defended the Philippine leadership of President Ferdinand E. Marcos by saying, "We're better off trying to retain our friendship than throwing Marcos to the wolves and facing the Communist power in the Pacific."

Secretary of State George Schultz has refused to accept the minimum economic necessities of life as a basic human right. That refusal is a cynical artifice to pervert the intent of Congress as articulated in the Foreign Assistance Act and to leave the victims of oppression to their fate. In a certain few cases—the Guatemalan Army, the Salvadoran National Guard and Treasury Police, the Phalangists in Lebanon—American administrations have actually rewarded the perpetrators of massacre by direct or indirect supply of more up-to-date weaponry.

But no American administration can forever ignore claims that a country whose Army massacred civilians has not met human rights standards. With public and congressional attention increasingly focused on the 1981 horrors in El Salvador, a new formulation surfaced when Undersecretary of State Richard Kennedy submitted a six-page confidential, "eyes only" memorandum to the secretary of state that October. "Congressional belief that we have no consistent human rights policy," wrote Kennedy, "threatens to disrupt important foreign-policy initiatives. . . . Human rights has become one of the main avenues for domestic attack on the administration's foreign policy." The administration, argued Kennedy, should take the offensive and make human rights "the core of our foreign policy" by redefining them as "political rights." "Political rights" he contended, "conveys what is ultimately at issue in our contest with the Soviet bloc"—"that where free speech and economic security do not exist, we will condemn all countries."

Making the rights of the individual a cause of constant concern in this country can have a profound effect on our foreign policy. Although anyone could see that the shah of Iran was one of the greatest abusers of human rights, the way which he left, leading to the hostage crisis, was disastrous for President Carter's foreign policies, because previous American administrations had visibly and repeatedly identified our power and prestige with the shah when nearly all the Iranians opposed him.

On the other hand, President Carter's political fortunes were damaged less by the downfall of Anastasio Somoza Debayle in Nicaragua. Carter's human rights policies there created a distance between our government and the dictator. When opposition to Somoza shook his hold on office, some of it encouraged by the administration's new policies, it helped to destabilize the region's almost feudal political structures. Having learned the lesson of Iran, President Carter avoided equating the United States interests with those of the precipitously declining autocrat's, and quickly labeled the successor government "acceptable." The United States suffered a diplomatic defeat but avoided a debacle as it succeeded in retaining political leverage.

While our electorate rejected many of Carter's programs when he stood for reelection in 1980, there was little evidence to suggest that his human rights policy was among them. And yet after Reagan became president, the only constituency that succeeded in stopping any of his early nominations was the human rights lobby.

Throughout Latin America during the early Reagan years, conditions deteriorated. Although Jeane Kirkpatrick, George Shultz, and Caspar Weinberger could not fail to see the inconsistency between their actions unleashing rightist governmental terrorism and their statements against "Soviet-supported freelance terrorism," they continued to overturn almost every aspect of Carter's foreign policy.

According to Kirkpatrick, his administration's human rights policy—which "opted to fight socialism with human rights"—so jeopardized the United States' strategic defense lines that it caused our country to become surrounded by "a ring of Soviet bases." This distortion blinded the ambassador to South America's intrinsic social and political backwardness and persuaded her that only oppressive military regimes should govern. In her opinion, those who challenged the status quo (including the Catholic Church) were either corrupt or Castroite terrorists. Therefore, Kirkpatrick believed, the failure to support military dictatorship because of human rights violations was playing into the hands of Soviet stooges.

Kirkpatrick, who has been championed as a possible vice-presidential candidate for 1988, claimed, for example, that the Somoza regime indulged in only "limited repression and limited oppression," even though Somoza's men killed more than thirty thousand people during his thirty-year regime. She claimed the Sandinistas were, from the outset, a Marxist-Leninist regime. Vilma Núñez, a justice of the Nicaraguan Supreme Court, complained to me in 1984 that the private landlord for the Supreme Court justices' chambers was overcharging them, but there was nothing that could be done. Some Marxist-Leninist country!

Kirkpatrick said the Somozas enjoyed "no monopoly of economic power." In fact, they owned more than 5 million acres of

Nicaragua's land, 25 percent of the arable land, as well as the country's biggest companies.

Kirkpatrick was not the only American politician to apply this standard to South America. Even after Secretary of State Henry Kissinger left office, he continued publicly to support the Pinochet government. His successor, Alexander Haig, said during his nomination hearing, "I do not believe we should in other than the most exceptional circumstances provide aid to any country which consistently violates the human rights of its citizens," yet excepted Pinochet's Chile from his remarks because the United States shared with that government "a belief in God."

Four months after Haig's statement, the Republican administration decided to sell arms to Argentina, Chile, and Guatemala, three of the hemisphere's worst military dictatorships and human rights abusers. Ernest Lefever, the rejected Reagan nominee for assistant secretary of state for human rights and humanitarian affairs, echoed Haig and Kissinger when he said, "Our policy should be concerned only with the external policies of other countries, and not to reform their domestic institutions or practices, however obnoxious."

Lefever is wrong. "Silent diplomacy is silence, quiet diplomacy is surrender," admonished Jacobo Timerman, the publisher who was jailed and tortured in Argentina without being charged with a crime. Timerman has also confirmed what the Chileans told me and many of us knew, that "the Carter human rights policy—an outspoken policy—saved thousands and thousands of lives in Argentina. The junta was afraid of Pat Derian, the assistant secretary for human rights." Robert Cox, the exiled editor of the *Buenos Aires Herald*, who left Argentina in 1979 after receiving death threats, has also affirmed that the Carter administration's condemnation of Argentine atrocities saved "thousands of lives."

Today an aggressive rights policy, equally applied to Communist and non-Communist countries, enjoys widespread support in the United States. Congressman Dante Fascell, chairman of the House Committee on Human Rights, reported that mail on Lefever nomination was very heavy—and overwhelmingly opposed to him on the grounds that his views on human rights ran counter to centuries of American law and thought. The very fact of public reaction to the nomination showed how times have changed. The position of assistant secretary of state for human rights has in the past been seen as unimportant, ineffective, and at best ceremonial. In today's political world such a position is significant, visible, and potentially lifesaving.

A perverse tribute to the significance of the human rights idea occurred during Congress' debate on aid to the contras, when the Reagan administration claimed that the Sandinistas' violation of individual rights required a military response. The administration's argument, that the United States should go to war to get rid of the Sandinistas because they closed down the newspaper *La Prensa*, exiled a bishop, and cracked down on domestic dissidents seriously misused a noble concept for a public relations purpose.

The question of how much pressure America should exert for human rights varies from country to country. We should try and influence each regime as much as we can, realizing that at times our power is great and at times nonexistent. The Reagan administration became appropriately harsh toward Chile and even toward South Africa as it realized we had nothing to lose by pressing them. On the other hand, if a summit by the superpowers can lead to arms reduction, it would be foolish to let that agreement collapse because the Soviet Union failed to make human rights concessions. Jeane Kirkpatrick and Henry Kissinger are correct when they say we need different standards for different countries and that pragmatism is an element of policy-making. Where we disagree is where and how the lines are drawn.

30

THE DEVELOPMENT of national consensus on human rights in the United States has significance beyond this country, and in spite of the actual policies of a particular administration or the swings in the relations between our country and the Soviet Union. This consensus translated into law through private litigation may have far-reaching impact.

For years American courts refused to hear claims concerning crimes committed by American citizens against foreign citizens in foreign countries. In the mid 1970s lawyers brought, in federal courts throughout the country, dozens of suits against the United States on behalf of Vietnamese citizens napalmed in Vietnam. The cases were uniformly dismissed.

But on April 28, 1982, a remarkable decision was announced by an American court. It is a case that could ultimately lead American courts to decide, in specific cases, that the United States government has acted murderously toward citizens of a particular country. A New York federal appeals court ruled that a former high Paraguayan police official—accused of kidnapping and torturing to death the dissident son of a politically prominent Paraguayan physician—could be sued by the victim's family in a United States court.

The case had begun six years earlier in South America. On the night of March 29, 1976, Paraguayan police officials awakened

Dolly Filartiga, daughter of a political opponent of the dictatorial government of Paraguay, and took her to the home of Americo Noberto Peña-Irala, Asunción's inspector general of police. There she was shown the mutilated corpse of her brother, Joelito. He had been whipped, slashed, and tortured with electrical devices. Pursuing Filartiga as she fled in horror from the house, Peña followed her, shouting, "Here you have what you have been looking for for so long. It is what you deserve. Now shut up or else." The message and warning were directed not at her but at her dissident father.

Dolly Filartiga tried to get a lawyer to help her bring Peña to justice. After much searching, she found Horacio Galeano Penome, a prominent Paraguayan lawyer, who agreed, against the advice of his family, to help file charges against Peña. For his trouble, he was arrested, shackled to a wall, interrogated for four hours and then disbarred, so he was unable to pursue the case at home.

But by a twist of fate, Galeano learned that Peña was in New York, was being detained as an illegal alien and therefore could be made subject to the jurisdiction of a New York federal court by serving him personally with a civil summons and complaint. The case was brought by Dolly Filartiga as executor of her brother's estate under the Alien Tort Statute, a federal statute that permits an alien to initiate a civil procedure against another in the federal courts for an offense committed outside the United States if that offense is a violation of the law of nations or a specific treaty to which the United States is a signatory.

With the aid of Peter Weiss, an American lawyer, a $2.5 million damage suit was filed in New York federal court against Peña, claiming that the torture and murder he had perpetrated violated the "law of nations" drawn from the International Bill of Rights (adopted by the United Nations and ratified by every member nation) and other international documents.

Peña's lawyers claimed the treatment of Filartiga was a political matter to be resolved in Paraguay and resisted the court's jurisdiction. They also claimed that Dolly Filartiga had lied. Her brother, they said, was not killed by the police, but by a butler in the Filartiga household. Peña produced the confession of the butler, Hugo Durata, which claimed that Durata had discovered his wife and Joelito in bed and that the crime was one of passion. But the Filartigas' lawyers submitted a photograph and evidence of three independent autopsies demonstrating that her brother's death "was a result of professional methods of torture." The trial court found that despite the butler's alleged confession in Paraguay, Durata had never been arrested, convicted, or sentenced in connection with his supposed crime.

Nonetheless, the lower court dismissed the case against Peña, stating it did not have the power to hear it, but the United States Court of Appeals for the Second Circuit reversed the lower-court decision and proclaimed, for the first time in American legal history, that American federal courts do have the power and jurisdiction to try purported acts of torture and to award civil damages if a violation of the law of nations as articulated in the United Nations Bill of Rights has been proved. It based its jurisdiction on a federal statute enacted by the First Congress in 1789. The statute traditionally applies to automobile and shipping negligence cases. It was the first time that statute was invoked for a foreign murder victim.

"Among the rights universally proclaimed by all nations is the right to be free of physical torture," wrote Chief Justice Irving R. Kaufman in a unanimous opinion. American federal courts can hear claims, he said, where an alien sues for a tort committed in violation of the law of nations, and the three judge panel found that "deliberate torture perpetrated under color of official authority violates universally accepted norms of the international law of human rights, regardless of the nationality of the parties." Thus, whenever an alleged torturer is found and served within our borders, the American court can hear the case.

Carried to its logical conclusion, the reasoning of the court demonstrates that if the American government violates international standards, by killing rebels in El Salvador, or by killing civilians and soldiers in Nicaragua, then American government officials who are responsible can be sued and held liable.

The case was sent back to the lower court for trial. Peña was then found responsible and ordered to pay $15 million in damages. No monies have yet been paid. A search for assets to satisfy the judgment continues but will undoubtedly prove fruitless. Unfortunately, the step the courts must take next—to force governments who sanction torture to satisfy money judgments—has not yet been taken.

Nonetheless, the case reflected a new willingness by our courts to enter into disputes involving foreign affairs, where basic liberties are at issue. Federal judges were emboldened by the Carter administration's strong stance on human rights, and frustrated by Congress' failure to confront the problem through treaty ratification. It was a similar frustration that led the Supreme Court to rewrite civil rights laws in this country.

Speaking of the decision, Filartiga's lawyer Peter Weiss said it could, if extended, have the practical effect of eliminating the United States as "a safe haven for human rights violators from other countries."

Added Bert Lockwood, director of the Cincinnati-based Urban Institute for Human Rights: "This litigation was clearly ground-breaking. We were getting international standards applied successfully within the U.S. courts for the first time."

Indeed, since then, the *Filartiga* decision has been used as a basis for applying international human rights standards to foreign refugees jailed in this country. Courts have ruled that all persons, whether or not United States citizens, are entitled not to be abused while detained during immigration procedures. This has been particularly relevant to this decade's refugees—notably the Vietnamese, Haitians, and Cubans.

A second watershed case has proved important for the development of world rights. In March 1981, a District of Columbia district court judge ruled that the government of Chile and Chilean officials could be sued here for the 1976 bombing that killed Orlando Letelier, Salvador Allende's ambassador to the United States, and Ronni Moffit, his associate at Washington's Institute for Policy Studies.

Unlike Joelito Filartiga, Letelier was killed in Washington, D.C., not far from the American government officials who helped Letelier's killers come into this country. A bomb placed in his car tore both Letelier's legs off—Moffit died a few minutes later. The blast was heard miles away—the car was demolished. But Chile's General Manuel Contreras, accused by Isabel Letelier of killing her husband, would ordinarily have been protected from prosecution here by the doctine of sovereign immunity. This doctrine had protected Paraguay in the *Filartiga* case. But the Letelier court held that the killings had so egregiously violated the law that sovereign immunity had been breached. As a result, it decided that the Chilean government and its generals, most notably General Contreras, could be sued for damages.

One year later the trial court rendered a $3 million damage judgment, and on October 15, 1983, Judge Morris E. Lasker of the New York federal court, brushing aside Chile's argument that the decision was unlawful, said that the Letelier family could satisfy the judgment by seizing the assets of LanChile, Chile's government-owned airline. This was the first time that a foreign government was punished in an American trial court for its violation of human rights.

Unfortunately, several months later the same federal appeals court that ruled that the Filartiga estate could sue, reversed Judge Lasker's decision in the Letelier case. The court said LanChile's assets could not be seized because Chile and LanChile were two separate entities and that Mrs. Letelier must look elsewhere for assets to satisfy the judgment. Judge Richard Cardamone, writing the appeals court decision, said naïvely that Letelier might still be paid because "Chile itself may decide as an act of international good will to honor the judgment of [the Lower Court.]" It is unlikely that Pinochet, who probably will be in power for many more years, will ever honor that judgment.

Cardamone also said "there may be a forum in South America or elsewhere" where Letelier's family could go. There is none. The U.S. Supreme Court did not reverse Judge Cardamone's decision.

In another extension of international human rights law, a federal judge in Los Angeles has ruled in favor of José Siderman, a former citizen of Argentina who sued the government of that country for damages resulting from torture.

Siderman, a Jew and an opponent of the government, was taken from his home on March 24, 1976, by ten men wearing masks and carrying machine guns on the night after military officers overthrew President Isabel Perón. The sixty-five-year-old man was tortured for seven days with a cattle prod and suffered two broken ribs. His captors then dumped him on a roadside, threatening him and his family with death if they did not immediately leave the country.

Siderman and his family fled to the United States and settled in Los Angeles. They filed the federal court action in late 1982 and served the government of Argentina in 1983.

Officials of the Argentine government who were served with a copy of the suit answered by sending a telegram to the State Department saying they rejected the jurisdiction of the federal courts. United States District Court Judge Robert Takasugi denied Siderman's claim for money for Argentina's wrongful taking of his property, but he ruled that federal courts do have jurisdiction over claims based on torture because they are not legitimate acts of state and ordered the government of Argentina to appear. When they refused, Takasugi cited the *Letelier* and *Filartiga* decisions and ordered a hearing to determine damages. The case ended when lawyers from William French Smith's Justice Department persuaded Judge Takasugi that the matter should be left to the courts of Argentina. The judge, under this pressure, said that in view of the fact that Argentina now had a democratic government, it was appropriate for the suit to be filed there.

The most important recent case of violations of international law found by our courts involved the Soviet Union. On October 15, 1985, a federal judge ruled that the Soviet Union breached international law by seizing and detaining Swedish diplomat Raoul Wallenberg in Soviet-occupied Budapest in 1945, and termed "suspect" Soviet assertions that Wallenberg, credited with saving as many as one hundred thousand Hungarian Jews during World War II, died of natural causes in prison in 1947.

The ruling by U.S. District Judge Barrington D. Parker came in a lawsuit brought on behalf of Wallenberg by his half-brother and his legal guardian. They asked for $39 million in damages and an order that the Soviet Union either produce Wallenberg or, if he was dead, his remains. Soviet claims to the contrary, the lawsuit charged that testimony of former Soviet prisoners and other evidence "established that Raoul Wallenberg did not die in 1947 and may in fact be alive today."

Judge Parker granted a default judgment to the plaintiffs after Soviet representatives refused to appear in the case, claiming immunity from suit in a non-Soviet country.

In a forty-page opinion Parker said he found "insufficient evidence ... to support a definitive finding as to whether at this time, Wallenberg is dead or alive." But he called Soviet assertions that Wallenberg died in 1947 "inconsistent with and at odds with credible and uncontroverted evidence presented by the plaintiffs. . . ."

Soviet Embassy spokesman Boris Malakhov had no comment on Parker's ruling. But he did concede, "I think that the case of Raoul Wallenberg was closed in 1957 when it was stated [by then-Deputy Foreign Minister Andrei Gromyko] that Mr. Wallenberg died of a heart attack [while a Soviet prisoner]." As to reports that Wallenberg, who would now be seventy-three, is still alive, Malakhov said, "There is no evidence except of rumours."

Parker found that the Soviet Union engaged in a "gross violation of personal immunity of a diplomat," one of the oldest and most universally recognized principles of international law," and said that the courts should intervene when there are "clear violations of universally recognized principles of international law. The violation of the diplomatic immunity of Raoul Wallenberg is only one such violation."

Torture and political murder, the subject of the *Filartiga*, *Letelier*, *Siderman*, and *Wallenberg* cases, have through the centuries been inextricably related to individuals considered to be traitors. In Roman law, which deplored the torture of free men, treason was a singular offense, the charge of which opened up one sure way of circumventing customary legal procedure and its safeguard against torture. The use of torture in treason cases freed the way for its use in other kinds of situations as well, some of them at or beyond the margins of the law.

Beginning with the eighteenth century, national states grew in size and power. Their strengths derived from their ability to mobilize vast resources and form a broader-based concept of governmental legitimacy. The legal profession and state legislatures, secure in their professional liberalism and enlightened jurisprudence, could, for most of the nineteenth century, afford to believe that increasing state power actually enhanced the security of its citizenry; that the state, however powerful, was simply the watchdog and guardian of preexisting and then constitutionally recognized individual rights, perhaps a bigger and stronger guardian than it had ever been before. But it also became easy for treason to become whatever the officers of the state said it was. Philosophical justifications for brutally punishing anyone who could possibly threaten the state led to an easy disregard of the law.

Few thinkers saw the French Revolution as the precursor of a newer and more ferocious kind of state. And very few of them could have imagined the extent to which that strength could lead, by the early twentieth century, to the abolition of conventional courts and the defiance of statutory laws. In the work of the revolutionary commissions in the Soviet Union between 1917 and 1922, then in fascist Italy and Spain, and finally in Germany under the Third Reich, torture for traitors reappeared under extraordinary revolutionary, party, or state authority and later, in some circumstances, under ordinary legal authority. The traitor, who was said to oppose the will of the people, came to be seen as more dangerous—and more repulsive—than the ordinary criminal. For example, Germany's Heinrich Himmler sanctioned the extralegal use of torture against all traitors—"communists, marxists, Jehovah's Witnesses, saboteurs, terrorists, members of resistance movements, refactory elements or Soviet vagabonds."

Because of these abuses we must commit to define treason more narrowly, and to expand the permissible limits of dissent if we are to ever hope to get legal systems back in the process of trying to reduce torture.

In the past our judiciary has been reluctant to accept cases similar to those of *Filartiga*, *Letelier*, *Siderman*, and *Wallenberg*. There is now a new feeling of promise. Today, if the courts follow and expand the precedent created by *Filartiga* and its progeny, the American judiciary may become a forum for foreigners killed or tortured by other governments. This optimism is tempered by Reagan's appointment of both federal trial and appellate judges who could be expected to vote the other way. But if our courts can develop a set of precedents prohibiting the violation of basic rights, it may be that an international consensus will follow.

With this hope we are now seeing the beginning of lawsuits in American courts charging our government with complicity in killings in Argentina, Korea, and Chile. In January 1987 suits were filed in Washington, D.C., against the Central Intelligence Agency, Lieutenant Colonel Oliver L. North, Admiral John Poindexter, and General Richard V. Secord for deaths they caused by supplying guns for the contra effort against Nicaragua. Several suits filed in Los Angeles on behalf of Salvadorans allegedly killed by American-trained personnel using American equipment may soon come to trial, although such a suit was recently dismissed by a federal appeals court.

It is still too early to tell if American courts will support an attack either on a president's foreign policy or his use of covert actions to achieve ends that are contrary to congressional intent. To do so the courts would have to break with traditional legal precepts that direct the judiciary to avoid such political questions. Here again the Reagan appointees may, at least for a while, carry the day.

But it is unlikely that American courts, no matter how they expand their jurisdiction over foreign killers, will stop many police chiefs or dictators from maiming dissidents. However, the suits may help stop the United States from being a refuge for dictators. These precedents were used by the government of Corazon Aquino in 1986 in suits filed in Texas, Los Angeles, New Jersey, and New York aimed at returning the assets of Fernando Marcos to the Philippine government.

Perhaps the most important value of the cases is that they help give publicity to specific acts of torture and thereby focus this country's attention, however briefly, on a state that abuses human rights. Paraguay's brutal terror is not often brought to our attention—the Filartiga case was important for reminding at least a very small segment of the United States of what happens nearly every day to dissenters in Paraguay. These civil cases can also help discover facts and sometimes embarrass this government when it gets too close to murderers. When on February 5, 1987, Armando Fernandez Lerios, a former official of the Chilean secret police, confessed in a Washington federal court to complicity in the Letelier murder, he admitted the continued publicity generated by the civil damage suit aggravated his "feelings of guilt," compelling him to contact the U.S. attorney. He is now giving additional facts that incriminate Contreras, Pinochet, and officials of our government.

CONCLUSION

WHERE DO WE go from here? How can we create internationally accepted standards and documents that do enforce personal and economic rights when no one can agree either exactly what they are or what priorities should be assigned to them, and when, as at present, there is so little effective enforcement machinery? How do we create and support international groups of private citizens that will send lawyers and other advocates into foreign courts to help those wrongfully accused of treason?

Although there is no international consensus on how to define treason, or what speech ought to be free, there is the beginning of a meaningful consensus in other areas relating to the protection of personal rights. Our Constitution's Bill of Rights and our courts' decisions expanding some of those rights are a starting point. Many of the basic principles that guided the founders of this country are the foundations for international documents that, if rigorously enforced both by international bodies and the foreign nations themselves, would protect men and women throughout the world.

The Universal Declaration of Human Rights, adopted and proclaimed by the General Assembly of the United Nations on December 10, 1948, is a model bill of rights for all human beings. But since the General Assembly has only advisory powers, the Universal Declaration did not create positive law directly binding on states. What it did do was to register an international agreement as to the essential minimum of human rights and the moral obligations of all member states. Some of those rights are life, liberty, and security of person; equality before the law and equal protection of the law; freedom from arbitrary arrest, secret detention, or exile; fair and public hearings by an impartial tribunal on any criminal charges; no punishment until proof of guilt in a public trial with all guarantees necessary for defense; and the inadmissibility of any confessions obtained by torture.

There are other freedoms found in the declaration that are not yet accepted by all countries, including ours. They include the freedom of movement within each state; the right to leave any country including one's own and to return to one's own country; the right to a nationality and the right not to be arbitrarily deprived of it nor denied the right to change it; the right to free choice of employment and to equal pay for equal work; the right to an adequate standard of living; and the right to freedom of thought, conscience, and religion.

Nearly all nations' constitutions speak of certain minimal individual rights that are very much like the rights first set forth in the Magna Charta over eight hundred years ago—yet, as we know, very few nations' government officials pay consistent respect to their words. The Soviet Constitution of 1917, the Chilean Constitution, and our own Constitution all state both the hope for a community where all people will live in dignity and the procedures to achieve those hopes. Few countries have legal systems like South Africa's, which is clearly and unabashedly built on terms to ensure that only the minority receive basic rights. The problem in most countries therefore, is not enacting more human rights legislation, but earning respect for those already on the books. Making foreign governments take rights seriously and trying to get them enforced is the role of human rights lawyers.

In this century we have been witnesses to the wholesale violation of human rights. These breakdowns are getting worse. Before the two world wars, the Holocaust, and the threat of nuclear war, Aleksandr Blok, the Russian writer, looking at the horrors of his nineteenth century, wrote, "The twentieth century more hopeless still, a haze where terrors hide beyond our ken." After World War

II, the Nuremberg War Crimes Tribunal declared that "aggressive war," "war crimes," and "crimes against humanity" were illegal. Yet the period since then has seen an unprecedented number of armed conflicts, many of them waged with savage fury and with no regard for international conventions.

Scholars and politicians years ago asked: Can war be controlled and made less inhumane (by actions such as banning chemical weapons and adapting rules for treatment of prisoners) or is Nuremberg a dead letter? The answer is both that war cannot be made much less inhumane and that the Nuremberg concept is not a dead letter. Even the Chileans paid ironic homage to it at their "Nuremberg show trial." It was also properly invoked by Raúl Alfonsín, the democratic president of Argentina, in 1984 when he brought that country's generals to trial for their genocide. It has some meaning.

What is international law about? Why should we place hope in its future? Nowhere has the source of laws protecting human society been sufficiently analyzed and defined. To make laws is a human instinct which arises among all peoples everywhere, often even before food and shelter have been ensured. There have been nomadic people who have ridden on horseback across continents, seemingly too mobile to form customs, apparently preoccupied with slaughter and devastation. There have been primitive people whose customs are primarily composed of what we call superstition. These people and societies have been thought to be without law, but that thinking was wrong; in fact, these nomadic and settled societies reached agreement as to how to order their lives and ordain penalties against violations.

We now have a proliferation of political and economic systems, each one making promises to its citizens. What system best guarantees the individual's rights will be the one that provides for the widest range of dissent as well as the greatest assurance of economic security. Yet states always take the easy way out. There are now mass arrests in Belfast, Afghanistan, and El Salvador, mistreatment of prisoners in the United States, inadequate due process in the Soviet Union, the violation of cultural and religious rights in China, Zaire, and Iran and suppression of speech and discrimination against women in nearly every country. These abuses continue to take place even though capitalist, socialist, and revolutionary movements have often been carried out in the name of the law, which promises to protect the individual.

Why then do many of us find it necessary to articulate a need for law, struggle for that rule of law, and yet find it usually impossible to achieve? Is Hannah Arendt as correct today as in 1951, when she wrote in *The Origins of Totalitarianism*, "The very phrase, human rights, became for all concerned—victims, persecutors, and onlooker alike—the evidence of hopeless idealism or fumbling feeble-minded hypocrisy"? Are we today paying lip service to high ideals while we continue to kill? And most significantly, is it realistic to work and hope for a meaningful global bill of rights? How can our actions through any of these remote international conventions and professional associations affect the fate of four members of a peasant family tortured and humiliated thousands of miles away by South African or Chilean or Afghanistanian security forces? Are all those words, documents, and organizations, with their attendant meetings and printed reports, finally meaningless?

I remember in high school reading the newly written United Nations charter and years later attending two meetings of the World Federation. I thought it all quixotic. But the world has significantly changed since then, and since Hannah Arendt gave her view of the effect of international human rights laws. It has become smaller and is much more of a community. The principle expressed by Cicero as *ubi societas, ibi jus*—wherever there is a community, there is law—applies to the present. No international society of even moderate complexity, whether it be composed of feudal, capitalist, or socialist governments, can exist without some adherence to law.

The outbreak of terrorism may help persuade all the superpowers that a better-regulated world is in their interest. Law is as vital for the sound control of world society as it is for a state. Most systems of law are constructed first to protect the community and its economic base and second to protect individual rights. Conduct that seriously threatens the survival of the community is considered by those who control most communities to be "treasonable." Those who control the state will make necessary laws to protect the state. A government that will not severely punish conduct it deems treasonable does not exist. International legal bodies can make definitions that are appropriate both for those dissenters who act treasonously and for state officials who overzealously persecute so-called enemies of the state.

The law sets up standards and rules by which the state, through its officials, agrees to exercise its powers and which, by definition, set limits on that exercise. Most authorities find it desirable to act by these standards. Thus, in England, France, the United States, and other developed capitalist countries, there has grown up a mass of laws and regulations that curb misconduct by state officials. State officers have legal power to act only in conformity with certain rules. Whether those rules give adequate protection to the people they represent will vary greatly in different situations, but the existence of rules provides some protection against totally unrestrained acts by state officers. To the degree that state officers act in an arbitrary manner, their authority becomes unstable and subject to the constant threat of revolutionary violence. When that happens, one of the necessary demands of the people is for a return to law.

The formal embodiment of individual rights into the conduct of relations between states is a comparatively recent development. Formerly, the official condemnation by one government of another government's repressive or barbaric domestic practices was seen as a form of outside intervention. Until World War II the prevailing norms of international intercourse inhibited even the most humanitarian of statesmen from making a demand for individual rights a formal constituent of foreign policy. Policy makers responsible for foreign relations have always been uncertain as to how the human rights factor could be reconciled with other national interests—strategic, political, and economic.

Both here and abroad due process rights often remain a political issue. In this country a vocal constituency attacks outrageous violations of human rights, and our foreign policy is sometimes tempered by that concern. In countries where critics are forcibly suppressed, the abuse of rights goes unchallenged. The shah of Iran's decision in 1979 to hold the twentieth-anniversary celebration of the Universal Declaration of Human Rights in Iran, and Ferdinand Marcos' decision to hold the "1980 World Peace Through Law" convention in the Philippines, were public relations exercises applauded by our government. The shah did it for the seal of foreign approval. Marcos attempted, by hosting the meeting, to head off the termination of American aid to his country. The fact that both regimes flagrantly violated the rights of their own people was overlooked by those regimes that sent representatives to the events and thus lent them legitimacy.

The decision to make momentous political moves on the grounds of human rights abuse will nearly always be suspect. When President Reagan dramatically reversed his position on the Philippines, citing Marcos' abysmal human rights record, it may be that he used the human rights issue as a façade to justify a change he felt was necessitated by American security concerns.

The sad truth is that respect for individual rights will often, if not always, be selective. When the shah of Iran was asked to leave the United States, David Rockefeller and Henry Kissinger spoke of their "moral outrage" at his ill treatment. Rockefeller and Kissinger neglected to express a similar feeling for the shah's individual victims or for the victims of other clients of America. Neither said anything about the boat people floating off the coast of Vietnam, about the peasants left on the roof of the embassy in Saigon, or about the guerrillas betrayed in Kurdistan.

What we can do is try to make our government servants in each of our three branches of government pay consistent attention to rights violations throughout the world. Congress could do so by ratifying the international covenants, including the Genocide Convention, by increasing economic aid levels, by reforming refugee practices, and by holding hearings continuously to oversee the executive branch's response to human rights violations.

If Americans bring sufficient pressure on their legislators, our Senate could immediately ratify the still-pending United Nations human rights covenant that seeks to establish international minimum standards for civil and political rights; for social, economic, and cultural rights, and for the elimination of racial discrimination. Congress might also take action to provide for all refugees, even if such provision creates expenses for our country.

Such ratification would put the agreements on a par with domestic statutes, and they could then be used as a judicial basis in our federal courts. That ratification could also be used to broaden our own civil liberties and be used as a building block for human rights advocacy in the United States. South African blacks or Chileans killed, tortured, or discriminated against by interests of

American corporations could file claims here. Our courts could entertain class actions by injured Nicaraguan citizens claiming that, but for the United States, there would no longer be a contra war.

A future Congress could also direct the courts to broaden their jurisdiction to hear cases of foreign or American citizens killed here by foreign governments and cases of foreign citizens killed by American personnel. Five international agreements—ranging from bans on genocide to racial discrimination—that have never been ratified by this country could become a basis for enforcing rights.

If American federal courts now begin to expand the rights of foreign citizens, they will also better protect the rights of Americans. A decision expressing a court's concern for jailed refugees is a precedent for a later court's concern for the jail conditions of Americans, both those who are detained prior to trial and those who are convicted.

We also should be more critical of our country's legal institutions. As supporters of the American legal system, we have often been so sure that our system is best that we discourage any outside evaluation of it. Amnesty International has as much trouble getting into our courts and jails as it does in countries thought to be less free. We can ask our jurists and congressmen to encourage international authorities like Amnesty and the International Commission of Jurists to scrutinize our practices more carefully.

We can also insist that the executive branch of government make the protection of personal rights a permanent, important part of our foreign policy. The application of the idea of linking human rights to foreign policy was not an innovation of the Carter administration. The United States was founded on a proclamation of "inalienable rights," and human rights ever since have had a peculiar resonance in the American tradition. In 1847 Albert Gallatin, the last surviving statesman of the early republic, told his countrymen, "Your mission was to be a model for all of the governments and for all other less favored nations, to adhere to the most elevated principles of political morality, to apply all your facilities to the gradual improvement of your own institutions and social state, and by your example to exert a moral influence most beneficial to mankind."

Alexis de Tocqueville, writing of our ideals in *Democracy in*

America, persuasively attributed the humanitarian ethic to the rise of the idea of equality. In aristocratic societies, he wrote, those in the upper caste hardly believe that their inferiors "belong to the same race." When medieval chroniclers relate "the tragic end of the noble, their grief flows apace; whereas they tell you at a breath and without wincing of massacres and tortures inflicted on the common sort of people." De Tocqueville recalled the "cruel jocularity" with which Madame de Sévigné, one of the most intelligent and cultivated women of the seventeenth century, described the breaking on a wheel of an itinerant fiddler "for getting up a dance and stealing some stamped paper." It would be wrong, de Tocqueville observed, to suppose that Madame de Sévigné was sadistic. Rather, she "had no clear notion of suffering in anyone who was not a person of quality."

American officials brought up in a society and a culture that embrace the concept of equality, surprisingly often act like Madame de Sévigné, as if extraordinary economic and political inequality is permissible because those who suffer for it, belonging to different political systems, are not persons of quality. Most of our present allies, on the other hand, will now no longer issue blank checks supporting us as we restore aid to some of the worst military dictatorships the twentieth century has seen. In Paris President François Mitterrand expressed "serious reservations" about Washington's Latin American policies, when we restored aid to Uruguay, Paraguay, Chile, and Argentina. "The people of the region want to put an end to the oligarchies that, backed by bloody dictatorships, exploit them and crush them under intolerable conditions," he said in an interview with *Le Monde*. "When they cry for help, I would like to know that someone other than Fidel Castro will hear them."

France at the time of the Chilean coup played an important role in protecting members of Allende's government. A decade after the coup it did even more. Outraged by the mass arrests and the systematic torture of political prisoners in Chile, Foreign Minister Claude Cheysson of France on May 18, 1983, denounced Chilean dictator Pinochet as "a curse on his people" and recalled the French ambassador. We, on the other hand, have done very little. When in 1983 the Argentine junta disclaimed responsibility for the *desaparecidos* ("disappeared"), the European Commission on Human Rights formally demanded an accounting; again, France withdrew its ambassador, and President Alessandro Pertini of Italy followed suit, declaring the "chilling cynicism of the communiqué . . . places those responsible outside civilized humanity." The United States remained silent for a month and then issued a pallid statement deploring the tragic events of the past.

Although one cannot help but be depressed by the number of flagrant rights violations in the world today, the individual rights picture is not entirely bleak. Never in recorded history has so much attention been paid to personal rights, never before have so many individuals, organizations, and governments worked so constantly to secure the obedience of government officials to law. And when individual states fail to give justice, the citizens of those states are beginning to think of international law forums. Members of British labor unions in 1983, frustrated by the policies of Prime Minister Margaret Thatcher, asked the World Court to protect their jobs. Individual supporters around the world of nuclear freezes and unilateral disarmament recognized a pressing need for universally accepted legal standards and a central international body in order to make arms reduction effective. And the United States suffered a significant defeat when President Reagan and Secretary of State George Schulz, while reaffirming their commitment to the rule of law, refused to admit the World Court had jurisdiction to hear Nicaragua's claims that the CIA mined its harbors.

Considering that regimes that systematically abuse human rights currently hold power not only in most of Central America but also in most of Asia, much of Africa, all of Eastern Europe, and much of Latin America, it would be foolish to suggest that the ideas of the international human rights movement have thus far made a substantial practical difference. Victims of human rights violations continue to be as severely abused as ever, and there is not much basis for optimism in the near term. Nor is it probable, for that matter, that the replacement of one presidential administration by another more committed to even-handed efforts to promote human rights would quickly produce any discernible decline in the worldwide violations of human rights. In the short run, however, such an administration would do well if it could simply re-

303

habilitate the image of the United States by dissociating us from the most seriously repressive regimes. Significant impact on the human rights situation in other countries will require sustained effort over a long period.

The most that can be said for what has been accomplished by the human rights movement is that the nations of the world today profess acceptance of the idea that their respective foreign policies must be concerned with abuses of rights by other governments. Surely, the exposure given to the human rights violations of long-established dictators in Haiti and the Philippines helped contribute to their downfall. South African and Chilean leaders also previously supported by the Reagan administration are now on the defensive as they argue that their countries are complying with minimal standards. That is no small achievement for a movement that is barely four decades old and that confronts so monumental a global task. Maintaining and building upon that momentum is necessary for more to be achieved.

The jailing and release of dissidents and treason and torture cases will appear and disappear in press headlines. But violations of rights will continue to impinge on American concerns, be they for humanitarian or selfish reasons. We now have established a body of domestic and international law that will be hard to reverse; precedents are set for our courts as well as our executive and legislative branches. It is now hard, if not impossible, to dismantle the international machinery—machinery that the United States can no longer influence as it once did.

Individual rights, which are on the international bargaining table, are an incentive to the Soviet and non-Soviet countries of the Third World, and are the subject of East-West competition. Even if polarization between the superpowers continues, the march toward an increased dialogue on individual rights and then a globally enforceable bill of rights seems inexorable.

This pattern of consensus, which came first with the awareness of injustice, then with the articulation of rights, then with changes of law, and then, we expect, with the ability to enforce a changed view, is based on experiences shaped during the 1960s when American dissidents, often with the help of lawyers, pushed and tugged this country into new directions. Drawing on a firm feeling that change was necessary, the law, at times ahead of the consensus, and at times behind it, helped define personal rights that were at first vague and unenforceable and then made them real and meaningful. Rights that did not exist at the turn of the century are now unalterably part of this country's legal system. The impetus for these changes comes with our increasing confidence that oppressive laws will ultimately fail and fair ones may, in the long run, protect all of us.

The world's peoples are desperately crying out. Amnesty International claims that one-third of the world's peoples live under governments that routinely employ torture. America's role in halting slaughter and oppression has been limited by political policy. Statesmen do not act morally unless they are compelled to.

We must try to respond to the pleas of those who face death. American citizens are starting to think as citizens of the world with an obligation toward future generations. In 1986, when people were still dying in racial violence in South Africa, the Senate and the House of Representatives finally ordered sanctions and six state legislatures passed divestment laws. American human rights lawyers worked full time in South Africa to create legal cracks and fissures in the wall of apartheid, both to help dissidents to speak out more freely and to reduce the horrors of prolonged detention.

If there is to be any hope at all in today's desperate race against state terror, we must work toward the creation of first the consciousness and then a consensus that will lead to a deep concern for personal rights—a concept that takes its roots in one of man's most ancient aspirations for a just and humane society, aspirations that first gave way to the law.

MARTIN GARBUS, one of the country's leading trial law-yers, has argued before the United States Supreme Court. He is a former faculty member at Columbia University and Yale University Law School. The author of *Ready for the Defense*, his articles have appeared in the *New York Times*, *The New York Review of Books*, the *New Republic*, and *The Nation*, as well as in scholarly journals. He has been a television and radio commentator on national and international events. Mr. Garbus lives in New York City with his wife, Ruth, a psychotherapist, and their two daughters.

FINE WORKS OF NON-FICTION AVAILABLE IN QUALITY PAPERBACK EDITIONS FROM CARROLL & GRAF

- Anderson, Nancy/WORK WITH PASSION $8.95
- Arlett, Robert/THE PIZZA GOURMET $10.95
- Asprey, Robert/THE PANTHER'S FEAST $9.95
- Athill, Diana/INSTEAD OF A LETTER $7.95
- Bedford, Sybille/ALDOUS HUXLEY $14.95
- Berton, Pierre/KLONDIKE FEVER $10.95
- Blake, Robert/DISRAELI $14.50
- Blanch, Lesley/PIERRE LOTI $10.95
- Blanch, Lesley/THE SABRES OF PARADISE $9.95
- Blanch, Lesley/THE WILDER SHORES OF LOVE $8.95
- Bowers, John/IN THE LAND OF NYX $7.95
- Buchan, John/PILGRIM'S WAY $10.95
- Carr, John Dickson/THE LIFE OF SIR ARTHUR CONAN DOYLE $8.95
- Carr, Virginia Spencer/THE LONELY HUNTER: A BIOGRAPHY OF CARSON McCULLERS $12.95
- Cherry-Garrard/THE WORST JOURNEY IN THE WORLD $13.95
- Conot, Robert/JUSTICE AT NUREMBURG $11.95
- Cooper, Duff/OLD MEN FORGET $10.95
- Cooper, Lady Diana/AUTOBIOGRAPHY $13.95
- De Jonge, Alex/THE LIFE AND TIMES OF GRIGORII RASPUTIN $10.95
- Edwards, Anne/SONYA: THE LIFE OF COUNTESS TOLSTOY $8.95
- Elkington, John/THE GENE FACTORY $8.95
- Farson, Negley/THE WAY OF A TRANSGRESSOR $9.95
- Garbus, Martin/TRAITORS AND HEROES $10.95
- Gill, Brendan/HERE AT THE NEW YORKER $12.95
- Goldin, Stephen & Sky, Kathleen/THE BUSINESS OF BEING A WRITER $8.95
- Golenbock, Peter/HOW TO WIN AT ROTISSERIE BASEBALL $8.95
- Green, Julian/DIARIES 1928–1957 $9.95

- [ ] Harris, A./SEXUAL EXERCISES FOR WOMEN $8.95
- [ ] Haycraft, Howard (ed.)/THE ART OF THE MYSTERY STORY $9.95
- [ ] Haycraft, Howard (ed.)/MURDER FOR PLEASURE $10.95
- [ ] Hook, Sidney/OUT OF STEP $14.95
- [ ] Keating, H. R. F./CRIME & MYSTERY: THE 100 BEST BOOKS $7.95
- [ ] Lansing, Alfred/ENDURANCE: SHACKLETON'S INCREDIBLE VOYAGE $8.95
- [ ] Leech, Margaret/REVEILLE IN WASHINGTON $11.95
- [ ] Lifton, David S./BEST EVIDENCE $11.95
- [ ] Macmillan, Harold/THE BLAST OF WAR $12.95
- [ ] Madden, David and Bach, Peggy/ REDISCOVERIES II $9.95
- [ ] Martin, Jay/NATHANAEL WEST: THE ART OF HIS LIFE $8.95
- [ ] Maurois, Andre/OLYMPIO: THE LIVE OF VICTOR HUGO $12.95
- [ ] Maurois, Andre/PROMETHEUS: THE LIFE OF BALZAC $11.95
- [ ] Maurois, Andre/PROUST: PORTRAIT OF GENIUS $10.95
- [ ] McCarthy, Barry and Emily/FEMALE SEXUAL AWARENESS $9.95
- [ ] McCarthy, Barry/MALE SEXUAL AWARENESS $9.95
- [ ] McCarthy, Barry & Emily/SEXUAL AWARENESS $9.95
- [ ] Mizener, Arthur/THE SADDEST STORY: A BIOGRAPHY OF FORD MADOX FORD $12.95
- [ ] Montyn, Jan & Kooiman, Dirk Ayelt/A LAMB TO SLAUGHTER $8.95
- [ ] Moorehead, Alan/THE RUSSIAN REVOLUTION $10.95
- [ ] Morris, Charles/IRON DESTINIES, LOST OPPORTUNITIES: THE POST-WAR ARMS RACE $13.95
- [ ] Munthe, Alex/THE STORY OF SAN MICHELE $8.95
- [ ] O'Casey, Sean/AUTOBIOGRAPHIES I $10.95
- [ ] O'Casey, Sean/AUTOBIOGRAPHIES II $10.95
- [ ] Poncins, Gontran de/KABLOONA $9.95
- [ ] Pringle, David/SCIENCE FICTION: THE 100 BEST NOVELS $7.95
- [ ] Proust, Marcel/ON ART AND LITERATURE $8.95

☐ Richelson, Hildy & Stan/INCOME WITHOUT TAXES	$9.95
☐ Roy, Jules/THE BATTLE OF DIENBIENPHU	$8.95
☐ Russell, Franklin/THE HUNTING ANIMAL	$7.95
☐ Salisbury, Harrison/A JOURNEY FOR OUR TIMES	$10.95
☐ Scott, Evelyn/ESCAPADE	$9.95
☐ Sloan, Allan/THREE PLUS ONE EQUALS BILLIONS	$8.95
☐ Stanway, Andrew/THE ART OF SENSUAL LOVING	$15.95
☐ Stein, Leon/THE TRIANGLE FIRE	$7.95
☐ Trench, Charles/THE ROAD TO KHARTOUM	$10.95
☐ Werth, Alexander/RUSSIA AT WAR: 1941–1945	$15.95
☐ White, Jon Manchip/CORTES	$10.95
☐ Wilmot, Chester/STRUGGLE FOR EUROPE	$14.95
☐ Wilson, Colin/THE MAMMOTH BOOK OF TRUE CRIME	$8.95
☐ Zuckmayer, Carl/A PART OF MYSELF	$9.95

Available from fine bookstores everywhere or use this coupon for ordering.

Carroll & Graf Publishers, Inc., 260 Fifth Avenue, N.Y., N.Y. 10001

Please send me the books I have checked above. I am enclosing
$_____ (please add $1.00 per title to cover postage and
handling.) Send check or money order—no cash or C.O.D.'s
please. N.Y. residents please add 8¼% sales tax.

Mr/Mrs/Ms _____

Address _____

City _____ State/Zip _____
Please allow four to six weeks for delivery.

FINE WORKS OF FICTION AVAILABLE IN QUALITY PAPERBACK EDITIONS FROM CARROLL & GRAF

☐ Asch, Sholem/THE APOSTLE $10.95
☐ Asch, Sholem/MARY $10.95
☐ Asch, Sholem/THE NAZARENE $10.95
☐ Asch, Sholem/THREE CITIES $10.50
☐ Ashley, Mike (ed.)/THE MAMMOTH BOOK OF
    SHORT HORROR NOVELS $8.95
☐ Asimov, Isaac/THE MAMMOTH BOOK OF
    CLASSIC SCIENCE FICTION (1930s) $8.95
☐ Asimov, Isaac et al/THE MAMMOTH BOOK OF
    GOLDEN AGE SCIENCE FICTION (1940) $8.95
☐ Babel, Isaac/YOU MUST KNOW
    EVERYTHING $8.95
☐ Balzac, Honore de/BEATRIX $8.95
☐ Balzac, Honoré de/CESAR BIROTTEAU $8.95
☐ Balzac, Honoré de/THE LILY OF THE
    VALLEY $9.95
☐ Bellaman, Henry/KINGS ROW $8.95
☐ Bernanos, George/DIARY OF A COUNTRY
    PRIEST $7.95
☐ Brand, Christianna/GREEN FOR DANGER $8.95
☐ Céline, Louis-Ferdinand/CASTLE TO CASTLE $8.95
☐ Chekov, Anton/LATE BLOOMING FLOWERS $8.95
☐ Conrad, Joseph/SEA STORIES $8.95
☐ Conrad, Joseph & Ford Madox Ford/
    THE INHERITORS $7.95
☐ Conrad, Joseph & Ford Madox Ford/ROMANCE $8.95
☐ Coward, Noel/A WITHERED NOSEGAY $8.95
☐ de Montherlant, Henry/THE GIRLS $11.95
☐ Dos Passos, John/THREE SOLDIERS $9.95
☐ Feuchtwanger, Lion/JEW SUSS $8.95
☐ Feuchtwanger, Lion/THE OPPERMANNS $8.95
☐ Fisher, R.L./THE PRINCE OF WHALES $5.95
☐ Fitzgerald, Penelope/OFFSHORE $7.95
☐ Fitzgerald, Penelope/INNOCENCE $7.95
☐ Flaubert, Gustave/NOVEMBER $7.95
☐ Fonseca, Rubem/HIGH ART $7.95
☐ Fuchs, Daniel/SUMMER IN WILLIAMSBURG $8.95

- [ ] Neider, Charles (ed.)/GREAT SHORT STORIES $11.95
- [ ] Neider, Charles (ed.)/SHORT NOVELS OF THE MASTERS $12.95
- [ ] O'Faolain, Julia/THE OBEDIENT WIFE $7.95
- [ ] O'Faolain, Julia/NO COUNTRY FOR YOUNG MEN $8.95
- [ ] O'Faolain, Julia/WOMEN IN THE WALL $8.95
- [ ] Olinto, Antonio/THE WATER HOUSE $9.95
- [ ] Plievier, Theodore/STALINGRAD $8.95
- [ ] Pronzini & Greenberg (eds.)/THE MAMMOTH BOOK OF PRIVATE EYE NOVELS $8.95
- [ ] Rechy, John/BODIES AND SOULS $8.95
- [ ] Rechy, John/MARILYN'S DAUGHTER $8.95
- [ ] Rhys, Jean/QUARTET $6.95
- [ ] Sand, George/MARIANNE $7.95
- [ ] Scott, Evelyn/THE WAVE $9.95
- [ ] Sigal, Clancy/GOING AWAY $9.95
- [ ] Singer, I.J./THE BROTHERS ASHKENAZI $9.95
- [ ] Taylor, Peter/IN THE MIRO DISTRICT $7.95
- [ ] Tolstoy, Leo/TALES OF COURAGE AND CONFLICT $11.95
- [ ] van Thal, Herbert/THE MAMMOTH BOOK OF GREAT DETECTIVE STORIES $8.95
- [ ] Wassermann, Jacob/CASPAR HAUSER $9.95
- [ ] Wassermann, Jabob/THE MAURIZIUS CASE $9.95
- [ ] Werfel, Franz/THE FORTY DAYS OF MUSA DAGH $9.95
- [ ] Winwood, John/THE MAMMOTH BOOK OF SPY THRILLERS $8.95

Available from fine bookstores everywhere or use this coupon for ordering.